# Pond Lane and Paris

Susie Vereker

**Other titles published by transita**

*After Michael* by Betty O'Rourke
*Elissa's Castle* by Juliet Greenwood
*Emotional Geology* by Linda Gilliard
*Forgotten Dreams* by Doris Leadbetter
*Scuba Dancing* by Nicola Slade
*Stage by Stage* by Jan Jones
*The Waiting Time* by Sara Banerji
*Turning Point* by Bowering Sivers
*Uphill All the Way* by Sue Moorcroft

**transita**

Transita books reflect the lives of mature women. Contemporary women with rich and interesting stories to tell, stories that explore the truths and desires that colour their lives.

To find out more about transita, our books and our authors visit **www.transita.co.uk**

# Pond Lane and Paris

Susie Vereker

transita

Published by Transita
3 Newtec Place, Magdalen Road,
Oxford OX4 1RE. United Kingdom.
Tel: (01865) 204393. Fax: (01865) 248780.
email: info@transita.co.uk
www.transita.co.uk

All rights reserved. No part of this work may be reproduced
or stored in an information retrieval system (other than for purposes of
review) without the express permission of the publisher in writing.

© **Copyright 2005 Susie Vereker**

British Library Cataloguing in Publication Data
A catalogue record for this book is available from the British Library

Cover design by Baseline Arts Ltd, Oxford
Produced for Transita by Deer Park Productions, Tavistock
Typeset by PDQ Typesetting, Newcastle-under-Lyme
Printed and bound by Bookmarque, Croydon

All characters in this book are fictitious and any resemblance to real persons,
living or dead, is entirely coincidental.

The right of Susie Vereker to be identified as the author of this work has
been asserted by her in accordance with the Copyright, Designs and Patents
Act 1988.

## ABOUT THE AUTHOR

Born in the Lake District, **Susie Vereker** has spent much of her life travelling round the world, first as an army officer's daughter then as a diplomat's wife. She worked in publishing in London, au paired in Germany, typed in Aden, taught English in Surrey and raised her three sons in Australia, Greece, Thailand, Switzerland and France. In the nineties Susie lived in Paris when her late husband was British Ambassador to OECD. Widowed in 2001 after a long happy marriage, she now lives in a Hampshire village that's been home – between postings abroad – for over twenty years.

Caught between her conventional upbringing, the duties of a diplomatic wife and the aspirations of the modern woman, Susie has led something of a chameleon existence. In Australia she was a sportswoman and young mother, in Greece a welfare worker and dabbler in archaeology, in Thailand a fund-raiser, in Geneva a magazine editor/journalist, and in Paris she concentrated on art history and writing. This is her first published novel.

Susie's life has been one of challenge and adaptation to different countries and customs, and this has been the inspiration for *Pond Lane and Paris*.

For more information about Susie and her work visit www.transita.co.uk

# DEDICATION

For my family, and for Sally, Mary & Susan, and writer friends all over the world.

# CHAPTER 1

LAURA SMILED GRIMLY AS SHE WATCHED the Bentley crawling up the rutted lane and around the bend by the oak tree. Eventually the chauffeur drew to a halt and hurried to open the door for her stepfather, who eased himself out and marched slowly towards her.

'Laura, my dear. Such a long time.' Julius flashed his impossibly perfect set of false teeth.

She steeled herself not to turn away as he bent forward to give her a dry kiss. 'Hello,' she said. 'You're looking very fit.'

Amazingly fit for a man of eighty-two. With his perma-tan monkey face and small-boned frame, he reminded her of one of those ancient American film stars you always thought were dead until they're resurrected on Parkinson.

Despite his tweed jacket and cavalry-twill trousers, Julius appeared out of place in the English countryside. His clothes were too new and too bright, particularly the yellow plaid socks.

Julius nearly tripped on one of the numerous loose stones on the path but otherwise moved with surprising agility. She led him into the sitting room where, in an attempt to be more hospitable than she felt, she had set the tea tray.

Once seated in her best armchair, he looked around. 'Nice vase of daffodils,' was all he found to say. His pale eyes were sharp behind half-moon glasses.

He shuddered when she offered him milk in his tea. 'Oh, no, my dear. Have to be careful with dairy produce at my age. I'll just take a little slice of lemon. But if you were to hand me one of those scones, I dare say it wouldn't do any harm, just this once. No, don't bother offering anything to Paul. He prefers to stay with the car, such a careful boy.' He went on to ask her questions about the garden but didn't appear to be listening to the answers.

Eventually she screwed herself up to say, 'About my mother's will, did the solicitors tell you I'd been in touch with them?'

His nose quivered. 'Ah yes, the Trust. It is all very difficult, my dear. I have talked to Tony – my accountant, good chap, used to be with his father, now he's taken over. Anyway, he feels I should preserve the capital intact in order to ensure maximum income – and there's not a huge amount of capital, you know. I'm only just able to live within my means as it is. After all, it was your dear mother's wish that I should be provided for until I die. Of course, it'll all come to you eventually but, alas, not yet, my dear. When I say all, there's not that much, and there's the question of my possible future needs. Nursing homes are so expensive, and, as Tony says, one should think of every eventuality...'

She forced herself to stay calm. 'Of course, I know, but I really would be grateful to have a little bit of my inheritance – however small – now, in advance. You see, I want to stay here and I don't seem to have the qualifications for a decent job – and it's very hard to start at the bottom at my age – so I had the idea of converting the cottage into a Bed and Breakfast place, but of course it needs roof repairs and a new bathroom and proper central heating, and as for the kitchen...' His attention appeared to be fading so she said in a sudden rush 'If you, the Trust, could perhaps let me have about ten thousand, that would be more than enough to pay my debts and set me on my feet. Then the bank might lend me some, possibly.'

There was a long pause. Eventually he spoke, his tone dry and remote. 'Didn't, er – your husband leave you any money? Thought there was some in his family.'

'No, there wasn't.'

Another silence.

'I'm sorry I couldn't come to the funeral, my dear, but I was in Switzerland.' His nose quivered again. 'I hope you got the wreath I sent.'

'Yes, thank you.'

'How long ago was it that he...?'

'William died fourteen months ago.'

'But he'd been ill for some years.'

'Yes,' she said bleakly. Any moment Julius would say something about its being a happy release for William. Which was what most people said or tried to say, if they brought up the subject at all. That is, if they hadn't already crossed the road to avoid speaking to her about the whole embarrassing business of death. For her, the real William had died eight years ago when he had a massive stroke, leaving behind a shell of a man who spent his day in a wheelchair. She couldn't explain to anyone how much she missed him, even the shell of him.

'But you're still a relatively young woman,' Julius was saying. 'You can start your life again. Sell this cottage. It's in an appalling state of repair. Take far more than ten thousand to put it right. I have a much better idea. Come and live in London with me. I am sure your dear mother would have wanted us to be together.'

She stared at him open mouthed, trying to disguise her anger and revulsion.

'D'you see,' he continued, his eyes filling with tears, 'I'm not getting any younger and I find my daily is getting rather careless and over-familiar these days, and very shirty if I ask her to do any extra time. And, though Paul is a nice boy, he seems very reluctant to do anything except drive and look after the car, not at all like the older type of servant who would do anything one asked. I'm sure you'd cope much better.'

'No, no, thank you,' she managed to say.

'But, judging by this very nice tea you have provided – the scones tasted home-made – you'd be an excellent housekeeper, my dear. And you do have nursing experience, not that I need nursing now, but you see if you came to look after me, it would mean I'd have to spend less on domestic help and it would save us both money, money that'll all be yours eventually, as I said.'

'Julius, I don't think we would get on,' she said through clenched teeth.

'But why not? I'm an easy-going man, easy to live with, and I have very simple tastes in food, hardly eat a thing. You needn't think you'd have to spend all your time in the kitchen. One really doesn't mind eating Marks & Spencer now and then. And the flat is quite near Harrods so shopping isn't difficult.' He paused and his eyes glinted. 'Ah, perhaps the proprieties worry you. I assure you, my dear, I am eighty years old, past all that long ago.'

Her patience ran out. 'It is not a question of propriety. It just wouldn't work. Quite apart from anything else, I don't like London. This is my home and I don't want to leave it. It's important to me, you see.'

'Perhaps you need time to think about it, but I am very much afraid that my hospitality is the only thing I can offer.' His eyes glinted again. 'Ah, silly of me. There must be a boyfriend around. A bit soon, perhaps, but no one would blame you, an attractive widow like you, sick husband all those years.'

Laura glared at him. 'There is no boyfriend, not that it's any business of yours. Now if you will excuse me, I have things to do. Like ringing up the solicitors.'

He hauled himself upright. 'Won't do you any good, my dear. Your mother's will was quite clear. I know it's hard for you to accept, but she felt you needed to be protected and that I was the person to do it. That husband of yours, he wasn't very good with money, was he? Threw it down the drain. That ridiculous business with the hotel in Greece.'

She could never argue calmly and rationally. Her voice grew higher and higher. 'For God's sake, that was years and years ago and it wasn't our fault... As for you protecting *me*, I've never heard... I mean, you're not protecting me at all. It's you who's protecting yourself. I'm sure my mother never meant it this way, for you to live in the lap of luxury while I...' She rose to her feet, scraping back the chair. 'Julius, I think you had better go.'

'I was going to take my leave anyway,' he said stiffly. 'My hosts will be expecting me. I'm staying with Rex. They say he'll be the Lord Lieutenant of Hampshire next year, d'you know.'

With a great deal of huffing and puffing, he left.

Enraged, Laura stared after him. When she had calmed down she reminded herself yet again that the world was full of people who had no money at all and no rich stepfather, wicked or otherwise. And, whether he liked it or not, Julius would be obliged to leave her something for her old age, unless he'd spent it all.

Meanwhile, as she had completely and utterly screwed up any chance of extracting any of her money from him, she would damn well manage on her own.

The Manager of the local National Westminster Bank had always admired Laura Brooke. A pretty woman, in a nice natural country way, he thought. She'd been to see him in the past now and then. Money problems, what with that poor invalid hubby of hers. Not that she was a moaner – coped pretty well, far too young for that lonely life, really. His wife's sister lived in the same village so he knew a bit about her. Looked younger than she was, Mrs Brooke, he thought, peering down at her file to note that she was in her mid-forties. Not too skinny, nice feminine figure. Her brown wavy hair was thick and untidy – the way she pushed it impatiently back from her face was rather appealing.

Clearing his throat, he said, 'I have studied your proposition for a prospective Bed & Breakfast business carefully, but, despite the fact you have catering experience, I don't think it's viable.'

'Oh, why not?'

He frowned, trying to ignore the distress in those blue eyes. 'You're not likely to attract the passing trade out there in St Mary Wield, are you? Even locals get lost finding your village. It's just too remote, Mrs Brooke, too remote by far. You might find a few guests willing to venture out into the depths of the country in July and August, but you can't accommodate enough people to bring in a decent income. And it's not as if there's any local sights or anything for the kiddies to do once they get there. In winter, well, you wouldn't get anyone at all in winter, you know. If the Bank were to advance this sum you require, I don't think you would be able to repay it. Unless you re-mortgage. If you offer the house as security, then we may well be able to help you.'

'No, no, I don't want to do that. Not the house.' She shook her head emphatically. 'But some B&B guests might like being remote and they could always go and visit Chawton. People are getting keener and keener on Jane Austen. I've heard there are busloads of American tourists.'

'Chawton is just too far. If you were nearer to it, or a bit closer to Winchester... As I said, you won't get the numbers you need to provide a regular return, and all that financial outlet won't have been worth while.'

Mrs Brooke began to argue her case quite sensibly but he could see she wasn't used to this sort of thing. Her voice went all high and strained.

Finally, with a fatherly smile, he sat back. 'In my opinion, your best course of action would be to sell your house to raise some capital, then buy a cheap flat somewhere. Then you could seek another form of employment, perhaps residential. For instance, I know there are many Retirement Homes that would value your considerable experience of caring for the sick.'

This prudent suggestion didn't seem to go down very well.

'But that's the very last thing I want to do.' She sounded really upset. 'Must go. Thank you anyway,' she gulped and rushed out.

The manager sadly closed the file.

Laura was glad of an excuse to take the day off from her latest miserable and badly paid temporary job – waitress in the Cosy Copper Kettle – to take a trip to London. She was determined to make one last desperate appeal to the solicitors before putting her house on the market. But the journey proved to be a waste of time and the train fare. High up in their plush modern City block, they were charmingly and politely dismissive. They could definitely not advance her any money without the approval of the chief trustee, Julius.

Dazed and disillusioned, she was walking slowly across Waterloo Station when she heard someone shrieking her name. Laura turned. Oh no, it couldn't be. Yes, it was. It was Bridget.

'Laura, what a piece of luck,' yelled Bridget, pushing past a group of startled-looking men with briefcases, 'Recognised you a mile away. Always look exactly the same as you did at school.'

Hardly a compliment, thought Laura who had been plain as a schoolgirl. Bridget, though, had been a teenage beauty in a solid athletic Amazonian sort of way. She had kept her looks and today she was wearing a wonderful suit, soft red with gold buttons and a short skirt. Too short for her goal-post legs, in Laura's view.

'Frightfully sorry to hear about your husband,' said Bridget without lowering her voice. 'Still, chap like that. Not much future. Only heard when we got back from Melbourne last month. You should have written. Now, when are you coming to dinner?' she asked all in the same breath. Her years in Australia had not in any way toned down the exaggerated plumminess of her diction.

'Well, I...'

'Got a wonderful idea. Come tonight. Now, this evening. George is away on business. Take pot luck with me, so we can have a proper chat.'

'That's really kind, but it's a quarter to five, and I have to get back, really. Before the rush hour.'

'Get back for what? You can do what you want now you're a widow.'

The thought that she was now totally independent for the first time in her life always unsettled Laura. She felt she should be used to the loneliness but she wasn't, not yet.

'Do you good. Be impulsive. Do come,' Bridget was saying and half an hour later Laura found herself in East Sheen outside the front door of an Edwardian semi-detached house.

'Here we are,' said Bridget. 'Had to buy in a hurry, as soon as we got back from Australia. Couldn't stay long in a hotel with our three monsters. The boys are having tea with a friend, thank God. I'll shove 'em straight into bed as soon as they get back.'

Bridget, who had tried to quiz her in a most intimate manner on the train, much to the interest of the other passengers, now pressed her into accepting an early glass of wine and a seat by the fire. The interrogation began in earnest. 'So what are you going to do?'

Laura explained about the failed Bed & Breakfast plan.

'Hm,' said Bridget. 'Why not try hotel management? You used to own a hotel in Greece didn't you. Before William's stroke.'

'Yes, but I don't have any references. And my CV is very bare. Dropping out of university to get married and owning a hotel that went bust isn't very impressive, even if it wasn't our fault. No one wants take me on as any kind of manager. I've been for about five disastrous interviews already. They took one look at me and my wrinkles and said no thanks, no recent experience. And I really can't face starting as a chambermaid or something at my age. Anyway, I want to stay in my own home.'

'Wrinkles? Nonsense, Laura, can't see a single bloody one,' boomed Bridget. 'God, look at me after the Oz sun... But tell me about this place of yours – sounds more of a millstone round your neck rather than an asset. Why're you so attached to it?'

Laura took another sip of wine and stared into the flames. It would sound trite to say that Pond Cottage was like an old friend. 'We were happy there... in the early days,' she said finally. 'And it's Alice's home. She was born there.'

'But I thought you had a shotgun marriage and ran away to Greece. That's what I heard. I was pretty offended not to be asked to the wedding by the way.'

Laura smiled. 'Sorry. It was very quiet, not shotgun though,' Thanks to the miscarriage, she thought. Aloud she said, 'But we did run away to Greece. At one point William tried working in London for a while – that's when Alice was born. But he didn't like it. London, I mean. So we went back to Greece. But all the time we were abroad I knew the cottage was there, like a security blanket.'

'So how old is Alice now? What's she doing?'

Laura was sometimes tempted to be economical with the truth when people asked her this question, because everyone else's daughter seemed to be reading Economics at Durham, if not Law at Cambridge. Or they'd just set up their own IT company and were making millions.

To Bridget she confessed that eighteen-year-old Alice was a nanny on a cattle ranch in Argentina and seemed determined to stay there. It had been a Gap-year job which, unfortunately, had turned into a permanent one.

'In the middle of the pampas or whatever? Isn't that a bit dull for a young girl?'

'Not if you're sleeping with your middle-aged rancher boss, it seems,' said Laura dryly.

Bridget laughed. 'So Alice has a man. What about you?'

'No.'

'Not at all? No one on the horizon?'

'No. Really, I had a happy marriage so I count myself lucky.'

'But unless you're a complete saint you can't have been all that happy after William's stroke, all day every day with an invalid.'

'Oh, I'm not a saint, just the opposite, but I got used to it... like plenty of other women in the same position. Got to accept the cards that are dealt. There isn't time to be unhappy when you're a full-time nurse. Anyway, it was much worse for him than it was for me, of course.' This speech was Laura's stock answer and the easiest thing to say. In fact, she'd often been miserable, resentful, desperate even, but she preferred not to dwell on her own inadequacies. Few people could understand the relentless burden, the frustrations, the sheer drudgery and the only too rare rewards of looking after the person who used to be William. Far better not to discuss her feelings, far better to suppress them.

'Was he, uh, completely paralysed?'

'Not completely.'

'But... no sex?'

'No.'

'So did you have a lover?'

'No time for that sort of thing,' said Laura primly. Nor any real temptation, she thought. Apart from Jack, of course, but he was out of reach. Maybe if he'd been less honourable...

Bridget stared at her incredulously. 'You haven't had sex for eight or nine years?' People often hinted around this matter but only a few asked a direct question on the subject. Laura had correctly predicted that Bridget would be one of them.

Bridget put down her glass with a bang. 'Unbelievable! High time you had a bit of fun. You're still jolly attractive in a country-bumpkin way. All you need is a decent haircut and a few new clothes and you'd knock 'em flat, well, flat-ish. I'll have to hunt around for a suitable chap. Let me think...'

She was not the first woman to make this kind of remark and occasionally one of Laura's friends would invite her to a ghastly party where she would be paired off with a dull elderly bachelor or wolfish divorcé. But she always refused any subsequent dates. She'd never found any of them in the least attractive. 'You don't have to fall madly in love to go out to dinner with a bloke, just dinner, for God's sake,' said one friend crossly. 'Anyway, you can't afford to be fussy, you know. Eligible chaps of your age are in pretty short supply.' To pacify such friends Laura usually said maybe she wasn't ready for a new relationship.

She explained some of this to Bridget.

'Got to start somewhere, can't stay in the nunnery for ever,' said Bridget, taking off her headband and tossing her hair. 'I'll have to find a tame man for you to practise on, while you're waiting for Prince Charming, that is.'

'Bridget, what I need is a decent job. What I *don't* need is the responsibility of a man in my life. Even my own daughter thinks I should live a little, spread my wings.'

Bridget snorted. 'Well, she's right there. So why are you so determined to bury yourself in the country? Crazy. You've got to wake up, rejoin the modern world. You're just putting your head in the sand, or the compost heap rather.'

Laura smiled sadly, 'Actually, after today I think I'll have to face it, I'm going to have to sell up. So if you know anyone who wants a so-called secluded rural retreat...'

'How many bedrooms?'

'Three. Or two and a half, to be honest.'

'I shall come and visit you, a tour of inspection.'

Then later, towards the end of the evening, a smug-looking Bridget said, 'An exceedingly brilliant plan has just occurred to me. Sometimes I'm quite surprised by my own genius. Can't say a word yet, but I may be able to solve all your problems in one fell swoop... D'you like Paris? And, if you play your cards right, there could be a man too.'

Yet another well-meaning busybody trying to arrange my life, thought Laura wearily.

## CHAPTER 2

NEXT MORNING A HEAVY-HEARTED LAURA telephoned the Winchester branch of Soames & Harker to put her house on the market. The manager and his assistant would call that afternoon, she was told by a refined-sounding young woman.

Today? Straight away? No, please don't come at all, she wanted to say.

She scurried round tidying and cleaning all morning, shoving piles of unanswered letters in the desk drawer and cursing the sun for shining through the window on the inadequacies of her housekeeping. Since William died her standards seemed to have slipped.

Then she rushed out into the garden to mow the lawns. The mower, too, was uncooperative and kept stalling at the young Spring grass. Come on you bastard, snapped Laura, giving it a sharp kick, after which the spluttering improved and the machine completed the task in a deafening roar of protest.

She had just finished when the estate agents appeared. Fortunately they were late. Owing to its obscurity, people often arrived late in St. Mary Wield. Laura brushed the grass off her jeans and shook hands politely. They were young men, both wearing Barbours, both nice-looking in an oily sort of way. One was tall and fair; the other, equally suave, was less tall, less fair, but similar. At first she found it hard to tell them apart but then she realised they had adopted different roles. Rupert the Fair played the enthusiast, the kind interrogator, while the one with big ears, whose name she hadn't caught, played the toughie.

'Lovely mellow bricks, these old cottages,' said Rupert. 'And the dormer windows, so typical of the area.'

Big Ears pursed his mouth. 'Purchasers tend to complain small windows make the interior dark.'

'Jolly nice view, Mrs Brooke. And the garden's a good size. Nice specimen shrubs.'

'Somewhat labour intensive. A purchaser looking for a weekend retreat may not find it very manageable,' said Big Ears.

'Cosy – nice atmosphere you've created, with the informal look. Oh, jolly nice beams,' soothed Rupert in a placatory manner when they went indoors. 'The real stuff.'

Informal is about right, she thought, suddenly aware that she hadn't hidden the overflowing ironing basket. In fact, too much clutter in general for modern minimalist Sunday-magazine tastes. Too many tattered cushions, too many unkempt houseplants struggling for space on the window sill, and far too many family snaps, particularly endless Alice-baby pictures taken in Greece. The photos had all been arranged for William, just in case he could still remember the past.

'Not all purchasers like low ceilings,' said Big Ears, ducking at the doorway. He frowned and tapped his felt-tip pen against his notebook. 'Have you bought, by the way, Mrs Brooke?

'Another house? No. I'm not sure how much I could get for this one.'

They stared meaningfully at each other and then went into a long rigmarole about how her house would be difficult to sell unless she put it on the market at a realistic price, an extremely realistic price. Even at this time of year, it could be a tricky one, what with no school nearby, no shop, nothing in the way of modern facilities. After a hasty conferral, they mentioned a sum.

'But that's not very much,' said Laura, sick with disappointment.

'No, but it might buy you a townhouse or bungalow in a modern estate which would be much easier to run as you get older.'

She snorted under her breath at the implication that she was verging on the geriatric.

'We don't actually have those kind of properties on our books,' Rupert continued impassively, 'but we could put you in touch with one of the Basingstoke agents.'

But in spite of the realistic price she was advised to set, few serious prospective buyers came round.

Three sets of people made appointments but didn't turn up. Either they'd got lost or hadn't bothered to ring and cancel.

'Quite normal,' said Rupert when Laura phoned him to complain. 'Londoners don't like these twisty narrow lanes and all the mud, you know,' he said. 'They just lose heart and go home.'

After a few no-hopers came a sharp-faced young woman driving a Mercedes. She teetered around in a black mini-skirt and stilettos, turning up her nose at the old-fashioned bathroom ('no en-suite, oh dear') and the unfitted kitchen, and opening all the cupboards and drawers with a loud sniff. She barely glanced at the garden. It seemed to Laura that she was invading, criticising and rejecting not just her cottage and possessions, but her second-self, her whole life.

After an hour the woman left without saying goodbye or thank you.

'That last one could be interested actually,' reported Rupert later. 'Talked about the cost of a complete modernisation of the house and garden – everything from double glazing to landscaping, a Japanese garden designer and a London interior decorator.'

'A Japanese garden?' Laura repeated, horrified. 'What does she want to do, cover it with blue gravel or something?'

'Mrs Brooke, we always advise vendors never to worry about what might happen to a property once it is sold.'

That night Laura prayed that Ms Stiletto-heels wouldn't make an offer for the house. Whatever her bank manager said, she couldn't bear to sell to a woman like that. Far better to cling on here, by her fingernails. She could even go back to work at the fish farm by the river. This had been the worst of Laura's temporary jobs: gutting slimy trout at dawn and packing them into boxes. A cold, smelly and repellent job and not well paid, but it provided an income of sorts. Maybe she could just hang on. Until when? Until your stepfather goes to meet his maker – whoever that may have been – said a nasty voice in her head.

Then she received a royal visitation from Bridget.

'Yes,' said Bridget, striding around the terrace. 'A perfect gingerbread cottage. Amazingly jungly at the back, all those fields and wild woods. Fabulous after suburban Sheen. And the furniture's so scruffy that tenants couldn't possibly do it any harm.'

Laura raised her eyebrows. 'I've had the estate agents round and they said it would be impossible to rent out. Except to the sort of hippie drop-outs who'd totally wreck the place.'

'Not much to wreck, is there? That's the beauty of it. You see, it all fits in with my master plan. That's why I've come to inspect you. Had the feeling your cottage would suit us down to a tee and it does. I need somewhere nice and dilapidated for the monsters to run wild, and this'd be perfect. So I want to rent it for a year, school hols only, while you're working in Paris. If you get the job and I'm sure you will. Oliver thinks you sound most suitable.'

Laura stared, 'Bridget, what are you talking about?'

'That is just what I'm about to tell you, if you'll let me get a word in. You see, my cousin Oliver is a frightfully distinguished chap who's just started working in Paris. He's divorced and he needs a sort of lady-watchdog, someone to keep an eye on his teenage daughter during the school hols – Charlotte's fifteen, a boarder at St Mary's near here actually. He's got cooks and maids and so forth, so you wouldn't have to do any work really. Wonderful job. I'd be tempted to go for it myself if it weren't for George and the monsters. Always adored Paris.'

'I see,' said Laura thoughtfully. Her heart was giving optimistic leaps.

'Best thing is you'd be back in your cosy cott half the year – downside is you'd only get four or five months' salary but we'd be paying rent too. So during part of the year you'd get two incomes. The interview's this Sunday. Thought you might find it easier if it's really informal, so you can meet Oliver over lunch with us. You can come, can't you?'

'This Sunday?' repeated Laura, suddenly panic-stricken. Having failed at so many of them recently, she loathed interviews.

'Yes, I mean it's a foregone conclusion. You couldn't be more suitable for the job, as I told him. Used to teenage girls, supervising large establishments in the past. Well, I gave the impression you ran a grand hotel rather than a glorified taverna. As for your appearance, if you tidy yourself up you can look quite ladylike and...'

Laura laughed weakly. 'Hold on. *He* might not think I'm so suitable, and what about the daughter? Supposing...'

'Course you'll get on with them. You're very easy-going. Remember that from school. Everyone liked you. And Oliver can be absolutely charming, mostly. I mean, he seems a bit austere, but it's all on the surface. He's a sweetie underneath. A lamb in the iron glove, as they say.'

Laura suppressed a smile. 'So what sort of age is he?'

'Oh, mid-fifties. Looks younger. Used to be a senior army chap, a brigadier or a general or something. Now he's doing something vaguely diplomatic, so he doesn't use his military rank. He'll have to explain – involves lots of initials. Now let's go and choose something for you to wear. Something a bit more elegant than that mac you had on the other day. You must have some decent clothes. Oliver's very meticulous, sort of man who notices things. You should aim for discreet smartness. I'm counting on you, Laura.'

Nothing in Laura's wardrobe was deemed suitable for the forthcoming interview so, after a failed shopping trip to Farnham where everything seemed both dowdy and expensive, she decided to borrow something from Melanie.

Driving along the winding, narrow Hampshire lanes, Laura thought about Melanie's husband. Jack was the man at the back of Laura's mind, the man she didn't allow herself to love. He was out of reach because Mel was her friend.

Nothing much had happened between Jack and Laura apart from the dangerous moment at their New Year's Eve party four years ago. Melanie had been drunk. She'd been drinking all their married life. Because of her loneliness, Jack said. He had left the City because of Melanie's loneliness.

That New Year's Eve Mel must have felt especially lonely because she drank heavily all evening and then, after midnight, she started to dismantle the Christmas tree, throwing baubles and tinsel at the guests. Then, in tears about the mess she had created, she rushed upstairs. Laura followed and managed to persuade her to go to bed, washing her face with a flannel and hanging up her dress. It took a while and when Laura came down again, all the other guests had left.

Alone and desolate, Jack was standing in the hall.

'Let's dance,' said Laura, moved by the miserable expression on his face. To comfort him she put her arms around his neck and they danced in the darkened room together to slow ancient Sinatra songs, with just the lights of a few candles.

It seemed forever since she had danced like this, alone with a man she liked. An undoubtedly attractive man. Then his lips were on her forehead and she knew that she had only to raise her face and he would kiss her.

After a while she did.

When he kissed her, the seal she had placed on her emotions shattered, and feelings she had forgotten or suppressed almost overwhelmed her. She recognised, with shock, how much she desired him. When eventually he pulled away all she could think of was how much she wanted to kiss him again.

They danced on, very slowly, very close. Eventually, he took her by the hand and led her towards the darkness of a small sitting room at the far end of the house.

Hesitating in the doorway, she heard herself say, 'Jack, we can't.'

The spell was broken. He stopped. 'You're right, Laura. Sorry, I...' Caressing her face, he said passionately, 'If we start, give way, we'd never be able to stop. It's a slippery slope, believe me. I'm sorry, but...' Then he held her close again as if he couldn't bear to let her go.

Her heart still thumping, Laura pulled away. 'Of course, just for a moment, I... But there's Mel and William.'

Leaving him standing there, she'd run away, driven home in a turmoil of worry and excitement, which gradually subsided into a dull pain as she turned into the driveway of the cottage.

William had been awake when she looked in on him that night. Hiding her guilty eyes, she wished him a happy New Year. He couldn't reply of course. He never did learn to speak again, but something made her feel he knew what might have happened.

After that Laura went to very few parties. She was always afraid that if she faced any more temptations, if she kissed Jack again, she wouldn't be able to resist the taste of him, and that he wouldn't be able to resist her. It was better to stay at home, be a sort of nun. Nothing noble about her behaviour, she thought, sometimes resentful, sometimes accepting. It was the only way to cope. William was her responsibility and she had to stick with it.

Occasionally she allowed herself to go to a wedding or a lunch party, and if Jack was there, she would watch him out of the corner of her eye, watch the other women surrounding him. And she would wait for him to come and stand next to her and talk to her. She was happy if he did that. His physical presence on just these occasional meetings sustained her.

He featured, of course, in her nightly fantasies. In bed she would lie awake concocting imaginary scenarios where they flew off together and lay on sunlit beaches and kissed on moonlit balconies, and then made naked, tender passionate love all night. But she was careful to remind herself that these were just daydreams. Nothing to do with real life.

When William died, Laura entered a long period of mourning, withdrawing from everyone. There was no thought in her head of anything else but William, her own grief and Alice's. Laura had no romantic daydreams at that time – it seemed to her that she would never feel anything for any man again.

But gradually, after Alice had gone abroad, Laura returned to the world, became less numb and, when she saw Jack, she had a sensation of reawakening. But she vowed that no one would ever know this, least of all Jack himself. Now that she was on her own, the temptation was greater. All the more reason to keep a distance between them.

And so now, eighteen months after William's death, Laura was on her way to see Melanie. Melanie, the pretty blonde overblown rose with the look of an upmarket barmaid. Rich, unhappy, alcoholic Melanie. Jack had told her that Mel's unhappiness stemmed from the fact that she was from Northern Ireland and she missed her family. She didn't like Hampshire or Devon or anywhere else Jack had taken her. Laura thought it a pity Mel never had a child to take her mind off her loneliness. They'd had all the tests apparently, but no reason had been found for their infertility. Then Mel had a miscarriage, or a late period she claimed was a miscarriage. After that she had started to drink more seriously.

Walking into the house, Laura decided Mel looked on better form than usual, but there was something on the kitchen dresser which could have been just orange juice, except that she was drinking it out of a mug. She drank all sorts of things out of a concealing mug – gin and tonic, whisky, vodka.

When sober, she was always welcoming. 'Of course, love, come in. Have a wee coffee. I'm just making some.'

Melanie's kitchen was untidy but basically perfect, just like everything else about her surroundings. They lived in an old farmhouse cleverly extended by Jack so that the seams didn't show.

Mel often liked to recount the story of Jack's success in his new profession of designer and builder after he had resigned from a promising – but in his view suffocating – career as a stockbroker. He'd begun by extending old houses, drawing his designs on the back of an envelope and scouring the country for old bricks and old joinery. His reputation quickly grew as he became popular with the country ladies like Antonia, Serena and Minty. 'Such a nice chap, one of us, understands exactly what one wants, an instinct for one's own personal taste.' 'Marvellous builder, full of ideas, rare as gold dust,' they would confide to each other.

His popularity was such that he was able to expand into building new houses, but he used old materials which made them look like seventeenth-century originals – without the inconvenience and draughts of the Old Vicarage and the Old Forge. Exactly what was in short supply and exactly what people wanted. Unlike some of the bigger developers, he never built houses on an estate all grouped together. He just had the knack of finding the right individual site, the right barn to convert, and persuading the suspicious planning committees that his houses would be an asset to the community.

As indeed they were, Mel would say proudly. 'My Jack, he always wanted to create something permanent and tangible, buildings that are real and good, far better than being a City suit churning investments around.'

Sometimes she was almost embarrassingly nice about Jack and other times she moaned about him. It rather depended on her alcohol intake.

Today she was in complaining mode, 'I said to him, you make enough dosh now. More than we need. The clients like a personal touch, mind. I told him he should give up his small conversions now he's so successful, but he's always afraid of another recession. That's my boy, a great worker.' Half way up the stairs she stumbled and then said, 'But he's never home and if you go to Paris, Laura, I won't have a friend in the world.'

'I'm sure that can't be true,' said Laura, with a pang of guilt. 'What about, what's-her-name, Caroline? Or I thought you liked Serena.'

'Toffee-nosed cows,' said Melanie gloomily.

'Oh, but what about the Red Cross Committee? Aren't you a member – surely some of those people must be friendly?'

'I was sacked. Just because I forgot to go to a few bloody meetings and mislaid their bloody raffle tickets. Lord save us, you'd have thought I'd lost the crown jewels or something.'

'What about Jack's clients? He's very popular.'

'Yes, *he's* very popular. Especially with the ladies,' said Melanie. 'Jack is much more understanding than their boring huntin' shootin' fishin' husbands. He's very sympathetic, so he is. As you know.'

Apprehensive, Laura waited for what she might say next but she fell silent.

When they reached the bedroom, she became more cheerful and thrust suit after expensive suit into Laura's arms. 'Try the blue – looks great on you, blue. I've grown out of that one. This whole cupboard's full of things that seem to have shrunk a wee bit. I'll give it to you. Have what you like. Perhaps the blue's a bit Tory Matron, though.'

Laura laughed. She stared at herself in the mirror and thought she looked good in an unobtrusive sort of way.

'Maybe you should try this black one with the short skirt – it's more sexy, give you more pulling power.'

'I'm not aiming for sex appeal – the image I want is genteel respectability.'

'Ah yes, better to hold your fire. After all, he could turn out to be a poison dwarf with two heads. You might not want to inflame his passions.'

'Mel, this is about earning a living, nothing else, OK?'

'So you say, Jane Eyre, so you say.'


When Ms Stiletto-heels made an offer somewhat below the asking price, Laura had great pleasure in refusing it.

'But Mrs Brooke...' began Rupert, sounding resigned, patient and clearly only too accustomed to dealing with difficult women.

'Just tell her I'm looking for something better,' said Laura.

## CHAPTER 3

'GOLLY, YOU DO LOOK SMART, almost too neat and pretty to be true. Hardly recognised you,' enthused Bridget, taking her by the arm and propelling her into the house. 'This,' she announced with the air of a proud mother producing a favourite child, 'is my dear old schoolfriend, Laura.'

Bridget's cousin, Oliver Farringdon, was handsome, very handsome if you liked the lean and hungry look, Laura thought. His dark eyes were speculative and she flushed a little as he looked her up and down while they shook hands. Tall and authoritative, with a determined chin and bony prominent nose, he was the sort of man one couldn't easily ignore in a crowd and in Bridget's small sitting room he dominated the scene. Though his hair was iron-grey, he gave an impression of youthful vigour and athleticism.

The daughter, Charlotte, was tall too, but limp and lanky rather than athletic-looking. Pale-faced, she was dressed in black jeans and a tight beige jumper that emphasised the boyishness of her figure. Her manner was cool and wary, like a nervous and over-bred greyhound. Whether this reserve was due to shyness or faint hostility, Laura couldn't tell. The girl stared out from under her dark fringe, and kept glancing at her father as if waiting for a signal as to what to do next.

After the introductions there was a silence that Bridget immediately sought to fill with chatter, but she was interrupted by the simultaneous arrival of three small boys brandishing plastic guns in each hand and shouting in loud Australian accents that must have been painful to their mother's ear. Two of them were wearing ragged cowboy outfits, and the third was dressed as a knight, or possibly a Space Alien, and they seemed to be in the throes of a violent battle.

No wonder their father spends so much time abroad, thought Laura uncharitably.

A flustered Bridget served lunch soon after. 'To calm the savage beasts,' she said.

Unfortunately the food did not seem to have a particularly calming effect and there was little opportunity for sensible conversation. The monsters seemed to make enough noise for thirty children. Charlotte kept giggling at their naughtiness, which encouraged further showing off. Mr Farringdon (don't use his military rank, Bridget said) didn't seem to find them so amusing.

After lunch Bridget instructed her guests to take the children for a walk in Richmond Park to feed the ducks while she organised the house, and so they all dutifully set off along the prosperous suburban streets of East Sheen.

As soon as the children had been released into the wide grassy slopes of the park, Farringdon fell into step beside Laura and began to ask her penetrating questions about her life. He listened carefully to her answers. 'I hope you are not expecting glamour and excitement in Paris,' he said seriously.

'I'm not expecting anything,' said Laura, her breath quickening. He was now striding along so fast that she found it hard to keep up with him, not helped by the fact that she was hobbled by her straight skirt and a pair of boat-like wellies lent by Bridget.

'What I want is someone who will supervise Charlotte quite closely. Too many temptations for the young these days.'

'I see.'

Giles, the eldest child, rushed back to her, his round face pink with exertion. 'Are we going to the nearest ducks or Penn Ponds?'

'The nearest ones – and wait till I get there,' said Laura quickly. 'Oh, look, the deer. How lovely, but don't go too near them.'

He stared at her scornfully. 'Course not.' Then he raced back towards his brothers.

Farringdon continued his train of thought. 'Charlotte's not a sophisticated child – she needs to learn to appreciate Paris, to be taken to art galleries and so on during the day, and then I need someone to stay in with her during the evening while I attend official social engagements.'

'I'm used to staying in.'

'So I gather from Bridget,' he said with a sudden smile that was full of understanding and approval.

Laura was charmed. She began to feel that she actually might have a chance of getting this job.

'You don't know Paris well, I gather. The Government has given me a good apartment in the sixteenth arrondissement. You would, of course, have your own bedroom but there's no spare sitting room,' he went on. 'I have domestic staff, so your duties would be entirely confined to Charlotte. I'm heading the British Delegation to the new Committee on European Defence. Naturally, there are social responsibilities attached to this job – I have the special rank of Ambassador – and I may ask you to act as hostess on occasions.'

Help, thought Laura. As he was describing the intricacies of diplomatic social life, she wondered if she should ask about the salary or time off, but it seemed inappropriate to mention such vulgar matters. Instead she decided to talk about the daughter. 'Charlotte is good with Bridget's boys,' she said, waving her arm towards the group ahead. When this remark elicited no response other than a faint snort, she asked, 'Does she, your daughter, have any career in mind?'

Farringdon ignored this question. 'She needs to concentrate on her GCSEs. It's essential she gets good grades, absolutely essential. She works hard at the moment, but her mother was a frivolous woman. Don't want that to happen to Charlotte. Young women these days can't afford to be frivolous, unfortunately.'

They paced on. Eventually Laura asked, 'Does she see her mother from time to time?'

'No,' he said.

Oh dear, thought Laura. She wondered who had instigated the divorce.

A little later she ventured, 'But I do think teenagers need a certain amount of freedom. And they behave better if one trusts them.' As soon as she'd made this sensible pronouncement she decided it sounded both pompous and bossy.

Farringdon shook his head. 'Never wise to be too trusting.'

There was a silence, and as they approached the children, he said, 'I'm seeing two or three other candidates this week. I'll let you know. My secretary will write to you.' His tone was cool and impassive, not particularly encouraging, she thought.

He didn't seem interested in watching the boys throw bread to the ducks and, without saying goodbye, he strode off towards the rugby pitches in the distance.

'Can I go with him? I like watching rugger,' begged Giles, tugging Laura's sleeve.

'No, stay with us. He prefers being on his own,' said Charlotte bleakly.

Driving home along the M3 Laura felt alternately optimistic and then full of doubts. Would he offer her the job and did she want it? She did, definitely. The salary was unlikely to be high. Living in someone else's house was never easy, and the General wasn't a cosy or comfortable man. Too authoritative and perhaps too severe. Although he might be OK once one got to know him – Bridget had proclaimed him to be a lamb at heart.

But no one else wanted her, apart from the fish farm. Too many prospective employers had rejected her. Oliver Farringdon seemed to be her only chance to escape from drudgery and keep her cottage. And he offered an opportunity to extend her horizons. It would do her good to get out of the country.

'Dad's gone now, Mum. Time you got a life,' had been Alice's parting shot before she went to Argentina.


Bridget was pleased with herself. It all seemed to have gone frightfully well. 'So what do you think,' she asked, handing Oliver a cup of tea. 'Laura's a dear, isn't she? And very discreet and unshowy. I'm sure she'd be terrifically diplomatic.'

'A charming woman', he said, 'but will she be up to the job? Years in the depths of Hampshire with a sick husband hardly prepare one for Paris.'

'But she comes from a sophisticated family,' said Bridget. 'Her mother was reasonably well off. Not that Laura's rich, quite the opposite. Poor as two church mice.'

'Is the mother still alive?' he asked.

'No, died ages ago and the thing is, all her money went to the second husband, which I always thought was jolly unfair. Let's hope Laura gets some eventually, when her stepfather pops off.'

Oliver paused. 'Mm,' he said.

'Course, William, her husband, never made a bean. He was a painter, you know. Much older than her.'

'A painter?'

Bridget was in sympathy with the dismissive tone of his voice. 'Yes,' she said. 'That's why they went to Greece – said he liked the light, if you please. I think he tried working in the City for a while, then he dropped out or was sacked, not sure which. In Greece he did use to sell a few paintings to the tourists, landscapes, that sort of thing. He sketched, you see, while Laura ran the taverna, er, hotel, I mean. She did all the work, while he sat about waiting to be discovered by the art world. He never was, though.'

'She sounds an exemplary person.' His tone was dry but it did not occur to Bridget that she might be over-selling her product.

There was a commotion as the children appeared saying they were absolutely starving, closely followed by Charlotte.

Bridget beamed at her. 'Charlotte dear, did you like my friend Laura? Such a sweetie, isn't she?'

Charlotte shrugged her shoulders.

'A thoroughly suitable person, ' said Bridget firmly. 'She's got a daughter a little older than you so she's used to teenagers.'

'I forgot to ask her if she speaks French,' said Oliver.

'She was quite brainy at school so I'm sure she does,' said Bridget, determined to arrange a crash course if this were not true.

Oliver smiled. 'Then I think she might do very well,' he said.

'I think so too. Don't you, Charlotte?'

Charlotte stood up and stalked towards the door where she paused dramatically. 'I don't care. What difference does it make?' she hissed. Then she rushed up the stairs.

Later that evening Laura was surprised and delighted to receive a telephone call from Farringdon offering her the job, subject to a trial period.

'But what about the other candidates you mentioned?'

'Decided not to bother with them after all. You seemed so eminently suitable.'

'How very kind.' She took a deep breath. 'Could you just, er, tell me the sort of salary you vaguely had in mind?'

He named a sum that was not overwhelming in its generosity but certainly more than she earned as a trout-gutter or waitress.

'How about spending the May half term in Paris?' he added. 'So you can see if you like us.'

## CHAPTER 4

LAURA WAS WAITING FOR JACK. She had changed into a clean shirt and clean jeans, and put on lipstick and a little scent. She despised herself for these unnecessary preparations, preparations she always made when Jack was expected.

When he arrived at her front door, she felt a surge of happiness, accompanied, to her annoyance, by a frisson of what was undoubtedly lust. Damn, she thought, kissing him hello in what she hoped was a sisterly way.

It struck her yet again what a pleasant looking man he was, weather-beaten face, blue eyes, square jaw, mousy-brown curly hair, greying at the edges, ordinary really. Yet his eyes were always bright and sexually alert. This sexual alertness of Jack's was powerful and difficult to ignore, though Laura tried. It wasn't a cold aggressive sexuality, just warm and friendly and interested. There was something extraordinarily appealing about Jack's friendliness, his energy, his warmth of character. Often, in the depths of her loneliness, she'd thought about wrapping herself up in his arms and staying there.

'So you're going to Paris?' he said, sitting down at the kitchen table and smiling in his you're-the-only-woman-in-the-world way. 'I'll miss you and so will Mel. She keeps talking about you.'

'Um, I thought she seemed a little better the other day.'

'No, she isn't better, as you so delicately put it.'

Laura paused. 'Does the doctor have any further suggestions?'

'No.'

'She won't go to a drying-out clinic?'

'No. She doesn't see a need for it.'

'Well, I was wondering, would you like me to try and persuade her to go to an AA meeting? I could even go with her, if it'd help.'

He looked up. 'You can try but it won't work. Didn't work when I suggested it. She's not like those people, she says.' His eyes were now blank, his voice dead and flat.

'Well, have a drink anyway,' said Laura. They both smiled at the irony of the offer.

'Trouble is,' said Jack, accepting a whisky, ' I find it hard to enjoy a social drink these days. And of course I don't keep any at home, not for myself. Though she buys it of course.'

'Can't you hide it or throw it away?'

He hunched his shoulders and then said, 'We passed through that stage a long time ago. There's only a limited amount one can do. Mel herself has got to want to stop...' He shook his head wearily. 'But let's change the subject. Tell me about the problem you wanted to see me about.'

So with endless apologetic preliminaries about how she didn't like to bother him but she didn't know who else to ask, Laura explained that her prospective tenant, Bridget, had decided some aspects of the cottage were a bit too dilapidated, even for her chaotic family, that they couldn't quite live with a leaking roof, or unreliable hot water. And they definitely couldn't cope with a dodgy heating system. After years in Australia they didn't like the cold.

'Of course, I could wait until the autumn to get a new boiler, but maybe it's more economical to do all the repairs at once,' said Laura. 'You see, I didn't like to ask you because you're a big firm and these are only small repairs, so I asked the little bloke from the next village and his estimate is so expensive I thought I'd just consult you to see if it was fair before I work out a way of borrowing the money. Sorry to bother you but I've been having sleepless nights over it all.'

'Just give me a list of what needs fixing, in order of priority,' said Jack, taking out his notebook.

Quicker to list what doesn't need fixing, she thought, but she confined herself to mentioning only the absolute essentials that Bridget had specified.

They made a tour of the house, during which Laura found herself uncomfortably close to him at times. In the bedroom when she showed him the loose window catch, he'd stopped and looked at her for a moment in a way that was not at all business-like. So she'd rushed out on to the landing and started babbling breathlessly about the roof. And he followed her, concentrating once more on his notebook.

Back in the sitting room Jack sat down again. 'We can do the job for you. No problem,' he said.

'But, er, how much would your estimate be?'

'Oh, we wouldn't have to charge you anything.'

'What? That's ridiculous. You can't run a business like that.'

His eyes twinkled. 'Laura, I do have a certain amount of experience in how to run a business, whereas...'

'Yes, of course but I *must* pay.'

'Look, we can scrounge good second-hand materials from our other sites or stuff that's fallen off the back of our lorries. For instance, one of my clients has just thrown out a perfectly good boiler because she wants the latest Aga. Apart from the plumbing, a lot of the work can be done by Charlie. He's a retired carpenter but he'll turn his hand to anything. In fact, I could take a hand myself sometimes. Then the cost of labour would be minimal.'

'But I insist. I must pay a proper price or I can't ask you to do the job,' she said.

'Nonsense.'

'Please, Jack.'

He shrugged his shoulders. 'All right then. Make it five hundred quid altogether.'

'But the other chap's estimate was six and a half thousand. How about if I pay you six thousand?'

He laughed. 'This is crazy. Buyers are supposed to bargain *down*, not up. Didn't anyone ever explain that to you? Anyway, I don't believe you've got that sort of money to spare.'

Laura thought of her overdraft. 'No, but I could borrow it. I'm sure the bank manager would change his mind if he knows I've got a tenant. Jack, I can't accept charity from you.'

He shook his head. 'No, my final estimate is five hundred pounds, repaid in instalments, as and when you can, when you've got some rent coming in or a salary. Take it or leave it. But if you don't employ my firm, I'll be bitterly offended,' he said smiling.

'But you're still not charging me nearly enough and I might not even get the job in Paris. I'm only on trial.'

'Laura, stop quibbling. We've got a deal, OK?'

'OK. I accept, you're an angel, a knight in shining armour,' said Laura and hugged him impulsively.

He held on to her and whispered in her ear using a sinister quasi Middle-Eastern accent, 'Strictly speaking, you should not become beholden to a strange man for fear 'ee will ask for somezing in return.'

She grinned and pushed him away, her heart thumping. 'Trouble with you is that you always turn me down,' she said unwisely.

'That's because I've got an addictive personality, like my wife. Only it's not alcohol with me. I was always afraid I might become addicted to you.' Though he, too, was talking in a joking manner, the expression in his eyes flustered her.

To disguise her feelings, she turned away. After a pause she said, 'About Melanie, I'll go and see her tomorrow about the AA. That's one thing I can do for you in return.'

'Right, thanks,' he said abruptly. 'But don't expect too much from her. I very much doubt she'll accept your kind offer.'

In the event, he was right. After dancing around the subject in a veiled way for about half an hour, Laura took a deep breath and blurted out her suggestion.

'No, thanks,' said Mel, her previously friendly mood evaporating immediately.

'But, Mel, it may sound boring but I know someone who went to AA and...'

'Mind your own business,' said Mel and her voice was full of suppressed rage. 'So I like a drop now and then. So does everyone. Laura, people like you are enough to drive anyone to drink, y'know. And that other bloody woman.'

'Who?'

'Some do-gooder called Prudence. What a name! A reformed drunk – they're the worst of the lot. All sanctimonious and "I know what you're going through and I am here to help you." A complete stranger. Rang me up out of the blue and blathered on about Alcohol with a capital A. How does she know what I'm going through? Bloody cheek. Don't know who put her on to me. Maybe it was that CPN woman.'

'CPN?'

'Community Psychiatric Nurse, some young fogey the doctor sent. Trouble is, those mad medics think anyone who has the odd wee drink is on the path to wrack and ruin. But I didn't think you were like that, Laura.' She paced around the room, her untidy blonde hair straggling down her back. 'If you really want to help, you should speak to Jack. Tell him to stay home more, talk to him about those women.'

Laura flinched inwardly. 'What d'you mean?'

'His clients. Not you, of course, I don't count you,' she said in a more kindly way, 'I mean women like that Mary, that stupid tart who thinks she's such a great lady.'

'Oh, her.'

'Yeah, her. Women think Jack's fair game, just because he's polite.'

'Course he's polite to his clients. That's business.'

'Yeah,' said Melanie, taking a swig from what may or may not have been a mug of coffee, 'I know that, you know that, but they, the tarts, think Jack fancies them. What d'you reckon?'

Laura turned away to hide her face. 'I think Jack's a sensible man who cares about you. And he'd be bound to avoid getting involved with female clients because it'd be bad for business. If men couldn't trust him with their wives, they wouldn't use his firm. And anyway, as I said, he's a loyal sort of chap, Mel. You must know that.'

'Yes, but he likes women. He stares at their legs, and their tits and...'

'Oh for God's sake, that's normal. If he chats them up, it's only in fun,' said Laura, feeling more and more guilty about her uncommitted sins.

'So you say, so you say,' said Mel gloomily, taking another gulp from her mug.

Next morning Melanie was feeling virtuous. Just to prove that she could, she'd held off the booze and driven to Farnham, done Sainsbury's, then gone for a wander. She'd managed to find a new dress in Monsoon which looked good. Long, Indian and droopy, it suited her, drawing attention to her bosom which was the best part of her and disguising the rest. And she'd bought a couple of bottles of vodka that were on special offer in the Wine Rack and saved a couple of quid at least. When she'd come home she'd put the vodka under the sink behind the Cif and the bleach, to save herself from temptation. Five minutes later she'd taken one of the bottles out again and, opening the neck with a satisfying clink, had sat down to have a tot, just a wee one, to settle her nerves after the long drive.

A while later, standing in front of the long mirror in the hall, she tried on the dress again to make sure it was all right. It was size sixteen, a size bigger than this time last year, which was scary. Looked good though – or would do when she had a tan – a thin black clingy cotton dress, summery and sexy, cut low. But there was white underwear all over the place, so pulling down the top, she removed her bra and rearranged the dress around her substantial bosom.

She leant forward to stare into the mirror. Too much cleavage showing now, Mel me girl, she said to herself. Won't do for Hampshire.

Behind her she heard a gulp. 'Uh, Mrs, I was knocking... Door was open so I...'

She spun unsteadily round to see one of her husband's new employees, a young plumber, just qualified.

'Uh, Mrs, uh,' he repeated incoherently, scarlet in the face.

A handsome young boy he was. She'd noticed him before, with his gold earring, blond crew cut and his muscular shoulders in a tattered grey tee shirt. His face was none too clean. Must have been peering down a drain.

She smiled. 'Hello, Gary. Like a drink?'

'No fanks.' Something, a bird perhaps, was tattooed on his arm.

'No fanks,' mimicked Mel, but he didn't seem to mind. Or perhaps he didn't hear.

He was staring at her, with glazed eyes, like a rabbit fascinated by a particularly attractive snake. He seemed to find it difficult to speak. 'Uh, the boss, he said, uh, you'd got a problem with... with the toilet, like.'

'Oh yes,' she said. 'Upstairs. In the guest bathroom. Water's always running. Will I lead the way?'

He cleared his throat. 'Right.'

'My husband said it needs a new ballcock,' said Mel with a glint in her eye. 'He could have fixed it himself, really.'

Gary followed her silently upstairs and along the corridor to the spare room, which was elegantly decorated in Colefax and Fowler and some rather unsteady stencilling done by Mel on one of her better days. She hadn't actually finished the hems of the curtains but they looked good. So did the bedspreads, made by a smart decorator in Alton on special order. Pity no one ever came to stay with them these days.

The en suite bathroom wasn't that big, so she stayed outside while Gary lifted the lid of the lavatory tank and peered at it. He muttered something about the van and then disappeared, returning a few minutes later holding a copper globe on a rod. Various lewd remarks ran through Melanie's mind but she restrained herself so as not to embarrass the boy. Then she remembered the leak under the sink.

'Cobblers' children have no shoes, as they say,' she began.

He turned and looked at her uncomprehendingly. She started to explain about cobblers' children's lack of shoes and builders' wives having nobody to do household repairs, but he wasn't paying attention. He wasn't even looking at her face. His eyes seemed to be fixed on her right breast which, she noticed in some surprise, had now escaped from the dress altogether and was protruding in magnificent abandon, all on its own. She felt quite proud of it, so bravely suspended there. It wasn't shy, this breast of hers.

Taking a step forward, she followed its good example.

He didn't retreat or shout for help. His mesmerised expression was rather sweet, bless him, she thought afterwards. At the time, she didn't think at all. She sat down on the bed and patted the space beside her invitingly. 'Right you are, young Gary,' she said.


When Jack came home, he found Melanie fast asleep in their bedroom, mouth open, snoring gently. She'd obviously had a bath as clothes were strewn around the room and she was wrapped in a towel. Seeing the inevitable glass of vodka on the bedside table, he decided not to waken her. There was no point. He wasn't angry any more, or rather his anger had turned into a dull, suppressed kind. He'd passed through the raging, shouting phase and the pouring-gin-down-the-drain phase and was now sinking towards accepting the inevitable, waiting till Mel reached the bottom and would then – maybe – accept help. He'd read about all these phases in a psychobabble handbook about what it feels like to live with an alcoholic. Not that he normally read that kind of bunk but the doctor had handed them out and, sickeningly, Jack recognised himself – and Mel – in these gruesome leaflets.

He went downstairs to the kitchen and found the worktops covered with Sainsbury's bags still full of groceries. Hastily he began to put the meat and eggs in the fridge. The good news and the bad news, he thought. Good – she had been sober enough to go shopping. Not wanting to risk losing her licence, Mel was usually careful not to drink and drive. The bad news was the soggy heap of formerly frozen prawns. He threw the whole packet into the bin.

He didn't bother to look for the till receipt to see how many bottles of spirits she'd bought and he didn't bother to search the house to check where she had stashed them. He did notice a chipped blue mug half concealed behind the curtain. Mechanically he picked it up and sniffed the contents. Gin this time. He left it where it stood.

No point in doing anything else. There was no point in getting angry either.

His stomach felt empty and he was in need of company. He returned to the Audi and drove out into the night.

# CHAPTER 5

Laura fed her ticket into the machine at the Eurostar terminal and the barricade opened for her. Like magic, she thought, full of sudden optimism.

She'd arrived far too early for the train, of course. Tugging her heavy old suitcase behind her, she waited in the queue for an expensive cup of filter coffee and sat down at the only free table. She sipped the coffee carefully, anxious not to stain her pale cream suit, another of kind Melanie's cast-offs.

Finally boarding was announced and, joining the expectant crowd, she made her way up the escalator and what seemed like a mile along the long platform until she found her place in the train, a sharp-nosed train with a distinctly French feel about it. As she stowed her luggage in the rack, Laura's spirits rose still further.

The confusing multi-lingual Eurostar magazine, written in stultifying touro-prose, did not hold her attention for long but she felt too restless and excited to settle down to her novel. Instead she played a game, guessing which passengers were French and which were English. It wasn't hard with the women – French equals short neat hair and short neat clothes. English equals somewhere between a sweet fuzzy disorder and drab anorak dowdiness.

In the centre table of the carriage three excitable French women (short and neat, dripping with jewellery) were holding a noisy business meeting. Beside them an Englishman (suit, no anorak) was droning boringly into a mobile phone. The pair of young lovers across the aisle seemed more appropriate passengers for this romantic journey.

Laura tried to remember the time when she and William were young lovers but, to her distress, she couldn't recapture her feelings. Instead her thoughts kept returning to Jack's face as he said goodbye.

She held her breath when the train slid down into the Channel Tunnel, but it turned out to be no different from any other tunnel, just longer. Of course, she wasn't exactly frightened of travelling beneath the sea but a small sigh of relief escaped her when they finally emerged into the bright sunshine of France. She sat back, watching the vast empty fields flash by.

The Gare du Nord was all cold winds, echoes and stale station smells. She hurried down another astonishingly long platform, worried that, despite Farringdon's promise to send his car, there would be no one to meet her. Beside the barricade, however, she found a small dark solemn-faced Frenchman with a board bearing her name. How grand, thought Laura, amused and gratified.

'*Bonjour, madame,*' he said, inclining his head politely and then, grabbing hold of her suitcase, indicated that she should follow him.

He bustled ahead to open the rear door of a large black Rover parked, with what surely must be illegal convenience, just outside the station. As Laura settled back into the leather upholstery she examined the opulent interior fittings of the car with some satisfaction. It made a pleasant change to be chauffeur-driven through the streets of Paris in a grand limo, rather than chugging around the Basingstoke ring road in her elderly Toyota.

The driver was keen to point out the sights. 'Boulevard Haussman, Galleries Lafayette, very grand surface.' Then, 'the famous Hermès... now Place de la Concorde. See, down there, l'Arc de Triomphe... River Seine,' he said with a proud flourish of his hand.

'Wonderful,' said Laura, overwhelmed by the elaborate beauty of it all. Not much was left to nature in Paris, she noted. Even the chestnut trees beside the road were firmly clipped into a neat green wall of foliage.

As they drove along beside the river past the *Grand Palais*, his voice took on a sepulchral tone. 'Place d'Alma. The underpass. *La pauvre princesse* Diana... the accident. It was that one, that pillar, number thirteen.' He waved his hand again.

'Oh dear.'

*'La tour Eiffel,'* he said, becoming more cheerful as they left the notorious underpass and drove up into the sunshine.

*'Merveilleux,'* said Laura, feeling she must attempt some French. She had borrowed tapes from the library but was not confident that her schoolgirl standard had much improved.

Finally they arrived in the serene boulevards of the seizième arrondissement. *'La Residence, madame,'* he said drawing up in one of the seemingly identical streets of elegant cream-stone apartment blocks.

Laura found Farringdon's name and pressed the buzzer that enabled her to enter the building – all inlaid marble and red carpets – and took the antiquated lift to the third floor. She hesitated for a moment outside a huge mahogany door and then rang the bell. It was answered by a skinny middle-aged man dressed in a white jacket, black tie and black trousers. His white hair was thick and curly, and he would have been good-looking if his features had been arranged in a more pleasant expression.

*'Oui?'* he asked with a frown, as if she were not the class of person he would normally expect to find on such a distinguished threshold.

*'Bonjour, je suis Laura Brooke. Je suis l'invitée de Monsieur Farringdon...'* she began haltingly.

'Ah yes, good afternoon, madame,' he said in English, 'His Excellency has spoken of you. The new lady for Miss Charlotte.'

Weird job description, she thought.

'This way, please.' His manner was no more friendly than before, but he did pick up her case.

'And what is your name?' asked Laura.

'I am Sebastien, the maître d'hôtel – butler, you say in English.'

Another world, she thought, looking around at the dark palatial rooms with king-size chandeliers drooping from high ceilings – ceilings about twice the height of those in her cottage. Valuable-looking oil paintings in heavy frames hung on the walls between panels of elaborate plasterwork. Persian carpets and traditional mahogany furniture added to the atmosphere of luxurious gloom, a gloom only partially dispelled by some Chinese porcelain table lamps throwing a discreet glow.

'Very nice, lovely,' said Laura, feeling a need to praise, however unsophisticated it might be to do so.

The butler led her silently down the passage to a door at the end.

'Very nice,' said Laura again, this time less sincerely. In fact it was a small dark room fitted with unattractive teak units and a hard-backed yellow armchair. Quite suitable for a governess though, she thought.

Having unpacked her few possessions, she was sitting in the drawing room, or salon, as she must now learn to call it, reading the *Insider's Guide to Paris* when Charlotte trailed into the room.

'Oh, you're here,' she said. The girl was only marginally more friendly than Sebastien.

'Yes, hello, Charlotte. How are you? When did you arrive?'

'Oh, ages ago. Dad brought me in the car,' she muttered, looking more waif-like than ever in black jeans and a droopy black sweater several sizes too big for her.

'Did you have a good journey?'

Charlotte shrugged her shoulders without replying.

After a pause, Laura asked, 'When will your father be back?'

Charlotte was half way out of the room before she turned and said, 'Dunno, 'bout six I suppose.'

Laura heard a bedroom door slamming at the end of the corridor, then some loud pop music. She wondered what to do next. Looking at her watch, she saw it was only five o'clock.

She wandered hesitantly into the hall. Sebastien materialised from behind a door, as if he had been hiding. 'You take some tea, madame?'

Laura returned to the salon. Finally tea was served, not by Sebastien but by a small fat woman in a blue overall. She was of Southern European appearance, with black bushy eyebrows meeting in the centre above vacuous black eyes.

'I Irini. I cook,' she said.

'I am very happy to meet you, Irini,' said Laura with what she hoped was a winning smile. It was clear the woman, too, wanted a look at her.

The cook grimaced briefly in response and then waddled out of the room, leaving behind her a smell of garlic and other less fragrant odours. Oh dear, thought, Laura. Not a ray of sunshine either. So there was a resentful teenager, a disapproving butler and a cook who smells. Welcome to Paris.

Still, the tea was good. It had been served on a silver tray loaded with white china with gold rims and gold crests, but the pot was too full and she managed to spill tea all over the tray. Hastily she wiped it with a tissue and then had to hunt round for a waste paper basket, wanting to dispose of the soggy mess before Sebastien caught her misusing Government property.

After tea Laura decided to take action. She knocked on Charlotte's door. There was no reply. The pop music was deafening. Sounds as if she has a live band in there, thought Laura. Perhaps she really has. An alarming vision of her new charge being drugged and gang-raped by a posse of dope-smoking rockers came into her mind. She knocked again.

Charlotte suddenly opened the door. 'Yeah?' she enquired truculently, swaying on her long legs. Apart from a pile of textbooks on the floor, the room behind her was astonishingly tidy, and the noise emanated from an extensive music system rather than drugged rockers.

'There's tea – are you going to have some?' asked Laura.

'No. Don't like brown drinks.' She made to shut the door again.

'Then, I was wondering if you could show me the way to the nearest chemist's,' said Laura quickly. She didn't actually need anything urgently but she was confident that no woman would turn down this request.

The girl gave a sudden shy, almost friendly smile. 'Sure, yeah. Right.'

As they walked down the street together Laura asked questions about Paris which Charlotte answered in muttered monosyllables as if the effort of talking was too much for her.

Then as they came around the corner of the boulevard, she suddenly sprang to life. 'La Muette. Yellow M – Metro. You can buy tickets in the Tabac, kind of bar. Pharmacies have a sort of big green cross. See, there's like two of them on opposite sides over there. I mean, it's a bit difficult not to find a pharmacy in Paris actually, one on every corner. All the French are massive hypochondriacs. Can you find your way back?'

All this was said in one great animated breath.

Laura didn't catch it all. 'What?'

'I said, if I go back to the apartment now, can you sort of find your way home alone?'

'No, I don't think I can. Would you mind looking after me for just a little bit longer?' asked Laura gently.

'Sure, OK,' said Charlotte with another sudden smile.

After the chemist, where Laura bought an unnecessary second toothbrush, and some equally unnecessary aspirin, they walked a little way down rue du Passy, gazing into all the glamorous boutiques, and drooling over the chocolates and patisseries – mega-*luxe* at mega prices, Charlotte said. Laura realised that she hadn't done anything as female and frivolous for years and it was fun. Under the sharp eye of a supercilious Parisian salesgirl in Morgan, Charlotte tried on an astonishingly short black skirt at an astonishingly high price.

'D'you think Dad'll say this is too expensive?'

'He might well, seeing as it costs about £20 an inch.'

'He's very stingy, Dad. Everyone else at school has got a proper dress allowance.'

Laura smiled, remembering how at a similar age Alice, too, used to begin all her sentences with Every One Else Has Got...

As they walked home Laura thought about Alice. She'd missed her so much when she first went abroad, but now she'd almost got used to their separation. There was both the physical and a certain psychological distance between them. Communication was so difficult with Argentina, what with the time difference and the phone lines being always engaged. Alice didn't answer e-mails either. Probably she was doubly uncommunicative because she imagined, correctly, that Laura disapproved of the romance with Roberto, her rancher boss whose wife was living apart, down in Buenos Aires. Actually,

Laura had been glad to hear about the wife. Her main hope was that said wife would return to the ranch, dislodge Alice and shove her on the plane to England.

Farringdon was already at home when they got back. He set aside his *Times* and rose to his feet, looking them up and down approvingly.

'Glad to see you girls getting together,' he said.

Still pompous but more friendly now, thought Laura.

*Tall, distinguished, very eligible and Not Married,* she heard her mother's voice saying. Laura shook her head. Despite his mature and handsome charms, she decided she was not attracted to cold-fish Farringdon.

Nevertheless she went to her room to try out the free sample that the girl in the perfume shop had given her.

Farringdon's conversation during pre-dinner drinks and dinner itself was smooth. He tended to talk a great deal. What he said was interesting and it was only necessary for Laura to supply a prompt now and then. Charlotte said nothing at all, and did not follow up any of Laura's attempts to include her.

The food was on the heavy side but tasty, and the wine excellent, but it was not a relaxing meal. Sebastien served each of the three courses at such frantic speed that Laura was afraid he would drop something. His demeanour was quite different when Farringdon was in the room – there was an almost grovelling politeness about the way he served his master.

After dinner, Charlotte dived off to her room, muttering something about English GCSE.

'Fat chance – probably studying Mills & Boon rather than Milton,' murmured Farringdon with an indulgent smile. 'Doesn't read nearly enough though and she doesn't take kindly to guidance about that or anything else.'

Laura warmed to him suddenly. 'Typical teenage... But in fact, she's been very helpful today.'

Farringdon raised his eyebrows. 'Glad to hear it.'

She described their shopping trip and he listened with approving attention for several minutes. Then he stood up and said abruptly, 'Now if you'll excuse me, I have some work to do.' It was as if he had allocated her only a certain amount of time and her appointment with him had come to an end.

Laura stood watching as he shut the study door behind him. Unwilling to sit alone in the salon yet again, she retired to her room and, feeling more and more like a Victorian lady, settled down to read the new Joanna Trollope. She left her door ajar in case Charlotte should wish to talk to her but at about eleven o'clock the thumping music suddenly ceased and everything was quiet.

Quiet, that is, apart from the noises that a strange building makes at night – creaks, groans, water glugging in the ancient pipes. The walls were thick but she could hear footsteps tapping backwards and forwards on the parquet floor above. And then there was the traffic in the street. So different from the quietness of the country nights at home.

She was glad to have her own bathroom as she wouldn't have wanted to meet Farringdon in the corridor in her faded cotton dressing gown. As she removed her make-up, she realised his bathroom was adjacent to hers and through the wall she could hear teeth being cleaned.

Irrationally disturbed by these intimate sounds, Laura went to bed.


To her surprise, she was left alone a good deal during the rest of the weekend. Charlotte remained in her room playing her inevitable rock music and supposedly revising for her forthcoming exams, while Farringdon sat in the study rearranging his meticulous papers or staring at his computer. Feeling superfluous, Laura passed the time reading or going for solitary walks around the streets. These walks involved window-shopping, architecture-gazing, and people-watching, and she enjoyed herself immensely. Her time would have been even more enjoyable had she felt able to stay out as long as she pleased, but there was always the feeling that she should be back at the apartment doing her job, whatever that was.

The servants had the day off on Sunday and Laura was at last given a task. Farringdon announced that he was going out to a drinks party. Meanwhile would she be kind enough to cook lunch for the three of them. The cook, he said, had left a joint of beef.

Not having felt welcome in the staff end of the flat, Laura had not even seen the kitchen before. She found it to be long, thin and L-shaped, a passage of a room, but well equipped, almost too much so. There were two fridges and two state of the art stoves and other more exotic machines all marked with cryptic icons instead of comforting English instructions. In the cupboards were huge catering-size utensils of every possible shape: fish kettles, giant saucepans, and mysterious cutters and grinders that looked as if they'd been there since the French revolution.

Fighting down a feeling of panic, Laura told herself that even if she hadn't cooked a Sunday roast recently, she'd done so hundreds of times in the past. She opened the nearest fridge. There was a joint of beef, clearly recognisable as such, though far too big for three. There were carrots and courgettes. She found potatoes and, after opening three drawers, a rather dud-looking peeler. And, eventually, a roasting pan of sorts. So far so OK.

She looked at the clock. This was ridiculous. She had taken half an hour just to equip herself. At one point she had thought of summoning Charlotte to help but decided it was best to make her own muddle without witnesses.

She stared at the matching ultra-modern ovens again. They seemed to have an extra knob, the purpose of which was obscure. She twiddled the left hand one, lights flashed and by some miracle the figure C.200 appeared on a little screen, accompanied by a reassuring hum. A reliable sort of temperature, thought Laura, relieved. After another ten minutes she flung the beef in the oven, hoping for the best.

It also took her an inordinately long time to lay the table in the grand dining room. The Government silver was arrayed in a series of heavy drawers, forty knives in one, forty forks in the other. She found stacks of at least sixty gold-crested plates in one cupboard in the pantry and several dozen cut-glass tumblers in another.

By one o'clock, the beef looked OK, though possibly overdone. The roast potatoes looked OK, though possibly soggy. The Yorkshire Puddings, however, had failed to rise very much at all and sat in a sodden row in the silver serving dish that Laura had found. She was scarlet in the face, the kitchen was in chaos, but she was ready.

By one thirty, Farringdon had not returned. Damn him, thought Laura.

At quarter to two she served lunch to herself and the hungry Charlotte who proclaimed it to be delicious and had three helpings. No problem with anorexia anyway, thought Laura, somewhat mollified.

At three o'clock, when they'd almost finished the washing up, Farringdon appeared. He had the grace to apologise, saying he had got caught in a traffic jam while driving through the Bois de Boulogne and his mobile phone turned out to have a flat battery. Not knowing whether to believe him or not, Laura served him the dried-up remains, which he ate without comment while reading the Personal Finance section of the *Sunday Times*. Then with another polite but not effusive apology, he retired to his study.

Laura fumed quietly for the rest of the afternoon and decided that she really could not cope with this kind of off-hand treatment. In the evening, however, Farringdon appeared to be in a friendly let's-pay-attention-to-Laura-and-Charlotte mode and announced he would take them out to dinner to make up for his non-appearance at lunch.

The restaurant Chez Géraud was small and cosy, with decorated earthenware plates adorning the walls and what seemed to Laura an exotic menu. She chose the terrine and then *canette de Dombe:* wild duckling from Brittany according to the helpful waiter, who seemed anxious to tell her which particular Breton marsh the duck came from so that she might fully appreciate its delicate flavour. Laura only understood half of what he said but hoped Farringdon was impressed by her communication skills.

With a quizzical amused expression on his face, he solemnly congratulated her on her choice and selected the same meal. He then ordered a bottle of expensive-sounding wine.

Really, he can be very charming when he chooses, she thought, and handsome in that dark blue shirt.

He began to ask her questions about her life and listened attentively to the answers. Charlotte said little as she ate her *steak frites* but her eyes darted from her father's face to Laura's as if she were watching a tennis match.

\* \* \*

On her last evening Farringdon drew her into his study. 'So have you enjoyed your stay in Paris, Laura?'

'Of course,' she said. 'Who wouldn't? It's wonderful.'

He leant forward, his eyes fixed on her face. 'And would you like the job with us or would you prefer to think about it? I very much hope you'll accept, and so does Charlotte.'

Does she, wondered Laura. She smiled. 'That's very kind.'

There was a silence and then they both began to speak at once.

'Please go on,' he said, 'say what you were going to say.'

'Well... about Charlotte, I suppose I'm rather worried that we, you and I, might not have the same ideas about handling teenagers. In my experience, one tries to bring them up to be honest, trustworthy and responsible, but one can't expect them to behave like young people a generation ago.'

He frowned. 'Actually, my main concern is just that. I want to ensure that Charlotte *doesn't* behave exactly like her mother.' He paused and then said heavily, 'Her mother was a stupid and promiscuous woman who deserted her child.'

'Oh dear.'

'That is why I chose you. To be a good influence, set a good example. Bridget told me how faithful you were to your invalid husband. I admire that. Rare qualities these days, virtue and fidelity.'

Oh, pass the sick bag, thought Laura, angry that Bridget had betrayed her confidences. She was tempted to say something shockingly coarse and improper to wipe the pious expression off his face. Instead she took a deep breath. 'Reverting to Charlotte, she is obviously a nice girl...'

'And I want her to stay that way. That's why she needs to be supervised. Kept from forming unsuitable relationships.'

Remembering she had failed to prevent her own teenage daughter from embarking on a highly unsuitable relationship, Laura could see the seas ahead positively bristling with minefields. Her doubts increased and she began to consider whether she should tactfully refuse the job.

Then he smiled and said, 'Charlotte's lonely in Paris, you see. Such friends as she has live in England. This new post of mine doesn't leave me much time to spend with her. That's why she needs you. It'd be a great weight off my mind if you were here.'

Laura's heart melted. He only wanted what he flatteringly saw as the best for his child and what was more normal than that? 'All right then,' she said in a rush. 'Thank you. I accept.'

## CHAPTER 6

NO SOONER HAD LAURA RETURNED TO ENGLAND after half term than her house was swarming with builders. Many more men than Jack had promised were hammering on the roof or propping up their ladders at every window, or in the kitchen cutting off the water for hours on end, or trailing up and down the stairs with spanners in their hand and mud on their shoes. Accompanying the workmen were thick clouds of dust and, above all, noise – cement mixers, power drills, hammers and full-volume local radio – from seven-thirty in the morning until four-thirty in the afternoon. She shuddered as she watched them tramp over her rosebeds to the pile of tiles they had stacked by the fragile new hedge. And she flinched as a mammoth delivery lorry tried to turn in her narrow drive and sunk its wheels into the lawn.

It'll be worth it when it's all over she kept telling herself, as the men sat in her garage drinking cups of tea and spreading crisp packets and fag ends all over the floor. She had invited them to use the kitchen but they preferred their own space outside, they said, to save her trouble, like. Whenever Laura felt like screaming illogically that they would save her trouble by just going away, she would take a deep breath and tell them – truthfully – how grateful she was and what a good job they were doing.

Jack visited the site most days, but with the workmen around they were never alone and he seemed concerned to maintain a professional and platonic approach. Now and then, though, his face took on a certain bright-eyed expression which Laura found herself half-acknowledging before she would quickly begin to talk about the roof repairs, or Melanie and how she was doing.

'Mel? Oh, much the same,' would be Jack's brief reply, before he, too, returned abruptly to the question of the roof.

Melanie stood in the hall one morning waiting for the postman's van to hurtle up the drive. She would recognise the noise of the engine straight away. Some days she opened the door and took the mail from the postman's hand and other times she let it slip through the letterbox to sit on the doormat for half an hour before she picked it up.

She hadn't had a drink this morning, just a couple during the night because she couldn't sleep and they were only wee ones that hardly counted. She thought that today she would try lasting till noon; then tomorrow she'd just have a glass with lunch and then by Friday she'd last till six o'clock in the evening, that's how she'd do it. Cut down a bit. Just in order to lose some weight.

All of a sudden she decided not to wait for the postman at all. She would go and sort the laundry and put it in the machine. That's what she'd do, change the sheets and make the bed all smooth for Jack, then he might come back into it. Recently he'd been sleeping in the spare room most nights. Said he was getting up early to take advantage of the light mornings, didn't want to disturb her. She tried to remember when they had last had sex and couldn't. He didn't understand how she longed for this reassurance that she was still alive and needed.

Then as she was stripping the bed and trying to find the clean double sheets – damn, they must be still in the ironing basket – she smiled to herself. Gary liked her anyway. Gary liked her a lot. He must do, otherwise he wouldn't take such an enormous risk because he'd surely lose his job if he were found in the boss's bed with the boss's wife. Jack was a tolerant man but he wasn't that tolerant.

She didn't think Gary would come back after the first time, but he appeared suddenly one day, looking very clean with his hair brushed, clearly apprehensive but clearly hopeful. So she took him in and they had sex on the sofa, with half their clothes on – that way it was quick. Then she said it was too dangerous for him, and also for her because she didn't want a divorce. So the brief encounter was over.

Sometimes she regretted this wise decision.

She heard the postman now and saw his red van. She stood back so he wouldn't see her through the window, then she wouldn't have to talk to him. You had to be polite because he'd been delivering mail to the village for ten years or more.

He left the engine running, he always did, and now she could hear his footsteps. There was a slither and four or five envelopes plopped down on to the doormat. Three of them were large and addressed in her own handwriting. 'Three rejections! In one day! Would you believe it? You would.' She was addressing these remarks to Phoenix, the little tortoiseshell cat who had come to supervise the arrival of the mail.

Mel opened the letters and saw the brevity of the ready-cooked replies from the women's magazines. 'Not quite right for us... but do try again.' She saved the largest one for last, the Mills & Boon. Then she decided she'd need a drink before tackling it. Secreted at the back of the larder was a full bottle of Smirnoff. She thought about diluting it, but not for long.

Sitting down at the kitchen table, she opened the envelope with trembling hands. 'A page,' she said to Phoenix who had jumped on to the table, seeking attention.

The editor had written almost a page, well, half a page. Pathetic to get excited but it was definitely a better quality of rejection. *There could be more Explicit Lovemaking*, she read. *A need for more spine-tingling passion. Try again.*

I can't try again, thought Mel, suddenly weary.

Try again, that's what the fertility clinic always used to say. But you feel better if you stop trying for what you can't have.

Her latest new career didn't seem to be taking off either. So here she was, dependent on Jack, as ever. In the early days she'd worked as a teacher of French, but she really hated it, teaching those awful bored kids. Mum and Da had wanted her to be a teacher because in Ireland, both sides of the border, it was a respected profession – not over here though. Apart from being a teacher she was a stockbroker's wife. A lonely job, that.

Then Jack was setting up his new business and she became a building contractor's wife. Jack said if you loathe teaching so much why not help me instead, as a bookkeeper. She wasn't bad at the office. But then the business expanded, and it all got a wee bit complicated and she made a mistake with the tax forms which put Jack in bad odour with the Inland Revenue. After that he hired a professional accountant and then more staff.

At that point Mel was ready to leave the office anyway because the fertility treatment took up so much time: a full-time job in itself attending clinics, having tests, laparoscopies, exploratory operations, more tests. Then there was an attempt at IVF. Then another. Heart-rending waits, heart-rending failures.

Eventually they packed it all in. By that time they were too old to adopt, and Jack had never been keen on the idea of someone else's kids. What he said was he didn't want to put her through any more hassle, knowing how picky and difficult the adoption authorities were. Always considerate, Jack, always protecting, always wrapping her up in a cocoon and trying to save her from herself.

She didn't go back to teaching. They didn't need the money and Jack wanted her to stay at home and do charity work like the other country ladies. He never understood that she wasn't like them. She just couldn't fit in. So she asked for a computer and he bought her the best available. But it didn't do her much good.

She looked at the rejections again. Then she got up to put them in her file, along with all the others.

There was a knock on the back door, quite loud. She went to answer it. Gary stood there, an expression of nervous expectancy on his handsome young face.

'I told you not to come back,' she said, not very firmly.

'Yeah, I know... but the boss, he ordered me to, like. He was sending me to the village anyway, something wrong with Mrs Dwyer's new bathroom, so he mentioned the garden tap here...'

'*Garden* tap?' repeated Mel breathlessly as his hand stretched out towards her breast. 'So why're you coming inside?'

His grinned. ' 'S'wot I was thinking about, coming inside.'

A while later when he had finally got around to fixing the garden tap she asked, 'How old are you, Gary?' She'd never thought to enquire before.

'Twenty-free.'

'Holy Mary, twenty-three! I'm practically old enough to be your mother.'

'No, you ain't. You're still young and dead sexy. Best tits I ever saw.'

She grinned. 'And what do you know, at your age? But, there again, you probably know more than I do. I s'pose you have a girlfriend?'

He looked embarrassed. 'Well, er, yeah. But, well, she's expecting, like.'

Lord save us, thought Mel, appalled. She took a deep breath. 'So when are you going to be a dad then?'

'I'm already a dad. This is our second. Ricky's four now.'
'Four!'
He beamed with pride. 'Yeah.'
She looked at him and shook her head. 'Gary, listen to me. You must not come here again. Never. You just can't afford to lose this job. I don't suppose your wife...'
'Me girlfriend.'
'I don't suppose your girlfriend has a job.'
'No, she stays at home wiv the kid and...'
She stared at him 'So you're supporting her and a child and one on the way.' Mel lost her temper because it was all so bloody unfair. 'If your girlfriend's having a baby then she needs loving and cherishing. You should be at home looking after her,' she shouted.
'But I'm at work.'
Mel failed to see the logic of this. 'A child is the most precious thing in the whole damn world. You don't know how lucky you are! Why don't you appreciate your family? Why don't you?' She hit him as hard as she could in the stomach but he didn't flinch.
As she made to hit him again, he grabbed hold of her arm. 'I do love Ricky, course I do. It's her, my girlfriend, she's a tricky cow. Like, she...'
'I don't want to know, and I don't want you here any more. If you ever touch me again, I'll tell Jack you made a pass at me and he'll believe me rather than you.'
Without a word he turned and left.
As the sound of his van faded away, she burst into tears.

When Jack telephoned Melanie late that afternoon, he realised from the aggressive abuse she dished out that she must be on her fifth or sixth vodka. He was angry for a moment, then a weariness came over him and he decided to delay his return for an hour or so, in the hope that by the time he got there she would be fast asleep. Instead he would go and visit Laura's cottage, just to make sure she was happy with the repairs and renovations.

Laura was looking tanned and slimmer in jeans and a faded blue tee shirt. She was wearing no makeup and a dirty pair of gardening gloves, but the evening sun was shining on her hair and she looked to him more desirable than ever.

He followed her into the kitchen and watched her as she washed her hands and carefully poured him a glass of wine, catching his eye from time to time and smiling. Her every gesture seemed to him significant. He shook his head. No, no, she wasn't flirting – she was just her normal friendly self.

They sat down on the newly repaired terrace.

'So how's it going?' he asked. 'No problems?'

She leant back and stretched her arms, soft brown arms that he wanted to feel around his neck.

'Wonderful, nearly finished,' she said. 'All I've got to do now is clean the place up and put my few precious possessions in the loft. Then it'll be ready for the invasion of Bridget and the triads.'

He smiled. 'So when are you starting this new job in Paris?'

'Next week.'

He was shocked. Selfishly he had half-hoped her plans would fall through, that she would stay in England. 'But I thought the school term didn't end until July.'

'Yes, but Charlotte has been allowed home early, because she's finished her GCSEs.'

Then they started talking about window frames and he promised to send her a painter, though she was arguing she could do it herself.

Finally, once she'd agreed with his suggestions about the house, he said she'd be glad to get away from it all. Seemed like the right thing to say.

She smiled. 'I don't really want to leave, but, well, perhaps in a way I do. It's an adventure. Haven't had an adventure since William and I went to Greece twenty years ago or more.'

The chatted on, discussing this and that. Finally Jack looked at his watch. 'I'd better get on home.' They walked towards the Audi. 'I'll miss you,' he said suddenly.

She smiled sweetly up at him. 'I'll miss you too. Couldn't have done it without you. I owe you so much. I'll pay you absolutely as soon as I can.'

'No hurry... Perhaps you could give me something on account, though.'

She looked worried. 'Thing is, I haven't been paid anything yet.'

'A goodbye kiss, I mean.'

She grinned. 'Thought you'd never ask,' she said light-heartedly and kissed him on both cheeks. She smelt of summer and tasted of all things desirable. Before she could turn away, he pulled her to him and kissed her full on the mouth.

For an instant she responded, then, flushed and laughing, she pushed him away. 'We shouldn't do that too often.'

We should do it the whole damn time, he thought, stifling an almost overwhelming urge to drag her off to bed and keep her there for ever.

Instead he said, 'Maybe not. I'd better go.'

Flushing, she smiled. 'Yes. I'll see you in September. Take care.'

'I will. Laura...'

'Mm?'

'I wish things were different.'

'I know but...' Her voice trailed away.

There was another pause. He felt unable to stay and unable to leave. He wanted to warn her to steer clear of Farringdon who sounded like a first-class prick. Finally he said, 'Beware of lecherous Frenchmen, won't you?'

She grinned. 'I will.'

'And Laura...'

'What?'

'Maybe you'd better change out of your wellies before you go to Paris.'

As she was laughing, he managed to start the car and drive away.

When he reached home, not in the best of tempers, he noted that the back door was open. 'Mel?' he called, as he flung his jacket on the kitchen chair.

There was a sort of moan from the hallway. He rushed towards it. 'What the hell? Oh my God, Mel. Are you all right?'

'No, not all right. Cut my leg. Fell downstairs. Jack, I'm sorry.'

It was like a murder scene. Melanie sat in a pool of red-stained laundry. More blood was oozing out of her leg on to the beige carpet and her left arm, too, was grazed and bleeding. With her right hand she was dabbing at the wounds with a bloody pillowcase.

Panic-stricken for a moment, he stood still. Then he pulled himself together. 'I'll call the ambulance, the doctor, then I'll...'

'No, no, it's not as bad as it looks, really. I'm OK. Just take me to Casualty in the car. Jack, I'm sorry, so sorry. My fault. Silly, I slipped. Carrying too much, carrying a pile of sheets down. Something tripped me up. Must have been Phoenix.'

There was no sign of the cat.

Jack knelt down and put his arm around her. 'Don't worry. It's OK. It's OK.' She reeked of alcohol but you couldn't be angry with someone in that state. Gently he examined her wounds. The worst was a deep gash on the shin.

He rushed upstairs to the medicine cabinet and found a bandage, old but still in its sterile wrapper, and half-empty box of plasters, most of them too small to be much good. He grabbed the packet of cotton wool that she used to remove her make-up. Back in the kitchen he poured some water into a glass cooking bowl and then returned to Mel. To his relief, when he began to wash them, the cuts began to look a little better, less extensive, more superficial.

She was brave and unflinching. All she said was, 'Jack, I'm sorry. About the carpet, it's ruined. Maybe some cold water, carpet shampoo under the sink.'

'Bugger the carpet,' he said.

As best he could he patched her up and, reckoning he could get her to the doctor quicker than any ambulance, drove her to Basingstoke District Hospital.

The visitors' car park seemed like half a mile from the hospital so he tried the Ambulance entrance where, mercifully, he found a place. Putting his arm around Mel, he led her limping to the door.

The strange medical smell of disinfectant and floor polish triggered memories of previous unpleasant visits to the hospital fertility clinic. He flinched inwardly and steeled himself for a long NHS queue, but, unlike the scenes in a television drama, the casualty department was quiet and empty.

A plump middle-aged receptionist filled in several pages of forms, anxiously pecking out the information on her computer keyboard. After only a short wait, they were whisked away into a treatment cubicle by a young nurse who ripped open a great many sterile packages on her stainless steel trolley, then cleaned Melanie's wounds with hearty efficiency. Eventually a solid female doctor, who also looked about seventeen, bustled in to sew up the shin with fine stitches of blue thread. The doctor had a kind face and very fat bottom, he noted as she bent over to concentrate on her work. While the doctor sewed, he held Mel's hand tight.

Forty-five minutes later, after a precautionary X-ray, they were on their way home.

'They said to take it easy and come back to have the dressing changed in three days. Nothing broken anyway,' said Melanie, who sounded completely sober by now.

'That's good.' Later he added, 'You were very brave.'

There was a long silence as they drove through the quiet countryside.

'Are you cross with me?' she asked eventually in a small voice.

'No. Not exactly cross.'

'The carpet...'

'As I said, to hell with the carpet. Mel, you've got to get a grip.'

'What d'you mean?'

With difficulty he summoned up his reserves of patience. 'You know damn well what I mean.'

After a while she said, 'I wasn't drunk. I just...'

'We'll see the doctor together next week, OK?'

There was another silence. Then she said even more quietly, 'You're not going to leave me, are you, Jack? Because I can't do it without you.'

'No, of course not.' But unhappiness settled heavily on his chest.

## CHAPTER 7

THIS TIME LAURA AND CHARLOTTE TRAVELLED on the Eurostar together. Charlotte, pale and sombre in a skinny black tee shirt and jeans, spent most of the journey reading teen journals full of advice about how to improve your orgasms and the sexual position of the month. She kept holding the magazines at an angle, presumably so Laura couldn't see what she was reading and disapprove.

Laura did disapprove, but mainly because she thought she herself was in more need of advice on the subject than Charlotte. Not that she wanted to read such trash. Of course not. And anyway just who are you thinking of having sex – of any variety – with? she asked herself.

Though Paris was exciting and different, Laura did not find her situation as cushy as a casual observer might have supposed it to be. The very fact that she had no domestic chores, and yet little time she could call her own, contributed to her sense of strangeness. The lack of privacy bothered her and, as she had predicted, it was difficult to adjust to someone else's way of life.

The staff were not easy. Sebastien, the butler, though polite enough, clearly disliked her, which was disconcerting. He had an unpleasant habit of materialising in front of her or behind her at unexpected moments, almost as if he were spying on her. She had the feeling sometimes that he had searched her room when she was out. Maybe he was jealous of her status as supposed friend and social equal of the Farringdons or maybe he thought she intended to take over the running of the residence. And maybe Irini's suspicious glares were due to the fact that she, too, was afraid of interference. Laura did, in fact, long to make some changes in the kitchen but she thought it wise to bide her time.

Apart from delegating to Laura the task of choosing the daily menus, Farringdon showed no signs of expecting her to take over the housekeeping. It soon became apparent that he himself liked to keep a firm eye on everything. For instance, Irini was made to produce all her grocery receipts, write down her costs in a notebook and submit it to him.

In turned out Laura was expected to do much the same thing. She was still unclear whether she was to be paid weekly or monthly and, as at the end of her first week she had run out of money, she decided to broach the subject.

'About my salary,' she began tentatively when she and Farringdon were alone after dinner. 'And I was wondering about my train fares and...'

'Ah yes, quite right. Slipped my mind before. I was about to ask you to submit a list of your expenses during the half term weekend,' he said, 'Just jot everything down, preferably with receipts and tickets if you've got them.'

'Right,' said Laura.

'Generally I would pay both yours and Charlotte's expenses such as snacks and museum entry, but if you go on your own, without her, then you would pay for yourself, of course. It would probably be best if you were to keep fairly detailed accounts to start with. Bit of a bore, but in Government service one has to keep fairly good records.'

'Of course,' she said stiffly.

'Is there anything else worries you?'

Quite a few things, she thought, but she smiled sweetly and made a neat set of accounts which she left on his desk when he was out. Next morning at breakfast she found an envelope with a cheque for the exact amount she had claimed.

As she walked to pay the cheque into her newly opened account, she pondered. It was hard to put her finger on why she did not like asking for money from Farringdon. He was, after all, her employer. It must be due to the fact that she'd been her own boss for too long.

At least Farringdon did not give orders about how Laura and Charlotte should spend their days, though each evening he liked to hear a report of what they had done. This was tricky as Charlotte much preferred studying Galleries Lafayette to visiting the Louvre. Finally Laura devised a bribery system – for every two afternoons spent in the shops or the cinema there had to be one afternoon at a museum or something else vaguely cultural. (Mornings didn't come into the equation so often as Charlotte was not an early riser.)

And so they passed their days together in reasonable if delicately balanced harmony. All the same, Laura could not rid herself of the sensation she was walking through a forest of hidden snares.

One evening she had just settled down to improve her French by watching the sexy male presenter reading the television news when she heard Farringdon's key in the lock.

'Oh,' she said when he came into the salon, 'I thought you were going to be out for dinner. I told Irini so. Sorry, they've gone off duty, both of them.'

Farringdon smiled, sounding just a little merry but looking as distinguished and handsome as ever in his dark suit. 'Rather a dull cocktail party, plenty of champagne but not much food. Decided to abandon it.' He looked around. 'Where's Charlotte?' he asked sharply.

'Gone out to supper with a schoolfriend, if you remember.'

'So she has, so she has.'

Smart shirt he was wearing, she thought, nice and crisp and blue, very becoming. All in all, it was quite surprising that he should come back from a party without a woman in tow. Unless perhaps they were put off by that cold manner he affected most of the time.

'I'll go and get you something to eat. Would an omelette be enough?' said Laura. She hurried off to the kitchen, determined to make a better go of cooking this time. To her relief there were eggs and butter in the fridge, but the only frying pan she could find had sinister brown stains and looked far from non-stick. She cracked the eggs carefully into a bowl and then skinned a tomato and chopped it along with some parsley. She even remembered to put a plate into the oven to warm. All this took some time as she had to travel what seemed like a hundred yards to the pantry to fetch implements and bowls. It really was the most illogically arranged kitchen. Then she went to the dining room to lay a place at the end of the long table.

She returned to the kitchen where she faced a new problem. The gas burners on the hob sulkily refused to self-ignite. Matches? Where would Irini keep matches? She was unable to find any and was about to return in humiliation to the drawing room to ask for Farringdon's help. For God's sake, woman, you ought to be able to cook an omelette, she could imagine him thinking. She tried the gas again. This time the burner sprang to life.

'Not before time, you bloody machine,' she muttered, as she poured the rewhisked eggs into the pan and, as the mixture solidified, placed the filling delicately in the middle. The yellow egg surrounding the red and green made a satisfactory colour scheme but her worse fears were realised when she tried to fold over the side of the omelette. It was irrevocably glued to the bottom of the pan.

'Save me, Delia,' she prayed. She stirred it around frantically and then scraped the resulting mixture on to the serving plate. It looked neither appetising nor adequate, but then she remembered seeing some smoked salmon at the bottom of the fridge. Hastily she chopped up a slice and arranged it over the top with another sprinkling of parsley in the hopes of disguising the leathery mess.

'Actually,' said a red-faced Laura, as she served Farringdon his dinner, 'I thought scrambled eggs might be nicer.'

He laughed. 'My favourite dish,' he said gallantly.

She could have kissed him.

'Pour us a glass of claret and sit down,' he said.

'But I've eaten.'

'Sit down anyway, please.'

He gave every appearance of enjoying the disgusting scrambled omelette and then asked for some cheese which they both ate, consuming a whole bottle of wine between them.

Farringdon became increasingly friendly and charming. 'I'm so grateful for your help with Charlotte. She's improved already,' he said and went on to talk about his hopes for his daughter. All this time he was looking into Laura's eyes as if she were the wisest and most sympathetic person in the world.

He really is OK when you get to know him, she thought after her third glass of wine. When he unbends a bit he's almost human. And rather attractive, if one were not his employee.

He helped her carry the plates out to the pantry. 'Just leave all washing-up for the maids,' he said airily.

'But...'

'Come on. Let's sit down and have a brandy. I need to discuss my plans for the summer with you.'

So they sat side by side on the sofa as Farringdon showed her brochures of luxury self-catering cottages attached to a golfing hotel on the coast where, he explained, they were all going on holiday in August. He would play golf, Charlotte would have golf lessons and she and Laura could swim and sunbathe, along with a bit of cooking, of course.

Oh dear, golf.

But also sex and sun, murmured an inner voice, unbidden.

His eyes seemed to be contemplating something along the same lines and, as they accidentally touched hands while reaching for the same brochure, Laura sensed a new awareness.

After another long glittering gaze from Farringdon, she thought it best to say goodnight and leave him to finish his brandy alone.

What's the matter with me, she thought as she lay awake. I lurve Paris in ze Spring time, sang her inner voice...Because my lurve iz here.

He's handsome enough, if you like that sort of thing, but Oliver is not my love in any sense. I don't have a love. Except perhaps Jack.

Jack is married, a lost cause, a total waste of time, and besides he's not here. Oliver is.


One evening Farringdon telephoned saying he was involved in a late game of tennis but a colleague of his was coming round for drinks. Could she entertain this person until he returned? Her name was something like Anise de Bourgeis or Annelise de Bougney, Laura didn't quite catch what.

The colleague, who looked to be about her own age, no, rather younger, was the epitome of all things Parisienne: tiny, slim with short well-cut black hair and large black eyes which dominated a pointed elfin face. She wore a simple cream linen shift, her only touch of colour being a pale blue and cream Dior scarf. Her heels were high and her skirt was short. In between were elegant legs clad in sheer stockings. Her shoes and handbag were of equal perfection. Laura herself had abandoned tights in the stuffy Paris summer and she was suddenly conscious of her pale ankles, and even more conscious of her flowery cotton frock which, even when she had first put it on, had looked slightly wrong. Now it seemed a disaster of frumpiness.

Judging by the girl's patronising manner, she was of the same opinion.

'What do you do in Paris?' asked Laura.

'I am a senior official in the French civil service.'

'Oh.' Laura was temporarily silenced by this conversation-stopping information. 'Your English is excellent,' she managed finally.

The girl smiled. 'And how is your French?'

'Well, I'm struggling a bit. For instance, I didn't quite catch your name, how do you spell it? It sounds like Annesse or Ahn-yes, but that can't be right.'

'Why, the same as English Agnès, of course, but with the *grave* accent. Maybe your great-grandmother or her maid were called Agnès, but here in France it is a fashionable and – how shall I put it? – upmarket name. I would recommend language lessons or you will not appreciate Paris,' she said firmly. 'And I will recommend a teacher, and also introduce you to my hairdresser, physiotherapist, and beautician.'

'Nice thought. I haven't had a facial for years.'

As if counting every wrinkle, Agnès examined her. 'One must have regular beauty treatment,' she pronounced. 'You will find we have excellent products available in Paris. We take such things seriously here.'

Agnès continued to give advice, until finally Farringdon telephoned again. This time he asked to speak to Agnès who listened and then said, 'But I think we should take them both. She is new, this governess-housekeeper person. I would like to be kind to her and to Charlotte.' Agnès then marched to the bell, rang for Sebastien and told him in an imperious tone that they would all be out to dinner.

Sebastien clearly disapproved of this sudden change of plan and opened his mouth to speak but Agnès had already turned her back on him. 'Come, Laura. Call Charlotte. We are meeting Oliver at Flandrin.'

'Flandrin?'

'A restaurant. Full of the *BCBG – bon chic, bon genre*, OK people, like the upper classes in your country but more fashionable. It will help you to enjoy the flavour of Paris.'

'You just take Charlotte. I'll stay here.'

She smiled in a friendly manner. 'No, no, I insist. I am making the invitation. I would like you to come too.'

As they walked down the street, Agnès stopped by an electric-blue super-mini VW which had been parked with Gallic flair – on the corner, half on the curb and half on a pedestrian crossing. She blipped open the door and extracted a small white long-haired terrier. 'Oh, Dougal, *mon petit ange*. Maman forgot all about you,' she crooned. The little dog wagged its tail in ecstasy while she attached a red lead to its matching red collar. After relieving itself on the wheel of the car, it bounced about in excitement as they proceeded down the boulevard. Having sniffed and watered every lamppost and doorway, it then had a more extensive call of nature and, urged on by Agnès, deposited a steaming pile on to the middle of the pavement.

When there was no sign of a scooper operation, Charlotte, who had maintained a sulky silence ever since Agnès's arrival, now raised her eyebrows and said in a loud whisper to Laura, 'Really, that's too disgusting, the way the French allow their dogs to do that. Just like I said, I was always treading in dog pooh when I first arrived.'

Agnès smiled impassively. 'I pay my taxes for cleansing services and it will be immaculate by dawn tomorrow. You will find our streets much cleaner than those in London.'

'Yeah, sure, in the early morning until the Frogs and their poncey dogs get up,' muttered Charlotte.

On arrival at the restaurant, Agnès was greeted reverentially by the head waiter. Waving her hand, she demanded an exterior table away from the main road and this was exactly what she got. They had just settled down to study the menu when Farringdon arrived, glowing with health after the exertion of tennis. Laura noticed that many female eyes followed him as he made his way to their table.

Rising gracefully to her feet Agnès kissed him coolly on both cheeks and invited him to sit on her right. They then began to talk shop. Laura didn't mind being excluded from their conversation as there was plenty to observe all around her. She noticed that Charlotte sat glowering at her food and seemed determined to eat as little as possible.

They were half way through the second course when a fat Middle Eastern woman pushed past their table and in so doing trod on Dougal's tail, causing a loud yelp of protest from the dog and an even louder harangue from Agnès.

'So careless. Some people have no idea how to behave,' she said. She ordered the waiter to bring a spare chair and hauled the dog on to it, where he sat looking mournful until she gave him a spoonful of her steak tartare.

Laura raised her eyebrows and asked if dogs were allowed indoors in restaurants too.

Agnès laughed. 'Of course. We Parisiens are crazy about them. In fact, you will find dogs are assigned better tables than non-smokers. We are not troubled by your Anglo-Saxon political correctness here.'

'Well, you're right but...' Laura was about to embark on a prim explanation about the difference between political correctness and normal hygiene, but Agnès had already turned back to Farringdon.

As the meal progressed Laura congratulated herself that she was enjoying the evening in spite of the fact that Agnès was a serious pain in the neck and also much better dressed, presumably cleverer and certainly far more successful than she was (though all these qualities combined in one prettier, younger woman were not endearing).

Something about their body language, however, suggested that Agnès and Farringdon were lovers and Laura couldn't help feeling a little piqued. This suspicion appeared well founded when, after the meal, he announced that he was going to see Agnès home.

'What a twit,' said Charlotte, as her father was driven away in the super-mini.

'She's anything but that,' said Laura, managing a light-hearted smile. After all, what did she care about Farringdon's sex life? 'Whatever you might say about her, she's not a twit.'

'No, him, Dad, for fancying her, I mean,' said Charlotte kicking at the lamppost.

## CHAPTER 8

THE ONLY GOOD THING ABOUT THE HOLIDAY was the fact that Agnès wasn't there, thought Charlotte. Otherwise it was a total waste of time. All her friends from school were going to villas in Greece or smart resort hotels in the south of France where there were water sports and discos. But here in crummy Brittany there was absolutely no one to talk to and nothing to do except sit by the pool watching topless Frog women working on their suntan or mincing around the golf course in their gold lamé shorts. And the sea was miles away, at least half an hour in the car and no buses. So you were just stuck in this isolated golf complex. Typical Dad to choose the type of holiday *he* wanted.

Charlotte had tried one golf lesson, but the other kids were French teenagers, all looking incredibly chic in their Ralph Lauren and not a single spot between them. They were either the same age as her or younger, and they were all much smaller.

Everybody of her own age was smaller, both boys and girls. Ooh, you *are* lucky, the girls at school would say, you're such a beanpole, you could be a model. But Charlotte knew you had to have the Look too – a model face with large eyes, Kate Moss cheekbones and pouting lips, and she just didn't. She was too ordinary: ugly on a bad-spot bad-hair day, passable on a good day with help from a bit of make-up, but nothing could make much difference to her deep-set eyes, sticking-out macho chin and far too big nose. All this looked fine on Dad, but not on her.

Charlotte considered her only good point was her legs. They were long and the right sort of shape, so people said. Well-meaning people like Laura often complimented her on her legs, but legs were clearly not enough. Not enough to attract boys.

They avoided her, Charlotte knew, because she was too tall, too flat-chested, and just not pretty or sexy. Anyway, the worst part was, she couldn't think of anything to say to them, even English ones like schoolfriends' brothers. She'd never had a boyfriend, probably never would. Probably be a virgin forever.

As for the French boys here, they were just impossible and cliquey, and they kept staring at her like she was a woman from Mars. That's why she totally refused to have any more golf lessons with them. Then Dad said he'd teach her himself, but that didn't work for two seconds. She was useless at it, and he just started to lose his temper, so she'd flung down the clubs and stalked away.

Trouble was, if she went back to the so-called cottage – one of the many concrete micro dwellings in the grounds of the chateau – she'd have to help Laura with the cooking or cleaning or something. Or talk to her. She didn't mind Laura actually, but sometimes they ran out of things to say to one another. She could see Laura desperately searching round for a new topic of conversation. Sometimes she tried a bit too hard, poor thing.

Actually Laura was good about driving her to the beach so they could swim and sunbathe, but neither of them had brought enough books. At least she had her CD player to listen to. Laura must have been a bit bored. She kept suggesting they visit the chateaux country but it was far too hot for that sort of thing, and anyway Dad didn't seem too keen to let Laura drive a long way in his car.

The only other good thing about it, thought Charlotte, was that she did get a superb tan. And although Laura kept raving on about sunhats and suncream and skin cancer, she seemed quite keen to sunbathe herself.

On the last day, Dad took them out to dinner at the chateau restaurant. Posh and pretentious with a bit of a scary menu, the sort of thing Dad likes. Odd thing was, he kept staring at Laura who had put on this blue dress, quite low-cut which, although it was unbelievably old-fashioned, did quite suit her now she was brown.

Charlotte began to wonder if he wasn't starting to fancy Laura. He was certainly staring at her chest. But there again, someone a bit frumpy like her couldn't compete for a second with the mega-cool Agnès, more's the pity. Not that she was crazy about the idea of Laura as Dad's girlfriend, but, like, *anyone* would be better than Agnès. Trouble was, Agnès had lasted an unusually long time.

Laura enjoyed the golf holiday more than Charlotte did but, despite the heat, she was pleased to return to the apartment in Paris. The holiday villa had been too cramped – all right for a family, but for her, a relative stranger, it had been too intimate. Being cooped up in a small space with Farringdon was not a comfortable experience. He was large and overpowering and she kept bumping into him at the wrong moment: like coming out of the bathroom, or into the sitting room when he was on the telephone to Agnès. Now you know he has someone else, you're beginning to fancy him, you contrary bitch, said her tiresome inner voice. 'Rubbish,' said Laura aloud.

Farringdon spent only a couple of days in Paris before he went away again. He was now going to stay with Agnès's family in their Loire chateau, leaving Laura and Charlotte behind. Laura was to be in complete charge while Charlotte took a part-time summer course at the Sorbonne. The cook and the butler would be on holiday too, so they would have only the Filipina cleaning woman, Conchita, to help. No great hardship, thought Laura, as Conchita, friendly and willing, was much easier to work with than the other two.

Laura felt strangely forlorn when Farringdon actually departed, not because she expected to go with him, but because she and Charlotte were being abandoned like Cinderellas in the empty city, while he went off to the cool of the countryside.

On Sunday Laura went out to buy bread for breakfast, plus a treat, the *Sunday Times*. This simple task proved to be more hazardous than she anticipated, as there was only one assistant at the bakers' and hence an unexpectedly long impatient queue. She stood admiring the wonders of French patisserie, but when it finally came to her turn she hesitated for a moment about which type of loaf to buy and also failed to understand about the centimes in the change. The assistant glared icily at her and the bejewelled woman behind clicked her teeth at the stupidity of the foreigner. Then the man at the paper kiosk was unaccountably disagreeable when she bought the newspaper. Disconcerted, Laura let it slip through her fingers on to the pavement, and, in trying to rescue the various parts, broke the top off the baguette she had just bought.

'Need a wheelbarrow for the *Sunday Times* these days, don't you?' said an English voice. A man, young and handsome, bent down beside her to help pick up the scattered sections. He addressed the news vendor, *'Un petit sac, s'il vous plaît, monsieur.'*

Sullenly, the man handed him a plastic bag.

'There you are, put the paper in this,' said the boy to Laura. 'Only way.'

When he smiled at her Laura caught her breath sharply because he reminded her so forcibly of William with his gentle blue eyes behind gold-rimmed glasses. Thin and tall, he was wearing a crumpled polo shirt and a pair of jeans, none too clean. He had fine patrician features, with blond wavy hair. In fact, he was so like William that she felt as if she had known him for ever.

He paced along beside her asking her the 'how long have you been in Paris?' questions. In return she learnt that he didn't live in the district but had been spending the night at a friend's flat. A female friend, I bet, thought Laura. She judged him to be one of those mild, amiable, little-boy-lost type of men whom women saw as no threat, but somehow or other they ended up, more or less accidentally it seemed, in one's bed, where they turned out not to be a little boy at all.

What do you know about it, virgin queen, muttered her inner voice. Maybe because he's like William?

When they reached the end of her street, she thanked the boy again and turned away.

Suddenly he called after her. 'Do you want to go to a literary evening? It's free?'

She hesitated. 'That's very kind but...'

'Here,' he said, striding after her and handing her a crumpled leaflet. 'Friends of mine, writers, are performing at the British Council. Bring your significant other, partner, friend, whatever. Do come. They're afraid no one will go, since it's August.'

The British Council sounded respectable enough so Laura thanked him and said they might well come.


Charlotte felt totally exhausted when she got home from the Sorbonne and then it turned out they had to go to some boring writers' evening. She could imagine how pointless and terrible it was going to be, just like the school play, only worse. But old Laura was determined to go, so they walked all the way to the 63 bus, which was like an oven, and then half way up to Les Invalides before they found the British Council, not the most glamorous place in the world, bit like a glorified library. As for the people, they were all youngish, as Laura had promised – or rather Laura's idea of young – but the men had beards and the girls had long straggly hair and long straggly skirts, just too sad to contemplate. At a table in the corner a middle-aged woman with a fat stomach was dishing out small glasses of red and white wine. Laura tried the red and said it was fairly rough. Charlotte never touched alcohol so she took a warm orange juice.

Then, weaving his way through the crowded foyer, *he*, the vision, appeared. He held out his hand to Laura. 'Hello again. Glad you could come. My name is Simon Axford-Lee, by the way.'

Laura shook hands. 'Laura Brooke, and this is Charlotte Farringdon.'

Charlotte gazed at him. He was just so perfect. She felt totally limp, almost faint, and her heart was thumping like crazy. Dropping her eyes, she managed to hold her hand out to shake his. His grasp was warm and strong.

'So what do you do in Paris, Simon? Are you a writer too?' asked good old Laura.

'Kind of. I do write a bit but I earn my daily bread as a waiter. The restaurant where I'm working now is closed during August, thank God.'

Laura looked all sympathetic. 'Yes, I know the feeling. I was a waitress too. In England.'

He stared in astonishment, obviously thinking her much too ladylike to have even heard of waitressing. 'So what are you doing now?' he asked.

Charlotte glared warningly and was relieved when Laura didn't make any silly jokes about being a babysitter or a substitute mother (as if). 'I work for Charlotte's father, a sort of housekeeper,' she said instead.

At that point a bell rang to announce the beginning of the performance. Simon ushered them into a large room where wooden chairs were set in a semi-circle. 'Grab the best seats. Quick,' he urged and disappeared back to the foyer.

Charlotte stared after him. Then she made an excuse and ran downstairs to the ladies to check her hair. Thank God, it was clean but there was a spot by her nose. Damn it. She fished for her new concealer, which hardly seemed to conceal anything at all. And she was wearing an awful girlie skirt because Laura had insisted the British Council might be formal. So embarrassing. Most people were wearing jeans, apart from the serious women in the droopy frocks. Simon's 501s were faded and not too clean, just right, and the body inside them... mmm.

She ran back upstairs. My God, there he was again sitting beside Laura. Charlotte realised she was going to have to squeeze past his knees to get to her seat. She took a deep breath and sort of smiled at him. He smiled back, a wide friendly smile, and Charlotte wobbled and nearly fell on top of him.

The poetry reading passed in a haze as far as she was concerned. After it was finished Simon was still talking to Laura when a hideous girl with greasy hair and thick glasses pounced on him and in a loud hearty voice invited him to go to a party 'with the crowd'.

He looked a bit shifty and said, 'Oh well, actually, I'm going to dinner with Mrs Brooke and Charlotte.'

The hideous girl, looking all upset, retreated back to her corner.

Laura smiled. 'Really, Simon, what a lie. I'm shocked.'

He looked embarrassed. 'Well, I didn't want to hurt her feelings but her parties are a bit grim and...'

Laura shook her head in mock disapproval. 'Ah, now I see why you've been paying us so much attention. You've been using us as a human shield against predatory females. Well, we've got to go, so you'd better walk with us a little way so as to keep up this great charade.'

Miraculously, he was still nattering away to Laura about poetry and writing when they were practically at the bus stop. Then he said suddenly, 'But actually why *don't* you come out to dinner, both of you?'

Laura looked extremely doubtful and seemed to be on the point of saying no, when Charlotte heard herself stutter, 'Uh, yes, we'd love to.' She didn't know how she'd dared. Her voice had come from nowhere.

Laura stared at her in surprise, then smiled saying maybe it would be OK, as long as she herself paid. He protested and after a lot of stupid over-polite arguing, it was agreed that they should split the bill.

His voice was nice, thought Charlotte, an accent Dad would approve of, upmarket Public School, but soft and musical rather than loud Hooray-Henry. She wondered why he was a waiter. He looked as if he should be something like a lawyer or merchant banker. Except maybe he wasn't smooth and laid back enough for that sort of thing. He talked really fast when he got excited, like now when he was talking about the poems.

The bistro Simon recommended was near the Rodin Museum, so that meant he and Laura got into a long discussion about Rodin during the meal. Charlotte didn't feel capable of talking at all. Nor could she eat anything apart from two pieces of lettuce.

Eventually she thought of something to say. She cleared her throat. 'Uh, I'd, I'd like to go to the Musée Rodin one day.'

Laura looked amazed.

It turned out that Simon was an absolute expert on Rodin because he had once thought of writing a screenplay about him.

'Tell you what, I'll take you both there. How about tomorrow?' he said enthusiastically.

Charlotte's strange voice came from nowhere again. 'Yes, good idea,' she said.

You had to admit it, thought Charlotte, old Rodin knew what he was doing. Absolutely fantastic figures and so realistic apart from their huge hands and feet. Rather masculine though. She wasn't at all comfortable staring at all this virility in front of Simon. Well, some statues were virile and some seemed to have mysteriously missing... parts. Even in her own mind Charlotte found the word 'penis' difficult. It was so medical, so...

She stared at the sculpture of ancient fat Balzac with no clothes on. Laura didn't seem to notice. Simon was raving on about how Rodin had been really controversial in his time and that he had been accused at the outset of his career of taking a mould from a real person's body. He certainly did one hell of a lot of sculpting. Apparently his models used to walk about in the nude all day, not just when they posed. That's how Rodin was able to do all the muscles rippling down the bodies, explained Simon. Charlotte thought about Simon's muscles rippling down his body.

Then there was one called The Kiss. She blushed at the sight of the naked couple and had to walk to the other end of the gallery. If only...

Charlotte seemed rather preoccupied and peculiar today, thought Laura, as they walked around the garden of the museum. Maybe she was overcome by Simon's charms. She certainly stared at him a lot. But a man in his twenties wasn't likely to be interested in a schoolgirl. Just as well, because he certainly wouldn't be Farringdon's idea of a suitable boyfriend.

Or maybe Charlotte was just exhausted by sightseeing in the heat. Laura felt pretty tired herself and decided they had better have a cool drink in the museum café before they went home.

As soon as she had gulped down her Orangina, Charlotte dived off to the ladies.

Laura decided to take advantage of this tête à tête to do a little investigation. 'So tell me about your writing, Simon.'

'Well, I'm trying to do a new screenplay.'

'What about?'

He took a sip of coffee and then began to play with the cubes of sugar, unwrapping the paper and then folding it neatly. 'I can't talk about it at the moment. It's going rather badly.'

'Oh dear... You know, William, my late husband, was a painter and he used to get very depressed about his work now and then. But it always came right in the end. Sometimes he had to put his canvas aside for a week or so.' This topic didn't seem to interest Simon, so she said. 'Tell me about your family. Is your father a writer? Or your mother?'

'God no. Dad wanted me to join a big bank or the civil service, or be an accountant or something when I left Durham. But I knew I couldn't face it. So I came to Paris to seek my fortune, and here I am, two years on and only a waiter.'

'So what do they think, your parents?'

'They don't know what I do. I told them I'm making contacts in the film world and doing journalism, writing ad jingles, all sorts of stuff I'm not. What happened was, I told them about a job I had with an advertising agency here, but I didn't tell them it was temporary. So they think I'm still fully and gainfully employed. Can't disillusion them. Not after all that money they paid for my education.'

'I see... But have you thought about going home and trying to find a job? It's supposed to be OK these days, the employment situation.'

'No, I can't go back to England. Not till I get something published. Not till I sell my screenplay.'

She studied him. 'So have you got a girlfriend here? Is that another reason why you stay?' She was suddenly aware that the question was rather intrusive.

'Sort of,' he said morosely, after a slight pause.

'Tell me about her.' Even more intrusive.

'Can't really talk about it.'

'Oh.'

'It's a difficult relationship,' he went on, obviously forgetting he didn't want to talk.

'Difficult?'

'Yeah.'

'Do you live together?'

'No, no, we can't. That's the problem. It's very difficult,' he repeated.

'So does she live in Paris, or somewhere else?'

'She lives here and in California. She's American, you see.'

Laura smiled. 'You make it sound like a drawback.'

'No, it's not that,' he said seriously. 'The main problem is, I hardly ever see her.'

Laura looked at him. 'Why not? Does she have another man?'

He flushed. 'Well, yes... She's married.'

'Oh dear.'

'It's impossible,' he blurted out. 'I never see her regularly. She just rings up out of the blue, whenever her husband's away. And then she comes round to my flat and... and then she just goes. Sometimes she only stays for half an hour. You see, I have nothing to offer her. He's rich, her husband, and I haven't even got a decent job. She'll never leave him.'

Laura shook her head. 'Has she got any children?'

'No.'

'Does she have a job, then?'

'Yes, she's in the film world. She does a bit of production and I think she's involved in casting. Anyway, she's going to read my script when it's finished and try to sell it for me.'

'That's good.'

His face cleared. 'Yes, she's terrific. She's very kind and very energetic, involved in so many things. But she never has any time...'

'So what sort of age is she?'

'Oh, older, a bit.'

'Late twenties? Early thirties?'

'Well, probably a bit more. About your age. Maybe older. I don't know. She's cool, very attractive. So are you, of course, but in a different way,' he added hastily.

Laura smiled. 'Well, she sounds an interesting woman, your Mrs Robinson.'

'Who?'

'You know, like the film *The Graduate*.'

'Oh yes, but don't say a word about what I told you. Please. Not to anyone at all.'

'All right,' promised Laura.

At that point Charlotte reappeared, complaining she had been waiting in a queue for ages but foreign women kept barging in ahead of her. Simon immediately turned the conversation back to Rodin and gave yet another long dissertation on the subject.

As they were saying goodbye near the river, he thrust a card into Laura's hand. 'Please,' he said, 'If you're giving any dinner parties and need a waiter think of me. I'd really like to get in on the diplomatic circuit. Much better paid than casual labour.'

She smiled and said she would certainly bear him in mind.

But when she saw Charlotte gazing after him with an expression of dreamy longing on her face, Laura though it might be wiser not to contact that particular young man again.

## CHAPTER 9

FARRINGDON WAS DISAPPOINTED BY AGNÈS'S so-called chateau. It was not the imposing pile he had expected – just a medium-sized, dark and crumbling stone house with vaguely gothic cone-shaped turrets at either end. He had also envisaged a formal French garden with little box hedges and straight rows of excessively tidy flowers, but instead there was a jungle of overgrown shrubs and heavy old cedars surrounding what may once have been lawns but were now more of a hayfield.

The interior was full of decaying antiques and gloomy portraits of cross-looking ancestors. The sofas appeared to have been stuffed with granite and the rose-coloured brocade curtains looked as if they would crumble at one touch of the hand. As for the plumbing: it appeared to date from the time the water closet was first invented, and often necessitated long embarrassing waits for the rusty tank to produce the trickle of water intended to flush.

On first acquaintance Agnès's mother, the Baronne, looked deceptively mild and almost English in her country clothes, but she proved to be as exacting as her daughter. She cross-examined him at some length about his antecedents and seemed disappointed that he was not related to a Lord Farringdon of her acquaintance. Then, however, she found Oliver himself in Who's Who which, along with the fact that he was a Major-General and Ambassador, seemed to go some of the way to satisfy her as to his eligibility. On a convenient bookcase in the corner of the salon were social reference books from numerous European countries including a well-thumbed copy of *Bottin*

*Mondain* which, Agnès explained with a smile, was the register of the French aristocracy and hence her mother's bible.

Plenty of *Liberté* in modern republican France, but not as much *Egalité* and *Fraternité* as one might have supposed, he thought with some amusement.

The Baronne was fiercely anti-American and, he suspected, anti-British, though she was too polite to say so to him. She made it clear that she did not approve of English as a means of communication and so most of the conversation took place in French, in which Farringdon was far from fluent. If Agnès used Franglais, as in *le look* or *le weekend*, she was harangued by her mother for desecrating the French tongue, upon which mother and daughter would start on a long circular discussion about language and culture. Agnès seemed determined to annoy by claiming, no doubt as devil's advocate, that English was the richer, more precise language. Aghast, the Baronne would then insist that her daughter's duty, along with that of every other French citizen, lay in being out there on the barricades, making the world understand that France was the last bastion of civilisation, bravely holding out against the invading McDonalds from across the Atlantic.

All this female argument became unutterably wearying, but there was no calming masculine influence as the Baron himself was on the Riviera with his mistress, according to Agnès. So there was no escape from the Baronne's rigidity and Agnès's teasing, and the yapping of the ghastly Dougal who had to be fed and watered and taken for walks in the stultifying summer heat. Occasionally they would drive out amongst the endless vineyards and visit some dreary relation of Agnès's. Oliver would just have to sit on yet another concrete sofa listening to the jabbering French. The whole thing was insufferably boring.

Even the sex was not up to standard. He had been allocated a room across the corridor from Agnès so he was obliged to creep over to her in the dark, trying to avoid the creaking floorboards and the heavy furniture placed strategically to crack him on the shin. Oliver felt far too old for that sort of behaviour and when he finally made it to Agnès's arms, she was uncharacteristically quiet and unresponsive. This and the heat affected his performance. It was clear they were both inhibited by the thought of the Baronne sitting bolt upright in her four-poster bed, listening out for every untoward gasp.

Oliver tended to blame Agnès for his occasional sexual failure. Though she was decorative and amusing, she had an acid tongue. It occurred to him he had never before spent this much consecutive time in her company. Holidays were a good test of a woman and Agnès had not proved to be restful company so far, not that he expected her to be. Relaxation was not her forte.

Apart from her sharp-faced beauty, Agnès's spiky wit had been the original attraction: that and the fact that she didn't give a damn for anyone else but herself. But who, in the longer term, wants to live with an egotistical porcupine, however bright and sexy that porcupine might be? Or was he being too harsh? Did her lively mind and body compensate for her lively temper? He would not yet cross her off the list of potential Mrs Farringdons, but she had lost ground. It was clear from the state of the chateau the family was far from rich, but that was a minor disadvantage. A greater worry was that, like so many women, she might turn into her mother.

When Agnès suggested they should pay a weekend visit to her father in Cannes, Oliver was highly relieved to escape to the south. However, the drive proved to be difficult, long and hot, with a series of horrendous traffic jams on the *autoroute*, and

Agnès's endless complaints about these facts began to grate on his nerves. When they finally arrived in Cannes, his temper was not improved when she informed him she had booked them in at the Carlton.

'My God, Agnès, I'm a civil servant not a millionaire. I really think we shall have to find a hotel suitable for mere mortals rather than pop stars and the jet set.'

She raised her eyebrows. 'Don't worry, *chéri*. Papa is paying. We are his guests.'

Thank God for Papa, thought Oliver, as he studied their room on arrival. It was the epitome of luxury, from the opulent gold-tapped bathroom via the emperor-size bed to the balcony overlooking the Mediterranean. There was a rose in the bathroom and a huge basket of fruit with a message from the manager offering them his most sunny thoughts. Oliver began to feel a great deal better, and as Agnès came out of the shower enveloped in white towelling, more aroused than he had done all month. He pushed her back on the bed and as she wrapped her legs around him, Oliver thought anew what an adorable, sexy little bitch she was.

And, if her father could afford all this, then she was indeed a rich bitch too. Oliver climaxed almost immediately.

Apart from the hotel and the pleasures afforded by the stimulating sight of so many beautiful women wearing so few clothes, Oliver did not find much to enjoy in Cannes. He disliked the crowds and the formality of the resort, particularly the beach itself which was divided into concessions, each fenced off by striped canvas awnings of different colours. According to status, each section had a smart restaurant or lesser snack bar, each a pontoon and several neat ranks of white sunbeds with decorative covers. There was almost no unfurnished area of sand in sight.

He had imagined that guests at the Carlton would have free access to the hotel's own section of the beach, but this did not prove to be the case. They were greeted by a beach manager in a nautical costume who was concerned to hear they had not reserved a sunbed in advance. The manager then asked which side of the pontoon they wanted to sit and commanded a junior attendant to show them to a place several yards from the sea. Oliver was annoyed to find that not only did he have to pay for the entry to the beach, but also, item by item, for the hire of the towels, the sunbeds and the umbrella. And the *plagiste* whose job it was to dig the umbrella into the sand then waited about for a tip.

And after all this expense, Oliver looked around and saw immediately that the other guests at the Carlton Beach were brash nouveau riche, not at all his type of person.

Ignoring him, Agnès spread out her towel on the sunbed, removed her bikini top and arranged herself at an appropriate angle. He watched. He knew she was aware of admiring male glances in her direction and yet totally disdainful of them. This contempt for the male sex was another of her attractions, of course. Reminded him of Elizabeth.

As usual, when thoughts of Elizabeth entered his consciousness, he pushed them away. Best thing, if you'd had a disastrous marriage with a faithless, nymphomaniac bitch was to forget about it. Otherwise you'd wallow in self-pity and recriminations and all that kind of bollocks... Always a mistake to let the wrong kind of woman get too close to you. Oliver closed his eyes in order to shut out the painful memories.

\* \* \*

At lunch they met Agnès's father, the Baron, on the terrace of the hotel where he gave them an elegant and expensive meal. He was a tall, thin, ascetic man, still handsome. The mistress, Elke, was Swedish, of a certain age, white-blonde, tanned, and apparently perfectly preserved – though her huge sunglasses and large straw hat made it difficult to be certain of this. She said little but smiled a great deal at everyone, especially the Baron who gazed at her with unqualified adoration. He did pay attention to his daughter, but all the time that Agnès talked, and she talked a lot, the Baron kept turning towards Elke, as if she was by far the most important person in the party. And he kept touching Elke: her hand, her face.

It was a none-too-discreet display of affection that disturbed Oliver. The old boy can't wait to get her back into bed, he thought sourly. It really was most indecent to see a middle-aged couple so sexually obsessed. More than middle-aged, the Baron must be in his seventies. Oliver shuddered inwardly and he began to wonder what would happen to the family money if, contrary to normal French practice, the Baron decided to marry his mistress.

When they were alone after lunch, Agnès launched immediately into a long and deeply unflattering criticism of her father's latest 'sluttish gold-digger' and would not leave the subject alone for the rest of the day. Even sex or an expensive visit to the Casino would not shut her up for long.

Finally Oliver had had enough. The stay in Cannes was becoming unbearable and when Elke, with the kindest of smiles, invited them on a three-day cruise on her yacht (apparently she had, after all, no need to dig for someone else's gold) Oliver declined, saying he really would have to return to Paris and his daughter.

He was a little hurt and offended that Agnès didn't look particularly sorry to see him go. But they said a cordial enough farewell to each other and promised to meet as soon as possible in September.

* * *

'Masses of things have happened,' said an unusually radiant Charlotte the moment her father, hot and exhausted from the long drive across France, walked through the door of the Paris apartment.

The ace news was that she'd passed all her GCSEs with mostly A grades. 'That's marvellous,' he said sincerely and was rewarded by a shy proud smile.

The bad news, she then informed him, was that Irini the cook had not returned from holiday, in fact, had given in her notice, and that Sebastien had broken his right arm.

'How damned inconvenient of them both,' said Oliver, muttering further more obscene curses under his breath. He was seriously concerned. He was due to host several important dinner parties during the next few weeks and he was also expecting a number of official house guests, Government Ministers who expected to enjoy a high level of hospitality. A cook could be hired temporarily, but it would be expensive and household efficiency would be extremely difficult to achieve without the smooth presence of Sebastien, damn the bloody little man.

Charlotte was babbling away. 'Laura's been doing all the cooking and Conchita has been doing extra cleaning. Sebastien, like, comes to work but he just stands there getting in the way and sort of subtly criticising the way Laura does things. And he's horrible to Conchita who can't understand a word he says, as usual, and she gets upset and in a muddle. So Laura tried to tactfully tell Sebastien to go home and rest, and that made him cross. He's coming tomorrow to talk to you.'

Oliver groaned. 'I can't even go on holiday without the whole bloody household falling apart. Where is Laura?'

'Gone shopping. She's a brill cook, Dad. Much better than Irini. And it's been good when Sebastian's been on one of his endless trips to the doctor 'cos then there's no one sighing and frowning all over the place and looking disapproving each time you sit on the sofa and dent a cushion.'

After talking to Laura, who had coped reasonably well with this minor crisis, Oliver decided that the obvious thing to do would be to ask her to stay on after Charlotte had gone back to school. Someone was needed to hold the fort until Sebastien recovered and another cook could be found. To his relief Laura agreed, on condition that the butler could be persuaded to stay at home with his broken limb rather than hanging around the apartment getting in the way.


Having been banished from the Residence – most casually and unsympathetically – by Monsieur Farringdon, Sebastien sat in his small flat in an unfashionable part of Paris nursing his anger. The plaster which encased his arm ensured that he was not in physical pain but his honour had been slighted. He saw no reason why he should not supervise the running of the Ambassador's residence, even if he could not actually do any physical work. Fate had played into the hands of the scheming Madame Brooke. The more he thought about her the angrier he became and when after a few long dull days Laura telephoned him for advice, he could hardly bring himself to answer her.

She was wanting to know the name of a caterer she could hire for a very important dinner party that Monsieur Farringdon was hosting for a very important person from the Government of England.

Sebastien took a deep breath. 'Yes, indeed, Madame Brooke, I will make all the arrangements. I know exactly what the Ambassador likes for such an occasion. I will telephone for you his favourite *traiteur*, who is an English chef, and order Monsieur's favourite menu. As for waiters, for twenty people you will need three persons to serve. Leave it to me, Madame Brooke. I will ask the chef to bring the waiters too.'

After he had put down the receiver he smiled for the first time for weeks. Maybe he would just be too ill to telephone anyone at all and then see how dear Mrs Brooke can manage to arrange this oh-so-important soirée. Let the guests from England wait for hours without anything to eat or drink.

Let Monsieur l'Ambassadeur see just how incompetent is the woman who has dared to assume she can manage the sophisticated arrangement of a diplomatic event.

## CHAPTER 10

AFTER CHARLOTTE HAD GONE BACK TO SCHOOL, Laura found herself running the household on her own. Now at last in the absence of Sebastien and Irini, she was doing a proper job of work. Housekeeping, even this upmarket sort, was hardly exalted or high-powered employment, but in an ambassadorial residence in a foreign country it was a challenge.

Looking back to earlier challenges, earlier lives abroad, she remembered the taverna where she and William had cut their teeth as hotel managers. Or, rather, where she had learnt the job and earned the money while he had painted. There it had been hot and sometimes difficult, fraught with Greek tantrums and inconsistencies. Laura had worked hard, resenting William's detachment, his absorption in his art.

Here in Paris life was cool and efficient just as long as you spoke French and knew exactly what to do. But she would have welcomed a little more detachment on Farringdon's part.

He would breath down her neck. 'Are there towels in the guest bedroom, Laura? Have you checked?'

'Yes, I've checked. I've checked everything,' she'd say patiently.

His temper grew shorter as the list of visitors and meetings and dinners lengthened, but nevertheless he appeared immensely grateful when she coped well with a succession of official guests whose every need was catered to with professional politeness. Bedrooms were immaculate, the bathwater was hot, men's shirts were ironed at a moment's notice, and their wives or 'partners' were politely taken to Galleries Lafayette or the Musée d'Orsay.

All this Laura coped with, and all the time Farringdon watched her closely, as if afraid she would get something wrong.

The main worry on his mind appeared to be the official dinner party for the new Minister of Defence. Farringdon had insisted the party should be at his Residence rather than at the grand professional Embassy in rue Faubourg St Honoré. Therefore it was even more important that the party should be a success. His own military honour and that of his mission was at stake. The new Minister was reputed to be a tricky, touchy fellow, a former left-wing university professor, who was only too ready to criticise what he saw as the Establishment, people like Farringdon.

Laura didn't feel equal to cooking a VIP dinner herself and anyway Farringdon had flatteringly asked her to attend the party. She knew her limitations: she could not both cater and attempt the part of immaculate hostess. In an effort to make Sebastien feel less marginalised, she had telephoned him for his advice and he'd agreed to fix the caterer and the waiters for her. The caterer, he said, was an English Cordon Bleu chef, which would be interesting for them all.

On the morning of the great party, Laura put the white wine and champagne in the pantry fridge, leaving the kitchen clean and empty for the caterer. She'd checked again with Sebastien and he'd said the chef would arrive around four o'clock to make the final preparations in situ. He, the chef, would bring absolutely everything, all the food, all the ingredients to make a delicious upmarket dinner for the twenty illustrious guests. Such a relief, thought Laura, not to have to worry about anything except making sure the apartment was looking its best.

She went to buy flowers, enjoying being able to spend as much money as she wanted, and constructed what she considered were some pretty but dull arrangements. Neat and tidy roses in shades of red to tone with the red curtains would be Farringdon's taste, she reckoned, certainly not ivy and grasses sprawling all over the table. Then she did a couple of vases for the drawing room, smiling to herself about the ladylike nature of the job.

After lunch she had her hair done, resenting every minute spent staring at her reflection while a cross young Frenchman vainly attempted to turn her into a smooth Parisienne.

Thankful that Agnès was away and therefore not to be among the critical guests, Laura ironed the nice safe black dress she would wear. Then she tidied the flat again, plumping up the silk cushions in the salon for the fifth time.

It was a little unnerving waiting for the chef. As the afternoon wore on Laura looked at her watch every five minutes.

At a quarter past four he had not appeared, nor had the waiters. She mustn't panic. Were they lost? Were they stuck in a traffic jam? Calm down, she told herself. There's still plenty of time. The party was not due to begin until eight thirty.

With nervous hands, she laid the table, a task the waiters would normally do. The cut glass and silver candlesticks looked elegant on the long mahogany table, but she was in no mood to admire her own handiwork. However many times she looked at her watch, the chef did not come. Not then, not at five o'clock or half past. She kept pacing out on to the balcony to stare down into the street at any vehicle that might possible be his but none of the cars or vans stopped near the apartment.

Ah, at last, that white car parking below, trying to back into a space near the apartment, it must be him. A man wearing a grey jacket and black trousers – quite fat, could well be a chef – looked around the street and then went around the back to open the boot. She held her breath. But he just took out a briefcase and disappeared purposefully into the flats opposite. Willing herself to keep calm, she ran back indoors, found the chef's mobile number in the house address book and telephoned, but a recorded voice told her to leave a message. She did so, without much hope.

She tried calling Sebastien. No reply, just a machine again. In a panic she phoned Farringdon's secretary, Elaine. Elaine sounded agitated too, saying she was in the middle of typing an urgent communiqué. She gave Laura a list of waiters to call but at this late stage another caterer might be difficult. 'Is Mr Farringdon there?' asked Laura fearfully. No, he was coming straight home from the international meeting.

There was no reply from any of Elaine's contacts, so Laura left increasingly desperate messages on various answering machines.

When Farringdon returned, his nerves were clearly on edge. 'Everything under control, Laura?' he barked.

Taking a deep breath, she explained that it wasn't.

His face paled. 'For God's sake, why the bloody hell didn't you check? You must always check all arrangements. Standard procedure, I'd have thought.'

Laura shrank back. 'Sebastien said he'd...' she stuttered.

'*You* are in charge at the moment. Not him.'

'But he...' Suddenly it dawned on her that Sebastien had deliberately dumped her in the shit, but this was not the moment to discuss this revelation.

Farringdon was glowering at her. 'Last thing I want to do is take the party to a restaurant. The Minister could accuse me of wasting Government funds,' he said.

Speaking with a calmness she did not feel, she said her plan was to walk down Avenue Mozart and buy something from one of the numerous local *traiteurs*. She'd often passed shops full of delicious looking ready-cooked food and could she take the driver?

'All right, go ahead,' he snapped. 'Might do as a fall-back position. But who's going to serve? Have you thought of that?'

Laura said she would do it herself, with Conchita who was still here, having been asked to stay on to wash up.

'Out of the question. You can't serve a five-course dinner for twenty people with a half-wit like Conchita – has to be done quickly and efficiently. The Minister has an after-dinner meeting... And I don't suppose for a moment that you have a waitress uniform tucked away in your wardrobe.'

'No, but... maybe one of the waiters will ring back. I'm going to take my mobile with me.'

It wasn't that easy to find elegant food for twenty people at a moment's notice. The first *traiteur* she came across had two large fish terrines which she bought, but they had nothing suitable for the second course. They offered her a fancily decorated whole salmon which she declined, thinking the meal would be over-fishy. The next shops were Greek or Chinese, far more upmarket than take-aways back home, but hardly suitable for a British diplomatic function. Oh God, she should have waited, bought the main course first. What if she couldn't find anything? All the offerings in the next *traiteur* consisted of various casserole dishes which just would not do at a Paris dinner. Then, joy oh joy, she came across a butcher who was still open. She could buy three or four fillets of beef, cook them, and serve them hot along with a selection of ready-made fancy salads.

Pudding was easy. The bakeries were full of delicious-looking desserts which could be tarted up with some fresh fruit.

With the chauffeur's help she transported it all back to the apartment, where, breathless and glowing with a sense of achievement, she quickly unpacked her purchases.

Farringdon marched into the kitchen. 'Well, first problem solved, that looks more or less edible, well done, but who's going to serve it?'

Flushing, Laura said she would try ringing round the list of waiters again.

As before, she had no success. She kept telling herself to keep a sense of proportion, for God's sake. Elsewhere in the world there were floods and famines and homeless people. No one would starve this evening. The official guests surely wouldn't mind if an unsuitably dressed woman served the dinner, rather than a team of efficient waiters. Or she could organise a buffet. They could help themselves.

In real life it would be perfectly normal. In this rarefied high-flown diplomatic Parisian world, it was not the way things were done, not considered *comme il faut*, but surely no one would care that much. Except that Farringdon *would* mind. He'd mind the loss of face. It would look as if he, a military man and not a career diplomat, couldn't organise his staff properly. The Minister might take offence that not enough effort had been made. And fellow Ambassadors amongst the guests would not be impressed.

She, Laura, was responsible for this mess. It was her job to organise an elegant diplomatic dinner and she had made a hash of it. As she rushed wildly around the kitchen arranging the food she willed the telephone to ring. Maybe there was a teenager, daughter of someone in the Embassy, who could act as a waitress. If only she knew the neighbours, they probably had a son who...

An idea suddenly flashed into her head. The boy, Simon. Yes! Yes! He was a waiter.

She ran to her room. Her address book stood on the desk, but, damn it, she hadn't bothered to transfer Simon's number to it. Her handbag? Where the hell was it? She scrabbled through the all the pockets, then, panicking, tipped it upside down on the bed. There amongst about ten scruffy bits of paper was Simon's card. Shakily she dialled the number. The phone rang for what seemed like five minutes and then yet again an answering machine kicked in.

In the middle of her message Simon picked up the receiver. 'OK,' he said, stopping her in mid-sentence. 'I'll come. And I'll bring a couple of mates. See you in half an hour.'

Overwhelmed with relief, Laura sat down with a bump.

Sooner than she had dared to hope, Simon appeared in a white jacket, accompanied by two small swarthy Frenchman, similarly dressed. She was reassured by his professional manner. He treated Farringdon with a suitable amount of deference and kept calling him 'Your Excellency' which went down well. Laura was addressed as 'madame' – she'd have found it amusing had she been less overwrought.

A now much calmer Farringdon still wanted her to attend the dinner, so she rushed to her room to change. At the last minute her black dress seemed to have shrunk, so she flung on a green silk jacket and black skirt, ran a comb through her hair and hurried back to the fray.

Simon and his colleagues were assiduous with the pre-dinner champagne, and the evening, long and boring by normal standards, was clearly a success. Farringdon headed one end of the long table and the Minister the other, and both were talking non-stop.

Seated in a lowly position in the middle, Laura didn't much enjoy herself as she was too stressed to make intelligent conversation in French to the elderly men on either side of her. Maybe they were puzzled by her status. Maybe they thought she might be Farringdon's mistress or partner, and rather than make a *faux pas* they mostly ignored her.

Sipping wine rather too steadily, she sat watching the waiters, afraid they might drop something or forget the plates or the wine, afraid that the food would not be up to scratch. It looked decorative enough but appearances could be misleading.

Then, still holding her breath, Laura found yet another thing to be concerned about. Her normally loose green jacket was tighter than before and now, she realised, far too much flesh was on display. Her bust seemed to be expanding along with her waistline. The only consolation was she could hardly swallow this evening. Pity in a way because the food was not at all bad – the Minister was wolfing it down.

Finally the ordeal was over. After the Minister had departed in a flurry of thanks and the other guests had left, Laura paid Simon and his colleagues.

'Thank you very much, *madame*. Was everything to your liking?' asked Simon, with an ironic bow.

She felt like hugging him but thought this would be inappropriate with the other waiters looking on. Instead she said that everything was very much to her liking and hoped she would see him soon.

'Well done, Laura. You coped very well with the great crisis. Calm under my attacking fire. I admire that,' said Farringdon, who was now full of charm and after-dinner brandy.

Laura supposed the remark about attacking fire was a kind of apology.

He insisted on pouring her a glass of Cointreau. 'The Minister was very pleased,' he said.

'I'm glad,' she said, in equally high spirits. Thank God that's over. And it even went well – certainly should have done, judging by the number of empty champagne bottles standing in a row on the pantry floor.

He took off his jacket and loosened his tie. Wow, she thought, smiling to herself, I mean, how relaxed can one get. He was wearing a plain lilac-blue shirt which rather suited him, especially as he had retained his Mediterranean suntan. She hadn't been too fraught to notice that some of the female guests had been gazing at him under their eyelashes, especially that Agnès clone in the chic black suit. Yet again Laura remembered how glad she was they'd been spared Agnès herself this evening.

'Nice boy, young Simon,' he was saying. 'I've decided to hire him as a temporary butler for another month. So many visitors, thought you could do with a hand. Not that you couldn't manage on your own, but he seemed a pleasant, willing young chap. You would be in charge, of course.'

'Oh?' If she hadn't been in such a good mood, she'd have felt irritated not to have been consulted. And what about Charlotte's crush on Simon? Farringdon wouldn't like his daughter to be romantically involved with the hired help, even if Simon couldn't be described as a bit of rough.

While Farringdon talked on she toyed with the idea of mentioning her worries, but then it occurred to her that Simon's job was temporary. He'd be gone before Charlotte came back to Paris for half term. So there was no problem, and to bring up the subject would just make herself and everyone concerned look a fool or untrustworthy, or both.

'I wonder if Sebastien got the date wrong,' Farringdon was saying meditatively. 'He had become rather hard of hearing lately, particularly on the telephone. One should really re-check everything.'

'I did, I did double-check with him but I'll bear in mind that I should be ultra clear,' she said, holding her peace.

'But you did very well in very difficult circumstances,' he repeated with a beaming smile. He continued to discuss the evening and what a triumph it had been. It dawned on her that despite his fifty-plus years and his world-weary sophistication, he'd been almost as nervous about the event as she had. It was as if he were a young executive having his boss to dinner for the first time. Now relaxed and triumphant, he was almost endearing, she thought. Underneath all those layers of stiff conduct and correct behaviour was a normal human being who needed the approval of others.

She had a sudden urge to lean forward and rumple his smooth dark grey hair. Deciding that this was a dangerous urge fuelled by her own intake of good wine, she stood up quickly and said goodnight. As she leant forward to pick up the remaining dirty glasses, she became aware that her cleavage was bursting at the seams and that he was staring with obvious admiration.

As she straightened up, he smiled at her, holding her gaze with a long, long look. Then, after a moment, he rearranged his features into a more politically correct expression. 'Goodnight, Laura, and thank you for everything,' he said.

Once in bed, Laura lay awake, adrenaline still pumping through her. She had an irrational fluttering feeling there was just the faintest possibility that Oliver – as she had now begun to call him in her mind – might come to her room. Which would be extremely awkward, as she'd have to ask him to leave. He'd go immediately, of course, but then she'd have to leave Paris because it would be too embarrassing to stay. And she didn't want to lose her job...

Of course he won't come to your room, she told herself. She jumped when she heard a floorboard creak outside. Then she heard Oliver's door open and close. Then the sound of running water. Was he having a shower?

For God's sake, calm down. He won't pounce on you uninvited. He's not the type. Not without a lot more encouragement than you've given him. So far. On the other hand, if you were to go to his room, maybe he wouldn't throw you out.

Horrified by her own train of thought, Laura pulled the bed covers up to her chin.

After a further uneasy half hour of listening to the rain, she fell into a restless sleep.

# CHAPTER 11

SIMON HAD BEEN PACING AROUND his small dark flat in the thirteenth arrondissement for almost an hour. Kiki was always late but he was always early. Early for Kiki anyway. If she arrived on time and he wasn't there he always feared she might not wait, that she'd rush impatiently away.

He'd already hoovered around a bit and thrown away a couple of half-eaten packets of stale biscuits and loads of coffee cups and Coke cans, so the sitting room looked passable if a little gloomy. He turned on a lamp but then turned it off again. He didn't want to illuminate the corners: the chaotic shelves and piles of books and newspapers that Kiki complained about.

Then he remembered the kitchen. Shit, supposing she wanted a drink or something? He quickly stacked the dirty plates in the sink and shoved the remains of a packet of Weetabix into the bin. Did he have time to take the rubbish down to the cellar? No, she might arrive and find him clutching a stinking black binbag.

He'd already changed the sheets, of course. She was fussy about that sort of thing, Kiki. Well, not that fussy, not always. She even liked sex in the back of her car, or outdoors, now and then. He never thought about her previous encounters in cars or woods, though sometimes she reminisced. He always tried to steer her away from these reminiscences. He didn't want to know about his predecessors, though he was not under any illusion that he was her first affair, or that he'd be the last.

These dark jealous doubts always vanished the moment she arrived, bubbling with life and sensuality and fun, shaking out her wild red curls and laughing at him.

But where the hell was she? She always looked surprised and hurt when he accused her of being permanently late. She'd shrug her shoulders and pout like Marilyn Monroe and then put her arms around his neck. 'Your watch must be fast, honey. You just couldn't wait for me to get here, could you?' Her American voice was extra sweet and low on these intimate occasions.

'No, I couldn't wait to see you,' he always said, and then, before she had time to remove her jacket – she always wore a smart jacket – he would push it half off her shoulders and begin to undo the buttons of her shirt.

'Wait. Like, this is a designer blouse,' she would say, giggling and starting to get breathless.

But he could never wait, once she arrived. Because he had already anticipated her arrival for so long. He would have been thinking about the white skin and the high round breasts and the mound of pale strawberry hair, neatly trimmed and so very exotic.

And the reckless excitement of her response to his love-making. All the time she'd talk to him, a wild monologue of appreciation and encouragement – and instruction. He didn't mind her bossiness in bed. It turned him on like crazy, like everything else about Kiki.

In his heart of hearts he knew her love for him was shallow, but he treasured it. One can't expect a free spirit to love in the same faithful boring way as mere mortal women. She was the kind the poets knew about and Simon was grateful. He felt blessed to have been touched by her magic. He imagined her like a kind of modern Venus, admittedly rather older than Botticelli's, rising from the pearly shell and into his arms.

Then he heard the doorbell. His heart pounding, he opened the door and in bustled Kiki in a cloud of scent and talk of traffic jams. With trembling hands he locked the door behind her.

There she stood in the middle of the sitting room, smiling her mischievous alluring smile, showing her small perfect teeth.

Without a word, he cut short her chat by kissing her open mouth. Then, while she stood, still laughing at him, he began the greedy ritual of undressing her right there. There was never time to get as far as the bedroom first time around.

As he pushed her back on the sofa, she stopped laughing and began to breath faster and faster, spreading herself before him like a feast. Then he was lost in her and, much too soon, it was finished.

As she lay below him, flushed and shining, he gazed at her ruefully. 'Sorry. A quickie. Next time...'

She grinned. 'I was right there with you. I'm a quick person too, as you know.'

He thought fleetingly of that film *When Harry Met Sally*. Meg Ryan's how-to-fake-an-orgasm performance in the restaurant must have made a lot of blokes uneasy. But Kiki claimed she never needed to fake it, 'not with you, Simon,' she would say.

There was a long pause while he gazed lovingly at her. Then he stroked her face and said, 'You're terrific, you know.'

'Mm. I know.'

After another contented silence, he said, 'Just after we make love you look about eighteen.'

'You're not wearing your glasses, honey. But flattery will get you everywhere. That's what I need. Give me more of that. More. More.'

He laughed. 'Kiki, you're so... honest. I love you so much.'

'Mm, you're cute too. You know, I think I'll take a shower – you're very hot today.'

Reluctantly he let her go. 'I'll come with you. Help you wash your back.'

'No. Fix some drinks and take them to bed. Today I can stay for Round Two.'


'How've you been?' she asked. He noticed she was wearing her bright sky-blue contact lenses. They gave her a strange blank look, like a *Star Trek* cyber woman, a beautiful unreal creature from another planet.

'I'm OK.' He smoothed back her wonderful hair. 'You're so great. You know that.'

She purred like a contented pussy-cat. 'I know, I know... Move over a little, honey – you're squashing my arm.'

'Kiki...'

'Wait. You don't have to rush. We have all afternoon.'

'Yes, but today I have to get back to work on time. I promised Laura. She's going back to England tomorrow and so we have stuff to discuss before she goes.'

'That's too bad,' drawled Kiki. 'The one day I make it all the way over here, you have to rush. She seems to have a strong influence. You must be quite close, you and Queen Laura.'

'Well, yes, she's nice. And not queenly at all. Why do you call her that?'

'Nice? That's what you said about her last time. Like, what do you mean by nice? You're meant to be creative. So describe her properly.'

'Laura? Well, she's chatty, easy to talk to and quite, um, maternal.'

She smiled in satisfaction. 'You mean sort of fat?'

'Not really. But she's not thin either, more rounded.'

'So she has big boobs?'

'A normal sort of size, I suppose. Hadn't thought.'

'Bullshit. I never met a guy who didn't think about a woman's boobs.'

'Look, Laura is nice and sympathetic, but I don't fancy her, OK? It's a working friendship. I don't think of her that way.'

'So why are you always talking about her? This pretty, soft, mommy-type with big breasts. You like her. You know you do. You love older women. All men are little boys at heart – they just want their mother.'

He thought it tactful to avoid saying that Laura was younger than Kiki, and, despite her kind nature, far from mumsy, quite fanciable in fact. 'I haven't said a word about Laura. In fact we, you and I, we haven't talked at all today. We hardly ever talk.'

'There you go again. Exaggerating as usual. You guys are never satisfied. If a woman talks too much, then she's a blabber mouth. But if a man wants to pour his heart out, then everyone has to listen till hell freezes over.'

Simon hated her generalisations. He disliked being called 'you guys', a typical example of the male sex, because it reminded him that he was just one of the numerous specimens Kiki had known. She was now talking about her husband. This was an even more tedious subject than men in general.

'Zak is just like that,' she said. 'Either he ignores me completely or he drones on and on about his business which has got to be the most boring thing in the whole world. Like, who in the hell cares about the wheat trade? And Zak is another guy with a mommy-fixation. D'you know he still calls her every week and...'

There was only one way to shut her up and Simon took it. He began to stroke her thighs and then very slowly and delicately around between them.

Kiki sighed and softened towards him.

Later, when she was just about to leave, he asked, 'Have you finished reading my script?'

'Your script? Not yet, honey. Now where did I leave my purse? This apartment is such a mess if you put something down for, like, one second, you can't find it.'

'But I cleaned up. Before you came.'

'I know, my darling boy. You do try. But for instance that tub of yours – it's terrible. A health hazard. Do something. Wash the shower curtain at least. The bottom part is so yuk, all covered in mould.'

'Sorry. But how do I wash a shower curtain?'

She laughed. 'Ask your mommy. Queen Laura will know. According to you, she knows everything.'

He decided to ignore this remark. He took a deep breath, 'About the script. I thought you said you'd read a few pages. What do you think of it so far?'

'Next time. We'll talk about it next time. I have to run now.'


Out in the street Kiki put on her sunglasses. She had already swathed her too conspicuous hair in a Jackie Kennedy scarf which she would take off as soon as she found a taxi. She chose a different taxi rank each time and sometimes she even took the metro. It was unlikely, though, that Zak would hire a private eye to follow her. He didn't have that much imagination. But on the other hand a gal has to be careful, even though it wasn't likely she would meet anyone she knew in this kind of neighbourhood, all grimy-grey dank buildings with brown-painted doors and horrible downmarket stores, not a designer boutique in miles. Why did Simon want to live here? He couldn't be that poor.

She smiled as she caught sight of her reflection in a mirror lining a shop window. Simon was right. She did look eighteen, well, maybe twenty-eight. Sex always made her glow. Too bad you couldn't put it in a bottle and take it like a tonic every morning. Then you wouldn't need a man. Or the beauty parlour.

Even in the early days Zak didn't make her glow that much. Because he never thought of her as a woman. More of an investment or a possession to admire from a distance. In fact, a first-edition trophy wife. Now, he bought real trophies: ornaments, pictures, that kind of stuff. So the house back home in California was like a museum, and the apartment here too. He never asked her if she liked the damn painting or the piece of the sculpture. He just went ahead and bought it. Still, Zak made money and for that, Kiki thought, may the Lord make us truly thankful. As she often said to herself in her philosophical moments, even a career girl needs to remember which side her li'l' ol' baguette is buttered.

Simon was so cute though, and it was nice to be worshipped. Everyone should have a little reassuring worship in their life, especially – and Kiki found another mirror to stare in – if they're past forty. Quite a while past forty if she was honest, which she wasn't too often.

She saw the yellow M of the metro station and checked her watch. Even if she took the slow ride to the sixteenth, she'd be in plenty of time for her exercise class with Philippe. He, the teacher, was quite cute too, and packed with muscles, but she'd lingered after the class once and he hadn't responded, so, like, definitely gay.

She did not often cheat on Simon, except with her husband now and then which didn't count and, besides, with Zak it was more then than now. But it was always good to look around for reserves. If Zak should suddenly notice one of the numerous little French ladies who surrounded him at work, then Simon would not be a good substitute to fall back on. A writer/waiter? No way. Even her sunglasses cost more than his weekly salary, for God's sake. Of course, she could pay for her own damn sunglasses but it was kind of convenient to have Zak pick up the tab until she got her next production assignment in Hollywood. Which must be any day now. Why didn't any of the studios return her calls? If you're not right there in town, everyone forgets you. It was pretty damn difficult to have a career in the States and a husband in Europe. Sometimes it seemed like she'd have to choose between taking care of Zak or taking care of her career. Right now Zak was a lot more profitable, so maybe she should be careful.

In any case, Be Prepared was Kiki's secret motto, so she kept her wits about her and her cyber-eyes wide open.

## CHAPTER 12

It was now October and Laura was back in England for a couple of weeks before half term.

As she stood outside her cottage surveying the scene, her euphoria at arriving home evaporated somewhat. The garden was a mess: a jungle of dead flowers, the surviving plants interspersed with displays of vigorous perennial weeds. And the lawn seemed to consist mainly of clover and dandelions. She supposed that the grass must have been mown occasionally or she'd be looking at a hayfield, but apart from that no one seemed to have done any gardening since she left the place at the beginning of July. So Bridget was not quite the conscientious tenant one might have hoped for. Policing the boy monsters must be a full-time job but all the same...

With some trepidation, Laura unlocked the house. To her relief, everything looked much as she'd left it, apart from a series of small grubby hand-prints on the wall beside the stairs. Could be a lot worse, she told herself, as she made a quick tour of inspection. Who cares about dust anyway?

She looked at the row of muddy wellies by the back door and the new extra row of hooks hung with children's coats, not too clean either. And the messy blue plastic basket full of toys – mostly cars and guns – in the corner of the sitting room. Well, naturally Bridget was entitled to leave the family's stuff here – she was still paying rent for the place as a holiday cottage. In some ways it was nice to see children's things around the place again – nevertheless, Laura couldn't help resenting these alien possessions. This renting and sharing business was a very peculiar thing.

Some of the furniture had been moved. Knowing it was illogical to mind about this, she pushed everything back to its proper place. Why she had to do this straight away she didn't know, but the cottage now felt more like home.

It was damp and chilly, though. She hurried to switch on the boiler, the second-hand bargain Jack's plumber had installed. Shivering she stood staring at the mysterious new programmer, then in desperation switched every control to 'continuous'. There was a pause while the boiler seemed to be in quiet contemplation, but, after a click and a hum and another click, it suddenly fired and roared reassuringly away.

So far so good, but she decided she'd have to keep her coat on for a while. The flat in Paris had been heated to sub-sauna temperatures since the first of the month so her blood was now far too thin for England.

She filled the kettle to make herself a cup of Nescafé. There was a whole jar, she noted somewhat mollified, but no milk, of course. She'd go shopping soon, if her poor old Toyota started after all those months in the garage. Laura decided ruefully that she was beginning to miss the convenience of city life already.

Nevertheless it was great to be home, back in England, back with familiarity and friends. She decided to telephone Mel straight away but, though she hung on for a while, there was no reply.

After some thought, Laura called Jack's office where a taped message advised her to try his mobile. Even a recording of his lovely familiar voice gave her a strange frisson. She hesitated. Calling a mobile during office hours seemed like an intrusion. But she needed to pay him back the money she owed and it would be more polite to give him the cheque personally, rather than send it through the post.

Polite? Who are you trying to kid? You just want to see him. Go on, dial his number.

Yet another recording informed her she had reached his voice-mail and invited her to leave a message.

'Oh, um, it's me, Laura, Laura Brooke, that is. I'm back home and I'd like to ask you and Mel to lunch. Please would you ring me, er, fairly soon because I'm not here for long.' She paused and then said, 'Goodbye. Thank you.'

Feeling ridiculous she put down the phone. Why hadn't she managed to sound more natural? She continued to lecture herself as she went out to the garage where she had to dig out a clump of grass to open the door. Which rather suggested that it had not been opened for some time despite Bridget's promise to start the car now and then. Not good news. Nor was it good news that the car was covered in a thick layer of dust. Sure enough, when a pessimistic Laura turned the key in the ignition, she heard that all too familiar hollow silence – a totally dud battery. She banged her fist on the steering wheel in frustration. Welcome to the real world, she told herself.

Then she heard the telephone. She rushed back to the house.

'Laura, wonderful to hear you.'

It was Jack. Smiling widely, all frustrations temporarily forgotten, she sank down on the nearest chair. She gushed that yes, it was terrific to be back and, yes, Paris was wonderful and would he and Mel come out to lunch. And so it was agreed. Then he asked about her cottage and she told him that it was marvellous, thanks to him and his men, but as for the damn car... Immediately he offered to come round with jump leads.

As soon as Laura put down the phone she felt guilty about trading on his good nature. I wasn't scheming, she assured herself. Nevertheless she then rushed upstairs to make face and hair presentable.

When she heard a car in the lane her heart beat faster. Was it his Audi? Didn't sound much like it on second thoughts. A white van pull into her drive, one of Jack's. With a stab of disappointment she saw that at the wheel was Charlie, the elderly carpenter who'd worked on the cottage last spring.

With minimum fuss and maximum efficiency he pushed the car out of the garage, and waving aside all offers of assistance from Laura, attached jump leads between the two vehicles. As the Toyota coughed reluctantly to life, she vowed to buy a new battery today. It was good to have earned enough money to pay for these luxuries.

'You're wonderful, Charlie,' she said.

Charlie gave her a bashful smile. 'Don't thank me. Thank the boss.'

'I will,' said Laura, happy at the thought.

Next day as she was waiting for Jack and Melanie in the pub, Laura looked around. It felt strange to be hearing all these people speaking English. The Cat and Fiddle seemed to have moved upmarket since her last visit which must have been an age ago. Certainly the food prices had moved up, and instead of the dumpy local lasses who used to dish out the steak and kidney pies there were now sprightly young Australian girls sporting red aprons, tee shirts and jeans. It all seemed staggeringly informal after Parisian white table cloths and black suits.

She was trying not to watch the door, but out of the corner of her eye she saw Jack arrive. Her heart thumped as she stood up to greet him.

He was looking tired and strained, she thought, but he gave a huge, warm smile. 'Laura! Wonderful to see you. Welcome back to civilisation.'

She laughed. 'Civilisation it is indeed.' Restraining herself from flinging her arms around him, she kissed him demurely on the cheek. 'Isn't Mel with you?'

'Sorry, but I don't think she's going to be able to make it.'

'Oh? Is she ill or something?'

'Probably more tired and emotional than unwell. She sleeps a lot at the moment,' he said, his face suddenly shuttered.

'Oh?' Laura hesitated. 'Shall I go and see her? I tried to phone.'

'She doesn't answer the phone these days. Going through an anti-social phase, I'm afraid. Won't see anyone. Even the faithful cleaning woman has finally given in her notice.'

'Oh dear. So it's worse, the problem.'

'Yes.'

'Can I, can I do anything to help?'

'No, I don't think so. You're very kind but they say she has to want to help herself,' he said flatly.

Laura felt a certain unbridgeable reserve between them and there was an awkward silence. Then she said, 'It's very nice to see you anyway.' She was ashamed about how pleased she felt at the prospect of having lunch alone with him.

He smiled more cheerfully. 'You too. I must say you're looking very smart. I like the new hair cut. So how was it over there in darkest Paris?'

She was beginning to tell him when they were interrupted by a loud female voice.

'Jack, dahling. What a piece of luck! I've been trying to get hold of you for yonks.'

Before them stood a tall, slim, sharp-faced blonde, elegantly dressed in tight beige trousers, a matching cashmere polo-neck and a deeply fashionable tweed jacket. She was carrying an Hermès Kelly bag and what was no doubt an equally exclusive briefcase.

Jack rose to his feet politely and introduced them. Her name, it transpired, was Arabella. After a quick scrutiny, Laura decided she was about fifty.

'Mind if I join you,' she said, sitting down without waiting for a reply. 'I was supposed to meet a chum here but she's let me down. Can't bear eating alone in a pub, but I must eat somewhere. If my blood sugar gets too low, I'm impossible. Now, Jack, what I was ringing you about was that client of yours over in Twyford. Hopeless woman. Can't make up her mind about the paint colours, and I've told her over and over again that I can't do a thing until it's been painted.'

'Bella is an interior decorator. She works with us from time to time,' put in Jack.

'How interesting,' said Laura politely.

Arabella fluttered her eyelashes at Jack. 'Now where was I? Oh yes, that woman. Well, I said we can't get any orders in for carpets and curtains until she decides and...'

'Bella, would you mind talking to Mike,' said Jack, sounding relaxed. 'He's supervising that job. I don't really get involved with the day to day running of projects now, I'm afraid.'

Bella pouted. 'But, Jack, I don't know if he understands about things like the importance of door handles the way you do – a personal touch is so crucial.'

'So is letting people get on with their job without interference from me,' he said patiently. 'Be an angel and call Mike, would you.'

'I think we have to go to the bar to order food,' interrupted Laura.

'I'll do it,' said Jack, leaping to his feet.

Laura opened her mouth and closed it. She had been about to say it was her treat, but then decided that no way was she going to pay for the dreadful Bella.

Bella glanced at the menu. 'How fearfully pretentious these country pubs are,' she said. 'I'll have a plain omelette and a green salad with balsamic vinaigrette, if they can manage that. If not, a ham salad will do. And let's share a teeny-weeny bottle of Chablis.'

As soon as Jack had gone to the bar, Bella announced she must trot off to the loo. Laura gazed crossly after her. Jack was being far too patient with the woman. Unless, that is, he actually fancied her.

'Oh Jack dahling, you're back,' said Bella as soon as she returned to the table. She crossed her long legs. 'Now even if you won't talk to me about Mrs Twyford, I'm sure you'd love to hear about my chum who wants to convert his stable block into holiday flats.'

It turned out that Jack was indeed interested and, with an apology to Laura about talking shop, he quickly noted down the name of Bella's 'great chum' and there was no pause in her conversation until the food arrived. During the temporary silence when she was picking daintily at her salad, Jack said, 'Laura works in Paris.'

'What as?' asked Bella, clearly not much interested.

'I'm a kind of governess or rather holiday companion,' said Laura.

'A governess? How archaic! Who for?'

'Oh, a diplomatic family.'

'D'you know the Maitlands at the Embassy and the de Vauregards who live in St Cloud and...' She reeled off a list of names and looked extremely unimpressed by Laura's lack of social connections. 'Poor you,' she said, 'I mean Paris is super and all that, but I've just remembered how dull the diplomatic world is. I was married to it once, so I know. All those officials are so formal and pompous. One just dies of boredom trying to talk to them.'

'Not at all,' said Laura loyally, though who she felt loyal to she didn't know. 'I mean, most of them are very cultured and well-informed.'

'In other words, impossibly dreary.' Arabella waved her hand in a languid manner. 'Still, *chacun à son goût*,' she said in an annoyingly good French accent. 'Personally I'd much rather have decent British country chaps like my Cosmo, or lovely Jack here.'

She fluttered her long eyelashes again as she said this, and Laura was suddenly suspicious. Maybe, just maybe poor Mel was right and Jack really did have a string of mistresses, this Bella woman being the latest.

He was smiling at them both, his eyes twinkling. More like his usual self, in fact.

Laura hoped that Bella might have to leave for an appointment with one of her numerous elevated clients, but she stayed and stayed. It was Jack who left in a rush. With a perfunctory goodbye, Bella departed soon after.

Laura realised she hadn't even given Jack the money she owed him. So she'd better post the cheque after all. Then it occurred to her to deliver it to his house right now. That would give her an excuse to see poor Mel alone and find out how she really was.

\* \* \*

When Laura arrived at Melanie's, she was pleased to see her car parked in the drive, but no one answered the front door bell. She wandered around the back of the house in case Mel was in the garden. 'Hello!' she called a few times. Then she saw that the back door was open, so knocking loudly, she went in. The kitchen was a shambles, with stacks of dirty plates on the draining board and even a couple on the floor beside another bowl of half-eaten catfood. There were two open tins of Whiskas on the dresser and what looked like a manuscript, or part manuscript, torn in pieces. Newspapers and letters were scattered around the pine refectory table.

Laura tiptoed into the hall – also a mess. 'Mel? Are you there? Are you all right?' Still no reply. She became anxious and, though it felt intrusive, crept up the stairs. 'Mel?' she called again as she stood outside the open bedroom door. Finally she poked her head round and saw to her relief that Mel was fast asleep, sprawled legs akimbo on the patchwork bedspread. On the floor half-hidden under the bed was a bottle of whisky.

She looked OK, though paler and fatter, less pretty than before. Her blonde hair was falling in sad soggy strings over her now rather puffy face. She was wearing jeans and a baggy navy sweater – in the past she used to be almost too smart and fashionable for the country, Laura remembered.

'Mel!' It came out more of a loud whisper than a shout. She didn't really want to wake her.

Mel's large bosom rose and fell, then she gave a little snore.

Losing her nerve, Laura retreated downstairs. She felt she must take some action, but what? She was standing uninvited in a friend's house. In fact, Jack had told her to stay away.

She looked around the kitchen again and decided that she really couldn't leave those plates on the floor. Having picked them up, she might as well put them in the dishwasher. But when she opened the machine, she found it full of clean crockery.

In for a penny, in for a pound, she thought. Cleaning an area of the worktop, she began to unstack the machine. Once it was reloaded, the room looked a great deal better. Laura checked the cat-food tins, covered them with foil and put them in the fridge. Then she took a sniff at the bottle of milk on the draining board. 'Yuck,' she muttered, tipping it down the sink and rinsing it out. The pile of dirty saucepans by the stove would take too long, so she filled them with soapy water and left them to soak.

She was searching underneath the sink for Cif or Mr Muscle when she came across a stash of vodka bottles.

Come on, you'd better go or Jack'll come back and find you here, she told herself suddenly.

She was about to drive away when she realised she'd forgotten the cheque again so, leaving the engine running, she ran back and posted it through the letter box on the front door.

'Laura?' It was Jack on the telephone.

'Yes?' she said anxiously, wondering if he'd guessed about her interfering Mary Poppins act.

'Thank you for the envelope,' he began. 'You really didn't need to repay it so quickly. In fact...'

'Thank you for all your help,' she interrupted. 'Sorry I forgot to give you the cheque at the pub. And thanks for the lunch too.'

She wondered if he would apologise for Bella's intrusion but instead he asked, 'Did you see Mel when you called?'

'She didn't answer the door,' said Laura evasively. 'Is she OK?'

'A bit better, I think. She did some housework at some point today, which seems like a step in the right direction. Or at least it could be.'

'Right,' said Laura. 'Well, give her my love. If you ever want to talk about it...'

'I talk about it all the time to the doctor and various other professionals but it doesn't get us anywhere,' he said wearily. 'I know you mean well, Laura, but it's something no one else can do but Mel, as I've said, far too many times.'

'Yes, but...'

'When are you off back to Paris?'

'Quite soon. Jack, I do hope that Mel can...' Her voice trailed off.

'Thanks, so do I. Look, I've got a call coming through on the other line. See you next time you're here. 'Bye. Take care.'

'Goodbye,' said Laura unhappily.

As she paced around the house, she lectured herself. Compared to Melanie's problems, she had nothing to be unhappy about. Except that Jack seemed more distant than before.

He's got a lot on his mind. What do you expect? If he doesn't want your help with Mel then keep out of it. Your motives are too mixed anyway. If you think there's still some kind of feeling between you and Jack, then the best thing you can do for all parties concerned is to stay away. It's not going to help Mel to recover if she finds out that you, one of the few friends she has, is carrying a torch for her husband.

I'm not carrying a torch for him. Not any more.

Are you sure?

She went to telephone Oliver to let him know when she was returning to Paris.

## CHAPTER 13

CHARLOTTE THOUGHT HALF TERM IN PARIS was going to be a drag, as usual. Dad wouldn't let her go and stay with Imogen whose parents had a flat in London. So she would miss Imogen's party. Everyone else was going. Just wasn't fair. Dad would never let her do anything she wanted.

As usual he sent the chauffeur to pick her up from the Gare du Nord – just in case she got lost on the metro, she thought bitterly. Not that she wanted to get the metro really, not with all her luggage, but sending the chauffeur was all part of Dad's over-protective bit.

Standing in the street outside the apartment block, she pressed the doorbell. 'Hi, it's me, Charlotte,' she muttered when an indistinct male voice answered the entry-phone. She noticed vaguely that it didn't sound much like Sebastien.

But as she dragged her suitcases out of the lift, she looked up and nearly fainted. It wasn't dismal old Sebastien who opened the door of the flat but, of all people, the hunky, amazing, fantastic Simon!

Simon in a butler's uniform, right here, in the apartment! The man of her dreams. The one she'd thought about day in, day out, ever since she'd met him in the summer.

'Welcome home, Miss Charlotte,' he said with a mischievous grin. How did he manage to wear glasses and still look so cool and handsome? She flushed and tried to think of something casual and witty to say in response but couldn't. 'So, er... how come you're here?' she managed eventually.

He explained that he was acting as a temporary replacement for Sebastien whose broken arm had turned out to be more serious than originally diagnosed.

'But I... I mean, why didn't Laura tell me? Where is she anyway?'

'Oh, she's gone shopping. She forgot something crucial. She said to say welcome home and she'd be back in a second. As for my job here, it was originally such a short-term thing that she probably didn't bother to mention it,' he said. He carried her suitcases all the way to her room and then with a polite kind of bow he asked, 'May I get you some tea? Is Earl Grey all right? Or a tisane: mint, vervain?'

'Tea?' repeated Charlotte. 'Uh, yes, please. Any kind, wonderful.'

'I'll serve it in the salon, shall I?'

She nodded dumbly. When he'd gone, she sat down on the bed with a thump. Then she remembered that she didn't even like tea.

As soon as she had forced down as much tea as possible, Charlotte retreated to her room. She decided she'd better wash her hair straight away. Thankfully she didn't have any spots at the moment, but it was going to be a serious problem having the love of your life under the same roof. Every day, every hour, she'd have to find something cool and sexy to wear. Like, she'd have to turn herself into a French girl. What a thought! Maybe she'd better postpone her hair and go shopping first because every single garment in her suitcase was dirty – she'd saved them up for Conchita to wash. Oh God, if Simon was in the kitchen he'd see all the washing – her knickers and bras hanging out to dry in the laundry room. He'd know exactly how small her boobs were even. She'd better hide her greying tattered M&S underwear – made even more grim by school name tapes – and zoom down to Passy Plaza. That lingerie shop wasn't as dead expensive as the rest. Maybe Laura would lend her some money.

It was all going to be mega tricky. But she couldn't wait to tell the girls at school. At last she had a boyfriend, kind of.

It was awkward, thought Laura, having Simon around that evening while Oliver was out on an official engagement. Next time she would insist on giving the boy the night off because it wasn't necessary for her and Charlotte to have a formal dinner served by a butler. The best thing to do would be to ask him to lay a place and join them.

This, with some initial reluctance, he did. 'You know, Laura, I really should stay the other side of the baize door, as it were. Or the others will resent me.'

Laura smiled. 'Don't be so stuffy. I'm in charge of cooking tonight, so sit down and shut up.'

Charlotte said even less than usual but she looked happy enough. Mostly she kept her eyes on her plate but occasionally she glanced surreptitiously at Simon with ill-disguised admiration.

Oh dear, thought Laura. 'So school was OK, was it, Charlotte?' she asked.

'Yep.'

'I don't suppose there have been any exams yet?'

'Nope.'

'How about the hockey team?'

Hunching her shoulders, Charlotte mumbled, 'Didn't play much.'

Laura tried another topic. 'Did you say you were going to the cinema in the Champs Elysées this evening?'

'Yep.'

'I've forgotten the name of the friend you're meeting.'

'Tania.'

'So what are you going to see?'

'*Shakespeare in Love*. It's been re-released. We're, uh, seeing it for like the third time actually. Tania's mad about Joseph Fiennes.' As if exhausted by this long sentence, Charlotte gazed firmly at her plate again.

But the ice was broken as Simon then talked about the film and what he thought about Tom Stoppard's screenplay, and the conversation became more animated.

'Tell us about your own film script, Simon,' said Laura.

He smiled happily, reminding her suddenly of William when people asked him about his painting.

'It's about an American, a man of about twenty-five,' said Simon.

'Right. Go on.'

'Well, the hero has an affair with an older French woman who teaches him the facts of life. But then finally a naïve young English girl saves him from her. Or the girl could be American, of course.'

'What else happens?' asked Charlotte.

'Well, that's it really.'

'Oh.'

'D'you think it sounds too much like one of those French movies with no plot except a rather gloomy love affair?' he asked anxiously.

'Well, actually, it reminds me of *The Graduate*,' said Laura.

'Oh, that was a generation ago,' he said. 'Anyway, this is set in Paris, so it's quite different. The French woman gives him culture lessons as well as sex lessons, broadens his mind. But maybe you're right. Like, maybe it needs more plot. In another version I wrote, the French woman's husband is jealous and plans to have the hero murdered, but the English girl finds out and saves him.'

'It sounds absolutely wonderful,' said Charlotte intensely.

Simon beamed at her. Then he said, with a flirtatious kind of wink, 'You know, Charlotte, you look good with long hair.'

Charlotte blushed. 'Having it cut tomorrow,' she mumbled.

Laura had followed this exchange with some amusement but also a certain disquiet. She hadn't expected to find Simon still here at half-term, but then surely not much harm could come to Charlotte's emotions in a week. By the Christmas holidays, Sebastien would be back and then young Simon would be out of their lives.

When a flustered Charlotte had rushed off to the cinema, Laura expected that Simon, too, would be in a hurry to leave, but he made some coffee and returned to the dining table.

'I know, shall we be daring and have a glass of brandy?' he asked.

She smiled. 'Why not? Servants are allowed a treat now and then.'

He poured the drinks.

After a moment's hesitation Laura said, 'Simon, I know you mean it in fun but it's probably better if you don't tease Charlotte or flirt with her too much. She isn't quite mature enough to cope with that kind of thing.'

'You're quite right. I'm sorry, madam, it was most incorrect. I forgot my place,' he said with mock solemnity.

'No, seriously, she's at rather a sensitive age,' she said, feeling a traitor towards poor Charlotte.

'Does she have a boyfriend?'

'I have no idea. How is your great love, by the way?'

'Kiki's... well, her husband is here at the moment – it's terrible.'

His tragic expression made Laura want to laugh but she managed to keep a straight face and ask politely, 'So how's it going, you and her?'

Simon poured his heart out yet again. The fact that he could hardly ever see her. The fact that they never spent much time together. According to Simon, her husband was sometimes unkind to her, and ignored and neglected her. But she would never leave him. That it was a hopeless love because he, Simon, would never be worthy of her. 'Sometimes I think I'm just her bit of rough,' he said, with a sigh.

Laura shook her head. 'You're not at all rough. Quite the opposite.'

'But you know what I mean.' He smiled sweetly. 'Sorry about all this. You're such a good listener, Laura. You see, you're the only person I can talk to about it. I've never confided in anyone else before. It's such a relief that you understand how I feel.'

I can quite see why Kiki likes him, she thought suddenly. He's a very attractive boy. All fair and touchingly vulnerable. In fact if I were twenty years younger...

Aloud she said, 'To change the subject, how's your screen-writing course?'

'It's good but I've missed rather a lot,' he said.

'Oh dear. Why? I thought you paid for all the lessons in advance and asked for the time off specially.'

'I did, but you see it so happens that the only morning of the week Kiki can come round with any regularity is Tuesdays and that's the day of the course, so I have to miss it.'

Laura shook her head. 'That's bad. It's important for you, the course.'

'So's Kiki. She's the most important thing in my life. I can't explain but she's like... like a bright shining star in a dark world.'

Laura suppressed another smile. 'But you said yourself that there probably isn't any future in it,' she said gently.

He took a large defiant gulp of brandy. 'No, but I don't care. I've got to be there for her. I can never give her up. When you find something good you can't just let it go.' Then he took his glasses off and rubbed his eyes.

Just the way William used to. 'You remind me of my husband,' she said.

He looked embarrassed. 'The one who died?'

'Yes, I've only had one.'

'Would you like to talk about him?' he asked awkwardly.

She smiled. 'No, no. Don't worry.'

'But it's your turn.'

Simon was unusual in that respect, she thought. Rather few men under thirty even pretended to be interested in other people's stories. 'No. It's OK. You'd better be getting home now, Simon.'

He stood up and began to clear the table.

On his way home through the Paris night, Simon felt compelled to take a detour. Tonight as on many other evenings he just had to walk down the boulevard where Kiki lived. He couldn't bear the thought of Zak being there. Against his will and common sense, he stopped outside the apartment building and looked up towards the third floor where there was a light in the salon. He knew which room was which because occasionally in the past Kiki had invited him to stay. Her bedroom was at the back overlooking a courtyard.

The curtains were open but he could see nothing. For ten minutes or more he just stood gazing up towards the building. Cars rushed past at the usual excessive French speed but the pavement was deserted, apart from a well-dressed old man walking a small white poodle. Both the dog and the old man stared at him suspiciously.

Ignoring them, Simon continued to gaze at Kiki's flat. He imagined her sitting there watching television, with her husband's arm around her. Or she might be writing, or reading. He didn't like to dwell on what else she and Zak might be doing. Anyway she'd let slip that he was more or less impotent.

He jumped. His mobile was ringing, sounding loud as a car alarm in his pocket. He pulled it out.

A miracle. It was Kiki. 'Simon! Is that you out there in the street? Are you, like, insane or something?'

'Yes, it's me,' he said happily. He looked up and could just see her face peering out of the darkened dining room window.

'You'd better come on up,' she said.

'But what about Zak?'

'He's out, a business dinner. But hurry. We don't have a whole lot of time.'

He dashed across the street, buzzed the entry phone and, not wanting to wait for the lift, raced up the stairs. The door of her apartment was open. Kiki closed it quickly behind him and put her arms around his neck, snuggling up to him. She was dressed in black, her red hair fanning around her lovely face.

'You're the craziest boy I ever knew,' she murmured. 'No, don't move.'

Then she sank to her knees.

After a while he gasped, 'I can't last much longer. Better go to bed.'

She stood up and, laughing at him, pushed him back into the small office by the entrance hall. She sat on the edge of the desk. Her short black skirt now seemed even shorter. As he took his glasses off, he noticed blindly that she wasn't wearing any underwear, just those stockings that stay up on their own. She always wore those stockings.

He gulped. 'Kiki, oh my darling.'

She held out her arms. He moved to kiss and caress her, but she said there was no time. She wanted him right now. Burning with lust and love, Simon obeyed her instructions.

A few minutes later, he said breathlessly, 'Sorry, just couldn't wait. You're so fantastic, you're just...'

Still panting, she pushed him away a little. 'Better go now, honey.'

'But I haven't seen you for ages. I want to hold you and talk to you, and hear how you've been...'

'No, you'd better go right now, before Zak gets back. He told me the dinner would finish early. He could be here any moment.'

'What? Oh my God,' His heart pounding, Simon grabbed his jeans and struggled into them.

'Take the stairs down. He always uses the elevator. If you meet him in the entrance hall, smile politely and pass by. He'll think you've come from a different apartment. Don't speak though. You don't want to get into a conversation with him.'

'But...'

She laughed at him again. 'Just go, honey chil', and be grateful.'

## CHAPTER 14

THAT NIGHT LAURA HAD BEEN LYING AWAKE thinking about love in general and love in particular. She was trying to remember whether she'd felt that intense, crazy, blotting-out-everything-else kind of love like Simon's. Without ever having met her, she guessed Kiki did not reciprocate poor Simon's adoration. In fact the woman sounded like a greedy, immoral bitch. All the same, if she were to be honest, Laura felt faintly jealous of anyone who had such a bold sex life. Or any sex life at all, for that matter.

Laura also felt a sneaking admiration for one who so successfully exploited men, rather than vice versa. Not that all men were exploitative. Her thoughts turned to William again. He was never exploitative. Too nice for that. He was her first lover, and she'd adored him and desired his tall, golden body.

After the initial dismay and shock, she'd been glad to be carrying William's child, not sorry to abandon her studies of mediaeval literature which had suddenly seemed dry and remote. Mad pheromones, as her mother called them, had engulfed her. Her mother was against William and pro abortion. She had brandished the metaphorical shotgun to try and prevent the marriage rather than encourage it. That was the source of the conflict between them. And the vile Julius, stepfather and Machiavelli personified, had fanned the flames of this conflict. 'Dear little Laura, so young, so fragile, doesn't really know much about the world' he would say, with a sickening smile on his face. 'Course little Laura doesn't want a baby, she's just a baby herself.'

William stuck by her. He needn't have married her but he had an old-fashioned sense of honour. She remembered his reluctant speech in the dark restaurant: 'All right then. Will you marry me?' he'd said miserably, as if each word had been forced out of him. The restaurant was so crowded and noisy she hadn't even been sure she'd heard right so she had to ask him to repeat his proposal. She'd said no, she wouldn't marry him, but then, a few days later, yes. Isolated by her family, Laura needed to cling to him.

She could picture her mother now, striding along Knightsbridge, a newly pregnant and queasy Laura having difficulty in keeping up with her.

'You'll regret it, Laura. You're only twenty – too young to marry, far too young to have a child. I know William is much older than you but he's very immature. If you wanted an older man, you should at least have chosen a man of substance, a man who amounts to something, rather than an artist, for goodness sake.' She made artist sound like tramp or drug-dealer. 'And his parents have no money at all, I gather. A low-church Presbyterian minister in Scotland with a Norwegian wife, you said. I don't suppose they approve any more than I do.'

They didn't approve, Laura knew. They didn't approve of anything.

Mama said, 'I've made an appointment at the clinic. Mr Smith – he's a gynaecologist – he will help you. I am sure he'll find suitable legal grounds. Don't forget, you call him mister rather than doctor as he's a surgeon.' Mama was keen on etiquette.

Laura had obediently consulted Mr Smith in Harley Street and allowed her legs to be suspended in the embarrassing stirrups, but something about his smooth grey hair and urbane manner irritated and repulsed her. Her baby was not going to be scraped out of her womb by a man like that, or anyone else, for that matter.

It was only a week later that she had a natural miscarriage – curiously painless, sad and strange. Laura told no one about her loss except the concerned and loving William who insisted on going ahead with the wedding regardless. In a pale daze Laura agreed. She didn't want to lose such an honourable man.

Immediately after the wedding they went to live in Greece where Laura wrote to her mother pretending she had only just lost the baby. At the time it seemed the only thing to do. They lived from hand to mouth – William sold a few paintings and Laura babysat for English families on holiday.

Eventually Laura's mother lured them back to England with the gift of Pond Cottage where later on Alice was born. In an attempt to provide for his new family, William tried another insurance underwriting job in London. It had been his profession before he turned to painting. But, inclined to be vague and absent-minded, and far too kind-hearted, he was sacked. Laura always suspected that Julius, a director of the firm, had engineered William's dismissal and said so. There was a massive quarrel – unforgivable things were said on both sides.

So they returned to Greece and, with William's redundancy pay, they bought a tiny white house which they converted into a tiny white hotel. Laura oversaw all the work while William painted. For a while they made a living of sorts, or rather Laura did, but then a new loud resort complex was built right next door, spoiling the peace of the setting. So her former guests no longer came and, though she worked and worked, Laura's dreams slowly died until they had nothing. Nothing except their daughter and their cottage in England, and each other.

Each other. But what did that amount to?

She loved William and he loved her, but somewhere along the way she'd lost her respect for him. Laura remembered only too well her mother's saying. 'Get rid of that husband of yours. He's a permanent passenger.'

Reluctant to admit she was right, Laura defended him violently. Another quarrel. Again Julius insidiously made things worse. He had a way of twisting people's words and turning them into daggers. 'I told your mother you said we should mind our own business and not interfere with your life, and she was very hurt. I told her you didn't mean to be so rude and cold. It's just your manner. But it upsets her, Laura, especially considering she's been so generous. We only want to help, you know.'

Then soon after her mother's heart attack and shockingly sudden death, William had a stroke and did indeed become a permanent passenger – in a wheelchair, locked behind a blank face. And Laura's life changed for ever.

Without the support of the doctor and the social services, and friends like Jack and Melanie, she would have gone mad. She never thought herself cut out for nursing the disabled but, by force of circumstances, she adapted. The presence of a child in the house sustained her too, and, somehow, they survived.

Or rather Laura survived, but she felt Alice had lost her childhood along the way. Alice went to board at St. Swithun's, already arranged and paid by her grandmother's will. Laura didn't want to send her daughter away to school – in fact she resented Mother trying to control matters from the grave – but Alice needed time and space away from the sick. Alice often went to stay with friends in the holidays, but she never brought anyone home to the cottage. Because of Dad.

Everything was arranged around William. All Laura's attention had been on him and not on Alice. Somehow, in the process of caring for her husband, she seemed to have neglected and grown further away from her daughter.

Laura minded about this a good deal, especially now when geography meant they were physically so far apart. Tonight, tossing and turning, she reminded herself firmly that Alice had been bound to leave the nest sooner or later. All the same, Laura would have preferred it to be later. Alice had grown up rather too quickly.

## CHAPTER 15

CONTINUING HER SEE-SAW LIFE BETWEEN FRANCE and England, Laura found herself back at the cottage in November. She rang Melanie several times and left messages on the answerphone. No one called her back. In accordance with her resolution, she did not phone Jack's office. If he wanted to see her, he would make an arrangement to do so, she reasoned. But she heard nothing from him.

She concentrated on trying to restore order to her garden before the winter set in. It wasn't much fun – icy-cold hands, damp knees and too much Hampshire mud – but she persevered with a grim devotion. The countryside was beginning to lose its charms. At this time of year the bright lights of Paris seemed more appealing.

At Oliver's request, she brought Charlotte back to the cottage for the exeat weekend. There was nothing whatever for a teenager to do in St. Mary Wield, but Charlotte seemed perfectly happy slumped in front of the television all day. They spent a crowded Saturday in Guildford where Charlotte tried on every pair of shoes in every shoe shop and eventually returned to the first to buy the first pair she had tried.

On the long journey back Charlotte said, 'You're very patient, Laura, thank you.'

Laura smiled. 'I learnt patience with Alice.' And William, she thought.

Then Charlotte suddenly said, 'My mother used to go to that theatre in Guildford sometimes.'

'Really?' said Laura. This was the first time Charlotte had mentioned her mother. 'Do you hear from her much?' she asked after a pause.

'Hardly ever. She's got a new husband and new babies now.'

'Where does she live? I've forgotten.'

'Brazil.'

'My daughter is in South America too,' said Laura.

'I know. You told me. D'you miss her?'

'Oh yes, very much. It's very difficult, trying to get through on the phone to her. It always seems like the wrong time of day or a bad connection. And she never e-mails.' After a pause she said, 'I expect you miss your mother too.'

Charlotte hunched her shoulders. 'Not particularly. Didn't see much of her when I was young anyway. She was always out.'

'How old were you when they divorced?' asked Laura gently.

'Eight.'

'How sad.'

'Don't be. I'm not at all sad myself. I hated the way they quarrelled. Hated her too. Not so much now. I mean, I don't care either way, really.'

The bleakness in her voice was distressing. 'I didn't always like my mother much either,' Laura said eventually.

Charlotte darted a glance at her. 'But you liked her sometimes?'

'Yes, of course. I loved her when I was small. Less once I grew up. She was a tough woman, rather disapproving and distant.'

'Like Dad,' said Charlotte.

'That's not fair. He's not distant. He loves you.'

'Yeah, you're right. Sometimes it's the other way round – he interferes too much.'

'Only natural – parents just want to help. We can't always stop ourselves.'

'Especially Dad,' said Charlotte.

They were silent for a while until they approached the outskirts of Farnham. 'So did you have nannies when you were small?' Laura asked.

'Loads of them. They didn't seem to last long in our family, what with Dad being so uptight and me being a pain.'

'Come on, Charlotte, don't fish. You're not too bad – for a teenager.'

Charlotte grinned. 'And you're not too bad – for a nanny.'


Soon Laura was back in France organising Oliver's pre-Christmas entertaining. It occurred to her that often these days he seemed to find a reason to bring her out a week or two before Charlotte's arrival. This time it was to train the new cook, another Filipina, kind-hearted but, Laura feared, of limited skills.

Laura was flattered to be given these extra weeks' employment and pleased to earn the extra money. When she thanked Oliver, he explained he had recently been given an allowance for a housekeeper and so could defray the cost of her salary.

'Oh, that's good,' she said, vaguely disappointed.

So you thought he'd asked you to come back early out of the kindness of his heart, just because he wanted you around, did you?

Laura bought and decorated a vast Christmas tree and taught the new cook how to prepare a turkey and made endless trips to forage for all the traditional English Christmas goodies. Oliver expressed himself as delighted with all her efforts, while the newly returned Sebastien grumbled about all the pine-needles and said that Laura had bought the wrong kind of tree.

She had no idea whether or not Oliver had reprimanded Sebastien after the dinner-party debacle. In any case, it was impossible to prove that it had been any more than a Franco-British misunderstanding, a confusion of dates. The only outcome seemed to be that Oliver decreed that in future only one person should be in charge of hiring staff for parties and that person should be Laura. This led him to make a rather tactless announcement to the effect that when Laura was in Paris she should be in charge of all entertaining and the selection of menus. Sebastien muttered about this under his breath but there was nothing he could do except sulk and glower and watch Laura even more carefully than before

She missed Simon's cheerful unthreatening presence. They sometimes met for coffee and gossip when they mainly talked about Sebastien and how uptight he was. Their other preoccupations, or rather Simon's, were either his screenplay or how much he loved Kiki. Laura supposed he was using her as a mother-confessor. 'You're such a good listener, Laura,' was his great refrain.

The script was under revision yet again and one day with a show of modesty he asked if she would read the first part. She protested she wasn't an expert but he said he'd value her opinion. Flattered, Laura promised she would, but maybe after the holidays. She told him Oliver was taking them skiing for Christmas, an exciting prospect that almost made up for the fact that, for the second Christmas running, her daughter would be on the other side of the world.

Simon didn't seem terribly interested to hear about Alice, so she didn't expand on the problems she had staying in touch with her.

During the last month every time Laura went out to a telephone box – she didn't want to ring on Oliver's bill – Alice was unavailable. When finally they'd managed to connect, the conversation was stilted at first. Alice said she was fine and

Laura said she was fine. And they both said, yes, their jobs were fine.

'How long are you planning to stay in Argentina, sweetie?' Laura had daringly asked.

'Dunno,' said Alice.

'So how is Roberto? And your charges?'

'He's lovely and they're a pain sometimes but mostly lovely too,' said Alice happily. 'And what about your Mr Rochester type?'

'Oh, he's OK,' said Laura. The heavy traffic thundering by drowned, she hoped, any catch in her voice.

'So d'you fancy him then, Mum? Sounds as if you do.'

Laura laughed heartily. 'Don't be silly, darling. Anyway he already has a girlfriend.'


The current state of the turbulent relationship between Agnès and Oliver was uncertain. Agnès had appeared only once at the apartment before Christmas. Laura remembered the occasion well. She had been roused from a deep sleep at around one in the morning by the sound of raised voices. In her dream-fogged mind, she thought someone needed her help. She'd got out of bed and wandered sleepily down the corridor towards the salon. Then she realised it was Oliver talking to Agnès. Laura was about to return to bed when she heard her own name.

'So there's no room in your holiday flat for me but you are taking that Laura woman?' asked Agnès in her imperious voice.

'Laura always spends the holidays with Charlotte, that's her job,' he said. 'Anyway, if you remember, you said you didn't want to go skiing. In fact last week you said you had absolutely no intention of seeing me again.'

'Evidently I've changed my mind. So why can't I share your room?'

'I don't think it is appropriate, not with Charlotte there. The flat's very small.'

'You English are so prim and hypocritical! Ah, I have an idea. I shall stay in a hotel. Too much family closeness can be cloying. Yes, on reflection, a hotel is a good idea. Then we can fight in private.'

Oliver gave what sounded like a forced laugh. Laura realised she shouldn't be listening to this fascinating conversation, but nevertheless she remained rooted where she was, standing in the dark corridor.

'So,' continued Agnès 'I believe there is a convenient hotel in Mottaret. The Mont Vallon, is it?'

'But that's a four-star,' began Oliver.

'Don't worry, chéri, I will pay for myself. As I always do. Dougal and I will be very happy together.'

'You're bringing that dog skiing?'

'But, of course. Dougal always enjoys holidays... Now are you inviting me to bed this evening or will it embarrass your servants?' asked Agnès silkily.

Not wanting to hear Oliver's answer, Laura retreated hastily to her room. She felt ashamed of her eavesdropping – an activity worthy of Sebastien.


A white Christmas in the mountains was a magical treat, thought Laura, breathing in the cold, high, invigorating air of Mottaret. The large chalet which housed Oliver's apartment stood on the edge of a nature reserve, beyond the bustle of the resort. The apartment itself had pine-panelled walls, red-striped curtains and sofas with red-checked cushions. Modern Alpine rustic decor – practical perfection in miniature. Everything you need from a modern kitchen to a breathtaking Christmas-card view over the fir trees and the mountains beyond. 'It's all so pretty,' she kept saying, much to Oliver's obvious gratification. Even Charlotte looked animated and cheerful. As for Oliver, away from Paris and the office, he seemed a different man, more relaxed, almost jovial by his standards.

Agnès joined the party the day after Christmas. Reputed to be an expert skier, she looked stunning in her tight silver ski suit clinched into her tiny waist with a shiny gold belt. Laura knew her own appearance was far removed from this vision of perfection. She'd tried the shops in Paris but all the ski clothes made her look like a Michelin man, a very expensive Michelin man at that. Finally she'd decided to take the easier option and go for cross-country skiing with its lighter, cheaper equipment and clothes.

After the first exhausting lesson with Jean-Claude, the terminally flirtatious ski instructor, every muscle in her body ached and groaned and asked to be released from this mortal coil. Laura's main hope was that soon it would be all over and she could go home and sit in a heap. But she had to summon up enough strength to visit the expensive little Huit à Huit supermarket – or superette, as it called itself – and forage, along with assorted Brits, Germans and Swedes, for some food for dinner.

The other three spent all day up in the mountains, leaving Laura feeling something of a Cinderella. Once she grew fitter, she began to enjoy sliding inexpertly around the peaceful cross-country track by the lake, but in the evenings she couldn't share the talk about how many steep and narrow runs the others had daringly conquered. Occasionally Agnès would turn to her and ask a patronising question about recipes or the local shops, as if to imply these were the only subjects likely to interest Laura.

\* \* \*

One day Oliver appeared back at the flat in the early afternoon. It turned out he had hurt his wrist. No, he didn't need looking after, he said. He'd go and buy the *Times* and spend the rest of the day in peace.

At around five o'clock, after Laura had provided tea and a rather delicious French pastry she'd been tempted by, Oliver began to look uneasy.

'Where's Charlotte?' he asked. 'The lifts closed half an hour ago. It's starting to get dark.'

'Maybe she's gone for a hot chocolate – or shopping. Anyway she was with Agnès, wasn't she?'

'Yes,' he said, pacing around.

She could see that he was visualising Charlotte with a broken leg or lost in the mountains or swept away by an avalanche. After another half hour Laura herself was beginning to worry.

Finally he picked up the phone to call Agnès at her hotel. 'Is Charlotte with you? She's not back yet.'

Laura stood anxiously beside him

As he stood listening to Agnès's reply, his hands shook. 'What? You left her in Val Thorens? By herself, on the other side of the mountain! That's highly irresponsible... No, whatever she may say, she doesn't know the resort that well. First time she's been there this season and she hasn't got a good sense of direction. She's only fifteen... No, I definitely do not agree that fifteen is old enough to ski alone. No one should ski alone. Basic safety rule... No, stupid girl's just lost her mobile so she doesn't have one. You could at least have given her yours before you abandoned her. Agnès, I don't give a damn about your bloody dog's ear problem.'

He slammed the receiver down. 'Agnès has coolly informed me that I'm fussing about nothing. She says Charlotte must have missed the last chairlift and be stuck on the wrong side of the mountain. If only we could be sure...' His face was ashen.

Laura's caught her breath as a cold wave of fear passed over her. 'But why didn't Charlotte ring from a phone box? She must know we'd be worried. Is it far away, Val Thorens?'

'Not that far. As the crow flies, it's about five miles. Not much further on skis. But by road you have to go right back down to the valley and up again. About thirty miles I suppose.' He shook his head. 'But, as you say, she would have phoned.'

Oliver called the ski patrols. No, they knew of no accident to a young English girl called Charlotte Farringdon. 'Are you sure you have the name right?' barked Oliver. 'Please phone me if you have any news... No, I do not think she will be in Dick's T Bar.' He turned to Laura. 'Damn that bloody Frenchman. Said a young girl would probably be drinking "beer with ze boyfriend".'

'But that's good news, isn't it? It's a clear evening. They would have found her if there'd been an accident. So she must be OK. And she's got money and a phone card.'

'What if she had an accident off-piste? They wouldn't see her if she had fallen off the edge of a path or something.'

'But surely Charlotte's a careful enough skier – she wouldn't leave the main piste, not if she's on her own.'

Oliver sat down suddenly. 'You're right,' he said uncertainly. 'Of course you are. In fact she was probably trying to phone when I was calling the emergency service. It's just that...'

'Look,' said Laura, trying to sound convincing, 'Somehow when a child is missing one always fears the worst, however unlikely the worst may be. You can't help it... You feel as if they're like pilots flying sorties behind enemy lines and you're at the air base watching for them to return. And if they're a minute late, you're absolutely certain they've been shot down. Or that's how I used to feel whenever Alice went anywhere by herself. Just wait till Charlotte starts driving, then you'll know what fear really is.'

He smiled a little. Then he poured them both a drink.

She made a half-hearted attempt to prepare the dinner, while Oliver stood in the hall looking out of the window across to the resort centre, the direction from which Charlotte would appear. From time to time Laura joined him, but there was nothing to see. Occasionally a young girl appeared crossing the car park towards them but it was never Charlotte.

When the phone rang Laura snatched it up. 'No, Agnès, she isn't back,' she began, sick with disappointment.

Oliver strode into the room and held his hand out for the receiver. His voice was icy. 'Agnès, we need to keep the line free. No, thank you, I don't think it is necessary for you to come round here. In fact I'd prefer it if you didn't.'

Eventually at six-thirty the telephone rang again. This time Oliver reached it first. He gave a long low sigh. 'Charlotte! At last. Where the hell have you been?' His voice was full of love.

Weak with relief, Laura leant against the wall.

After he'd finished his long searching conversation he turned to Laura. 'She's OK,' he said in a muffled voice. 'She's down in the valley at the railway station. Got stuck on the wrong side of the mountain, as we thought. Luckily she just caught one of the few buses down but it took an hour. Said she tried to ring from Val Thorens but there wasn't time. She's getting a taxi back up here again. Another forty minutes, poor child.'

'But she's OK?'

'Perfectly all right.'

'Thank God, thank God' she said emotionally. 'We'd better let Agnès know.'

'To hell with Agnès.'

'No, really, Oliver. We should call her.'

'Very well, Laura. Whatever you say.' He dialled the hotel. 'Agnès? Yes, she's safe. No thanks to you. I'll have to cancel our dinner this evening. Rather spend it with Charlotte.'

There was a pause and then he said sharply, 'Well, if your dog has a problem and you've decided to go back to Paris tomorrow that suits me fine. Goodbye.'

Laura smiled to herself. Next week, when he'd calmed down, no doubt Agnès would be back in favour again.

A tired but cheerful Charlotte was welcomed like the prodigal daughter. Champagne and then a great deal of wine was drunk and dinner was eaten. Charlotte was made to tell every detail of her story. How Agnès had left her at the foot of the cable car indicating with a vague wave of her hand the direction Charlotte should take when she eventually returned to Mottaret.

'But it's a complete maze of lifts over there. What the hell was she thinking of leaving you alone?' said Oliver.

'She wanted to get back early and I don't ski as fast as she does.'

'Bloody woman,' he muttered under his breath.

'Well, at least she treats me like an adult, unlike some people,' said Charlotte. 'I just made a mistake and then I realised, but there were loads of big queues and I missed the last chairlift. Only by about five minutes. I was really stressed out.'

Laura shook her head. 'You did very well not to panic,' she said.

'Yeah, well I did panic just a bit, till luckily this English bloke who was stuck too told me about the bus. I thought Dad would go ballistic if he had to pay for a two-hour taxi ride for me. Probably cost a fortune.'

'About seventy pounds, I imagine,' said Oliver dryly.

'No way! Amazing. Dad I'm sorry about the eight quid for the bus and then there's my share of the taxi up. I'll save up and pay you back the twenty quid and...'

Oliver laughed. 'Never mind.'

When Charlotte had finally finished her story and disappeared to bed saying she was exhausted, Oliver offered Laura a glass of Genepy. As she sipped the strange-tasting green liqueur she reminded herself about the effect of alcohol at altitude, but then ignoring her own advice she accepted another glass in celebration.

Oliver ran his hands through his hair. 'My God, what an evening.' He drew back the curtains and looked out towards the mountains. 'I need to unwind,' he said. 'Let's go for a walk around Lac de Tueda. There's a good moon tonight.'

Laura put on her snow boots, warmest gloves and her new white anorak with its thick furry hood.

'You look like a polar explorer,' said Oliver with a smile as they set off into the cold night air towards the frozen lake.

The stars were bright above. Laura said, 'I've just realised you never see them in Paris, the stars.'

'No, there are several things you don't see in Paris,' he said.

The snow was crisp under foot as they marched along the path in companionable silence. Soon they were out of sight of the village surrounded by the snowy fir trees. It was totally quiet and still. A very romantic setting, she thought, fuzzy after everything she had drunk.

Suddenly Oliver stopped. 'Thanks, Laura. You were wonderful.'

She smiled. 'But I didn't do anything. Charlotte rescued herself.'

'No, but you were there,' he said. 'Unlike Agnès.'

Laura shook her head. 'If you remember, you told her to stay away. Maybe you shouldn't be too hard on her. Not having children, she probably doesn't understand why we got all neurotic.'

'But it's typical of her. She's always so damned casual. She should never have left Charlotte on her own.'

'No, but – '

'People forget how dangerous the mountains are.'

'But it was good weather and, when it came to the point, Charlotte coped fine. The whole experience has probably taught her a useful lesson.'

'Maybe,' he said.

They paced on. 'It's so frightening, isn't it?' said Laura after a while. 'When teenagers start to fly the nest – even if it wasn't deliberate in this case – it's so hard to let them go, so hard to acknowledge that they can manage without one.'

He stopped. 'You're a wise woman, Laura,' he said with a smile.

For a moment he held her gaze, then in silence they walked back towards the village.

It was dark in the doorway of the apartment block but she could see him staring down at her. Suddenly, he leant forward and kissed her quickly on the mouth.

Before she had time to respond, he drew back. Then without a word he opened the door for her.

'Sorry,' he said indistinctly. 'I'm going for another walk, by myself. To clear my head. See you tomorrow. Goodnight.'

'Goodnight, Oliver,' said Laura, hoping he couldn't see her burning face.

Once in bed she lay awake. What was all that about? Was he just grateful or what? It had all happened so fast that she hardly knew what she felt except that it had been a surprise, quite a pleasant surprise at that. She smiled to herself. It must have been the Genepy. Closing her eyes, she fell asleep.

Next morning, mildly overhung, Laura managed to serve breakfast in her usual brisk manner and Oliver behaved as if nothing had happened. But a few minutes after he and Charlotte had left to go skiing, he returned on his own. 'Forgot my gloves,' he said casually.

'Oh,' said Laura, continuing to stack the dishwasher.

'Laura, sorry about last night. I overstepped the mark.'

Flushing, she said awkwardly, 'That's OK. No problem.'

He gave her a quick embarrassed smile and rushed out again.

As she finished clearing up the flat, it occurred to Laura that she was tired of being told she was a wise woman and a good friend and a good listener, all that. She wouldn't mind being treated as a sex object for a change. Nowadays men even felt obliged to apologise for kissing her.

## CHAPTER 16

'MONET WAS JOLLY KEEN ON WATER LILIES and that old green bridge,' remarked Bridget, marching around the Musée Marmottan.

'Jolly keen,' agreed Laura, smiling at this insightful critique. 'Keen as mustard, in fact.'

Bridget looked at her. 'Are you teasing me, Laura?'

'Of course not. Wouldn't dare. Seriously, you must get Oliver to take you to Monet's garden in Giverny. It's all been replanted to look just like the paintings. It was the Brits who did the planting, of course.'

'How riveting,' boomed Bridget. Her voice seemed extra loud in Paris. 'And I see Monet was a train-spotter too. Must have made a packet if he sold all this stuff.'

'I suppose he did in the end, but they weren't too popular at first, the Impressionists. There was an art jury who rejected some of their paintings. They said they weren't good enough for various exhibitions in the late 1800s. Like, d'you remember Manet's *Le Déjeuner sur l'Herbe*? That was turned down too.'

'Manet as opposed to Monet? Don't know why they had to have similar names, jolly confusing. But if that's the painting with the naked ladies having a picnic in the woods with the fully-clad chaps, then I certainly remember it. I always thought the men should be naked too. Wouldn't be allowed these days, too discriminatory.'

Laura laughed. 'It's so lovely to see you, Bridget. Life tends to be a bit correct and serious in Paris.'

'Well, I had to come and find out how you're getting on with my oh-so-correct and serious Cousin Oliver. Or perhaps you're already having naked picnics with him?'

'Not in winter,' said Laura with a grin.

Having dumped the boy monsters at home with a new au pair, Bridget was spending a long weekend in Paris. Oliver had specially asked Laura to stay on at the end of the school holidays to cope with this visitation.

Since the ski holiday she had occasionally sensed new suppressed frissons in Oliver's presence, but nothing was said and he made no further moves. If it hadn't been for the occasional glance held a fraction longer than normal she would have dismissed the quick friendly kiss as just that. As for Agnès, she had not been seen recently, but she was often temporarily out of favour. Or she could even be away on business. So her absence might have no significance whatsoever.

What do you know about these things anyway? Laura asked herself frequently. Not very much at all. Nevertheless, she felt that her relationship with Oliver was not exactly as it had been.

Bridget, who clearly saw herself as a matchmaker, appeared to be on the watch for signs of romance, so Laura was particularly careful to act the professional housekeeper and, of course, Oliver wouldn't dream of displaying any familiarity towards her when other people were around.

'Thought you might have nailed him by now,' said Bridget one evening when Oliver was out at an official party.

Laura smiled. 'If you mean Oliver, sorry to disappoint but it's not on the cards. Besides, he does have a French girlfriend.'

'Just see her off. That's my advice.' Bridget tossed her blonde head. 'He'll never find any one more suitable than you. In fact, I shall tell him so.'

'Bridget, please keep out of it.'

'Ah-ha! So there is something to keep out of. I thought so. I have a sixth sense for these matters. But never fear, I can see things are at an extremely delicate stage. I shan't say a word, not a word. But if you want me to give this French girl a good parting kick in the derrière, just let me know.'


'What a crowd!' whispered Bridget, as, dressed in their best little black suits, they walked into the first of the five vast ground-floor reception rooms of the British Embassy residence in rue Faubourg St. Honoré. 'Which one is the Ambassador's wife?'

'That one, in grey silk,' said Laura. 'The small elegant blonde.'

The Ambassadress's tired eyes glazed over as they approached her to shake hands. She smiled vaguely at Laura. 'Remind me who you are.'

'Laura Brooke. I work for Oliver Farringdon and this is his cousin, Bridget Prior-Hughes. I don't know if he's here yet. He was coming separately.'

'How nice,' said the Ambassadress, brightening up a little. 'Dear Oliver. I saw him earlier, I think, possibly in the ball room... *Ah, bonsoir, Monsieur le Ministre*.' She had turned to greet someone much more important.

Bridget and Laura backed away and went in pursuit of a green-uniformed footman bearing a tray of champagne.

'Oliver says that Ambassadors' wives generally fall into three categories: the keen, the resigned and the stark staring bonkers,' whispered Laura.

Bridget laughed. 'Wonder which category that one falls into.' She looked around again. 'Wow!' she exclaimed, 'Versailles in miniature only nicer. And you say there are yet more reception rooms upstairs. Look at all these yellow silk walls. And all this gilding, fabulously ornate. Ceilings must be at least thirty feet high. I expected it to be grand but no one told me it was a palace.'

'Yes, amazing, isn't it? Apparently the Duke of Wellington bought it fully-furnished from Pauline Borghese, Napoleon's sister,' said Laura, who had mugged up a few facts. 'In the next door room is Pauline's bed. And there's a naked statue of her in the hall.'

'Do show me,' said Bridget, elbowing aside some fat French dowagers and their elderly escorts.

After inspecting the historic four-poster, Bridget stared around again, gawping at the scene.

Laura said, 'Sorry I can't introduce you to anyone. I hardly know the Embassy people. They swim in a much more important fish pond than I do.' Then she suddenly stopped. 'Oh, hell. What on earth's he doing here?'

She was staring at a dapper old man who was helping himself from a tray of smoked salmon canapés.

Bridget studied him. 'I say, isn't that your wicked stepfather?'

'The very same,' said Laura grimly.

Julius looked up, his face breaking into a cadaverous smile. 'Laura, my dear. What a pleasant surprise!'

'Hello, Julius,' she said, trying to avoid being kissed on the cheek and not succeeding. As his skull-face brushed hers she shuddered a little. 'Bridget, I believe you remember Julius.'

'Of course I do,' said Bridget gaily, and launched into yet another isn't-this-a-fantastic-room conversation.

'What are you doing here?' asked Laura when Bridget stopped for breath.

'Just catching up with Paris,' said Julius airily. 'I always pop into the Embassy while I'm here. Leonard and Aurelia are very old chums of mine. I'm on my way to the champagne country, actually, to try the latest vintage, staying with the Pol Rogers, d'you know

Suddenly in the crowd Laura caught sight of Oliver making his way towards them. Reluctantly she introduced Julius who seemed fascinated by the information that there were no less than three British Ambassadors in Paris, one for France and two attached to international organisations. Protocol, correct form, and snobbery were Julius's main hobbies, Laura remembered.

'What did you say they were called: was it bilateral and multilateral ambassadors?' asked Julius.

Oliver explained. 'Well, obviously bilateral ambassadors deal with international relations between Britain and the country to which they are accredited. Multilateral ambassadors deal with Britain's relationship with various international organisations. Of the multilateral ambassadors, the one with the highest profile is the chap at the United Nations in New York, of course. My own mission is somewhat smaller,' he added with uncharacteristic modesty.

'Ah, but you are doing a very valuable job, I'm sure,' said Julius.

Smarmy little toad, thought Oliver. Aloud he said, 'Yes, we achieve a great deal in a quiet sort of way.' Looking over Julius's head, he saw Bridget and Laura being swept away by a loud blonde woman, a minor Embassy wife whose name he had forgotten.

Laura was looking pretty this evening, he thought. Even rather chic. Maybe she'd had her hair done. That sort of thing changed a woman.

Blinking behind his half-moon glasses Julius was running through the names of all the important people he knew in Paris. He was explaining the parentage of each person as if he were a bloodstock agent discussing a string of race horses.

Oliver was about to say he must move on and circulate when Julius clutched his arm, 'So Laura is working for you? She can be a bit difficult. And impulsive. But, of course, she's a wonderful girl.'

'Difficult? Hardly sounds like the Laura I know. And she's doing a very good job,' said Oliver stiffly. The old boy sounded a bit tight, obviously been quaffing too much ambassadorial champagne.

'She's not a maid or skivvy, you know.'

Oliver stared, 'Of course not.'

'In fact, she's not the sort of person who should be working for her living at all, certainly not as a housekeeper.'

'She's not a housekeeper,' began Oliver.

'D'you know, she married the wrong man,' said Julius, lowering his voice confidentially.

Oliver had to bend down to hear what he was saying.

Julius continued, 'My wife never liked Laura's husband. A spendthrift, a drop-out. But I'll see her right when I go. Finally, that is,' he added with a cackle.

Oliver presumed he was referring to his eventual demise. He looked like a walking corpse already, but these thin old men often lasted well past their sell-by date.

Julius tapped his nose. 'She'll be a fairly wealthy young woman eventually. If she gets my money too, as well as her mother's. She has to treat me right though. You mark my words. It's not good that she's working as a skivvy. She should be living with me, d'you know. Then she would have more status. As my heir.'

Oliver listened carefully to all this. He was remembering a conversation he'd had with Bridget when he first met Laura. Something about all Laura's mother's cash going to the creepy stepfather. It would be interesting to know how much was involved.

'Julius, may I call you Julius? Let me find you another glass of champagne,' said Oliver, with a friendly smile.

That night after sex with Agnès, Oliver dressed quickly. Then he sat down on the bed beside her as she lay naked under the covers. She was at her best at these times, relaxed and unusually gentle. This sunny mood never lasted long though.

He took her hand. 'I have something to say. I think we need a break from each other.'

Agnès smiled lazily. 'A long break or a short one?'

'A long one.'

'This must be at least the tenth time you have suggested this. But you always return for more in the end.'

'On the contrary, normally you're the one who insists it's all over. And then you change your mind.'

' "Treat them mean, keep them keen." Isn't that what you British say?' She stretched out her arms.

Oliver snorted.

'You yourself are not exactly a dove of peace, chéri,' continued Agnès.

'Maybe not, but one can change.'

She stared at him. 'What a strange thing to say. People never change, not from the age of about eighteen. Not from the age of five, in most cases. You, for instance, will always be the original smug stuffy arrogant Anglo-Saxon prig.'

'And you, my dear, will always be a smug stuffy arrogant French bitch.'

Agnès laughed. *'Nous sommes très proches.* We are so alike, so well-suited.'

'I don't think so,' said Oliver, putting on his coat. 'There may be more to life than sex and war.'

'But what else is there, my love? At least we are not dull together.'

He shook his head firmly. 'Goodbye, Agnès. Incidentally, I've taken my shaving things from the bathroom.'

She sat up. '*Mon Dieu*, what a definitive step! But don't worry. Tomorrow I will buy you a new set in case you change your mind.'

'I won't.'

'But you will... one day. You always do,' said Agnès, lying back.

Oliver stared at her pointed breasts and thought for a moment that she might be right. Then, pulling himself together, he bowed formally from the doorway. 'Goodbye, Agnès. And, uh, thank you for everything.'

As he left, he placed his key on the hall table.

The night before Laura and Bridget were due to return to London, Oliver invited them both out to the local brasserie.

At the last minute Bridget claimed to have a headache. 'You go without me,' she said faintly, clutching her head with her hand.

So Laura gave her a couple of aspirin and left her in peace. On the way to the restaurant, it occurred to her that Bridget's headache might be of the diplomatic variety.

Oliver ordered two rounds of Kir royale – champagne with Ribena, as he called it – and then some wine. Then he urged her to choose from all the most expensive items on the menu and generally acted the perfect generous host. Between them they ate a huge *plateau de fruits de mer*, a dish the size of a teatray piled high with oysters, crayfish, crab, giant prawns, clams, mussles and other mysterious tiny shellfish. Laura wasn't sure how to tackle everything on this mound of seafood, but with the new improved relaxed Oliver it didn't seem to matter. She tore the prawns apart and ate them with her fingers and after swallowing the oysters one by one she tipped the juice from the shell into her mouth, tasting the sea. All the time the waiter kept filling up her glass. As she was sucking the delicate flesh from the crayfish claws she caught Oliver watching her, studying her with an intense dark stare. The scene reminded her irresistibly of seduction in the manner of a historical novel – foreplay in the tavern, Tom Jones about to bed the inn-keeper's wife.

'What are you smiling about?' asked Oliver.

'Oh... nothing. I'm just enjoying myself.'

'Me too,' he said.

All evening he was full of charm. 'Lamb in the iron glove' had been Bridget's muddled metaphor. Inappropriate anyway, thought Laura. Lamb wasn't the first creature that sprang to mind. Not that she could think of a better one. Hawk? Hawk or dove, whatever, he was looking especially good with his skiing tan. Handsome, and growing more so after each glass of wine.

Once back at the flat Laura accepted some Cointreau, and they talked some more, side by side on the sofa. She was giving a long dissertation about her trip to the Musée d'Orsay with Bridget when she realised he wasn't listening. He was just watching her. He's going to kiss me again, she thought suddenly. Maybe that's not such a good idea.

But when it came to the point it did seem like a quite a good idea after all. There was nothing gentle or tentative about Oliver's kiss and, after the initial shock, Laura found herself responding.

After a few flustered minutes, she pushed him away and said formally, 'Oliver, I'd better... I mean, thank you for the dinner, and everything.'

'Thank you for everything too,' he said with a twinkle. And then, against her own advice, she was pulled into another decisive and passionate embrace. His hand ran down over her breast and she felt what was undeniably a wave of lust.

This was a mistake. Definitely a mistake.

Breathing hard, she pushed him away and whispered urgently, 'Maybe this is getting a little, uh, incorrect. Don't want to spoil our working relationship.' Considering it was the heat of the moment, she managed, she hoped, to sound suitably light-hearted. Then, swaying a little, she rose to her feet. 'I probably won't see you in the morning if you're going to the office early, so goodbye and thank you and, er, see you at Easter.'

Oliver stood up. 'Goodbye, Laura. I may come to see you in England. Before Easter. If that would be all right.'

'Oh. Er, yes,' she said, flushing again. 'Well... goodnight.'

'Goodnight again,' he repeated, gazing thoughtfully down at her. 'See you in England.'

Leaving him standing in the middle of the salon she raced down the corridor to her own room and shut the door firmly.

She stared at herself in the mirror. And what do you think his intentions are now? she asked herself.

Hot and restless, she lay awake for a long time brooding nervously about the answer to this question. After an hour she concluded that if he intended to come to her bed it would not be tonight.

Of course he won't. You ran away again.

I had to. This new dimension, it's awkward for my job if he and I...

As usual, you sound like a frightened virgin. You're scared of any kind of intimacy.

It's just that I need to be sure he's the right person.

Maybe you should chill out. Be more casual and modern about sex.

I can't. Anyway nothing is ever casual with Oliver. I ran away this evening because it was the last chance to pretend it was just another harmless little kiss that means nothing.

Maybe, maybe not... What about Jack, though? Did that mean something?

Yes, yes, of course it did, but that's in the past.

So you say.

One has to be realistic.

Absolutely. So that brings us back to Oliver. What are you going to do about him?

Nothing much has happened. Nothing will. So shut up and let me sleep.

## CHAPTER 17

Back home, busy with English pursuits like gardening, Laura began to miss Paris. And maybe Oliver. In spite of his promise, or request, to come and see her in England, when he did actually ring the cottage and suggested taking her out to lunch she nearly dropped the telephone in astonishment.

'There's something I'd like to discuss,' he said mysteriously, before ringing off.

As usual, Laura was in a quandary as to what to wear. Not jeans, she thought, but she'd left all her new chic clothes in Paris. She didn't possess anything suitable for an expensive restaurant, if that was what Oliver had in mind. Not that there was much choice in this part of Hampshire.

Hoping he would favour the upmarket-pub option she selected a short tweed skirt with navy tights – flattering to the legs, she reckoned – and found at the back of her wardrobe a navy cardigan with gold buttons. It was what shop assistants called a classic, bought in a sale but never worn because it made her look about ninety. Nevertheless it was clean and tidy and would have to do. Her equally boring white shirt was on the small side and rather too thin for late January.

So why not wear a sweater? Or are you thinking of the scene when he undoes all those buttons.

She smiled to herself. Maybe I am.

What if he just wants to discuss Charlotte's A levels?

We'll see.


Oliver seemed out of place in the cottage, too large, too restless, but he looked wonderful in faded beige cords and an equally faded tweed jacket. Of course, he always had the right clothes for the right occasion.

'Where are we going?' she asked, putting on her Barbour. She'd sponged the ancient mud off the hem in his honour.

'Oh, I've brought lunch with me,' he said. 'What they call a "posh picnic" in a smart deli near Waterloo station. God knows what it'll be like, but there's plenty of wine to wash it down.'

A bit cold for *Déjeuner sur l'herbe*, thought Laura with a private smile, wishing she had chosen the jeans option.

She settled back in Oliver's Mercedes, watching him. He drove well, though a little fast in view of the narrow lanes and the excessive amount of mud on them. She asked him where the car had come from.

'Oh, I keep it here, at home. That's where I'm taking you for our picnic. My house is empty at the moment. I don't rent it out.'

'Right,' said Laura, thinking about the significance of an empty house. Aloud she remarked, 'I forgot you'd have another existence, away from Paris. But Charlotte mainly talked about a flat in London.'

'That's not home,' he said.

'So where is your house and what's it like?'

He smiled at her. 'Wait and see. It's not so far.'

'So you live in Hampshire too? Why didn't you tell me?'

'Didn't seem relevant till now,' he said.

As soon as she saw Oliver's country house quietly hidden away at the end of a long lane, Laura was beguiled by its traditional charms – all mellow bricks and dormer windows and red gabled roofs of different heights sprawling in every direction. Like her own in fact, but very much bigger. The garden was huge, three or four acres, mostly trees and shrubs and vast lawns. It was tidy but bare, hardly surprising given the time of year. Oliver said there'd be a carpet of daffodils later on and then bluebells in the wood.

Laura made suitably admiring comments about that, the view and everything else she saw. The house was called Manor Farm and had, he said, been extended over the centuries to become a so-called gentleman's residence. Most of the farm land had been sold. Now there were only a few fields left and some woods which provided, he told her, a bit of rough shooting.

He unlocked the front door and led her inside. The rooms were filled with attractively battered antique furniture and shabby sofas of an indeterminate colour. Faded rugs covered the wooden floors, the bookcases were full of dusty leather-bound books, and dismal landscapes hung on the walls. The atmosphere was of a little-visited museum. A wonderful old house, a sleeping beauty, she thought. Not frigid, just a little austere and desiccated. But it would only take a little loving care to bring it to life. It was also physically cold. She shivered in her short skirt, reluctant to take off her coat.

Oliver said, 'Sorry, I've only just turned up the heating. Let's go and sit in the kitchen. The Aga's on so it should be warmer in there.'

The kitchen was less welcoming than the rest of the house. She presumed that Oliver's ex-wife had chosen the nineteen-seventies melamine look, and nothing had been changed since.

He hadn't yet shown her the upstairs rooms. Maybe he was saving that for after lunch.

They sat down at the pine table – she'd managed to give it a quick wipe when Oliver was out of the room. He produced red wine and taramasalata, houmous and pitta bread, plus a ready-mixed salad, quite a delicious one with apples and walnuts. 'Jolly good for Waterloo station,' she said with fake heartiness, but nervous tension prevented her from eating much. She had another glass of wine.

Here she was on her own, with Oliver circling around her like a bird of prey. Was he going to drop down from the heights and scoop her off to his lair? Come to think of it, she was already in his lair.

Or was this just another polite social occasion? Either way, why was she so on edge? Most women of your age would take the situation in their stride, she told herself.

After lunch Oliver lit a fire in the drawing room. The logs were damp and, though the paper burnt quickly, the wood stubbornly refused to catch. After the fifth attempt, he managed to achieve a sulky glow but it made little difference to the temperature in the room. As she sipped her coffee, Laura shivered again.

'Sorry,' he said. 'You're still cold. I've got some old sweaters upstairs. I'll get you one.'

So she was left alone. Kneeling down on the hearth rug, she put another log on the fire. It hissed and gave out a puff of grey smoke, looking as if it was about to expire at any moment. She found an ancient set of leather bellows and used them to blow gently until eventually a few small flames burned with faint enthusiasm.

Oliver returned with a mottled brown Shetland sweater. It was huge and shapeless, and no doubt looked wonderful on him. On her it would look like a sack of old potatoes, but she put it on all the same. It smelt very faintly of damp and mothballs.

There were other ways of keeping warm, she thought, as she put it on. Bet Agnès wouldn't dream of wearing a sack. She'd have much more interesting suggestions.

Laura took another sip of coffee. Even the coffee was cold now. Suddenly Oliver leant forward and took the cup from her hands.

His eyes were fixed on her face. 'Laura,' he said huskily. Then he cleared his throat.

She tried not to panic, waiting for the next move.

'Laura, will you marry me?'

She stared at him in astonishment, opening and shutting her mouth. She had been expecting every kind of suggestion except this one.

'I, er, I...'

Then he kissed her, not forcefully as in Paris, but respectfully and gently. After a moment he pulled back, looking, for once, not at all sure of himself.

There was a long silence.

She tried to speak. 'I'm very... it's... Well, you've taken my breath away,' she muttered, shivering even more violently than before.

Suddenly he stood up. 'Maybe it's colder in than out. Would you like to walk around the garden? I know you love gardening.'

No, she wanted to shout, for once in my life I don't want to look at the damn garden.

But she found herself borrowing some ancient Wellington boots and following him outdoors. As they traipsed around the dank flower beds, her sense of strangeness grew. They were marching away from the house and down to the end of the garden where there was a stile into the field. Without a word he led her up to the top of a hill behind the house.

'These are my fields,' he said, waving his hands at the rolling Hampshire countryside, 'as far as those woods down there.'

She smiled, finding her voice at last. 'So you're master of all you survey.'

He took her face in his hands. 'Not quite,' he said. Then at last he kissed her, almost roughly this time, but before she had time to respond he drew away again. 'So what do you say?'

'I hardly know.' She was breathless and confused. 'We, we haven't known each other very long.'

'Yes, we have. We've lived together for over six months, on and off.' He smiled. 'You've made a big difference to my life, and to Charlotte's.'

Laura shook her head. He was being so gentlemanly. How could she say that, actually, instead of tramping around the countryside she wanted to be taken to bed and passionately convinced of the rightness of all this.

She looked up at his anxious face and then stared down again. 'You, you've made a big difference to me too, but... it's a bit sudden,' she mumbled.

'Not so sudden, is it? I think you know I find you very attractive and you're not the kind of woman who one can have as a bit on the side.'

She flushed. 'But...'

'But what?'

'I just don't know what to say.'

'Well, at least you haven't said no.'

Half way down the hill, she asked, 'What about Agnès?'

'Told her it was finished.'

'I see,' said Laura.

Silently they walked back to the house. As he helped her over the stile, he held on to her hand, but not for long.

'I'll take you home now,' he said. 'Give you a chance to think.'

Laura blinked. Again she had been steeling herself for the seduction scene. Maybe he's waiting till he gets back to the cottage, she thought. He probably thinks I'll be more relaxed on my own ground.

On the way back in the car, it occurred to her that her bedroom was very untidy. Why she was attaching so much importance to these unimportant matters? There's much more at stake than sex, she told herself firmly.

To her astonishment, when Oliver delivered her to the cottage, he gave her a polite kiss on the cheek and said, 'I'm going to London. Ring you soon.' Then he got into the Mercedes and drove away.

When next day he did telephone, Laura had, after a sleepless night, decided to stop acting like a wimp.

'Why don't you come down for the weekend?' she asked in a rush.

'Did you say for the weekend or at the weekend?'

'For.'

'I see. I was going back to Paris tomorrow. A meeting.'

'Oh... couldn't you stay on a bit?'

'Do you think that would be a good idea?' he asked enthusiastically.

'Yes.'

'Maybe I'll send my deputy to the meeting in Paris then. OK?'

'Fine,' said Laura.

As the weekend drew near she wasn't sure it was such a good idea after all. If everything went wrong then she couldn't go back to Paris and work for Oliver as if nothing had happened. Far, far better to take things slowly and carefully, as he seemed to want to do.

Of course, she didn't have to commit herself to anything. Inviting him to stay didn't mean she wanted to marry him. Spending the weekend together didn't even necessarily have to involve sharing the same bed.

Get real.

OK then. Sex will probably take place. But even if I've abstained for ten years, it can't have changed that much.

Next day Laura had a brilliant idea. She would go and buy a book on the subject, do a bit of revision.

She made a special journey to W.H. Smiths in Winchester but they didn't seem to have much choice in the Health and Lifestyle section. She picked up one possibility and then put it quickly back on the shelf. Far too embarrassing. What if the Vicar was buying some parish stationery and saw her rifling through sex handbooks, or, even if W.H. Smiths was vicar-free, what would the cashier think?

Then she remembered Charlotte and her teen magazines. That'd be the answer. They'd assume she was buying something for her daughter.

Laura stared bemused at all the garish headlines on the magazine stand. 'The sex that will blow your mind and how to get it.' 'The new missionary position that will guarantee an orgasm Every Time.'

She changed her mind. All these handy how-to hints didn't seem much to do with love. If it was love with her and Oliver, she would know.

He was due on Friday evening at eight o'clock. She'd invested in a bottle of whisky and some of Sainsbury's best Burgundy to cover any potential embarrassment. They'd have dinner and the rest would follow quite naturally, preferably in the dark. It couldn't be that difficult, seducing a man who likes you. In fact, thinking back to the past, it was pretty easy.

Then once they'd established some kind of intimacy the rest of the weekend would be OK. It wasn't as if they were strangers.

But when he did arrive – a whole quarter of an hour early – Laura felt extraordinarily shy. 'Hello, do come in,' she said gaily, trying to over-compensate.

'Hello, Laura.' He sounded almost as peculiar as she did.

Then, with flourish, he produced some champagne and a small jar of caviar.

'Wow, thanks,' she said, still in her gauche schoolgirl mode.

She had some trouble in finding champagne glasses which were dusty and the wrong shape anyway – globes instead of flutes. He didn't seem to mind.

After two swiftly swallowed glasses she felt a great deal better. So much so that she nearly forgot to cook the vegetables. She was dithering about in the kitchen when Oliver came in.

'Can I help?' he asked.

'No, no. It's fine. I'm fine.'

'Laura, don't you think we've waited too long?'

'Well, sorry. I mean dinner will be ready in a moment. I...'

Before she could continue he took her in his arms. 'Laura.' Then he kissed her hard and purposefully.

She staggered backwards until she was leaning against the wall. For a wild moment, she thought it was going to be sex on edge of the kitchen sink.

'Better turn off the stove,' he said, breathing hard.

'What?'

'Just to make sure nothing burns.'

Then he ushered her upstairs and stripped off her clothes before she had time to think. The last thing she remembered before it became a hot blur in her mind was the fact that she wanted to turn off the bedroom light but he wouldn't let her.

Afterwards she felt a certain sadness. It wasn't what she had expected somehow. It didn't feel like love as she remembered it. Passion, yes. He wanted her badly, no doubt about that. He hadn't wasted time on preliminaries, hadn't allowed quite all her inhibitions to melt away.

She smiled at him, trying to disguise these feelings. Obviously unaware of any doubts, he looked extremely pleased with himself, and her. That reassured her. She was just so out of practice. It would be OK in time.

He ruffled her hair. 'Shall we have dinner now?' he said happily.

After the fourth time they had made love in the course of the weekend, Oliver fell asleep almost immediately. Laura lay back in triumph. She was doing better she thought, gazing at him in the dim moonlight that shone through the curtains. She had become accustomed to his powerful, almost rough lovemaking. William had been a gentle and artistic lover, so very different. Oliver didn't seem much interested in foreplay but Laura was reluctant, too shy in fact, to criticise his technique. Besides, she now found his very impatience erotic. She felt much desired. That, after all these years of celibacy, was becoming a powerful enough aphrodisiac.

After lunch on Sunday she wondered if he would take her to bed again but he suggested a walk. As they trudged down the lane together, she began to feel self-conscious What if she met one of her neighbours? She had been widowed for some time now so it was perfectly reasonable to be going for a walk with a strange man, but Laura didn't feel ready for gossip on the subject. She turned right on to a footpath beside the pig fields, not so scenic as Oliver's woods, she thought, but almost as peaceful.

She began to tell him about the little stray piglet she'd found on the road once and how difficult it had been to catch. 'I was wearing my best shoes and they got all muddy. It ran so fast, zigzagging about – I had to throw my coat on top of it and pounce, a sort of rugby tackle. And, you know, when I was carrying it, the poor little thing felt just like a human baby, the same sort of weight. Reminded me of the Duchess in Alice in Wonderland. And then when I got to the pig pens I didn't know which sow to give it to. I was afraid if I chose the wrong one she might kill the piglet and so I had to phone the farmer and...'

Oliver didn't appear to be listening to this fascinating story. He took her hand. 'So what d'you say, Laura?'

'Well, I think it's good that pigs are reared in open fields nowadays.'

'I'm not talking about bloody pigs, for God's sake.'

'Oh, sorry.' She smiled up at him. 'Well,' she said cautiously, 'I'm very much looking forward to coming back to Paris at Easter.'

'I'd like us to get married before then.'

She caught her breath. 'Don't you think we should take it a bit more slowly?'

'No, I don't. We're both old enough to know our own mind,' he said. 'No point in hanging around. After all, there'd be no big formal wedding to arrange.'

'But, well...'

'You keep saying "well".'

'Do I? Sorry. I just thought there was no rush. We live together anyway in Paris, and now, well – oh, dear, I'm well-ing again...'

'Laura, I don't want you in Paris as a mistress. I want you as a wife. It wouldn't be appropriate for you to live under my roof in any other capacity.'

'But these days it's normal... I thought you told me one of your fellow Ambassadors was living with a partner.'

'He's not the British Ambassador,' said Oliver loftily. 'Anyway, we need to think of Charlotte. She holds you in very high esteem. I want things to stay that way. I don't want her to catch me creeping across the corridor to your room. And I don't want the servants, people like Sebastien, to lose their respect for you.'

'I see what you mean.' The Sebastien argument was convincing. She could just imagine the sneers and sniggers behind the kitchen door. He'd see her as Oliver's fancy woman.

They walked on.

'Talking of human babies,' she began warily, 'you wouldn't want any more children, would you? Because...'

'God no. I'm far too old. It'd be quite ridiculous. I always felt sorry for my contemporaries who married young trophy wives and then found themselves deep in nappies.' He stared at her. 'You weren't thinking of babies, were you?'

'No, no, I'm sure I'm too old too,' said Laura, relieved.

She jumped as a pheasant rose up in front of them and flew away, whirring and squawking in terror.

'Stupid bloody bird. Wish I had a gun,' said Oliver absently.

She said, 'So you're going back to London tonight.'

'Yes, catching the first Eurostar in the morning. Can't stay away from the office any longer.'

They walked back along the footpath without speaking. There was so much she wanted to say but for once in her life she tried to make an effort to think things through before she spoke. It wasn't until they were back in her own kitchen that she finally said, 'Oliver, I'm so honoured that you want to marry me, but I can't give you an answer yet.'

He smiled down at her. 'Let's go to bed. I've ordered a taxi at six o'clock.'


Today it felt better, almost like love, thought Laura. She lay naked in her bed, listening to the sound of the taxi driving away.

She grinned suddenly. It almost seemed as if Oliver was trying to screw her into accepting him. His persistence was immensely flattering. Not like William who had more or less married her out of politeness.

Another difference was that her mother would approve of Oliver. Unbidden, her mother's voice drifted into her mind. 'May I point out the advantages of being Mrs Oliver Farringdon,' Mama would purr. 'The diplomatic, an apartment in Paris, a lovely country house in Hampshire, a ski chalet and even a flat in London. Think of my grand-daughter, too, how much she would benefit from all this.'

Alice. She had never liked poverty. That's probably why she was still in Argentina with the rich old rancher. But Oliver would give Alice a proper background, something to come home to. Then maybe she'd return to England, go to university and meet lots of nice English boys of her own age.

But am I in love with Oliver, truly, madly, deeply?

Does it really matter? Aren't you too old for truly, madly, deeply? You're enjoying the sex anyway, judging by all that heat.

She smiled to herself. Yes, I am but... but maybe it's going to my head, the physical stuff. I can't think straight.

You think too much, that's your problem. There are all kinds of love. We can't all be Romeo and Juliet. Anyway, look what happened to them.

Laura turned over and thumped the pillow. What about Jack? What would he say?

Jack would want you to be happy.

But will I be?

## CHAPTER 18

'JACK?' SAID LAURA, HOLDING TIGHT on to the telephone. 'I tried to ring Mel but she wasn't there. I've got something to tell you. I'm getting married.'

There was a silence and then he said, sounding bleak but sincere, 'Congratulations. Who to?'

She told him.

'And when's the happy day?'

'March the fifteenth.'

'So soon.'

She rushed on. 'We're getting married in a registry office and just having a blessing in the village church. And a small party at Oliver's house which is a bit bigger than this, well, quite a lot bigger, but not far away. Will you come, you and Melanie? Sorry, I know I'm completely incoherent but...'

'Of course I'll come,' he said. 'Mel is away though. In a clinic. One of those drying-out places. She may be there a while.'

Poor Mel, thought Laura, poor Jack. 'Oh... but that's a step forward, isn't it?'

'Maybe. Hope so, but I'm not that optimistic.'

'I'll go and visit her, shall I?'

'That would be kind. She's rather dislocated at the moment.'

After another pause they both started talking at once.

'This man of yours, I hope he's good enough for you.'

She laughed weakly. 'Come on, Jack, that's a bit corny.'

There was another silence and then he said, 'So what would you like for a present?'

'A present?'

'A wedding gift, you know.'

'Oh... we don't need anything. Not at our age. Oliver. He's quite well-off.'

'I see. But, all the same, I'd like to give you something.'

'No, really, Jack. Just come to the church. I'll send you an invitation.'

After she'd put down the phone, Laura walked to the window and looked out on to her garden. It had been an awkward, stilted conversation – he sounded so distant, like a polite stranger. She felt like bursting into tears which is not, she told herself firmly, the proper state of mind for a mature bride-to-be.


A few days later Jack appeared on her doorstep early one evening.

'Congratulations, again,' he said, kissing her hello in a fraternal manner.

Refusing to recognise any emotional jolt, she smiled gaily and led him into the cottage.

'So where's your fiancé?' he asked, looking around.

'In Paris. He has to work.'

He smiled. 'If I were him, I wouldn't leave you alone for a moment.' He handed her a flat parcel wrapped in navy blue paper and tied with gold string. 'Here, this is for you.'

She laid it on the kitchen table and opened it carefully. It was a small exquisite drawing of a young woman's head – eighteenth-century in style. 'Oh, Jack, it's lovely.'

'She reminded me of you... I didn't know what to get you. I spent an afternoon messing about in Winchester then at last I found her.'

'Thank you very, very much. It's lovely,' she repeated, giving him a quick hug and kissing him on the cheek.

Before she could turn away he took her by the shoulders, studying her face. 'Now, Laura, tell me all. You're looking very pretty, by the way.'

She smiled. 'You look nice too.'

He did. She'd also forgotten about his direct gaze.

Pulling away gently, she turned and fixed her attention on opening a bottle of wine and pouring them both a drink. Then, as they sat at the kitchen table, she launched into her story. When she had come to the end of a well-edited version, he said, 'So you've only just got engaged and you're getting married in a month? This may sound intrusive, Laura, but we've been friends for a long time. Don't you think you're rushing things a bit? What's the hurry?'

'Not much point in hanging around at our age.'

'But why get married? Why not just live together for a bit longer, see how it works out.'

'Oliver's a bit stuffy, the traditional type, doesn't approve of cohabitation.'

He raised his eyebrows. 'How gentlemanly.'

'Absolutely. He's determined to marry me. Even his daughter seems pleased, which is good. They need me, I think. It's nice to be wanted and needed, you know.'

'Any man would –'

'Rubbish. There's not a great queue of admirers, I'm afraid.

He shook his head. 'Seriously, Laura. You've led a rather sheltered life. I seem to remember you used to avoid people, especially men.'

She smiled. 'That's just not true, not fair. We were very gregarious when we were young, William and I. You can't run a hotel without meeting people.'

'No, but after that you were a sort of hermit for ten years. Again forgive me for saying so, but you're a bit unworldly.'

She thought it best to try and keep the conversation light-hearted. 'But I'm a Parisienne now and no one can accuse a Parisienne of being unworldly.'

He stood up and began to pace about. Then he turned and said, 'I just think you should have allowed yourself a bit more fun and freedom before you got married again.'

'You're making it sound like a jail sentence. Of course, I'd be the first to admit that marriage isn't a piece of cake, but –'

'Farringdon's much older than you, isn't he?' interrupted Jack.

'He's a young fifty-five and perfectly healthy. Very sporty in fact.'

After a pause he said, 'I wonder why his first wife left him.'

'I don't know who left who. But she, well, he said she was unfaithful. And Charlotte sides with her father, as far as I can tell.'

'Hm, I wonder...' He picked up his wine glass and twiddled it around. Then he drank some. 'Perhaps it's more the speed of the whole thing that worries me. You rushed into your first marriage, Laura, and now you're doing the same again.'

'Well, my first was happy so there's no reason to suppose a second one wouldn't be.'

He paused again and then said, 'Were you really that happy with William?'

'Yes, of course I was.'

'Sorry,' he said. After a moment he continued, 'It's just... Well, I'm jealous, I suppose. I've hardly seen you recently and when you're living permanently in Paris we shan't see you at all.'

'Oh, we'll be back. We'll only be there about two or three years.' It was strange saying we again she thought. 'And you can come and stay with us in Paris, you and Mel.'

'I hardly think that would be a good idea.'

'Of course it would,' said Laura, not at all sure this was so. 'How is she, by the way?'

His face closed the way it always did when Mel was mentioned. 'Hard to tell. I won't go into how difficult the last few months have been. But do go and visit her, if you like. She said she'd love to see you.'

Quite soon, he departed. Laura sat down at the kitchen table with her head in her hands. Then she looked at the portrait again. It was beautiful but oddly disturbing. It would have been better if he'd given her something domestic like a kettle or a casserole dish. She felt suddenly drained and insecure. The distressed expression in his eyes had shattered her fragile peace of mind.

Melanie's clinic was in such an obscure part of Hampshire that Laura got completely lost. Eventually she found it – a grand Victorian monstrosity of a house situated miles from anywhere in the middle of an extensive park. The open gates were guarded only by a cattle grid so it was not a prison, she thought, but it was clear that the place had been selected for its remoteness. The only signs of life she'd seen for about half an hour were a few sheep grazing in the distance.

Inside the clinic was all soothing pale cream walls and long corridors close-carpeted in a careful beige. Laura was shown to Melanie's room by a middle-aged woman in a grey suit who spoke in the firm but hushed tones of one used to dealing with troubled minds.

Melanie sounded almost normal though there was something odd about her eyes. 'Laura! The blushing bride. Congratulations!' she said. Laura hugged her.

'Tell me all about Mr Right,' insisted Melanie.

'Later. I want to hear about you first.'

The grey woman gave a polite smile and departed.

Melanie made a face and shut the door after her. 'Not a ray of sunshine, that one. Major Barbara, I call her,' she whispered. 'So what do you think of my cell?'

'Pretty nice,' said Laura, looking at the restrained luxury around her. 'And a bathroom with a bidet too. There's posh for you.'

'Absolutely. Poor Jack, it's costing him an arm and a leg. Think of the price of a suite at the Ritz and double it.'

'Heavens... I must say, Mel, you're looking much better.' She was very pale in fact, but Laura felt encouragement was called for. 'So what do you do here all day?'

Mel sighed. 'We have these terrible meetings where we confess all our past sins.'

'And?'

'That's it, really. We attend a group discussion in the morning and talk about a Higher Being and the Twelve Steps. Then there's lunch followed by more discussions in the afternoon. It's harrowing, Laura, I tell you. There's nothing to do but go over and over how terrible you've been to everyone, how one's bad behaviour has affected other people. They even make you write it down – everything, all the binges. If you can remember them, that is.'

'You've never been terrible to me. In fact, you were very kind.'

'Thanks, Laura. Thanks for that. That's the first nice thing anyone's said about me for ages. You can't imagine how cruel people are to each other in the group, all in the name of honesty.' She looked as if she were about to break down.

Laura said hastily, 'Oh dear... But isn't there any one nice, any one you can talk to?'

'If you mean the other inmates, they're a mixed bunch. A doctor, a grandmother, a lorry-driver. Don't know who's paying for him. I can't seem to get on with them. They're so spiteful, some of them, so self-centred. The only person I like is a Welsh girl, Donna – a bit intense but she has a sense of humour. But she's going home soon. As for the rest...'

Laura said, 'I hope I'm not interrupting anything. I was told it was OK to come on a Wednesday.'

'It is. It's our afternoon off. We're suppose to walk around the park and stare at the bloody sheep.'

Laura smiled. 'Poor Mel. But it's worth it. You're much better, aren't you?'

'I am. Almost cured now. The withdrawal part – cold-turkey – was the worst three days of my entire life. Awful, awful vivid nightmares. I'm never going to touch another drop. But the shrinks have told me I need to stay here at least two months. They're just raking in the cash, I told Jack. But he believes them. He's been so patient, I don't want to let him down. He's a good man, Laura.'

'I know.'

'When I think what I've done to him...'

'Mel, maybe a walk isn't such a bad idea.'

Mel walked to the window and then she turned and said, 'What I'd really like to do is go into Winchester to buy some books. There's nothing at all to read in this place. It's either Dean Koontz or endless ghastly American psychobabble books about how to improve your life and set goals and be a better person, and take one step at a time and...'

Laura wasn't sure that excursions were allowed but Mel said airily that at any stage she could pack her bags, call a taxi and leave. Her stay at the clinic was completely voluntary, she insisted. She also claimed that an occasional change of scene was recommended.

While Mel was signing out at the reception desk, the grey-haired woman said, 'We must ask Mrs Brooke to stay close beside you to support you in the town, mustn't we, Melanie?'

'Oh, ye of little faith. Laura Brooke is one of my closest friends, the most reliable person I ever met, is that not so, Laura? She'll tie me to the mast as we drive past the sirens. All the pubs in the world won't lure us on to the rocks, Barbara, I promise you. My salvation will be entirely safe in Laura's hands.'

Barbara pursed her lips.

'Besides,' said Mel in a wheedling voice, 'I went out on a trip before, did I not? And I resisted temptation like one of the holy saints.'

'Yes, but that was with your husband.'

'Laura is a tower of strength. She'll look after me.'


'How about Stockbridge? We could have tea there instead,' suggested Laura nervously as they drove out of the gates. Somehow a village would be a lot safer than Winchester, she thought.

'It's books I want, not tea. You don't know what it's like in that mausoleum. If I don't have something decent to read I won't be able to last the course. I'll go completely off my head.'

'Yes, but couldn't Jack take you to Winchester?'

'He's too busy with the business. He usually visits in the evenings and anyway he hates the way I dither about in shops.'

'But if you give me a list, I could...'

'I can never decide what I want until I get there, you know how it is,' said Mel, who was clutching a large empty basket, books being so heavy, she said.

Later Laura asked, 'What does all that mean – a Higher Being and the Twelve Steps?'

Mel sighed. 'Oh, it means you can't conquer the illness, alcoholism, on your own, you need help from others and possibly what they call a Higher Being. And it takes twelve steps to conquer it. Needless to say, you take One Step at a Time,' she said, emphasising the words theatrically.

'So what are they, the steps?'

'Frankly, Laura, I'm sick to death of talking about it,' said Mel. 'Can we please just forget about the whole bloody shebang and have a nice day out.'

Negotiating the Winchester one-way system, Laura parked the car in the Brooks Centre and as they walked up the pedestrian precinct towards Waterstone's, Melanie began to look increasingly cheerful. 'See how much good this is doing me, Laura? Acting like a normal person.'

After spending almost an hour in the shop, she bought a pile of books.

'Let me help you carry them,' said Laura.

Mel stuffed the Waterstone's bags into her basket. 'No, I'm fine.' Then she said, 'Will we have some tea after all?'

Laura had a moment's doubt and then she realised that there must be several cafés in Winchester that didn't serve alcohol.

After a few ladylike cups of tea, Mel said that actually what she really needed was a couple of new bras, what with the laundry facilities at the clinic being on the slow side. So they went to the lingerie department of Debenhams and Mel took ages, selecting about ten bras to try on. 'It's always difficult with my oversized boobs,' she confided.

While Mel was safely ensconced in the fitting rooms, Laura went to find the ladies. She had an uneasy feeling that the dull pain in her stomach meant the start of what her mother used to describe as 'that difficult time of the month.' She hunted all over the store and then she found a sign saying 'Toilets Closed for Refurbishment'.

'Try that new shopping centre, dear. Ever such nice lavs there,' advised an elderly shopper. Laura raced across the road. But when she arrived back in Debenhams, Mel was nowhere to be seen. In a panic, Laura dived into the changing rooms, peering behind the curtains and shocking a fat old woman in a state of undress.

'Madam, madam, what are you doing?' shrieked the assistant.

Laura waved her arms. 'Where's my friend? She was here a minute ago.'

A disapproving expression came over the assistant's face. 'If it was that Irish lady she said she didn't like our bras after all – wouldn't even try them on, which was a shame. She just left them on the counter and...'

'Did she say where she was going?' interrupted Laura.

'No, madam,' said the assistant crossly.

Laura rushed out into the street where she paced up and down, cursing herself under her breath. She was very much afraid that Mel had dived off to the Wessex for a quick vodka.

After hunting frantically around for ten agonising minutes, she suddenly caught sight of her trotting down the street, clutching yet more shopping, orange Sainsbury's bags this time.

'Mel! Where on earth have you been?'

Avoiding Laura's eye, she said quickly, 'Sorry to desert you, Laura. I tried them all on, but the bras in that place were no good. Not a single one. Typical of bras, isn't it? Can't trust them. You think you've found one that fits and then the eejits change the style. So I gave up and went to Sainsbury's. You'd think the food at the clinic'd be decent at that price, but it's just so dull, hardly better than school. So I bought some biscuits and chocolates... oh and some bananas and orange juice too. Just to keep me going. One needs a few wee treats after all that soul-searching, you know.'

For some reason this detailed list made Laura even more suspicious. 'Can I help you carry that stuff?' she asked.

'No, no, I'm fine.'

But when Mel stacked her basket into the back of the car, Laura heard the sound of bottles clinking together and it seemed unlikely they were bottles of orange juice.

On the way home from the clinic, Laura debated with herself as to whether she should have tackled Melanie, but it seemed too awful to accuse a friend of being deceitful, of lying, in fact. Or maybe she should have told the nurses about the potentially worrying purchases. But then again maybe it was something Mel would have to deal with herself or maybe the nurses would automatically check. Then Laura wondered if she should ring Jack, but the whole idea of telling tales was offensive. All the same, she had the feeling she was a moral coward, that she should have done more to protect Mel from herself.

Back at the cottage she changed her mind yet again and telephoned the clinic, asking to speak to Barbara. Barbara had gone off duty but Laura managed to get hold of another nurse or psychiatrist, she wasn't sure which, who listened calmly to her story and promised to look into the matter.

'I may be maligning Melanie. She may be perfectly innocent. You won't tell her I rang, will you?' pleaded Laura, feeling immensely guilty. 'Has anything happened? I hope she's OK.'

'Please don't worry, Mrs Brooke,' said the nurse. 'Just leave it to us.'

'But is she OK?'

'Just leave it to us,' repeated the nurse ambiguously.

## CHAPTER 19

WEDDINGS DON'T ALWAYS BRING OUT the best in people, thought Laura, remembering all the complaints she ever heard on this contentious subject. Now that formal weddings had become ever more elaborate and expensive, the upmarket problem pages were full of middle-class moans about the high-handed behaviour of the Other Family – whether the bridegroom's parents should nowadays contribute to the cost and, if they did, how much say should they have in the planning of the event. Second and third weddings of older couples only added extra sources of friction: endless quarrels about which ex-wives and new partners should be included on the guest list and what their role should be on the day.

But as she and Oliver were mature adults, without any parents to cope with, their small wedding should be simple and pitfall-free. Or so she hoped. They wouldn't even have to worry about inviting Oliver's ex as she was safely in Brazil.

Oliver had quickly agreed to Laura's suggestion for a quiet wedding in England followed by a large reception in Paris – he said he'd invite enough official guests to be able to put the Paris party on his entertainment allowance. Laura told herself this pragmatic approach was perfectly sensible.

She planned to ask about thirty people to Oliver's house after the church ceremony. Then there was the question of what she should wear and small things like the invitation cards, her bouquet and the flowers for the church. Then would Oliver want to hire a limousine and a professional photographer or should they drive themselves everywhere and ask someone like Bridget's husband to take happy snaps?

Laura knew she couldn't afford to fund all this with her meagre savings. Anyway she wanted to send Alice the air fare from Argentina, so that she wouldn't be beholden to Roberto, her middle-aged lover. Also, since Alice was a raunchy dresser and unlikely to possess anything suitable for an English country wedding in March, it might be advisable to offer to buy her something respectable to wear.

When Oliver came back for the weekend, Laura raised all these delicate subjects over dinner. Having cautiously outlined her plans, she was rather hoping he might begin discussing the financial aspects, but he did not. Finally, towards the end of the evening she forced herself to say, 'What do you think is the best way to pay for all this? I'll be responsible for what I can, my outfit and the flowers,' she began.

'It's normally the bride's family, isn't it? But, of course, you can send the bills to me. On the other hand though, maybe we should ask your stepfather to cough up for the reception,' he said. 'After all, he snaffled all your mother's money.'

Laura flushed. 'The last thing in the world I want to do is crawl to Julius. It would completely ruin the whole thing for me. You don't understand, I just can't bear him,' she said vehemently.

'All right, all right. Calm down,' said Oliver, patting her hand. 'But you should at least put him on the invitation list.'

'I don't want him there.'

'Laura, this isn't like you. One often has to invite people one doesn't like. It's just one of those things.'

'Oh all right,' she said, ashamed. 'But just as a guest. I'd rather have no party at all than ask him to pay.'

'OK, OK, we'll have a little reception and just get the caterers and people to send their bills to Paris.'

'Not everyone will want to do that.' Steeling herself, Laura took a deep breath. 'Oliver, I hate to ask this, but could you please give me some money in advance so I can fix everything? I seem to have spent most of my salary on paying off my overdraft and fixing up the cottage. As I said, I want to pay for my suit and hat myself but...'

'Do you really need something new? You've got clothes in Paris, surely.'

She glared at him. 'But a wedding is a special occasion.' I'm sounding like a bimbo, she thought suddenly.

He smiled. 'Just teasing. Personally I prefer you without clothes. Come to think of it, we do seem to be wasting a lot of time with all this talk.' He held out his hand and, after a moment's hesitation, Laura took it.

Later, after they had made love, she put her arms around him and said, 'About the wedding expenses...' More bimbo behaviour, she thought.

'How much d'you need?'

She told him.

'That much?' He smiled indulgently. 'I'll give you a cheque before I go.'

This he did, and a generous cheque it was. But the episode made Laura uneasy.

She even discussed it in a veiled manner with Melanie on her second visit to the clinic.

'Oh, you'll get used to it, holding out your hand for money. I do it all the time,' said Mel. 'Men like it. Makes them feel important, good providers and all that. These young girls who earn a fortune don't know what they're doing to their husband's egos.'

Laura smiled. 'That seems rather an old-fashioned view.'

'Well, I can afford to be old-fashioned with a generous husband like mine. Jack has always looked after me, always wrapped me in a cotton-wool cocoon.' She frowned and said earnestly, 'Not that I'm trying to blame him in any way. Everything is entirely my own fault – that's what they teach you here. When I think of what I've done to him, the terrible strain on the poor man...'

'So how are you getting on? Will you be able to escape before my wedding?'

Mel looked at the floor. 'They're not very keen on me going out now. They say it puts me in the way of temptation. I had a wee bit of a lapse the other day. They say I'm not strong enough yet, and maybe I'm not.'

She spoke as if she were reciting a lesson learnt in class or a mantra that she must repeat to convince herself.

Laura had been worried that Mel would somehow find out that she'd betrayed her to the shrinks after the visit to Winchester, but Mel showed no signs of hostility. In fact she was more subdued altogether this time.

'Do they give you tranquillizers here, to help you?' asked Laura, voicing her thoughts.

'They don't, apart from when you're drying out. They just try to brain-wash you instead.'

'What d'you mean?'

'Oh, nothing... So tell me about your wedding, Laura. I hope you're buying a lovely lacy trousseau with La Perla knickers? And what about embroidered tablecloths for dainty diplomatic tea parties?'

As they talked on, Mel became more lively, more like her old self. Her parting shot was to the effect that marriage wasn't easy and that Laura would have one hell of a lot of adjustments to make. 'And don't let him continue to treat you like an employee. Start as you mean to go on,' she added.

Laura thought about this on the way home but could not foresee any real problems. The fact that she'd lived in Oliver's household already was an advantage. She knew him well. He wasn't the easiest person in the world, but she understood how to cope with him. Being married would not be so very different. In fact, her new status should make their relationship a great deal easier.

Laura, the wife, Laura the stepmother – she wasn't losing her independence, she was gaining a whole new life. Tonight she would telephone Oliver in Paris and tell him how happy she was.

'Agnès, what a surprise,' said Oliver doubtfully.

It was late, about nine o'clock one evening. Tomorrow he would be returning to England to marry Laura. Everything had been arranged: the simple ceremony in Hampshire, then in a week's time the reception in Paris. He was just checking his accounts and packing his suitcase ready for the early train when the doorbell rang. He had to answer it himself as the servants had gone.

The last person he expected to see was Agnès, who'd sounded icily remote when he rang to tell her about his engagement.

This evening she was all suspiciously sunny smiles. 'May I come in?' She looked at him from under her eyelashes.

'But of course.'

As he took her coat he noticed her scent and the fact that she was wearing a tight-fitting suit, inevitably short and black, with apparently no blouse under the low-cut jacket. Following her down the hall to the salon he could not help being aware of the fact that she was an equally alluring sight from the rear. He realised regretfully that this was nothing to do with him any more.

'I came to say goodbye and to toast your health,' she said, extracting a bottle from her briefcase. 'This is a quite special Calvados from the estate of my cousin in Normandy.'

'How sweet of you. Where are you going?'

'Nowhere. But you, chéri, are about to embark on the long and difficult voyage of matrimony. Before you depart I thought I should like to spend a few quality moments with you, as our dear friends the Americans would say. And I have even bought you a second gift,' she said, presenting him with a small parcel.

He opened it to discover a leather-bound book.

'It is my family history, all the ancestors. My mother wrote it and had it privately printed at enormous expense. I thought you would find it interesting. I wanted to give you something personal.'

'Er, how very kind,' said Oliver. 'I shall look forward to reading it.' Extraordinary present, he thought. Still, it wouldn't be difficult to hide it on the top shelf of the bookcase.

Agnès settled back on the sofa. 'So tell me your plans. Where are you and your bride going for the *lune de miel?*'

'Geneva, a long week-end.'

'Unusual choice for a honeymoon. I hope you will have good weather in March. It can be rather gloomy and foggy by the lake.'

'I have a few meetings at the U.N., so it seemed convenient,' said Oliver. He was about to say that they were taking Charlotte skiing again during the holidays but it seemed more tactful not to mention that particular subject.

'Meetings! Oliver you cannot combine a business trip and a honeymoon. How many meetings? Don't tell me you will be at the United Nations all day and every day while poor Laura is languishing on her own.'

'No, in fact, she isn't staying long in Geneva. She's coming back to Paris separately – wants to look after her daughter who's over from South America.' Oliver wasn't going to tell Agnès that he was not best pleased about this arrangement. He supposed it was reasonable for Laura to want be with her child, but it was not very convenient for him.

Agnès smiled. 'Not a very romantic honeymoon with all these daughters around.'

'Oh, we like it that way.'

'How nice.' She was silent for a moment and then she said, 'I can see it's economical for you, marrying the nanny, though I have to say it's a bit of a cliché.'

Oliver thought it beneath his dignity to reply that actually he had received an allowance towards Laura's salary as a housekeeper. This would now be replaced by a marriage allowance, but he would, he calculated, be marginally less well off than before.

Agnès was still making loaded remarks. 'Your bride is so domesticated and such a good cook.'

'Laura is a very wise and effective person with a strength of character you couldn't begin to understand and –'

'She has a nice bosom, certainly.'

He sighed. 'Fold away your claws, Agnès. Let's talk about something else. How's it going at the Ministry?'

She pursed her lips and then she said, 'Refill my glass and I'll tell you.'

So, gossiping comfortably about matters of state, they drank some more Calvados. Then Agnès said that she needed to inspect his bathroom cupboard because she had lost a tiny pot of some outrageously expensive Dior face cream and it might just be there. He protested there was nothing in his room that belonged to her, never had been, but she seemed determined to check.

She was taking a very long time, he thought. He began to read a section of the *Times* he'd missed earlier. After a while he walked down the corridor to investigate.

His bathroom door was shut. He sat on the bed and waited, and then he knocked. 'Is everything all right?'

'*C'est magnifique,*' she called. 'Come in.'

Cautiously, he opened the door and peered round.

Half covered in bubbles she was lying back in the bath soaping one of her elegant legs with his sponge. She smiled. 'It's such a wonderfully ornamental bathroom, all this marble. One just could not resist making use of it for the last time.'

He drew in his breath. 'Agnès, what are you playing at?' he asked hoarsely.

'Oh, the same games, the same games you used to enjoy so much. It would be fun, I thought. And you are still a single man. This is my other present to you – a stag night. Isn't that what you British call it? We don't so much follow the custom in France though it is becoming more fashionable. I knew you would be too staid and boring to arrange a stag night for yourself. See how thoughtful I have become. Why don't you join me? At least let me wash your back. You want to be nice and clean for your wedding, don't you?'

He took a step backwards. 'Sorry, no. Bad timing. Please go.'

'Very well. If you are determined to be dull and virtuous...' Smiling, she lay back. 'But if you ever get bored with the dutiful

Laura, do telephone me. Though, of course, I may soon make other arrangements myself.' She waved her naked arm languidly. 'Before you go, just pass me that towel, my darling.'

Oliver did as he was told.

## CHAPTER 20

As Bridget said, the ceremony in England and the party after it went 'jolly well', though much of it was now indistinct in Laura's mind. Beforehand she'd been nervous, full of doubts, but the fact that she was organising her own wedding carried her through.

She was also distracted by the great excitement and happiness of seeing her daughter again. Alice only arrived the day before the wedding so there was a great rush to buy her something to wear, and to catch up with her news. Alice was full of stories about anything and everything to do with Argentina – only on the subject of her man did she show any reticence.

Talking to Alice, shopping, last minute calls to the caterer and the florist, last minute gossip with friends, rushing over to Oliver's to check on the house and garden – all these preoccupations meant Laura had little time for misgivings about the future.

Oliver had been pleased with her efforts, so gentlemanly, so handsome, so much admired by everyone. This general approbation had helped to bolster Laura's conviction that she was doing the right thing. Only Jack looked less than happy. He'd sat at the back of the church, had one drink at the party and then left early, saying he had to go and visit Melanie who was still incarcerated in the clinic.

And after all that discussion, Julius was abroad and so declined the invitation. He sent a set of brandy glasses as a present – the mean old bastard, muttered Laura under her breath. But his absence ensured that she actually managed to enjoy her own wedding.

The so-called honeymoon weekend in Geneva had been brief but passionate enough. Lustful enough anyway. In her heart of hearts, Laura considered that its brevity had been one of its advantages. She felt that as they were an older couple embarking on a marriage of convenience (though she only rarely acknowledged this to herself), they might need to measure out the passion carefully, in case it didn't last. Men and women, she thought, needed sexual passion to carry them through the quarrelsome stage until they reach the kind, safe, loving friendship that makes a happy marriage. She also thought that, though some couples had love, passion and friendship from the beginning, she and Oliver might need to work at some or all of these.

Tonight at the reception in Paris, as she stood shaking hands incessantly, she began to long for the end of the evening. Oliver's drawing room – her drawing room now, she realised – was full of distinguished grey-haired men and well-preserved bejewelled women in black dresses. In most cases the sexes were divided, the men talking importantly to each other and women murmuring in their own polite groups. Agnès, of course, was not gossiping with other women. Looking slimmer and more chic than ever, she'd arrived with a tall and handsome young man, stayed for fifteen minutes and then departed, announcing that one was expected at dinner elsewhere, the implication being that one's dinner elsewhere was a pretty important affair.

Ironically, Agnès had been one of the few guests she recognised. As crowds arrived and departed, Laura was amused by the attention she now received in her new role. People she hardly knew treated her like their oldest friend, and with a great deal more respect, as if, by virtue of marrying Oliver, she had become a much more interesting and worthwhile person.

Some people, mostly men, also complimented her on having such a charming daughter. Women were distinctly less enthusiastic, though one frail old grandmotherly type said Alice would be a nice friend for 'little Charlotte'.

Laura hoped that her daughter was behaving. Alice had poured herself into a long cream-coloured satin sheath, so tight she couldn't wear any knickers, or so she boasted. Out of the corner of her eye Laura could see her surrounded by a gaggle of over-excited males of different ages and nationalities. All bust and bottom, Alice was an appalling flirt and, much as Laura loved her, she was not the easiest person to tour around Paris with. Men pursued her relentlessly and instead of giving them the cold shoulder, Alice pouted like a young Brigitte Bardot and thrust out her hips.

Oliver was the only man Alice didn't vamp. Laura sensed she didn't like him much. Only natural. No only child wants to share her mother with anyone else. Although Laura had been overjoyed to see her and was dreading saying goodbye, she couldn't help admitting that Alice's impending departure would make settling in to married life a great deal easier.

As for Charlotte, it was hard to tell what she felt about all this. The only thing she showed any enthusiasm for was her new very grown-up black suit. She was now standing alone on the edge of the crowd. Her long legs looked wonderful and she'd rounded out a little and become less waif-like recently. Her new gamine haircut was an improvement too, but the hostile expression on her face was so uninviting that it was hardly surprising she was alone. As soon as she could escape from the door, Laura intended to go and rescue her.

The England party had been OK, thought Charlotte. Quite small and informal. Better than tonight anyway. Mind you, the whole idea of Dad and Laura was a shock. Charlotte supposed she should have seen it coming. On the whole she was cautiously pleased.

As Charlotte looked around, her eyes came to rest on Alice. Her new stepsister was not at number one in her personal top of the pops. Alice was matey enough when they were alone, but in company she was inclined to hog everyone's attention, being so pretty and sexy and so damn aware of it. It wasn't just that she knew how to attract men – tiresome enough in itself – but Dad and Laura fussed over her too, Laura especially. 'What would Alice like to do? What would Alice like to see?' Alice had this habit of standing with her curly blonde head on one side looking at people all sincerely as if she were drinking in their every word. In Charlotte's view, though, Alice was a complete fluffy. And a rude fluffy at that, Charlotte didn't like the way she was always making faces behind Dad's back.

'Good evening, Miss Charlotte,' said a voice in her ear. 'May I get you another glass of champagne?'

She spun round. 'Simon! Uh, great to see you. You're not in uniform,' she added stupidly.

'No, tonight I'm a guest. Something that your maître d'hôtel heartily disapproves of, I'm sure.'

'Oh, Sebastien disapproves of everything on principle,' said Charlotte.

At that point Sebastien himself came creeping past, glancing at them both suspiciously. They both giggled like naughty children.

'So how are you enjoying the party?' asked Simon with a wink.

'Not much. How about you?'

'Not much,' he said, 'but more so now I've found you.'

She flushed, and opened and shut her mouth.

He smiled. 'You look terrific tonight. You've turned into a swan, in fact.'

Charlotte flushed again. Then she found her voice. 'Yeah, well, you mean, like, I was an ugly ducking?' Cool reply, she thought, smiling more confidently. ' Laura bought me this suit. Nice, isn't it?'

'As I said, you're gorgeous. Laura looks great too. She's such a sweetie, isn't she? I was amazed to find out she had a daughter of eighteen.'

'So you've met Alice.'

'I have. We didn't have a great conversation. Bit like talking to candy-floss, I thought. Oops, sorry, forgot she's your new sister.'

'Don't worry,' said Charlotte happily.

'Maybe she'd be OK if we bought her one of those tee shirts that says "Natural blonde, please speak slowly".'

Charlotte giggled again.

'Just had an idea. Would you like to go out to dinner or a movie tonight?'

She stared at him. 'What?'

'I said let's go out somewhere.'

'What, now?'

'Well, I'm sure Alice will be dining with one of the wolves circling round her. If you and I go out too, then Laura and Mr Farringdon can have some peace when the party's over.'

She gulped. 'I'm not hungry but the cinema would be brilliant. But I'd have to ask Dad and...'

'Leave it to me. I'll fix it up with Laura.'

'But Dad...'

'She's your stepmummy now, you know, and maybe she's just a bit more approachable,' he said.

Charlotte felt it again. The same feelings she'd always had about Simon. Your feet just didn't touch the ground. All those songs, those soppy lyrics, those poems, they were right.

He took her to some terrible adventure movie and afterward she couldn't remember the plot at all. He was so gorgeous, so easy to talk to. She couldn't get over the fact that they were able to chat together in a perfectly natural manner, almost natural anyway. Maybe it was because she was older now or maybe it was just the champagne.

When they came out of the cinema the rain was pouring down but he smiled and took her hand and then they ran down the Champs Elysées to the metro. It was just like the love scene in a film. He insisted on showing her right back to the door of the apartment block – he said he promised Laura – and then, standing in the open doorway, his lips brushed her cheek.

When he'd disappeared Charlotte stood in the hall for a moment, her heart pounding away. Then she crept up the stairs to the apartment. Equally quietly she unlocked the door and tiptoed along the corridor to her room. She half expected Dad to pounce and interrogate her. But he and Laura were obviously otherwise occupied. She tried not to think about that, because the whole idea of anybody over thirty making love appalled her, let alone her own father and Laura.

Once safely undressed in her own bed, she lay wallowing in thoughts of Simon, remembering his every expression, his every word, playing every scene over and over again in the video of her mind. She knew he didn't love her, she knew he had someone else. None of this mattered – what was important was just being with him now and then.

\* \* \*

'So where've you been this evening?' asked Kiki.

'Laura's wedding reception,' replied Simon, stroking the hollow part of her back. He loved that curve between her shoulder blades and her buttocks. It was fun to play with her body after sex, when she was all warm and compliant.

'Queen Laura got married to freeze-dried Farringdon?'

'Yes, I told you.'

'Well, bully for her. She did OK for herself. You were later than I thought though. Must've been a good cocktail party.'

'Not bad, but you told me to come after ten-thirty so I had to fill in some time after the end of the reception. Seemed like a good idea to go and see a movie,' said Simon.

He couldn't be bothered to tell her about Charlotte. Kiki would get all stroppy and assume – wrongly of course – that he had designs on the girl. He had no desire to go into long explanations about her being a harmless young kid.

Kiki turned over. 'You should paint over that stain on the ceiling. Why don't you ever fix anything in this dump?'

He smiled. 'Sorry. Too busy writing or working... or making love to you.'

She smiled up at him, her expression softening.

'Talking of movies, Kiki, about my revised script, have you read it yet?'

She was now studying her crimson fingernails. 'I read the beginning.'

'And?'

'It's good. I like it.'

He smiled happily. 'How far did you get?'

'Honey, I don't have a whole lot of time at the moment. Damn it, this nail varnish is chipped already. Supposed to be a new long-lasting kind.'

'But what do you think about it so far, the script?'

'Like I said, I love it.' She rippled her fingers along his chest. 'But I just don't know how much it'll appeal in the US. My instincts say you need to make it more American.'

'But it's about an American boy adjusting to French customs and culture.'

'I know, and that is kind of interesting. Plenty of people here would find it really great. But back in the States I don't know that the average guy in the street can relate to Europe, that's the problem. Tell you what, you just write me a three-page summary of the plot, no make that two pages, double-spacing, and I'll look at it again.'

'So, Charlotte, is he your boyfriend, that yummy Simon bloke?' asked Alice next day.

Charlotte flushed. 'Not exactly. We just go out sometimes.'

'But you fancy him rotten, don't you?'

'Uh, no, absolutely not – he's just a friend.'

Alice raised her eyebrows. 'Could've fooled me.'

'So have you got a boyfriend?' asked Charlotte, hoping to distract her.

Alice grinned. 'I certainly have, but he's no boy. He's forty-five actually – moody, dark and very, very sexy. Mind you, almost all Argentinians are sex on legs. Kind of like Italians but taller – they really adore women, and so handsome with it. Get you into the sack soon as look at you, know what I mean.'

'Oh, absolutely,' said Charlotte with what she hoped was a sophisticated sigh.

'You want to be careful with the Latin types,' added Alice. 'The French boys probably chase you, do they?'

'Well...'

Alice grinned. 'Anyway, I bet old Mum has given you a good talking to about the facts of life. She sat me down the day after my sixteenth birthday and explained all about safe sex for the birds and the bees. So funny. Didn't tell her I'd been shagging a boy from the next village for about a year. Mind you, now I've got a brilliant lover, I realise he was a disaster, that boy. I should've picked a more experienced bloke first time – it's very important to get your sex life off to a good start. Some people say it affects your whole attitude to men.'

Charlotte looked at her in unwilling admiration. 'What's your Argentinian called?'

'Roberto. Dear Roberto, he's taught me such a lot, so before I go if you want any advice at all about lurve, just fire away.'

'Thank you, I will,' said Charlotte. Though no way would she confess her virgin state to Alice, she thought.


'Charlotte, I've got a goodbye present for you,' said Alice mysteriously. 'Come along. I'm just finishing my packing.'

Charlotte followed her to the spare room where a battered suitcase stood on the bed crammed to the brim with clothes and shoes and make-up spilling out of plastic bags. Lying beside the suitcase on the rumpled bedspread was a black slip-dress, short and insubstantial.

Alice held it up invitingly. 'Too small for me,' she said, 'I mean, with my big boobs it's just a bit too revealing, but on you – well, you've got that tall skinny model figure with legs up to your armpits – the blokes won't be able to take their eyes off you.'

Charlotte hesitated.

Alice said, 'I've never worn it – bought it in Buenos Aires in a hurry and realised it was a mistake the moment I got home. Roberto hates me in black anyway. You know how it is. But I promise it won't look tarty on you.' She gave a disarming smile.

'Thanks,' said Charlotte, 'thank you very much.'

Alice waved a warning finger. 'Don't wear it unless you're with a guy you really fancy, because it's the kind of dress that turns 'em on like crazy. You just wriggle your shoulders and then one strap falls down – accidentally, of course – and then the other, know what I mean?'

'Sure,' said Charlotte nonchalantly.

Alice fumbled in her handbag. 'Here, take these Durex too. Don't like to waste them. I bought them just in case. Didn't need 'em in the end – I've been so damn virtuous here.' She winked. 'I wouldn't want Roberto to know that I'd been contemplating playing away, though. He gets so-oh jealous. If he finds French condoms in my suitcase, he'll probably thump me. Better to ditch any incriminating evidence in advance, I always say.'

Charlotte stared in surprise at the four packets in her hand.

'Put them somewhere safe,' advised Alice. 'I don't think you should wave them about under your Dad's nose, do you?'

So when Laura had taken Alice to the airport, Charlotte went back to her room and made sure the condoms were still in a very safe place. The black dress was on the bed. She put on some sheer black tights and took off her bra. Staring at herself in the mirror she stuck out her chest. Miles away from Page Three material but maybe, just maybe, they'd grown a tiny bit bigger and at least they didn't sag. Some of the girls at school had long droopy boobs already.

Then she put on Alice's dress – it slid over her shoulders and hung alluringly over her body, managing to make her look nicely curvaceous rather than too straight and skinny. Charlotte sighed in satisfaction and then, still staring at her reflection, she tried an Alice-type pout plus a wriggle of the shoulders. One of the straps fell down obligingly. Charlotte smiled at herself from under her eyelashes.

## CHAPTER 21

LAURA IMAGINED THAT ONCE SHE HAD got over the wedding, and the novelty of being married, her life in Paris wouldn't change that much. The only difference, apart from moving bedrooms, would be that she'd live there all year instead of just the school holidays.

However, she had overlooked several aspects, one being that since she was no longer employed by Oliver she would no longer have a salary.

When she told him she was thinking of finding a job, he looked shocked and said this was not a good idea for a woman in her position. Ambassadors' wives should either be employed in something high-powered and impressive, or not at all. But when she hesitantly suggested that as far as her daily spending money was concerned it might be an idea to have a joint bank account in Paris, he said this would be unwise, though he didn't specify why. He thought it best for her to continue to use the separate housekeeping account. When she went on, with some reluctance, to mention that as an Ambassadress she would need a few more suitably smart clothes and maybe have her hair done occasionally, he offered to add a small dress allowance. Later in the day, she saw him checking his records on the computer, with pie charts and flow charts and columns of figures zooming around the screen.

She found all these financial discussions distasteful and vowed that if she ever came across a suitably ladylike job she would take it. Except that she feared that if she couldn't use the latest software she couldn't get a job and Oliver would not permit her to practise on his precious computer in case she somehow deleted all his files.

There was another small matter that bothered her and that was the way he watched her at parties. If she found herself alone talking to a man, however young, however old, Oliver would stride up and whisk her away.

Maybe it's flattering, this jealousy, she told herself finally. He seemed proud of her in some ways, which was endearing – he liked to watch her dress and, more particularly, undress. And, of course, he liked to make love to her – which was good, except somehow there was not the same joy that had coloured the early times with William. But that was a lifetime ago. Maybe her memory was adding rosy tints, maybe it hadn't been that blissful anyway, just youthful enthusiasm. Or maybe, she thought as she lay awake listening to Oliver's quiet snoring, she was now too old for joy.

Anyway sex wasn't that important – she had managed without it for years. She now had a marriage and a role to play, that was the thing.

This role seemed to consist in being constantly well-dressed, a strain in itself, and giving or attending endless dinner parties and lunches with people she did not know, further strains on her repertoire of small talk and on her waistline. Eating for Britain, she told herself. Sometimes it was hard to find common ground if she was sitting between, say, a Chinese embassy official with fractured English and a retired French general with a hearing problem. On these occasions she felt a longing to escape.

The wives of Oliver's foreign colleagues were kind and welcoming, but they were mostly older, kind grandmothers who had different concerns and different conversations. Once she had asked them about their families and their holidays, they didn't always find much to say to each other, and Laura felt like a cuckoo in a flock of wiser birds. They were chic and smart with not a grey hair among them (grey hair not being permitted by Paris coiffeurs), infinitely better groomed and more youthful in appearance than their contemporaries in England, and from an entirely different world. None of them seemed to mind their husbands' heavy gallantries towards Laura and even Oliver seemed to accept that sort of thing as de rigueur.

Of course there were many positive aspects of being Madame l'Ambassadrice, like the invitations to the fashion shows with the wild paparazzi and the amazing models, both species being even more extreme in the flesh than they appeared in the newspapers.

As she wrote to Alice, *'My French has greatly improved but my figure continues to suffer badly. It's daunting how the Parisiennes remain so slim. I try to look reasonably smart but it isn't easy. I even attended a small informal fashion show the other night where I discovered I had to sit in the front row with the other ambos' wives, all dressed up to the nines. As the parade of near-naked beanpoles passed in front of us (all pale as death but madly beautiful in an unreal kind of way), I was too embarrassed to take my chewed biro out of my handbag to mark any garments I fancied – or didn't fancy like the hideous "low-necked violet crêpe bouclé jacket over a midi orange taffeta skirt." As you can imagine, Oliver was extremely relieved to hear that I hadn't placed any orders.'*

Aware that this new elevated role was removing her further and further from reality, Laura made an effort to stay in touch with her few 'normal' friends in Paris, people like Simon.

Today, picking her way along the dingy streets to his apartment, she pondered about his relationship with Kiki and wondered belatedly if it had been a mistake to allow him to take Charlotte to the cinema that evening. It would have been Victorian to say no, but she was uneasy about Charlotte's crush on him which showed no signs of abating. That was one of the reasons for this visit – to deliver another tactful lecture about not leading Charlotte astray. The other reason was to return his film script which she had finally got round to reading.

Simon had warned her that his downmarket flat was in a state of terminal chaos but, as she looked around her she found it hard to say anything polite. It was mystifying how personally neat he was despite living in such a tip. Reams of typewritten pages stood on a table in disorganised hillocks beside bulging files and scattered newspaper cuttings. Covering the floor and the scruffy furniture were stacks of books, discarded sweaters, several odd shoes, cans of coke, sweet wrappers, half-eaten biscuits and dirty coffee cups. There was only one smart item in the room – a dark grey Toshiba laptop, its screen glowing like a star in a compost heap.

'Great computer,' said Laura, relieved to be able to find something to praise.

He smiled proudly. 'It was my big investment last year,' he said. 'Fully paid off now, thanks to you giving me a job.'

She couldn't resist brushing down the chair before sitting down.

'It's so brilliant of you to read my script,' he said. 'What d'you think of it? I'm biting my nails.'

She began to open the elastic bands on the folder. 'The thing is, Simon, I'm not an expert.'

'Don't want an expert. I need a gut reaction from the average cinema-goer.'

'Maybe you should ask Charlotte.'

'She's a bit young. Come on, Laura, I'm terrified. Stop torturing me – what do you really think of it.'

'Mm. I like it. It has a lot of depth.'

He sighed with relief.

'I'm trying to identify with the older woman,' she said. 'It all depends who plays the part in the film. Does this person have to be French? If you could make all the characters American it might be easier to cast and sell. There'd be loads of possibilities.'

He frowned thoughtfully. 'That's kind of what Kiki said. But the whole point is, it has to be set in Paris.'

'So why not make the older heroine American but a long-term resident, a world-weary sophisticated expatriate? Middle-aged Hollywood actresses would fight for the part.'

He beamed. 'That's brilliant, Laura. The woman could be a former schoolfriend of the boy's mother. The mother says, like, "look up my old friend when you go to Paris, dear – she's married to a really important French guy," and he says to himself who wants to meet a boring old friend of Mom's but then, when he calls on her and sees a beautiful middle-aged sexbomb, he's gobsmacked.'

Laura laughed. 'Absolutely. But the husband needs to stay French. Americans like a French villain,'

'I agree. And the young girl could be American too. A student. Actually I'd already thought of that, but casting an American actress as the older female lead is a stroke of genius, Laura. Can't think why I missed it myself. I just had this fixed idea that she must be French.'

'William used to say he got too close to his own work sometimes.'

He's probably forgotten who William was, she thought. Sometimes even she forgot him.

They talked on about the script. Finally as she was about to leave Simon asked politely, 'So how is it going at the Residence? How is my best friend Sebastien?'

'Still snooping for France,' said Laura with a smile.

'I'm so grateful for all your help,' he said. 'Dare I ask – would you read a bit more of it for me?'

Laura said she would, then she had a sudden flash of inspiration. 'I don't suppose you'd have time now and then, if you weren't too busy, to give me a mini computer course. I want to get a job and I really need to update my very limited skills.'

Simon beamed. 'Sure. It'd be great to be able to do something for you for a change. Come any time, any day.'

Oliver looked up over the top of the *Times*. 'Where have you been?'

'I went to see Simon.'

'Simon... did you meet him in a café?'

'No, at his flat because...'

He lowered the newspaper and frowned. 'Laura, I don't think it is appropriate for you to visit Simon's apartment.'

'Why on earth not?'

He sniffed. 'People may get the wrong idea.'

'About what?'

'You're an attractive woman and people may say – '

'Oh, for heaven's sake, Oliver. Simon is light years younger than I am. He's hardly more than a boy. No one could possibly think... and anyway no one we know lives anywhere near Simon, so the problem doesn't arise.'

Oliver's voice grew colder. 'A woman in your position has to be particularly careful. You don't want his concierge to think the worst.'

She stared at him. 'Simon doesn't live in the kind of building that has a concierge. Don't be so pompous. If I want to go and visit my friends then I will.'

He shuffled the newspaper and then put it down again. 'What were you doing there anyway, all this time?'

'If you must know, I was returning part of his screenplay to him. He asked me to read it. And I've brought some more back with me – which I'm also going to read and discuss with him. So now you know.'

She left the room, shutting the door behind her with a bang.

That night Oliver had an official dinner to which wives were not invited. She decided to pretend to be asleep when he returned, her back turned to his side of the bed. Nevertheless he pulled her towards him. Mutely she accepted his cognac-laden embraces, deciding this must be a form of apology.


'Let's have some wine,' said Simon, jumping up.

Laura peered at the keyboard. 'Help. That e-mail I was typing has completely disappeared. Most peculiar. Where's it gone?'

Simon leant over and clicked the mouse.

'Sorry, said Laura. 'I'm such a klutz... No wine, thanks. Might finish me off completely.'

'No, no, do you good, give you courage. I'll just pop over to the supermarché. Back in a sec.'

Laura panicked. 'You're leaving me all alone with this machine? What if I make some terrible boob and delete your script, your masterpiece?'

'Chill out, Laura. I've got back-up copies. To be on the safe side, don't empty the waste bin – the one on the screen, I mean.'

'OK,' she said dubiously as he disappeared down the stairs. Poor boy, she thought. He's obviously bored stiff having to devote his Monday afternoons to a Mrs Rip-van-Winkle technophobe. She hardly dared make a move in his absence in case those comforting blue clouds disappeared and the scary black screen underneath reared up with its threatening messages about MS-DOS, whatever that might mean.

She was just reading the first chapter of *Windows for Dummies* yet again when she heard his key in the lock.

'That was quick,' she said, without looking up.

'And who the heck are you?' enquired an American voice coolly.

Laura rose to her feet. Before her stood an attractive woman with sharp green eyes peering out from under artfully tangled red hair. Tanned, slim, and dressed to kill in shocking pink with matching stilettos, she was, on second glance, not that young. Ah-ha, thought Laura.

'I'm Laura Farringdon. And are you Kiki, by any chance? Simon has told me so much about you.'

The woman drew in her breath. 'Yup, that's me.' Her face was unsmiling and aggressive. 'What are you doing here? I thought you just got married,' she said, spitting out the words.

For an alarming moment Laura feared she was about to be attacked. She was half way through a hasty explanation when Simon reappeared.

'Kiki! What a surprise.'

'It sure is,' she said. Then she turned on her heels and swept out.

A flustered Simon raced after her. Laura could hear a fierce argument at the bottom of the stairs. At the top of his voice Simon was shouting, 'But I love you. You, only you.'

Fun for the neighbours thought Laura, amused. She was just wondering how she was going to get past them to leave the building when they both returned.

'Guess I wasn't too friendly,' said Kiki with a strange half-smile. 'Sorry, Laura. Kind of a misunderstanding.'

'That's OK. Look, I'm just going.'

Kiki held out her hand. 'But I need to apologise. Maybe I could give you lunch one day. Like, we're neighbours, aren't we?'

'Lovely,' said Laura, thinking it was the last thing she'd want to do.

'We have so much in common,' said Kiki with an ironic glance at Simon.

When Monsieur Farringdon, returning unexpectedly early, demanded to know where madame was that afternoon, Sebastian gave an exaggerated pursing of the lips and, sliding away his eyes, frowned as if in deep thought. 'I don't believe that madame told me where she was going.'

'Well, what time will she be back?'

'I do not know, sir.' Then he said confidentially, 'I believe that she is in the habit of visiting Monsieur Lee on Mondays. Would you like me to give you the telephone number?'

'Monsieur Lee?'

'Simon, that is.' Sebastien kept his voice suitably neutral.

'Ah,' said Monsieur with a frown.

'Would you like me to give you the telephone number, sir?' repeated Sebastian unctuously.

'No,' snapped Monsieur. 'Just bring tea for one please.'

Sebastian withdrew, smiling to himself. It should not, he thought, be difficult to plant another such seed now and then. After all, it was not correct behaviour for madame to consort with a young man such as Simon, a former member of staff, not correct behaviour at all and it was his, Sebastian's, loyal duty to bring the matter to the Ambassador's attention.

## CHAPTER 22

CHARLOTTE HAD JUST COME BACK TO PARIS and the long summer stretched ahead of her. She couldn't face going away with Dad and Laura in case they let their hair down and got all lovey-dovey, though there wasn't much sign of that at the moment. To her mind they seemed pretty distant for a newly married couple, but probably at their age that was normal.

Anyway she really was getting too old for parental holidays so she had cunningly arranged some work experience. She'd told Dad that the careers mistress at school had advised her to get a temporary job in a French environment and Dad was always keen on her improving her CV and doing the right thing. Right thing or not it was unbelievably boring addressing envelopes for Médecins Sans Frontières with a load of middle-aged women, but it gave her the excuse to stay alone in the flat in Paris for two weeks with just the staff to look after her.

Full of a strange restlessness, she had her own agenda of what she wanted to experience in the summer holidays. Stuff they'd been talking about at school, things that had been on her mind for a while.


Charlotte put on the soft black slip dress with the shoe-string straps. Now that she was so brown the dress was even more becoming. Her skin in the mirror looked clean and shiny, so did her hair. And her eyes.

Everything she'd bought from the traiteur was sitting in the fridge, waiting for Simon. She laid the table and then she went down to the cellar for a bottle of wine. Which one should she choose? The oldest one, the red one with the picture of the chateau had a slightly murky look perhaps. The cellar light was on a time switch. Charlotte suddenly feared all the lights would go out and that rats would jump on her. She punched the light-button again. She'd never like the cellar with its German writing on the door. Used to be a prison in the War, Dad said.

Hastily she returned her attention to the wine racks. Then her eye was caught by the bottles of champagne. That was the answer. She would put it in the freezer to cool down quickly and then maybe that white wine over there, 1994 it said. Quite old, so it better be used up.

Returning along the sinister corridor carrying the bottles she met the temporary concierge who gave her a strange look. Charlotte realised the dress was not the kind of thing one normally wore in the cellars.

Once back in the apartment, she remembered scent. Women should always wear scent, eye make-up and earrings, Simon said once. Simon says. It sounded like the game.

He was late. She could feel her whole body shaking with nervous anticipation.

The door-phone rang and, soon, there he was. So tall and lean, so sunnily handsome with a lock of blond hair falling over his eyes and tangling with the frame of his glasses.

Her heart stopped.

'Hello, you,' he said. Then he kissed her on both cheeks. 'Pwoah! You look fantastic – what a dress!'

She felt herself blushing from head to foot.

'Is Laura here?' he asked, looking around.

'No, they're away till tomorrow.'

'Where's old Sebastien?'

'Oh, the staff have gone home.'

He looked at her again as if suddenly reassessing the situation. 'So where would you like to go for dinner?'

'I don't want to go out. I've got it here – well, it's in the fridge. You needn't worry. I didn't actually cook it.'

He laughed and gave a kind of bow. 'Miss Charlotte, this is very kind of you.'

She handed him the champagne to open and they went to the salon and sat down, not on the same sofa but at right-angles to each other. Simon chatted away in quite a jolly manner but Charlotte couldn't think of much to say in reply. Didn't seem to matter as he was happy to be listened to, she could tell.

Dinner started off a bit stiff and awkward, but then he began to imitate Sebastien, dashing off to the kitchen and then serving everything with a bad-tempered flourish which made her laugh. The fishy terrine from the *traiteur* wasn't as nice as it looked – too much mayonnaise and a strange sticky cardboard texture. She couldn't eat anything anyway, not even the strawberry tartlets which normally she loved.

After they'd put the plates in the dishwasher, Simon stared at her with an amused, quizzical kind of twinkle – he'd been looking at her this way all evening – and then he said, 'Shall we go out for a drink somewhere? There's a pub in the Champs Elysées that's quite fun if you want a Brit atmosphere or if not...'

Charlotte, who was swaying a little after the unaccustomed alcohol, took a deep breath and finally blurted out, 'Actually, I sort of wanted to ask you a favour.' She tried to remember to flutter her eyelashes.

He smiled. 'Anything for you, my lovely.'

'That's just it. Like, can we go back to the salon?'

So he took her hand and sat her down on the sofa. 'What's the problem?'

'I, I can't tell you, lost my nerve.'

He looked all concerned. 'Charlotte, if there's something the matter, I'd be only too glad to help.'

'Could you turn that light off,' she said suddenly.

He did so. There was only one lamp on now, on the far side of the room.

Without looking at him she took a deep breath and blurted out, 'You see, now I'm sixteen I don't want to be a... a virgin any more so I thought I'd ask you to... well, I thought you'd know what to do and I'd rather it was you than, like, some awful drunk boy in the back of a car. Alice said the first time is so important – I sort of want it to be special, you see. Well, I hope you see... I mean, you don't have to, of course.'

After she'd spoken she could hardly believe she'd said all that, though she'd rehearsed it so many times. She felt her face grow redder and redder.

He stared at her in astonishment and there was a silence which seemed to last for ever. He doesn't want me, she thought, in a sick shock of embarrassment.

Eventually he took her hand. 'I'm very honoured to have been selected for this tempting role,' he said gently, 'but don't you think it's better to wait until you're a bit older, until you fall in love?'

'But, you see, I *do* sort of really, really... lul, like you,' she said, staring miserably at the carpet. 'Please don't laugh. I know you don't feel the same way.'

'Charlotte, I'm not laughing.'

'Maybe you don't want to,' she whispered

After another age he said, 'Actually, I confess that I do, very much. Like any man would, sitting alone in an apartment with a beautiful sexy girl. In fact, I've been thinking about you recently and this evening when you opened the door wearing that dress, I was, well, I was stunned.'

She smiled, half-scared, half-relieved. 'Really?'

'But...'

'Simon.' She leant towards him.

Very gently he took her face in his hand and kissed her on the lips. Instinctively she opened her mouth and they kissed some more until she was breathless and deliriously happy.

He drew back suddenly. 'But what about Laura... and your father? Trouble is, they trust me.'

'They don't need to know. Nothing to do with them.'

After another long wonderful deep sexy kiss he murmured, 'If we... promise me, if we make love, you'll wait for right person next time. You won't say yes to every man that asks, will you? And they will ask, believe me.'

She stared at him. 'Of course I won't sleep around. Is that what you think of me?'

'No, no,' he said hastily. 'Look, I'm going out now, to find a late-night chemist. I'm not equipped. Come to think of it I saw a dispensing machine in rue de la Pompe. Not far, about ten minutes. When I come back, you may've changed your mind, which would be OK.'

'Equipped?'

'You know, safe sex.'

She put her arms around his neck and muttered into his collar, 'You don't need to go. I've got some... some things, er, you know, contraceptives hidden in my room.'

He grinned and shook his head. 'My God, you went and bought condoms? That was very brave.'

Her burning face still buried in his shoulder, she said, 'Alice gave them to me. Four packets, is that enough?'

He gave a stifled yelp of laughter. 'Yup, if there's three in each one, that should do it.'

They kissed some more. 'What happens next?' she whispered.

'It's very hard to resist you when you look at me like that, all soft and shiny-eyed,' he said.

For an awful moment she thought he was about to change his mind and leave. She remembered about the shoulder straps. Shrugging, she let them fall.

He drew in his breath and then he stretched out his hands to pull her dress down a little further so that her nipples were almost but not quite exposed. 'You're so lovely,' he said helplessly. Then he ran his knuckle delicately along the top part of her breasts. Electrified, she closed her eyes.

'Is there a zip?' he murmured reaching around behind her back.

'No – it's very kind of stretchy, this dress.'

'So it is.' He pulled it slowly down to her waist. 'You didn't sunbathe topless,' he said, stroking her white skin.

Mutely, she shook her head.

Then he kissed her so fiercely that she was utterly lost. He drew back and, almost as if it were accidental, his hand brushed her left knee. As he progressed upwards, she felt her thighs begin to fall obediently apart.

Abruptly he tugged her skirt down.

Confused, she opened her eyes again. 'Don't... I mean, don't stop.'

He began again, slowly and carefully, until eventually his fingers were skimming lightly over the soft folds between her legs, and she was burning with an overwhelming, almost unbearable excitement.

'I think I'd better take you to bed now,' he murmured. 'If you're sure.'

She gulped. 'Yes,' she whispered.

He looked down at her then he said seriously, 'It would be wrong if you'd had too much to drink. Say "she sells sea shells".'

She stared at him, astonished. 'What?'

'Go on. Say it. I'm testing you for sobriety.'

'She sells sea shells on the she shore, I mean, sea shore,' Charlotte heard herself repeat like a stupid but well-behaved child.

He smiled. 'Not bad,' he said. Taking her hand, he led her along the corridor.

In a moment of irrational modesty she'd pulled up the top of her dress, but once in her room, she stripped off completely and dived under the bedclothes so he wouldn't be able to see her. 'The condoms are at the back of the top drawer – in a little blue sponge bag, underneath my scarves,' she mumbled from under the sheet.

There was rather a long pause, during which time her courage began to fail. But finally he lay beside her, quite naked, and all over again he began the caressing and the murmurs of encouragement until she lost herself once more in a wild mindless wonderful fever.

Then, suddenly forceful, he pushed into her with a few determined nudges.

She gasped at the pain and shock of it and lay still. After a few stunned moments, she began to try to follow his rhythm, but, just as she felt she was about to understand, he groaned and pulled away.

'Sorry,' he said looking down at her with a remorseful smile. 'You're too lovely. Couldn't hold back.'

She smiled uncertainly.

'You were terrific,' he said.

'Was I?' She felt elated and relieved.

'Are you OK?'

'Fine.' When nothing further seemed to be happening, she asked, 'Um, is... is it over?'

' 'Fraid so. For the time being.' In a matter of fact way, he handed her a box of Kleenex. 'I'll get the champagne – don't think we finished the bottle.'

Still naked he disappeared and then returned with two glasses and the half-empty bottle. Lying on her back she watched him. He really did look very strange, with his brown arms and his white body and his thing. Even on closer acquaintance, she still couldn't give it a name.

Using the flat space between her breasts as a table, he poured her a glass. 'A toast to Charlotte's lost virginity,' he said with a flourish.

Grinning, she picked up the glass and, propping herself up on her elbow, took a sip. Somehow she expected to feel completely different, but her room, everything was still the same. Apart from Simon's being there, of course.

'I hope it wasn't too painful for you, was it?' His voice was all tender and concerned.

'No, not really.' She didn't like to say that, compared to the fantastic, overwhelmingly exciting preliminaries, the sexual act itself had been less earth-shatteringly wonderful than she'd expected, more animal than romantic. In fact, the whole procedure struck her as faintly comical. The more she thought about it the funnier it seemed. She began to giggle.

He smiled. 'Ssh, Charlotte. It's not polite to laugh in these circumstances.'

'Can't help it... so funny...'

He pinched her nose. 'What's funny, little one?'

'Sex,' she spluttered.

He began to laugh too. 'You're so right. Sorry, I'll last longer next time. I promise you, you won't always laugh. After a bit more practice together, we won't be able to speak for hours afterwards – we'll just lie swooning in the languor of spent passion.'

She smiled happily at him. 'Oh, are we going to try again?' It was such a relief that he wanted to.

'Yes, my beautiful Charlotte, oh yes.'

'When?'

'Quite soon,' he said.


Simon was too late to catch the metro home. In the taxi his triumphant post-sexual euphoria had begun to evaporate into a cloud of guilt. He really shouldn't have succumbed, but she was so sweet, so innocent, so pretty. Not so innocent any more, thanks to him. The second and third times it was still a bit painful and funny for her but he'd made her happy, seemed like she'd come even. Which made him happy too. She was so touchingly sexually naïve, a refreshing change after Kiki.

Kiki, oh Lord. She must never know. Still, there was no reason why she should.

Charlotte, Charlotte. Maybe he shouldn't have encouraged her, shouldn't have said all that stuff about passion. All the same, it would be hard to stay away from her, especially as she was such a quick and appreciative learner, especially as she was crazy about him.

Those shiny eyes, those slim hips. He groaned. Oh my God, she was his former employer's daughter, hardly more than a child. Laura had warned him off Charlotte a long time ago – he had betrayed Laura's trust. He'd also betrayed Kiki and generally behaved like a shit.

He shook his head. Then again, maybe he was being unfair to himself. After all, it was Charlotte's idea – she'd come on pretty strong. She was a young modern girl who more or less knew what she wanted.

All the same, he'd have to extricate himself from the situation. Not straight away or she'd be hurt. He'd have to see her at least once more. Or maybe twice.

## CHAPTER 23

OLIVER ROSE TO HIS FEET AS SOON AS LAURA walked into the room. 'This is filth,' he said explosively.

'What is?' asked Laura, alarmed by his tone. They were making a flying visit to hot and sultry Paris between holidays and, feeling exhausted, she had just returned from the hairdresser to find Oliver reading in his study.

'This play of Simon's. I find it most objectionable that he should ask you to have to plough through it and I shall tell him so.'

She stared at him. 'It's a film script, not a play and it was in my briefcase. You must have taken it out.'

'I did and I regret it. It's very low-level stuff, not the sort of thing you should be wasting time on. I really don't know what he's playing at, that boy. I shall have to have a word with him. Bloody cheek asking you...'

'The point is, Oliver, this has absolutely nothing to do with you,' she shouted, suddenly losing her temper. 'If I want to read stuff by my friends then I will. It's not your business.'

'Seems he's making a pass at you, getting you to read sordid sex scenes between a boy and an older woman, so it *is* my bloody business. You are my wife and I...'

'Exactly. Your wife. Your equal partner. And Simon has absolutely no designs on me. You sound ridiculous, Oliver.' She snatched the manuscript out of his hands, turned on her heels and stalked out of the room.

A little later she heard the front door slam.

Nothing was said about anything when Oliver returned from the office. He was silent and remote, seated in his study reading official papers. During dinner he hardly spoke. Still furious, she went to bed early and pretended to be asleep when he lay down beside her. Soon, to her immense irritation, he began to snore. Why was it that men always seemed to be able to sleep, regardless? Too upset for a proper night's rest, Laura tossed and turned, coughing periodically.

When she belatedly joined him at breakfast, he was calmly eating a croissant. He looked up at her warily, but all he said was, 'Would you like a grapefruit today – they're quite good.'

Pulling back her chair, she sat down. 'Look,' she said, determined to try and clear the air even if he was prepared to let things slide, 'look, if it really upsets you I'll meet Simon on neutral ground but I am going to continue to read his stuff. I must continue to see my friends.'

Oliver smiled, almost placatingly. 'Yes, yes, of course you must. Neither of us should forget our friends.'

*Dear Melanie,* wrote Laura. *Haven't heard from you for ages. How are things in Hampshire? We had a good holiday and Oliver played a lot of golf.* How banal, but she could hardly write that she'd felt alternately neglected and bored, or overpowered by Oliver's jealous attentions. *Went to stay with friends of Oliver's at their villa which had a fantastic pool but not many other diversions apart from eating. Fear have put on yet another kilo and Parisian pencil skirts have all shrunk.*

Oliver's friends, mostly rich retired Army types, had been polite but mainly indulged in the do-you-know-old-Buffy-Frogmore-who-lives-in-Gloucestershire-near-Highgrove type of conversation at which Laura was not adept. They all seemed to be married to achingly chic middle-aged French women with gilded tans and smooth hair miraculously unaffected by humidity, and unbearably flat stomachs enhanced by sophisticated beach ensembles. She'd been caught out again at a dinner party last night – it was so hot that Laura had dressed in an old floral sunfrock, but all the French women were immaculate in carefully accessorised black linen.

I don't fit in with them, the hearty braying English or the brittle French, she thought. I don't really fit in with Oliver at all. She sometimes had the feeling she didn't measure up to his expectations – he didn't think she was smart enough, slim enough, chic enough for the kind of people he liked. She felt he was watching her all the time, sizing her up, seeing if she passed muster. 'Laura, your hair is a bit of a mess,' he'd say. Or 'Laura, you were rather silent last night,' would alternate with 'Laura, one mustn't hog the conversation, you know.' Holidays were such a strain, she thought, with Oliver around all day. In Paris at least she had some time to herself, some time when she wasn't under scrutiny, under pressure.

It was typical that Julius, that great arbiter of the social scene, should show up in the south of France. Oddly, he seemed to reassure Oliver of her social acceptability.

*Mel, you remember the loathsome Julius, my stepfather? He was staying with allegedly grand 'chums' nearby and kept appearing at the villa at drinks time. He acted as if he and I were close and cosy family.*

One evening Julius sat quaffing gin and tonic, waving his tortoise head around sizing up the villa, just like all the rest of them. He was discoursing on the social life of the Riviera and name-dropping so thick and fast that Laura had ceased to listen long ago.

'Caught a glimpse of you in Cannes last week, Oliver old chap,' he said. 'Saw you having lunch with the Baron de Bougneis and his daughter. Oops,' he said, with a mischievous smirk. 'Little Laura wasn't there. Am I talking out of turn?'

'No, of course not,' said Laura crossly. 'I was invited but I didn't feel well, bit of a cough, thought it was too hot to go into town.'

She knew he was lunching with Agnès and her father. Quite right, no reason why he shouldn't see Agnès now and then. After all, he met her at work on a regular basis. There has to be trust in a marriage, as she'd told him after the Simon episode. And they had agreed they should make time for their old friends. Old friends definitely did not include Julius, of course, but Oliver seemed to like him.

*Oliver thinks we ought to keep in keep in his good books, he said. To my horror, when Julius mentioned that he was going to be in Paris in the autumn, Oliver asked him to stay. Fortunately Julius refused. He said he always stayed with Leonard and Aurelia at the Embassy as they are so well placed with all those guest rooms and all those servants.* Oliver's face was a picture, she thought. He didn't like being reminded that there is a much grander British Ambassador in Paris who lives in a palace rather than an apartment.

*But actually our main guestroom is really very nice, so you and Jack must come over some time – don't forget.*

Of course, they wouldn't come. Jack wouldn't risk Mel disgracing herself and thereby disgracing Laura. In a way, though, thought Laura with a smile, a drunken Mel would liven the place up a bit. Not that one should joke about alcoholism. Poor Jack, so patient, so kind, how did he manage to keep his cool? How did he manage to stay so loyal? Every time she started to complain to herself about Oliver's annoying behaviour, she reminded herself about Jack's long-suffering staying power.

# CHAPTER 24

MELANIE HADN'T HAD A DRINK ALL MORNING, her hands were shaking and she looked and felt like a dead cow. Yesterday Jack had come home early and found her worse for wear, with five empty whisky bottles on the kitchen table. She'd explained truthfully that she was just about to go to the bottle bank but he'd hit the roof, saying he went the other day and how come there were so many new empties already. Then he'd issued yet another ultimatum. She must go back into a clinic NOW, he said. He'd find a new treatment centre if the last one was no good. He started raving on about the Priory, or a new kind of boot-camp, or the Minnesota method; then he said something about her helpful ex-alco friend Donna, an American called Ruth, and another person and another. By this time her head was reeling. One thing she knew was that she didn't want to go back to a prison-like clinic.

Give me a chance. I'll show you, she'd said. I'll go to the bloody AA. Give me one last chance.

So today she was making a big effort to find the local AA meeting hall which was in an old seedy part of the town she'd never penetrated before. It was difficult enough to find the church itself and then there was only one peeling sign saying 'Church hall in Randall Lane.' After another ten minutes of wandering around in the pouring rain – damn it, why had she left her umbrella at home? – she found herself hurrying down a dingy passage with high windows on either side. There wasn't a soul in sight to ask and besides she didn't feel like communicating with anyone.

She was going to be very late. Then at last she saw another sign to the hall above some worn stone steps leading down to the bowels of what looked like a factory building. Down to hell in fact, she thought grimly.

When she opened the door at the bottom of the steps she found herself looking down on to a dark Dickensian room full of cigarette smoke. About thirty people sat around a long wooden table – their faces looked both vacant and scary. Choking at the smoke and the faint smell of bodies in second-hand clothes, Mel backed away up the stairs.

No way, she said to herself as she ran down the street to the car park. No way. In the car, she took a couple of huge swigs from the half bottle of vodka she'd stashed in the glove compartment. Then she got her little stirrup cup out and had a proper drink. Or two. She had been trying not to drink before noon lately, but today she needed something to steady her nerves.

Driving home, she felt a little better. She'd have to concoct a good story for Jack as to why she didn't stay. She took another swig. During the last months he'd been putting more and more pressure on her to go back into treatment. No wonder she felt on edge. She'd done well when she came out of that last clinic, lasted several months even, but then something happened that really upset her.

It was Phoenix, the cat. She got caught in a discarded roll of barbed-wire. Mel searched for five days and when she found the poor little thing she was almost invisible at the bottom of the hedge – a scrap of fur, matted with mud and dried blood. It looked as if she'd tried to bite her own leg off, the one that was held by the wire.

There was a crow standing by, ready to peck her eyes out.

Horrified, Mel had dragged some branches over her to protect her then she'd run home for the secateurs and back again to Phoenix. She'd managed to cut her free and then she'd run panting back again through the fields, carrying the wounded animal in her arms. Almost unable to speak in her distress and panic, she'd phoned Robin, the vet, but inevitably he was out on a call. Finally she'd raced through the lanes to the surgery to meet him. He still didn't arrive. She had to wait in the car for twenty minutes while poor scrawny Phoenix lay beside her barely breathing.

Robin arrived eventually and was all sympathetic, but it was too late. Mel knew that already. He said he'd deal with the body, unless she wanted to bury it herself.

'No,' said Mel. 'You take care of her.'

On the way home she'd stopped at a branch of the Wine Rack. Stacked from ceiling to floor, all those shiny bottles surrounded her, winking their temptation.

She only bought half a bottle of whisky.


Today, driving home along the country lanes, Mel remembered Phoenix and her awful lingering death. She took another swig from the bottle on the seat beside her. Then another. It was raining down even harder now. She put the windscreen wipers on to full, but the visibility was poor. Swish-swish they went at a million miles an hour, the noise irritated the hell out of her. Still, she was nearly home now. Relax, relax, she told herself.

When the sharp turn at the bottom of the hill loomed up, she turned the wheel and, in a moment of suspended horror, suddenly realised she wasn't going to make it.


When she opened her eyes again, she blinked in confusion.

Someone, a woman, was speaking. 'Are you hurt?'

The car door was open and someone was peering at her through the rain. 'Shit,' said Mel. 'Shit.'

The woman was wearing a navy plastic raincoat with the hood up. Water was dripping all over her face. 'Do you need an ambulance?' She had an American accent, all efficient and commanding.

Mel shook her head to clear it. Unbuckling her seat belt, she staggered out of the car and leant against it. 'Shit,' she said again.

'Are you OK?'

'Fine,' said Mel uncertainly. She looked at the car. 'Holy Mary.'

The front wheels were in a deep ditch but apart from a dent in one wing it appeared to be undamaged. The same could not be said for a fence nearby which was leaning at a rather peculiar angle.

'You'll need a truck to pull you out of that,' observed the woman.

'Don't worry. Thanks a lot,' said Mel. 'Please don't wait. I'm OK. Not far from home.' Then she peered inside the car to see if she could find the vodka but it had disappeared. She staggered around to the back, remembering she'd also bought some whisky in Sainsbury's. A quick nip would restore her equilibrium.

She scrabbled around in her shopping bags, hoping that neither of the bottles was broken. Fortunately there they were, safe between the kitchen rolls and the lavatory paper. She was just unscrewing the neck of the Johnny Walker when a hand landed on her shoulder.

'You're harming your poor body,' said the woman. 'You don't need that.'

'Oh yes I bloody well do,' said Mel.

The woman held out her hand. 'Give those bottles to me.'

Mel was astounded. 'Sorry, did I miss something somewhere? Exactly who are you and why in the name of God are you taking it upon yourself to tell me what to do?' Good on you, Mel, she told herself.

'You're Melanie. Right?'

'Yes, but...'

'I'm Ruth and I'm your friend.'

'The hell you are. Never seen you before in my whole life.'

'I'm also a friend of Donna's. I was just on my way to see you – she sent me.'

'Did she now? Old Donna. How's she doing?' Mel remembered her as being the only bearable inmate at the clinic all those months ago. A frail-looking girl, youngish, a good dry sense of humour. They'd agreed to keep in touch but Donna stopped ringing a while ago.

'She's in much better shape than you are,' said Ruth, still holding out her hand for the bottles.

Sanctimonious bitch, thought Mel. 'Ruth,' she said, with heavy sarcasm, 'it was *so* kind of you to help but mind your own damn business, *please.*'

'Give me those bottles or I'll call the police and have you arrested for drunk driving.'

Mel stared at her. Then she slumped back against the car. 'OK, take them.'

'Now I'll drive you home,' said Ruth.

Befuddled, Mel followed her to an old Ford estate car parked off the road a little way back.

Ruth drove competently, following Mel's directions. She was a middle-aged woman, dark-hair, dark-skinned, handsome rather than pretty. Mel couldn't be bothered to ask what she thought she was doing following her around the country.

Back home, Ruth decided they should call the local farmer and have him deal with the car. He'd know whose fence had been damaged so Mel could offer to pay. 'That way we don't have to bother with insurance companies,' she said.

'How come you know so much about farmers and stuff?' asked Mel wearily. 'And how d'you know Donna?'

'I live in the country, in Wales,' said Ruth.

'An American in Wales. OK, I'll buy it. So what are you doing here?'

'I'm from Hywyl Farm, a community of recovered alcoholics, and I've come to find new members to join. We need people and people need us, people like you. Donna said you're a teacher. We need someone to teach our kids. So you're, like, destined for us. It's all quite simple. Part of a larger plan, as we see it.'

'Sorry, Ruth, thank you and all that, but weirdo communities are not my scene.'

'Let me guess. You've been an alcoholic for several years and, you know, alcoholism is not a disease that you can conquer on your own. You need help, just like with any other sickness –'

'Spare me the sermon. I've heard 'em all. Anyway, I'm not into all that stuff. Far better to drink than to have to listen to bloody shrinks boring the pants off you all day long.'

'I am not about to argue, Melanie. I used to be a drinker, just like you. We try conventional treatments. They don't work. So the community is your last chance.'

Mel stared at her. Apart from being American, she looked more or less normal. Her clothes were conventional middle-class gear, no hippie beads or anything. Without her coat though, she was a rather odd shape, tiny thin legs and a big chest sticking out of her grey sweater. As she stalked around the kitchen, peering at everything with her round black eyes, she reminded Mel of a determined pigeon.

'I need a drink.'

'You don't. Go pack a suitcase. You are going to leave a note for your husband to have him pay the farmer for dealing with the car. Write that you've joined the new treatment programme.'

'Ruth, watch my lips. I'm not going anywhere.'

Ruth picked up her mobile. 'OK, I'll call the police. Like I said, you're way over the limit. They're bound to prosecute.'

Mel shook her head slowly. This woman was nuts. 'You're threatening me. In fact, you're kidnapping me.'

Ruth smiled. 'Yes, dear.'

Dear? Yuck, thought Mel. Then she thought of a way out. 'I need to call my husband. He wouldn't want me to go away.'

'Jack knows about my visit. He knows you need help.'

The ground fell away from her feet. Mel clutched the back of the chair. 'He knows? He set me up?' The scheming bastard.

'Yes. This is what we call an Intervention. He planned to meet us both here later on. He didn't foresee the car crash though. Maybe you'd prefer to leave before he finds out about it. Lucky I was early, don't ya think?'

Mel sighed again and walked unsteadily to the window. It was still raining. Then she turned and said, 'I suppose the weather can't be any worse in Wales. So what, apart from wellies, will I bring with me for this little holiday? I guess it'll be extortionately expensive. Like all these places.'

'Oh the community doesn't use money. It's free – if you work.'

'But I haven't taught in years.'

'The other teacher will help you. As for what to pack, jeans, sweaters, simple country clothes are all that's necessary. Residents are not permitted cash, credit cards or mobiles, and use of the communal telephone is restricted. You'll be surprised how cheap life is when you don't drink.'

Lord save us, thought Mel, it'll be self-sufficiency and vegetarians and free love. The latter thought cheered her faintly.

But then what if it was all lesbians or something? Not that she had anything against consenting adults and all that, but... 'I suppose you're not a nunnery?' she asked aloud.

'Oh no,' said Ruth with a smile. 'The community believes in equal opportunities for everyone, even men.'

'Then what have I got to lose?' said Mel meekly.

As she packed her suitcase under Ruth's watchful eye, she managed to hide some cash in her walking boots. There must be pubs, she thought, even in Wales.

## CHAPTER 25

*D*EAR *MELANIE*, WROTE LAURA AGAIN. Of course she was writing to Jack too. *You didn't reply to the letter I wrote last summer and Jack said nothing in his Christmas card. Not that I wrote any Christmas letters myself this year, so here goes. How are you? How's life? As for France, all going well here.*

Is it? she wondered.

*The seasons have passed in the correct Parisian manner – the mass migration to the coast for the summer holidays, the Rentrée when the citizens return at the beginning of autumn (all on virtually the same day, so causing an immense traffic jam), then Christmas parties and the New Year.*

She paused, reflecting on the last few months. It was now February which meant that they'd been married nearly a year. Oliver was talking about a first anniversary party, but she'd managed to push him off the idea, saying she'd rather go out to dinner *à deux*. She didn't see him much alone these days – he was so busy.

She couldn't write *Dear Mel, My new husband is alternately cold and mean, or jealous and possessive. And so arrogant, all those people who kowtow to him, all this 'Good morning, your Excellency' goes to his head. Perhaps it's reminiscent of his time in the army, he's used to ordering people around. As you foresaw, I have to remind him I am no longer his employee.*

*But he has his moments. We still have sex – is once a week enough for newly married people of our age? – but even then it sometimes seems he's trying to avoid touching me with his hands, as far as possible. He certainly never hugs me on non-sexual occasions. And he flinches if I try to touch his face. To be absolutely truthful, there are some weeks when we have no physical contact at all if there's been some kind of a row. His is a chilly sort of passion.*

No she couldn't write any of that, of course. Because maybe her own passion was lukewarm too.

The periodic lack of physical closeness in her marriage made her all the more aware of deeper cracks in their relationship, cracks of which Oliver seemed oblivious. He was engrossed in his work, his sport, the formal socialising, and Laura played the old-fashioned supporting wife who sat on the edge arranging things. As she'd known in advance that he was a traditional retro man, she felt she had nothing to complain of. It's not as if he beat her physically, and she was strong enough to combat any verbal bullying that came her way.

She was afraid of turning into one of those women who keeps a list of grievances against her man, wounds stripped bare and raw, examined every day so they no longer heal.

But it was hard to make allowances for him when he treated her like an army recruit who needed toughening up. For instance, she still brooded about his behaviour when she was ill in the autumn. She'd had a bad cough for some weeks and finally forced herself to make an appointment with the doctor. That day she was feverish and light-headed, hardly able to speak. With barely concealed impatience, Oliver had delivered her to the surgery in the car – the chauffeur was away.

'You'll have to take a taxi back,' said Oliver, dropping her near the door. 'I'll never find a parking space around here.' She felt too weak and ill to protest.

At the surgery, the doctor listened to her chest and then insisted she have an X-ray immediately. This involved a long walk through the streets to the laboratory, an ordeal she could hardly remember. Finally she made it home and collapsed into bed with the medicine she had been prescribed, six packets of no doubt over-strong pills and linctuses for scary-sounding chest infections like chronic emphysema and pulmonary embolism.

Later the doctor rang up with the results of the X-ray. Unfortunately he spoke to Oliver rather than directly to her, and told him that there was absolutely nothing to worry about, a well-meaning reassurance which Oliver took to imply that she had been making an unnecessary fuss.

'Even the French say there's nothing the matter with you. Why on earth are you still coughing?' was his attitude. He didn't actually say that what he needed was a healthy wife to run his household but it was obvious that that was what he felt.

Laura soon recovered, but the incident seemed to her to illustrate that she was only acceptable as a wife if she was fit, looked good and performed her proper duties in a proper manner.

His possessiveness was still a problem too. He opened her mail now and then 'by accident', sometimes blaming his secretary. But he had allegedly accepted that her visits to Simon were completely innocent. All the same, she'd finally given up the computer course. It wasn't worth the sulks. Marriage is about compromise, she told herself yet again. Be positive. The warmer, happier periods should grow longer for them both once he felt more secure – he needed to feel that she was a woman who could be trusted. She had to make allowances for the wounds left by the infidelities of his first wife.

Allowances had been made in all directions and things were improving. Recently he had been kinder, more solicitous. He'd even given her a credit card which was an amazingly generous gesture for a man like Oliver, a big trusting confident step forward. And she had been touched when he bought her a bunch of exotic orchids that she'd admired in the florists.

Whenever she felt angry with him, she reminded herself about the orchids.

He was playing tennis on the indoor courts in St. Cloud – two evenings a week – which no doubt made him feel better, fitter. It'd be nice if he invited her to play occasionally, but then she wasn't much good at tennis. In fact, it now seemed they didn't have much in common, apart from Charlotte.

Charlotte was a great consolation. Laura was looking forward to her arrival at half term. Her presence made them seem like a family. Laura loved her almost as much as she loved Alice and in return Charlotte was an affectionate child in her own self-contained way. Not a child any more, Laura reminded herself. Ever since last summer Charlotte had suddenly changed and grown up. She was now a beautiful young woman – shy and coltish still, but sometimes she glowed with a youthful sexuality that was almost disturbing. Not that she was overtly seductive like Alice, it was more that there was a new light in those demure brown eyes. Laura saw no sign of a special boyfriend in Paris or anywhere else, but, if one existed, she and Oliver would undoubtedly be the last to know.

Laura had suggested she bring a schoolfriend or two to keep her company at half term but Charlotte said she wanted peace to work on her A-level revisions. If she needed a break she'd go and see Sophie. Laura had never met this French girl, Sophie Simone, but she lived somewhere over on the other side of Paris and Charlotte often spent time with her during the holidays. As Oliver said, it was good for her to practise her French.

'Why, Laura, hi! Great to see you!'
'Hello, Kiki.'

She was enveloped in politically-incorrect fur, a mink coat and a mink hat. Her sharp eyes peered out in a manner reminiscent of a pretty little rodent. Laura wasn't sure how they had become 'buddies' but Kiki kept inviting her to lunch 'to apologise for that little ol' mix-up' and finally, in desperation, Laura had accepted. They'd got on surprisingly well. Though totally self-centred, Kiki had a wicked sense of humour – a refreshing change from the heavy conversation of international functionaries and their clever, serious wives.

'Cold, isn't it? Let's have a coffee at La Ronde, all nice and quiet,' said Kiki. Typical environment for her to have chosen, thought Laura. Staffed by the most supercilious waiters in Paris, La Ronde was an expensive café-restaurant where the drinks cost twice as much as anywhere else.

'So how've you been?' asked Kiki, having told Laura every detail of her winter sun holiday with Zak.

'Oh, all right,' said Laura.

'And how's *Simon*?' asked Kiki archly.

'I'm sure you must've seen him more recently than I have. I gave up the computer course. Apart from anything else, he kept forgetting to be there.'

All raised eyebrows and pursed mouth, Kiki scrutinised her face. 'Really? That's interesting.'

'How d'you mean?'

'Well, like sometimes I call Simon and say I'm coming around to see him and he's, like, too busy, says he's all tied up with your computer lessons.'

'Oh.' Laura couldn't think of anything to say.

'Now just what is that boy up to?' asked Kiki meditatively. 'I even began to think maybe it wasn't so innocent between you and him after all.'

Laura shot a glance around the café – still quiet and empty luckily. 'Don't be ridiculous, Kiki. Of course it is. Simon's crazy about you. He was always telling me how much he loves you.'

Kiki shook her red curls. 'Sorry, there I go again. But you know when a man gets kind of less enthusiastic about sex you start to get suspicious.'

'Mm, perhaps... So what d'you do when that happens, Kiki?'

'Well, the French say one needs more ammunition – new sexy underwear, sexy night gear. Paris is full of it. Artillery of the night, I think they call it... Or there's a more direct American method.'

'What's that?'

'Kick him in the balls and then go claw her eyes out.'


Scarlet-faced, Kiki sat in the sauna, enjoying for the moment the familiar baked-resin smell and the penetrating heat. The sweat was running down between her breasts which were modestly covered by her black swimsuit, unlike those of the two Frenchwomen who had just come in.

'*Bone-jewurr*,' said Kiki who vaguely recognised the older one as being a member of the health club.

'*Bonjour, madame,*' they echoed and then ignored her completely.

The club was nearly empty today so why in the heck did these women have to be in the sauna the same time as she did? And why did they have to roll down their swimsuit tops? Kiki heard that in Scandinavia and Germany everyone took saunas completely nude which would be even more gross. She hated the idea of stripping in front of other women.

The French didn't seem to mind *where* they stripped. In the doctor's surgery they never offered you a gown. Even if your only problem was a sore toe, you were supposed to sit around stark naked with the door wide open while nurses and doctors wandered in and out.

She peeped covertly at the Frenchwomen's breasts. Both were small, tending towards flat, but with relatively large dark nipples, unlike her own pink rosebuds, as corny old Zak used to call them way back in the days when he noticed that kind of thing.

Kiki smiled to herself. The women were still acting like she didn't exist. One of them muttered scornfully to the other *'une Americaine.'* The other said yes, the *Americaine* was always at the club and didn't speak a word of French. Kiki smiled to herself again. She didn't speak French much because people always laughed at her pronunciation, but these same people often underestimated her real good understanding of the language.

After another peek, Kiki decided the women were sisters. Both were thirty-something, dark and attractive – in as much as anyone can look good covered in sweat with a towel around her head. The younger one with a pointy face was especially pretty. The older sister was asking about the lovebite that had been exposed and Mademoiselle Pointy Face raised her eyes to heaven as if to say 'don't ask'. Then Pointy Face was talking about having a few days off while her office was being decorated – a far less interesting topic of conversation, thought Kiki, who asked in English if they minded her putting some water on the coals. With a shrug, they agreed, but then the hiss of heat was so intense that Kiki couldn't stick the place a moment longer. After a shower, she took another dip in the pool. She stared at herself in a passing mirror and thought she might have gained a pound. Better not cut that exercise class later on then.

After another tiring session in the sauna, this time alone, she went to the relaxation area which consisted of a row of nine or ten daybeds. Kiki put her towel down on one near the window and lay back, closing her eyes.

Hearing voices, she opened them slightly. The French sisters again, sauntering in wrapped in the regulation thick white towelling robes. Ignoring her again, they lay down on adjoining beds at the other end of the room.

They were in the middle of a murmured conversation. 'So having surprised Fabien during a cinq-à-sept, I am thinking of revenge,' said the older one. 'I shall take a lover myself, perhaps an Englishman this time.'

Kiki hid a smile. She was familiar with the term *cinq-à-sept*, the two hours a Frenchman set aside for dalliance between leaving the office and arriving home to spend the evening with his family.

Pointy-face was asking, 'Why an Englishman?'

'I believe they are more faithful, more reliable than our compatriots. And I'm told they are less exacting about one's appearance. It would not be a catastrophe for an Englishman if the lace on one's bra did not match one's *slip*.'

Pointy-face gave another tinkling laugh. 'You may be right about that, but I'm afraid they're just as unfaithful as men of any other nationality. For instance, on the eve of Oliver's wedding, he and I...'

'Really? The diplomat?'

'Ssh! Be a little discreet.'

'I told you, the *Americaine* doesn't speak a word of French – anyway she's asleep.'

Kiki thought of giving a delicate snore but then decided that would be way over the top.

The older one asked, 'I forgot, whom did Olivier marry?'

'The housekeeper. *Mon Dieu*, I told you a hundred times.'

'Ah yes. How extraordinary! But, I meant to ask you before, why did you not marry him yourself? He sounded quite suitable, even by Maman's rigorous standards.'

'I thought of doing so, but finally the idea of a foreigner did not attract me.' She sighed. 'Besides, the behaviour of husbands is not encouraging. Yours is a serial adulterer and our dear Papa is worse.'

'You are too cynical, little sister. As I am, perhaps. I fear Papa's treatment of Maman has blighted your approach to men.'

'For God's sake, spare me the psychoanalysis. And as regards the opposite sex, forewarned is forearmed, as the English say. But, seriously, dear Oliver is not really the type one should marry. He is inclined to be domineering. Really, one has far better control over a man if he remains a lover rather than a husband.'

The older one drew in her breath. 'So, despite the new wife, you are still lovers?'

'Ssh, you are asking too many questions.'

'Agnès...'

They lowered their voices still further but Kiki had heard enough. Was this fascinating, or what!


'So you see, Laura, I thought I should tell you,' said Kiki sanctimoniously.

Shivering uncontrollably, Laura had sunk into a chilly void. Then she found her voice which came out in a kind of croak. 'There are lots of diplomats here, every country in the world has an embassy and then there are all the international organisations. Maybe it was somebody else.'

'Somebody else called *Oliver*?'

'Olivier is quite a common French name.'

'Maybe, maybe not. But, like, how many diplomats by the name of Oliver, *or* Olivier, have just married their housekeeper? And she was talking about an Englishman. It seems like one hell of a coincidence.'

'So you said twice already,' snapped Laura.

'Don't get all aggressive with me, Laura. It's not me you should be angry with. I'm doing you a favour. I didn't have to come here, but I like you and, in my opinion, a woman has a right to know.'

I wonder if poor old Zak knows what she gets up to, hypocritical cow, thought Laura savagely. But Kiki was right. One shouldn't shoot the messenger. With an effort she said, 'Sorry. So what did they look like, these women?'

'No one looks great in the sauna, but they were attractive in that scrawny French way. Flat-chested though. You wouldn't believe it.'

Laura was still shivering. 'What about her face, the one who... Was she pretty? Mid-thirties, short dark hair, dark eyes?'

'Yes, guess so. Couldn't see much of the hair because she had a turban on her head. But, yeah, her face was pretty, sort of pointy.'

Laura let out a long trembling sigh and sank down into the nearest chair.

Kiki said, 'That would describe a million Frenchwomen but I heard her first name. I even wrote it down somewhere... Oh, I remember, in my little Prada notebook.' She scrabbled in her handbag. 'Darn it. I left it at home. Let me try and think. It was a designer name.'

'What d'you mean?'

Kiki shook her head. 'Same as one of the dress designers, you know.'

'Was it Agnès, by any chance?' whispered Laura.

\* \* \*

In a daze Laura walked home. Could she really believe Kiki, Kiki of all people, not the most sensible, reliable person in the world? Trouble was, now it all fell into place – Oliver's unexplained absences, his cool-hearted lovemaking, his spasmodic guilty attention to her. The credit card, the orchids. Flowers! How classic, how corny! And Agnès – though she always looked smug and pitying, maybe recently there'd been an extra triumphant gleam in her bright little eyes.

Waves of hot resentment washed over Laura. Back at home she paced around, hardly aware of what she was doing. She wanted revenge, she wanted to... When he got back from the office she would... would what? Kick him in the balls, like Kiki said? Not that, Laura couldn't bear screaming matches, nor would she cut up ties or slash his suits, or dish out his wine to the neighbourhood, though the idea was tempting.

It came to her that what she really wanted to do was leave. As quickly as possible.

At seven-thirty he had still not returned and then she remembered he was going straight from the office to the tennis court. On an impulse, she telephoned the wife of one of the other regular players. Somehow she wasn't surprised when the woman said that, didn't she know, the game had been cancelled this evening.

That does it, thought Laura, blind with anger. She grabbed a sheet of the official crested paper and wrote shakily: *I gather you are still seeing Agnès. Our marriage was a mistake anyway. Will organise tidy divorce. L.*

Full of trepidation about the enormity of what she was doing, she put the note in an official envelope, sealed it and placed it on Oliver's desk. Then she snatched it up again when she heard the floorboards creak behind her.

Heart in mouth, she spun around to find Sebastien standing in the doorway. *'Bonsoir, madame,'* he said.

'Oh, er, Sebastien.' She held the letter tight. Then she stuttered, 'Did the Ambassador leave any message as to where he was this evening?'

'No, madame,' he said impassively. 'Madame, excuse me, I have a request ask you. May I tomorrow purchase a new clothes brush, that is to say, a roller brush for cleaning clothes?'

Laura's head reeled. 'Roller brush?'

'Two of Monsieur's suits are covered in white dog's hairs which are very difficult to remove with the normal brush.'

Dog's hairs? What was he talking about? Then, flushing angrily, she realised whose bloody dog it must be.

Flinging the letter down on the desk again, she snapped, 'Call me a taxi, Sebastien. In half an hour.'

He frowned. 'Yes, madame. About the clothes brush...'

But Laura had already left the room. In a hurried rush before she changed her mind, she scrawled another note for Charlotte who was due to arrive tomorrow. *I am very, very sorry but I've had to leave your father. He will explain. I hope you can understand. Please come and see me – absolutely any time you want. All love, Laura.*

Hastily she flung some clothes into a suitcase and asked Sebastien to take them down to the taxi. His face was stern with disapproval, presumably because she hadn't told him in advance that she would not be in for dinner. 'What shall I say to His Excellency, madame?' was his parting and unanswered query.

On the way to the station to catch the last Eurostar of the evening, thoughts of practical matters darted into Laura's panic-stricken mind for the first time. Fortunately Bridget was skiing this half term so she wouldn't be using the cottage, but would there be a late train from London to Winchester? Then would there be taxis at Winchester in the middle of the night? She *could* stay in Oliver's London flat, but it wasn't ideal, psychologically, to remain on his territory. Then she had an inspired idea. Stay one night at the Ritz or the Savoy, have a hugely expensive late dinner from room service, and put it all on Oliver's Master Card. For the first time since Kiki's revelations, Laura smiled momentarily.

The taxi stopped at a set of traffic lights and then progressed slowly along the brightly lit Paris streets. Digging her fingernails into her hands, she waited anxiously for the left turn that led up to the Gare du Nord.

Even in the Eurostar departure lounge, she was still afraid that Oliver might come racing after her and it wasn't until the train smoothed its way out of the station that she began to feel better. In fact she felt so much better that it suddenly occurred to her that she had been waiting for an excuse to leave Oliver.

But later as she sat back in her seat gulping a celebratory glass of wine, she began to question the wisdom of her wild impulsive decision to leave so rashly and so suddenly. In particular she was assailed by heavy waves of guilt about Charlotte. Yet again the poor girl had been abandoned.

She was in a terrible state, almost incoherent, thought Simon holding Charlotte tight in his arms. She'd suddenly appeared on his doorstep in floods of tears.

He'd forgotten that she'd be back for half-term. Didn't admit that to her, of course. He hadn't meant this affair to last as long as this – over six months now – but he couldn't bear to hurt her. Every time they met, he'd been meaning to say it was over but she seemed so desperately vulnerable. Even more so this evening, with this extraordinary news about Laura doing a bunk.

'So what did your father say? Why has she gone?'

'He won't say a word.'

'But he must have told you something.'

'All he said was she'd be back sooner or later, but I don't believe him – see this note she wrote me.'

He read it through. 'So if you can't get anything out of him, why don't you ring her?'

She looked at him through her tears. 'D'you think that would be a good idea?' A while later, she asked, 'Could you ring her for me?'

'No, I really couldn't. It's to do with your family, not me.'

'He always screws everything up for me, Dad. Always.' She began to cry again.

He took her in his arms and whispered into her soft dark hair. 'Poor poor Charlotte.'

They remained on the sofa. Then like an automaton she began to take off her shirt. Always surprised by the creaminess of her skin, he touched her shoulders and then ran his hands down the length of her delicate body to her astonishingly small waist, so young, so soft.

She put out her hand and led him to the bedroom. As she began to remove the rest of her clothes, he rifled through his bedside drawer. 'Charlotte, sorry, I wasn't expecting you, not organised this evening. I've run out of condoms as usual. Better go and get some.'

'Don't leave me. I need you,' she begged. So he kissed her again and again until her tears dried up. 'Anyway,' she whispered, 'it's a safe time of the month, it'll be OK.'

She was almost luminous, darkness and light. No sane man could possibly resist her, he told himself as he pushed her back on to the bed. It was better than ever this time. She was so passionate, so responsive, that he almost lost control, but, to be absolutely sure, he withdrew at the crucial moment, spilling himself on to her smooth flat stomach.

She smiled up at him, 'I love you, Simon.'

'It's mutual,' he said. At the time, he meant it.

## CHAPTER 26

AFTER A FEW EERILY QUIET DAYS AT HOME without receiving a single phone call from either Oliver or Charlotte, Laura rang Bridget.

'What d'you mean, you don't want to let your house any more?' asked Bridget indignantly.

Laura's hand shook as she clutched the telephone. 'The thing is, I've left Oliver. Actually I'm in England now already. I'm just warning you about the holidays. Sorry, but you won't be able to use the cottage.'

'Oh,' said Bridget. 'The boys will be very disappointed. I'd planned a party with an Easter egg hunt in the garden.'

The children's feelings were clearly the only thing that mattered. There was a long disapproving silence and then she said, 'Why, what has he done? For goodness sake, aren't you a bit old for this kind of melodramatic behaviour?'

'Sorry, can't talk about it. Just thought I'd better let you know. Goodbye,' said Laura sharply and put down the phone. Damn. She was on the edge of tears. She'd intended to be all cool and calm, but the slightest hint of criticism, the slightest opposition, any kind of problem, pushed her to the edge of self-control. Yesterday the car wouldn't start and that seemed like the end of the world. She hadn't called Jack this time though. She hadn't called him at all. She wanted to, of course, but she knew it would be yet another mistake.

She sat down with a large glass of red wine, her second or was it the third? Alcohol won't solve any problems, she told herself as she corked the bottle. It didn't solve any for Melanie.

At least Mel wouldn't disapprove of her. The great thing about Mel was that she didn't disapprove of anything. Laura decided to ring her next day when Jack was sure to be at work.

She got the answerphone as usual. 'Please leave a message,' said Jack's endearingly familiar voice 'or try Mel on...' Puzzled, Laura scrabbled to write down the number with an area code she didn't recognise.

She called it. To her surprise an American voice answered, 'You've reached Hywyl Farm. Please leave your name and number. We'll get back to you right away.'

Reluctant to talk to a machine, Laura tried three times, once in the afternoon, once in the evening and finally about nine in the morning when surely Mel would be in. Still the answerphone replied. So eventually she left a message asking Mel to ring her at the cottage.

It was not Mel who called the next day but the same American woman who gave her name as Ruth, no surname. 'Members of the community don't use the telephone too much,' she pronounced, 'but Melanie is whole and well and sends you her greetings.'

'I don't understand...'

'Peace and happiness to you, Laura,' said Ruth and rang off.

The days passed and there was still no word from Oliver. It was a very peculiar situation. She'd thought he would run after her, apologise on bended knee, and beg her to come back to Paris and start afresh. And, because she had to, she would steel herself to refuse, explaining it was all over. She rehearsed what she would say again and again – she had made a mistake, they should never have married.

But then she began to realise that apologies were not his style. He was all pride and stiff upper lip. He had probably told people she'd gone to England because of some family crisis or other. She imagined him stoically carrying on his life as if nothing had happened. He might not even tell Agnès about her departure. They would both sit there over dinner discussing the menu and current affairs in their oh-so-civilised way. Then later Oliver would take her to bed. Maybe he'd be more passionate than usual, but Agnès wouldn't know why.

Or maybe he loved Agnès all along and was only too glad to have the coast clear.

Laura shook her head fiercely. She was driving herself crazy imagining all these scenarios. She'd been sleeping badly, tossing and turning half the night, going over and over in her mind what had happened and what she'd done, and the consequences of it all. Sometimes when she was watching solitary television in the evening she managed to relax for half an hour but mostly she rushed around in a flurry of constant nervous activity. Her house was very clean anyway, she thought grimly, and she'd already lost weight. So it wasn't all bad news and, despite all her negative emotions, she still felt a sense of relief. Though it would be frowned upon by the world in general, leaving Oliver seemed right.

The only person who seemed wholeheartedly to approve of her actions was Alice. 'No way, Mum!' she said on the phone. 'You left him! How cool! You did the right thing. Oliver, well, he gave me really bad vibes. Sorry and all that.'

'But you hardly knew him.'

'Yeah, but, well, he just wasn't, you know... well, he was just so uptight and kind of, like, turgid.'

She wasn't prepared to say much more but Laura was comforted by these words of support.

Bridget rang again. 'I've spoken to Oliver but he won't say a word. More or less told me to keep out of it. But I feel one must do something. It's so sad for you both.'

Laura groaned inwardly. 'Um... kind of you to want to help, but, as he says, it's our affair, not anyone else's.'

'Well, I hope I'm not talking out of turn, but perhaps you should go back and try and solve your problems. Oliver is a good man underneath it all, believe me. Just think of poor Charlotte and...'

'Bridget, thanks. We'll talk another day. But not about Oliver, OK?'

Laura put down the phone quickly. Trouble is, she was only too aware of the terrible effect all this would have on poor Charlotte.

She wrote to her at school inviting her to come to lunch any Sunday, but there was no reply. Then Laura telephoned Miss Hardy, the housemistress, to leave a message. Still no word from Charlotte. Finally she called the housemistress yet again and, with some hesitation, explained the situation more fully.

The woman later rang back to say that Charlotte was not ready to see her. She did not advise that Laura should turn up at the school unannounced because it was important to give Charlotte a chance to come to terms with things in her own way.

'But how is she?' asked Laura anxiously.

'Very subdued,' said Miss Hardy. 'I'm afraid it's been a great shock to her.'

Miss Hardy had no doubt been trained in dealing tactfully with separated parents and was clearly trying hard not to sound disapproving. She hadn't succeeded though.

\* \* \*

One cold, wet and windy March evening Jack arrived, as day after day she'd been hoping he would – even though she had no right at all to think of him.

After he had wiped his feet and taken off his soaking wet jacket, they stood looking at each other. Then, despite all her resolutions to the contrary, she flung herself into his safe arms and buried her face in his neck. His skin was all cold and damp from the rain but he smelt good – wool, aftershave and fresh air.

Holding her tight, he repeated her name gently, 'Laura, Laura.'

She managed, just, to avoid bursting into tears. They remained without speaking for a while and then she disentangled herself.

'How about a drink – would wine be OK? It's all I have,' she said all in the same breath. 'How did you know I was back?'

'Mel told me about your message.'

'Yes, where on earth *is* Mel?'

'A long story. Tell me yours first. Laura, what are you doing here?'

She took a deep breath. 'I've left Oliver.'

'I see.'

She couldn't tell from his face what he thought.

'Why? he asked eventually.

'Another long story. I've been stupid. I mean it was a big mistake but I can't talk about it, not yet.'

Jack got up and disappeared into the kitchen. After a few minutes he came back with a bottle of wine and two glasses.

Laura sighed. 'Oh sorry. Typical of my current state, I offered you a drink and then forgot to pour it. Keep forgetting everything at the moment.'

They went to sit by the open fire. All relaxed, he settled back in the sofa. Attempting to keep an appropriate, not too intimate distance, she chose the old armchair opposite.

'So tell me about Mel,' she said. Easier than talking herself, she thought.

Staring into the flames, he explained that Mel had gone to stay on a farm in Wales where it was difficult to communicate with her but as far as he could tell she was happy, happier than she'd been for some time. A few months after her stay in the clinic, she'd gradually started to drink again until things were as bad as before. Worse, in fact. He'd talked to someone called Donna, a friend of hers, who advised him to arrange a meeting, a deliberate confrontation – they call it an Intervention – with an American counsellor, an alcohol expert. He wasn't sure what happened but when he got home that afternoon he found a note saying that the car was in a ditch, and that Mel had joined a bunch of what she called non-drinking weirdos in darkest Wales.

'A bunch of weirdos? Does she mean a commune? Hope they're not some fearful cult,' said Laura.

'No, apparently not. They're a new organisation, though, not much known about them.'

He said he'd gone to visit her to make sure she was safe. He'd been worried about the idea of the community, but there was no sign of New Age hippies or yellow-robed fake Buddhists. Just an assorted bunch of earnest, well-scrubbed, ordinary-looking people in jeans. Mel was sober, which was a good start. She wasn't ready to come home yet, she said, but would let him know when the time came. Meanwhile would he mind staying away? She was teaching in the school, which she enjoyed. All the same, he thought she was quieter, less lively. Then again, doctors at the other clinic said recovering alcoholics can sometimes remain depressed and unstable for quite a while.

'Well, just so long as it works in the end,' she said, sifting through her own mixed emotions.

'Nothing seemed to work for long though, not in the past. So I'm not that optimistic.'

After a while Laura said, 'It must have been awful, for Mel and for you, I mean, the last few years.'

'Yes... not much fun watching someone destroy themselves. At times it was hard to think about anything else except what was happening at home. At one stage I got totally obsessed with trying to prevent her from drinking. Idiotic really. I tried to impose my own willpower on to her. Unsuccessfully, of course.'

She watched his face. He still loves her in spite of everything, she thought sadly.

There was another silence. Then he asked again if she wanted to talk about Oliver. Not yet, she replied. He offered to take her out to dinner and she said it was a vile night outside and she wasn't really in the mood and how about if she cooked them both spaghetti carbonara which was about all she could rustle up.

Bringing the wine with him, Jack came to talk to her in the kitchen. He didn't get in the way or interfere like Oliver would. He just sat there smiling and comfortable, telling her the gossip in the village and beyond, not too far beyond, just as if they were two normal people. She supposed he was trying to cheer her up.

During their frugal supper, he was so kind and sympathetic that eventually she began to talk about her marriage. Not to moan about Oliver, just to repeat that she'd made a mistake, she didn't fit in with his life, they didn't have much in common, better to end it swiftly before too much harm was done. This was how she'd planned to explain the situation to the world in general, so she might as well rehearse her statement. She began all right, fairly calmly, but then her eyes began to water and her voice grew higher and higher. 'You see,' she said finally, 'the awful thing was, I began to realise I was much, much happier when Oliver wasn't there.'

He put his hand on her arm. Then after a while he asked, 'Is that the whole story? Or was there something else? Or someone else?'

Without meaning to, she found herself pouring out more and more. In an emotional garbled rush, she told him all about Agnès.

He shook his head. 'These things happen sometimes. She may have led him astray temporarily. We men are weak creatures, easily tempted. It probably isn't serious.'

She dug her nails into her hands. 'As far as I'm concerned, it's pretty damn serious when a man sleeps with another woman during the first year of his marriage, the night before his wedding even... But anyway it just wasn't going well. I can't... I can't explain without whingeing... Oh I don't know, it's just a mess.'

Jack shook his head and said nothing.

'Are you sticking up for him?' she said sharply.

'No. I'm on your side, of course I am. Fact is, I've always thought Farringdon sounded like a first-class prick.'

She laughed momentarily in sudden relief.

'So what are you going to do?'

'Well, arrange a quickie divorce... I don't think he'll mind.'

'I bet he *will* mind.'

She remained silent, then she said, 'It looks bad, giving up so soon on a marriage, doesn't it?'

'Oh for God's sake, you should never worry about how things look. All your close friends know that you don't normally give up. You've never been a deserter, quite the opposite. But whatever you decide to do, I'll stick by you. It's not as if you're the only woman in the world who's left her husband.'

'I know.' She took a gulp of wine. 'You haven't actually said "I told you so", but you were right. I shouldn't have married in a rush. I should have just lived with him for a while.'

'You weren't to know he'd turn out to be a shit.'

'No... but,' her voice trailed away. After a pause she asked suddenly, 'Were you ever unfaithful to Mel?'

He sighed ruefully. 'Yes, sometimes, not often. When things got bad. I suppose it was a form of release. Not that that's any justification. But it didn't mean anything to me or to the few women involved.'

'How do you *know* it didn't mean anything to them?'

'Well, I just chose the kind of woman who was looking for occasional recreational sex rather than love.'

'Not that terrible Bella person?'

He smiled. 'Not her. Have to draw the line somewhere.' He shook his head and suddenly said slowly, 'Once though, a long time ago, there was someone who mattered and I broke it off after a few months because of Mel. I'd been bloody stupid and she was hurt, very hurt, the woman. I swore then I'd never get involved in any kind of serious affair again.'

'Did Mel know?'

'No, I'm pretty sure not. But her drinking got worse around then, and I began to wonder if it was because she'd found out. She never said anything though. Not a very edifying story, sorry. It's difficult for someone like you to understand.'

'Look, I do understand. I'm not in a position to make moral judgements on other people. Anyway, how d'you mean, someone like me?'

'Well, an honourable person.'

'A prig?'

He smiled tenderly. 'Not a prig. As I said, a good, decent person.'

She groaned. 'You've got me all wrong. And if I'm so virtuous, why is my life such a mess?'

He stretched his hand forward to touch her arm. 'Nothing is ever particularly fair.'

'I know, sorry. For a start, you've got far worse problems than I have.' In an attempt to pull herself together, she pushed back her chair and began to clear the table.

After dinner they sat side by side on the sofa. They were talking of mundane matters now – Jack's business and how it was going. Laura couldn't help wishing yet again that he was not the husband of one of her friends because tonight she would very much like to be taken to bed. She felt a need to do something wild and not at all honourable and virtuous. Recreational sex, was that what he called it?

Suddenly he took her hand. 'Did you hear what I just said?'

She flushed. 'No, sorry. My mind wandered for a moment.'

'I said what are you going to do about money. Can I lend you some?'

'No, no,' she said hastily.

Then she told him about her job interview tomorrow, with the local estate agents. She probably wouldn't get it but they were looking for someone to show houses part-time, better than nothing. She was back at square one really, but she was determined to get a job of some sort, however lowly. At least she'd had recent work experience, though she couldn't exactly ask for a reference from Oliver. She smiled to show that this remark was a kind of joke.

He looked at her thoughtfully. 'So you really have left him?'

'Oh yes,' she said.

'Good.'

They looked at each other for a long while and then Laura, needing to break the tension, got up from the sofa to put another log on the fire. She remained beside it kneeling on the floor, her back turned towards him. Suddenly she felt his hand caress the back of her neck. It was a quick gentle touch but intensely intimate, intensely arousing. She didn't turn towards him.

'I should go,' he said.

'I know.'

They both stood up and Laura went fussing out into the hall to look for his coat. Mutely she handed it to him and with the other hand opened the front door. A blast of cold air blew in. The weather had deteriorated still further and the rain lashed their faces. She shut it again quickly.

'Awful night. Why don't you stay? You can have Alice's room. You may be slightly over the limit anyway. Stay till the morning.'

He looked down at her. 'If I stay, it won't be in Alice's room.'

Then he kissed her, a brief passionate kiss. Eyes closed Laura responded, sinking towards him.

'I want to stay, but I have to go, my love,' He turned to open the door.

'Of course you must,' she whispered.

When he'd gone, she returned to the kitchen and began to wash the saucepans in an agitated manner, scrubbing them round and round. She wiped the table again and put the remaining glasses in the dishwasher.

Finally when everything was immaculate, she went upstairs to bed, but, as usual, she was unable to sleep.

* * *

She thought he wouldn't visit her again, but he appeared now and then on his way home from work. He wouldn't stay for dinner, just a glass or two of wine. They talked a great deal about their problems. Laura told him she hadn't heard a word from Oliver and was thinking of starting divorce proceedings soon, but Jack advised her to wait, a cooling-off period would be a good idea, he thought. Maybe when she'd thought everything through, weighed the alternatives, then she might want to contact Oliver, give her marriage another go.

She couldn't help being depressed by this sensible advice. Jack even suggested marriage guidance counselling. With a grim smile, Laura said that would not be Oliver's scene.

They discussed Melanie too, and Jack told her how he blamed himself for not wanting to adopt a baby in the early days. If they'd done so, maybe Mel would have been happy, not so lonely. And then maybe he shouldn't have become so tied up in the business. Or if they'd gone to live in Ireland maybe she would never have become an alcoholic. Laura said she thought that ultimately Mel was responsible for her own behaviour. Jack agreed, but he didn't seem convinced.

They talked about many other matters – more cheerful topics like Laura's new job with the estate agents. To her surprise she'd been selected, but disappointingly it only amounted to three afternoons a week at the moment, and she didn't get any commission, just a flat fee for showing people round. To make him laugh she told him how odd some of the houses were, like the country mansion with the green projection room where, according to neighbours, the staid-looking occupants showed blue films. That reminded him of strange houses he'd been obliged to build, for instance an Arab client had wanted a six-foot-long aquarium built into the bedroom wall. Then she told him stories about the funnier side of Paris life, and about Bridget and the monsters, and about the creep Julius who still looked all too healthy. Jack asked her again if she was all right for money and she said she was, which was more or less true at the moment, but her savings were disappearing in a frightening manner.

They discussed everything, in fact, except the sexual undercurrent between them. During all these visits they didn't kiss again apart from a swift goodbye, but desire was there in his eyes and she could not disguise it from hers. One evening when he had stayed later than usual and they were standing in the darkened hallway, she nearly screamed: I'm fed up with being so bloody well behaved, why don't we go to bed and to hell with everyone else?

So go ahead, put your arms around his neck and seduce him, said an inner voice. He wouldn't be able to resist if you really put your mind to it.

He suddenly asked, 'Laura, do you mind me appearing here so often?'

'No, of course not. Good thing I don't have any close neighbours, though, because otherwise...'

'Otherwise people might think we're having an affair?'

She flushed. 'Yes.'

'You could tell them I come around because you're an old friend, and you're unhappy. But, that's just an excuse. Really I come because I want to.'

She held her breath, looking up at him.

'I come here because we've got this precious time together,' he said seriously. 'Sooner or later Mel will come home, and sooner or later you'll go back to your husband. But just at the moment I can see you and breathe the same air, and it's keeping me going.'

'Jack...' She put her arms around his neck and kissed him on the mouth. Then, after a while, she drew back and said fiercely, 'I won't go back to Oliver.'

'It's early days.' Then he kissed her again. 'You shouldn't do anything rash, on the rebound,' he whispered, but his hands held her tightly. 'The very last thing you need at the moment is an affair.'

These wise words of his were in contrast with his actions as they clung to each other. He began to caress her breast.

Breathlessly, before she weakened any further – and she already felt she was clinging by her fingernails on the top of a tempting slippery slope – she pushed him away. 'What about Mel?' she said miserably. 'Jack, I don't think I can stand it much longer, this strange game we're playing, you and I, whatever it is.'

He drew back. 'I'm sorry, you're right. If you'd prefer it that way, I won't come and see you again.'

'No, I think it's better if you don't,' she heard herself say. The words came out sounding sharp and hostile, far more so than she intended.

He said, 'If you need me, just ring.' Then he left.

After he'd gone she sat down and wept for herself, for Jack, for Mel, for Oliver and Charlotte, and the whole stupid mess.

## CHAPTER 27

CHARLOTTE FELT MORE AND MORE FRIGHTENED EACH DAY. She was in London at the beginning of the Easter holidays, staying with a friend, she had told her father. But in fact she was alone in the Putney flat.

For the last two weeks she had prayed for that familiar dull pain, but it never came, nor did the blood. Every morning she had woken up with the feeling that it must happen today but when she dived to the loo – and she dived there pretty often – there was nothing. Nothing at all.

Finally she took the bus to the shopping centre. She chose Boots because they were anonymous but she was terrified that she would somehow be standing in the queue with one of her schoolteachers or a friend of her father's – completely unlikely in London, of course.

She picked up a wire shop basket and, with a dull sick feeling of fear in her throat, searched around the aisles until she found the right place. At last there in front of her was the 'family planning' section and on a lower shelf what she was looking for, the pregnancy tests. She darted a quick glance around the shop. Suddenly a middle-aged woman materialised from nowhere and stood beside her, peering through thick glasses. Charlotte froze and then retreated quickly back along the aisle to stare at the shampoos. With some vague idea about looking for camouflage, she went to the back of the shop and put two large boxes of Kleenex into the basket.

It took another five minutes before she could bring herself to go back to her goal. She now saw that there were three brands of pregnancy test, but she couldn't face studying and comparing them in public. Quickly she chose the Boots version as it had the most discreet packaging. She hid it under the tissues in her basket and then rushed to the check out.

Certain that everyone in the queue was staring at her, she arranged her purchases on the counter with trembling hands. She'd thought that maybe if she stacked the pregnancy test between the Kleenex boxes it would be fairly inconspicuous. It wasn't. She felt as if there might well have been an announcement on the loudspeaker, A CUSTOMER IS BUYING AN OWN-BRAND PREDICTOR TEST. IS IT BUY ONE, GET ONE FREE THIS WEEK?

But the cashier, young and dyed-blonde and sulky, was silent and indifferent. She didn't seem to know or care that she could be checking through Charlotte's future across the counter.

## CHAPTER 28

DURING THE LAST FEW ANXIETY-RIDDEN WEEKS, Laura had been living in a strange solitary limbo of meaningless activity, showing houses, job-hunting, spring-cleaning and gardening. And trying to plan her future. It seemed to her that now the cottage was in a reasonable state of repair, she could think again about taking paying guests on a B&B basis but she had to find out about the rules and regulations involved.

She had still heard nothing from Oliver and she made no decision about him, no steps towards arranging the divorce.

And Jack did not call again, which was a good thing, as she told herself for the umpteenth time. Often her eyes strayed towards the telephone and she thought about calling him, but what was the point? It would only prolong the agony for them both, she told herself. They had said everything there was to say.

One day just before Easter when she was outside looking at the damp spring grass and wondering if she could afford to have the lawn mower serviced, Laura had a marvellous surprise. Charlotte suddenly telephoned and asked in a small voice to be fetched from Winchester.

As she raced along the green country lanes, Laura formulated words in her mind, words of apology, words of explanation, but when at last she saw Charlotte standing on the station forecourt, she swept her into her arms without speaking.

Paler and thinner than ever in jeans and a black sweater, Charlotte clung for a moment and then turned away to heave her scruffy rucksack into the back of the car.

Laura said, 'I'm so very happy to see you. I thought you'd be in Paris for the holidays by now. Is all well?'

'Uh, yuh.'

On the way back, Laura tried to continue some kind of light conversation but Charlotte had clearly sunk back into her earlier silent self and would not reply. After a while Laura decided she was right, they couldn't talk about anything important yet, so maybe it was better not to talk at all.

Back at the cottage Charlotte accepted a cup of tea, which was unusual, but she wouldn't eat any ginger nuts, normally her favourite. She pushed the plate away with an abrupt gesture as if the biscuits were poisonous.

Deciding that it wasn't the moment to comment on this, Laura settled down at the kitchen table and hesitantly began the speech she had prepared.

'I'm very, very sorry about everything, darling, but, the thing is, your father and I should never have married. We made a mistake. He's a good man but we... I don't fit in with his life, and, well, I feel terrible, really terrible and very guilty but I thought, rather than let things drag on unhappily, that the best thing would be to...'

Suddenly Charlotte pushed back her chair with a loud scrape. 'I don't give a shit. What matters is I'm pregnant.' Then she burst into tears.

'Oh, my poor darling,' said Laura after a shocked pause. Oh my God, she thought, and moved to put her arms around Charlotte.

'Are you sure? Have you seen a doctor?'

'No... did a test.'

'How many weeks since...?'

'Six.'

'Charlotte, it could still be a false alarm then. Worry, stress, it could just be that, you know. It does happen sometimes, especially at your age.'

'But the tests were positive. I did two.'

'I see.' Laura hugged her tighter. 'Have you told Oliver?'

Charlotte shuddered. 'No.'

Laura paused for a moment, wondering if the whole crisis could be kept away from him. Then she asked gently, 'Supposing you really are pregnant, who's the father?'

'I can't say,' sobbed Charlotte. 'He doesn't know yet.'

'Darling, tell me, please. We have to sort this out.'

Charlotte said nothing.

Laura's mind raced. 'It can't be Simon... is it?'

Charlotte whispered, barely audible, 'Yes'.

A wave of anger left Laura breathless for a moment. Simon, what a bloody fool! How could he do this to a schoolgirl, barely more than a child? She forced her voice to stay calm. 'We'll go and see my doctor here. She's a nice kind understanding woman. She'll arrange a proper test. And then, if it's positive, we'll get hold of Simon.'

Of course, the official hospital test confirmed it – Charlotte knew it would, although she'd cherished some kind of illogical hope that she'd wake up one morning and find it had all been a bad dream, the worst dream in the world.

The lady doctor was all kindly non-judgmental briskness and thrust stacks of leaflets into her hand. Charlotte hadn't read any of them. The doctor mentioned ante-natal clinics on the one hand, but she'd also said something veiled about Charlotte's mental state, whether she was really strong enough to face an ordeal like childbirth at her age. The word 'termination' was floated in the air. Termination, abortion, whatever way the doctor put it, it didn't sound good.

It took a great deal of courage for Charlotte to phone Simon. She only managed to bring herself to do so because Laura nagged and nagged and finally dialled the number for her, pushing the receiver into her hand.

Charlotte tried to put it down again before he answered. In fact she prayed he would be out. But one look at Laura's determined face told her that sooner or later she would be forced to speak to him. Better to get it over with, Laura kept saying.

Startled, she heard Simon's voice answering the telephone. She cleared her throat. 'Hello,' she whispered.

'Charlotte! Is that you? Great to talk to you. So glad you phoned – I've just had the most wonderful news. My screenplay has been accepted.'

'That's... that's terrific,' she said blankly.

There was a small silence. 'Did you take in what I said? Hope you're pleased for me. You sound a bit odd.'

'Oh, I am. Congratulations.'

'Yes, it's wonderful. I'm going to America. For the rewrites.' His voice was full of happiness and hope.

'When?'

'Saturday. In fact I'll just pop in and say goodbye before I go. Or you could come and see me off, eleven fifty, Charles de Gaulle airport.'

'But I'm ringing from England at the moment. I'm not in Paris.'

'I see. Shame about that. Well, in that case, maybe I'll have to say goodbye now.'

Charlotte took a deep breath. 'I could... I could come with you. To America.'

He laughed. 'If only. But it looks like our lives are moving on in separate ways. You're a great person, Charlotte. I'll always remember you. But when you've finished your A-levels and you get to university, you'll meet all sorts of new blokes and forget all about me.'

'I won't ever forget.'

'Like I said, nor will I. It's been wonderful,' he said cheerfully. 'You're a great girl with a great future and I think...'

Charlotte suddenly put the phone down.

Eventually she was obliged to confess to Laura that she'd failed to break the news and so Laura said grimly she would take matters into her own hands and telephone him herself.

Charlotte didn't want to sit on the sidelines during this phone call, so she wandered out into the garden and stared at Laura's tulips and the other spring flowers that were all over the place creating an atmosphere of rural prettiness totally alien to her current mood. Occasionally she looked back towards the house – waiting. Let him ask for her. She wasn't going to run after him. No way.

Eventually a harassed-looking Laura came to find her.

Charlotte's heart sank still further. 'He's not too thrilled, I guess,' she faltered.

'No. I gave him a piece of my mind. Of all the damn irresponsible – '

'He didn't want to speak to me?'

'He's going to ring you back when he's got his act together, whatever that means.'

'Right. Did he say anything else?'

'He said he was very, very sorry and he sends you his love, and that he would pay for the abortion.'

For a moment Charlotte thought she was going to faint. Taking small painful breaths, she said, 'Was that all? Was that all he said?'

'Well, he kept repeating he was sorry.'

A wave of cold nausea hit Charlotte, blanking out all her emotions. Then after a pause she stammered out one of the random things that had been on her mind, 'Alice told me you married her Dad because you were pregnant.'

Laura spoke slowly, 'Yes, well, no. I actually had a miscarriage in the end, but my parents thought I was pregnant and I didn't tell them about losing the baby. It's hard to explain why. But anyway I was twenty rather than sixteen, but I was young and immature, and far, far too young to marry.'

'Actually I'm seventeen now. The other day.'

Laura looked stricken. 'Did I forget your birthday? I'm sorry.'

'Doesn't matter. Who cares?'

They paced around the garden in silence.

'I have to be straight with you, Charlotte. In common with most young men these days, he doesn't want to get married. He doesn't want the baby.'

'He said so?'

'Yes, he did, and anyway I think marriage in these kind of circumstances would be a terrific mistake.'

After another long pause Charlotte muttered, 'But you don't have to have a husband. I may... I may want to keep the baby anyway.' Actually she wasn't sure of this but she thought she should air the possibility because she had the impression that was what people did these days. It didn't seem real though, the idea of the baby. She couldn't visualise it as a living thing growing inside her.

'I see. Well, we'll have to talk about all the options. What's best for you.'

After another circle Laura spoke again, 'As I told you, he's offered to pay for an abortion. So he damn well should. You can have it on the National Health – on the grounds of your age – but privately might be quicker and more comfortable.'

In her heart of hearts Charlotte had known that this was all he would offer. Half of her had fantasised that he'd fly to her side and promise to take care of her for ever. The other half, the sensible womanly half that was already developing knew all along that he didn't love her, that he had feet of shifting sands; that, though he thought of himself as a gentleman, taking on the burden of a pregnant teenager was not part of his game-plan.

Laura was saying, 'It's not as if he's stable financially. He's had some kind of advance payment for his script, though I think final acceptance still depends on the quality of the rewrites. So he hasn't exactly made it to the big time. And it isn't a steady job.'

Charlotte took a deep breath and said emotionally, 'It wouldn't matter to me. I don't care about money.'

'No one cares about money at your age but, the point is, whether Simon is solvent or not is immaterial because – '

'Because he's in love with someone else, isn't he?'

'Charlotte, I don't know. Possibly.'

'I'm going for a walk by myself. No, I'd rather be on my own.' She stomped out of the garden and away down the lane, tears flooding down again.

Laura thought it best to avoid talking about the situation during supper in the hope that Charlotte might eat something but she managed only half a spoonful of peas and nothing else.

Then putting down her fork, she suddenly announced in one long rapid speech, 'I've decided. I do want to keep the baby. What I thought was maybe that you could look after it. I'll have to leave St Mary's and go to the local Sixth Form College probably. Though maybe it won't show too much before I take A-level. Then I'll take a Gap year to have the baby and go to university after that. Or the year later. It should work out OK.'

Laura looked at Charlotte's pale wan face but then she steeled herself to say, 'No, I'm very sorry but I really couldn't cope with a baby. I have to earn my living. I've only just started this new job.'

'But Dad, he would support us.'

'Just about the only thing I'm certain of is that your father would hit the roof. An unmarried mother, his precious daughter – a baby at seventeen! He thinks it only happens to half-witted girls from inner-city slums. Can you imagine what he'd say?'

'Yes... But once he saw the baby he would love it.' Her voice faltered.

'I'm not so sure about that,' said Laura grimly. After a pause she went on, 'Charlotte, you're just too young. And if you think there would be this tie between you and Simon...' She saw that she had hit home. 'Darling, I'm sorry to be brutal but he really does *not* want this child. I'm pretty sure you'll never see him again, let alone be able to force him to pay maintenance, especially if he's in America.'

'You don't know that for certain.'

'No, but – '

'I thought I could count on you, Laura. I thought you were the one person in the whole world who'd understand and stick by me. I mean, I just can't believe that you're not supporting me.' Charlotte burst into tears again, but when Laura went to put her arms around her she pushed her away.

'I am supporting you, darling,' said Laura, distressed, 'but I have to tell you looking after a child is a full-time, exhausting and demanding and sometimes rather boring and lonely job.'

'I know but – '

'The point is, you *don't* know. You have no idea what it entails. The baby would be solely and entirely your responsibility and you'd have to give up your bright future, postpone university, and so many other things about being young and free that you might never get back. You'd have to tell your father. You'd have to get him to give you an allowance until such time as Simon could be forced to help. You see, I can't support you financially because I can hardly support myself. The only thing I can do is offer you a home, but Oliver probably wouldn't allow you to live here now that we're separated. And as he holds the purse strings, you'd have to do what he said.'

'So you won't help me.'

More and more agitated, Laura searched for words. 'I *will* help but I can't look after a baby. You could stay here, if your father will let you, as I said, but I'd very much prefer not to have a continuing financial arrangement with him. I'd much rather have a clean break.'

Charlotte turned on her and said furiously, 'So in fact you don't really want me here.'

'Charlotte, I – '

'Why did you have to leave Dad? This would be so much less awful if you were together. It's just not fair.'

'I'm sorry but – '

'It's not fair on him or me,' she repeated. 'Anyway – anyway, it's partly your fault I'm pregnant.'

'What on earth d'you mean?'

'It happened the night you left Paris. I was so freaked out – I went to see Simon and I just wasn't thinking straight and –'

'I don't think – '

Charlotte's voice grew higher and higher. 'But maybe you're right. A baby needs a proper family. I know what it's like to be part of a broken home and I wouldn't want any child of mine to go through what I have. I thought you were different, but seems to me you're just like my mother.' She stopped for breath and then shouted, 'And, and I bet you wouldn't talk about abortions if it was your own grandchild, your own flesh and blood.'

'Wait...'

But Charlotte had already run up the stairs to her bedroom.

After a while Laura went up and knocked gently on the door. When there was no answer she whispered, 'Charlotte, we'll talk about it in the morning. I will support you, but we have to think everything through as calmly as we can. To work out what's best for everyone.'

A while later, the phone rang. It was Simon wanting to talk to Charlotte. Laura called her and then went to bed, leaving her downstairs whispering and weeping into the telephone. Not long after, Charlotte's bedroom door slammed again with such force that the whole cottage shook and shuddered.

In her own bed Laura lay awake. Of course she couldn't blame herself for the pregnancy, but then maybe she should never have brought Simon into the household. Weak and beautiful people of either sex always cause trouble. She *had* foreseen problems, all sorts of problems. Not this one though. In this day and age, it was ridiculous that intelligent girls should make these mistakes. Except of course it was the oldest mistake in the world and one she'd made herself.

All through the night she tossed and turned. She'd been too forceful towards Charlotte, too domineering. Just like her own mother had been, though now she was beginning to understand her mother's feelings and to forgive her. Her mother had seemed to be against her, now she understood the opposite was the case.

But the moral climate had changed since then. She must let Charlotte make her own decision. However inadvisable it was, the girl had a right to keep her own baby.

Maybe you should change your mind. For Charlotte's sake, maybe you should agree to help out with the baby at least part of the time. And for Charlotte's sake, maybe you should go back to Oliver. He was unfaithful but then so were you, in your head. That last time that Jack came around, if he'd stayed you would have made love. So, St. Laura, you are not perfect.

But I didn't...

Face facts. Jack will stick by Melanie. He always has. The best thing you can do is patch it up with Oliver and take care of Charlotte.

But I'm not sure that I even like Oliver.

You liked him once upon a time, not so very long ago. You may like him again. You haven't given this marriage much of a chance. Make it work. See it through. At least until Charlotte is older. She's so vulnerable.

But what about the baby? It'll be dependent for years. I'd have to look after it until she gets a decent job or finds a crèche, or gets married even.

Then you'll just have to hang on in there. At least that's something you're good at. Normally.

I can't face all this self-sacrifice, not again. And anyway what if Oliver doesn't want me back?

He will. He'll give up Agnès if you ask him to. He could have married her but he chose you. He loves you.

You reckon? Well, he's got a pretty funny way of showing it.

Give him a chance, Laura, give him a second chance.

What about the baby?

Give it a chance too.


Finally she fell asleep, waking with a guilty start at around nine o'clock next morning. As she passed along the landing she saw that Charlotte's door was still shut. The lie-in would do her good

– she must be absolutely worn out, poor child. As soon as she appeared, they'd have another talk.

Laura crept anxiously around the house all morning. It was nearly eleven when she received a phone call from Tom Bone, a local farmer. 'Hope I'm not intruding, Mrs Brooke. Oh, sorry, I mean Mrs Farringdon.'

She groaned inwardly. It seemed ironic that people in the village were only just getting around to remembering her new married name.

'But,' continued Mr Bone, 'there was this young lady, wanted to go to Winchester. She was in the phone box by the pub, said she was ringing for a taxi but when she saw me she jumped out, hitching-hiking like. So I took her with me, seeing as how I was going to the garage. I mentioned it to my wife just now and she said I should telephone you in case it might've been your step-daughter. Mentioned your Alice, y'see, the young lady. I don't rightly know if I ever met your step-daughter so I wouldn't recognise her. My wife, she says I shouldn't go around picking up hitchhikers anyway, but seeing as how this one was in the village and nicely spoken like... Only she seemed a bit upset...' His voice trailed away.

'Was she tall and thin, about seventeen?' asked Laura urgently.

'That's right. Wanted to go to the station, so since it weren't too far out of my way, I took her there. Quite early in the morning, it was.'

Laura swore inwardly, but she thanked him and then rushed up to Charlotte's room. Sure enough, it was empty. Typically, she'd even made the bed.

## CHAPTER 29

THERE WAS NO REPLY FROM THE LONDON FLAT. Laura tried again and again. Finally she left an answerphone message: 'Charlotte. We need to talk. You can keep it, if that's what you want. I've changed my mind. I would be prepared to help in the way you asked.' She'd chosen her words carefully so that the cleaning woman who kept an eye on the flat wouldn't understand.

Having left the message, Laura felt suddenly sick at heart. In trying to do the right thing, maybe she was making yet another major mistake. But she forced herself to write a letter to Charlotte as well, in case the message somehow went astray. In the letter it wasn't necessary to be so cryptic so she said more specifically that they'd work something out, that she'd help with the baby while Charlotte continued her studies.

She didn't write that she would go back to Oliver. Nevertheless her conscience continually attacked her on the subject. Any sane person would give the marriage another chance, she knew, for the sake of all parties involved. Especially Charlotte, of course.

Laura waited in vain for four days, but however much she stared at the phone it did not ring. She called the flat very early in the morning and late at night but there was no reply. She didn't dare make any other calls out in case her line was engaged at the one moment Charlotte chose to ring.

Finally, unable to bear the suspense any longer, Laura drove up to London.

The flat looked clean and tidy, and apparently unoccupied, but when she opened the fridge she saw a bottle of fresh milk and a bunch of grapes. The cleaner might have brought them but it seemed unlikely.

The answerphone was blinking its red light to indicate a message. Laura played it back, but there was a just an elderly woman's voice saying idiotically, 'Er, sorry, wrong number'. There were no other messages. So hers had been erased.

She sorted through the mail which had been placed on the desk in the hall. By the cleaner? It had all been opened, but her own letter wasn't there. So that meant Charlotte had received it, had been here. So why hadn't she rung?

Laura went slowly into the bleak empty sitting room and sat down. Maybe if she waited until the evening Charlotte would appear... unless she'd already gone back to Paris.

Laura told herself she should have rung Oliver at the beginning of this drama. She couldn't wait much longer before doing so.

Suddenly she heard a key in the lock. She jumped up and rushed into the hall. Her heart dropped. It was Oliver. Alone. Obviously in a furious temper, he looked tired, strained and much older.

'Where's Charlotte?' she asked without preamble.

'I don't know. What the bloody hell is all this about a baby?'

'She told you?' faltered Laura.

'No one has told me a damn thing but it doesn't take a rocket scientist to work it out.' He glared at her. 'Your message, your letter. You knew all about it so why on earth didn't you tell me?'

'She got my letter?'

'No, I opened it today when I arrived. Needed to track down where she was. And what do I find? A major family crisis that no one sees fit to tell me about. My daughter is pregnant. And you of all people actually seem to be encouraging her to keep it. For God's sake, Laura, you must be out of your mind.'

'Oliver, I'm sorry. I...' She decided not to argue about reading other people's mail.

'So where the hell is she? She's got to be made to see sense, get rid of it. Or is it too late for that?'

'No, no. She's still in the early stages.'

'That's one small mercy. Then ring a clinic, for God's sake. Get her over there straight away. Now. Immediately.' He was spitting out the words.

'I agree but – '

He stopped pacing and shouted, 'If you agree then why haven't you done something about it? What did you mean in this bloody stupid letter of yours?' He took it out of his pocket.

She took a deep breath. 'I agree about the abortion but she needs to make the decision herself.'

He snorted angrily. 'Bugger that social-worker claptrap. She won't thank us later for letting her wreck her life. And, while we're on the subject, who's the father, might one ask?'

She told him. There didn't seem much point in holding anything back.

Oliver exploded again and said predictable things about wringing Simon's bloody neck. Then he turned on Laura and said he blamed her for the whole situation, she should have kept a better eye on Charlotte, dealt with her with a firmer hand. For God's sake, that's why he hired her in the first place.

Laura's voice grew higher. 'If we're going to shift the blame around, one might just as well say that you and Agnès are responsible – Charlotte ran to Simon when I left Paris. Apparently she was too upset to worry about birth control.'

Oliver sat down, head in his hands. 'What a bloody stupid mess.'

'It certainly is – but we have to find Charlotte. Look, I've brought her school address book with me. I'll try and contact one of her friends.'

'Then we'll call the police.'

'I really don't think – '

'Laura, anything might have happened.'

But Charlotte's friends knew nothing, or so they said. The police promised to put her on the missing persons list but it was probably nothing to worry about, a seventeen-year-old often disappeared after a family row, they suggested. She could even be with the boyfriend in Paris.

Then Laura called Simon's flat but the phone appeared to have been cut off, nor was she able to get through to Kiki.

By this time, it was getting late.

Oliver suggested abruptly that they should go out and get something to eat, an offer she declined, saying she'd rather go back to the country in case Charlotte showed up there.

She picked up her handbag. 'I'll call you as soon as I hear anything. I'll be off now.' Nothing would persuade her to spend the night under the same roof as Oliver. She turned to him. 'Will you do likewise?'

He didn't reply.

'Oliver?'

'What?'

'Will you call me as soon as you hear anything?'

'All right,' he answered distractedly.

Just as she was leaving, he said, 'About Agnès, you got the wrong impression, I assure you, only half the picture. I'm sorry.'

She stared up at him. He looked so wretched that, for a moment, she wavered. Then she said, 'Maybe you should have said that before. I left several weeks ago, if you remember.' She was trying to speak calmly but her voice shook.

'I'm sorry. I was angry that you'd left in a hysterical rush without speaking to me. I was waiting for you to come to your senses and explain yourself.'

'Me come to my senses! Of all the arrogant – '

He interrupted her. 'Thing is, I'm not actually *seeing* Agnès, as you put it in your note. Not in the sense you mean.'

'But you were seeing her that night, the night I left,' said Laura, 'when you were supposedly playing tennis.'

He stared at her. 'No, I wasn't, I wasn't seeing Agnès *or* playing tennis. The tennis was cancelled because we had a late council meeting. I rang and left a message for you with Sebastien to that effect.'

'Oh, he didn't tell me,' said Laura uncertainly, not knowing what to believe. Then she snapped, 'In what sense were you seeing her then?'

'It's just business. She's a colleague so I have to get on with her. I wrote a letter to you explaining that but I tore it up. Should've sent it, but your jealousy seemed to be so unreasonable at the time.' He put his hand on her shoulder. 'I don't suppose you... would you consider coming back to Paris, at least for a while, see how it goes?'

She pulled back and said furiously, '*My* jealousy! So it was unreasonable to mind about Agnès. Did you or did you not sleep with her the night before our wedding?'

He looked away and said after a pause, 'Yes, I'm sorry.'

'That's awful. Sickening.'

He dropped his gaze. 'I agree and I'm sorry, very sorry, but it was an aberration, meant nothing. She doesn't... I don't love her but I've slept with her on two other occasions since you left. Not before that though. Not when you were in Paris. I've regretted it, taking up with her. It won't happen again, not if you come back.'

Laura opened and shut her mouth. She was angry but, with this genuine apology, the first she'd ever heard from Oliver, some of the wind had been taken out of her sails. He looked so miserable, so unusually humble, and it seemed as if he was telling the truth. Maybe Kiki had got it all wrong that Agnès was an ongoing affair. And Sebastian forgot the message that night. Perhaps deliberately. But why this long silence from Oliver during all these weeks?

She hesitated, confused for a moment. Then, remembering his strange cold behaviour and the loneliness of her marriage, she said slowly, 'It's too late. Half-misunderstanding or half-not, we never talked about it or anything else. It's not just Agnès, it's everything.'

As his grip tightened, she shrugged him off . Slamming the door behind her she ran down the stairs in a wild panic.

Calm down, calm down, she told herself as she tried to unlock the car with shaking hands. He's not going to chase after you. Not Oliver.

But maybe you should go back and comfort him, said her conscience. He's very unhappy. 'I just can't. I just can't,' whispered Laura aloud.

Easter passed in a flurry of phone calls about Charlotte, between Laura and Oliver, Laura and Bridget, and Laura and anyone else she could think of who might be able to help find her. It now seemed impossible to eat or sleep or do anything except stare at the phone, willing it to ring.

Then early the next week her prayers were half-answered. Oliver called sounding a little happier. He'd gone back to Paris to find that there was a letter from Charlotte, postmarked London, saying she was OK, but nothing else, no address.

'Oh thank God for that', said Laura, sitting down with a bump. 'So maybe we'll just have to wait till she writes again.'

Then suddenly in mid-April Miss Hardy, the housemistress, rang. 'Good morning, Mrs Farringdon. Charlotte says she has left two of her A-level text books at your cottage, so would you be kind enough to post them to her.'

'Charlotte's back *at school?*' asked Laura, astonished and hugely relieved.

'Yes, of course. As planned, she came back a few days before the beginning of term to join our A-level revision booster programme. We've always been concerned that she's very much on the young side, but she is a strong candidate and –'

'Can I speak to her?'

Miss Hardy gave an embarrassed little cough. 'I'm afraid she doesn't seem to want to contact you directly. That's why she asked me to make this call on her behalf.'

Laura tried not to mind. 'Well, anyway tell her to call her father in Paris immediately. He's very worried he hasn't heard from her.'

'I'll pass on the message, Mrs Farringdon, but meanwhile can I just get you to jot down the names of the books she needs?'


When Laura rang Oliver to tell him the good news, she couldn't help being moved by his emotional gratitude. A while later he phoned back to say he still hadn't been able to talk to Charlotte but he'd spoken to the school without telling them anything about the pregnancy and would she mind going to investigate? He'd go himself but Charlotte would probably rather talk to her. Fundamentally, this was a female problem, he thought.

Laura smiled for the first time for weeks and agreed that fundamentally it was.


As soon as she had finished her morning's work, Laura set off for the school. When she arrived at the converted Queen Anne mansion she parked the car behind the new classrooms block and went in by one of the side entrances to avoid speaking to any nosy teachers or matrons.

All was quiet. She had timed the visit deliberately to coincide with the period when all the girls would be out at the games pitches involved in hearty healthy outdoor activities.

Aware of that curious sweaty-chalky school smell, she crept up the narrow staircase, all squeaky polished lino and faded yellow paint. Charlotte's tiny study was empty. Feeling like an intruder, Laura sat down and looked around her. The place was bleak but, apart from the stains of ancient ink on the desk, absolutely immaculate, with books and files in neat rows. Charlotte had taken down all her old posters and now the only decoration was a pin-up of a young rock-star type Laura didn't recognise. He looked a bit like Simon.

She chose a battered, much-thumbed copy of Jane Eyre and began to read. It was hard to concentrate in the silence. After half an hour, she heard footsteps in the corridor.

Charlotte, desperately young in her navy uniform, appeared surprised and none too pleased to see her.

She flushed. 'Laura. Why did you come?'

Laura stood up, but Charlotte didn't look as if she wanted to be kissed hello. 'I brought your books.'

'Could've posted them.'

'I know but I need to see you. What's been happening? We've been so worried, your father and I.'

Charlotte turned away to stare out of the window. 'Yeah, I bet. Well, I had an abortion. Just like you wanted.'

'But I left a message on the phone and wrote a letter saying I *would* help look after the baby.'

Tears in her eyes, Charlotte gazed coldly at her. 'I never got any letter.'

'Well, your father opened it but – '

'So Dad knows. Terrific. That's all I need,' said Charlotte, heavy on the sarcasm.

'He was bound to find out sooner or later. Charlotte, I'm sorry you never got my message.' It came to Laura that maybe Oliver had deliberately deleted it.

Charlotte blinked. 'Bit too late now, isn't it?' Her voice was getting higher.

'I'm very sorry about the abortion.'

'Huh.'

'But maybe it's just as well.'

After another silence Laura said, 'It was very brave of you. Have you told anyone here at school?'

'No, of course not. Don't want to tarnish the precious family name, do we?'

'So where were you all this time?'

'With friends of Simon's. They fixed me up with the clinic. Simon paid. It was quite all right, if you like that sort of thing.'

'Oh my God. And now?'

'Now, after A-levels, I've decided to lead my own life. And, don't worry, I'm not going to inflict myself on you ever again.'

Laura flinched. 'Darling, I'm sorry about everything. You've gone through a hell of a lot and I feel terrible... I would've gone to the clinic with you. Stayed with you all the time. I do wish you'd rung me. I could have helped.' She desperately wanted to hug Charlotte.

'Huh, a big help, I'm sure.'

'But I'll always be there if you need me, in the future.'

'What d'you mean? Are you going back to Dad?' Charlotte sounded suddenly light and hopeful.

Laura paused. 'No... No,' she repeated firmly, realising that this was how it had to be. 'I can't, I'm sorry. I know it's hard for you to understand but I really can't. I made a mistake. Your father and I, well, we just weren't right for each other, and I know I can't make him happy, not in the long run. I feel terrible about it, about him and about you. But this doesn't, needn't change things between you and me. I'll be there in the cottage. You can come and stay any time.'

'Don't worry, I know you don't mean that. Goodbye, Laura,' she said stonily and walked away down the corridor.

Back home Laura called Oliver who was extremely relieved to hear about the abortion and kept saying so over and over again. He also kept repeating how grateful he was to her.

She was about to say goodbye when he asked offhandedly, 'Are you coming back to Paris?'

Laura paused. 'No,' she said.

'I see.'

She took a deep breath. 'I think we should go ahead with the divorce.'

'I see,' he repeated.

'I'll consult my lawyers, shall I?'

'If that's what you want.'

'I do,' she said and put down the phone.

She felt immensely guilty but liberated. Recently she'd become more and more depressed, afraid that her guilty conscience and sense of duty, particularly about Charlotte and the baby would somehow lure her back into Oliver's life. Now everything had changed.

Given that Charlotte was clearly so miserable, Laura was ashamed of own selfish sense of freedom but, whatever the emotional and financial cost, free she intended to be. After all those unhappy years with William, she just could not sacrifice the rest of her life to Oliver.

## CHAPTER 30

EVERY DAY THAT PASSED LAURA THOUGHT ABOUT JACK and wondered if she should call him. She had an excuse, a business matter. She was busier than ever showing houses, but the work was not regular or especially profitable. So in order to earn additional money, she was still investigating the Bed and Breakfast idea and had now received a copy of the latest Tourist Board advice. After wading through all the bumph, she gathered that a second bathroom would be essential. The obvious thing would be to ask Jack to arrange the building works and yet contacting him would only put her in his debt again.

Contacting him would also cause further temptations and emotional complications that she couldn't cope with at the moment. She was in the throes of separating herself from Oliver and had finally screwed up courage to write to the solicitors about a divorce.

The Senior Partner, a Mr Mackenzie, replied to her letter saying that matters would be put in hand, writing in a postscript that he was sorry to hear her stepfather had been unwell. This news did not make Laura herself feel especially sorry. Her conscience mentioned that she should visit Julius, but the days passed and she did not do so.

It was only a week later that she was awakened at six in the morning by a telephone call from Roehampton Hospital.

'Mrs Farringdon?'

'Yes?'

'There's no easy way to tell you this but I'm very sorry – your dad passed away here last night.'

Laura shook her blurred head in disbelief. Her father had died when she was a baby. 'I think there's been a mistake.'

'No, I'm sorry, dear, Julius went suddenly. A stroke. He was admitted during the day but he didn't last the night. I'm sorry we didn't get through to you before. We had a the wrong telephone number.'

Laura drew in her breath. 'But he's not – '

'It's a great shock always,' continued the nurse kindly.

'But how did you find me?'

'In his records, next of kin.'

'I see. So what do I do?'

'Sit down, have a nice cup of tea, dear. Then when you're feeling better, could you come and see us at the ward? We'll take you through the procedure.'

'Today?'

'When you feel up to it, dear.'

She had for years been expecting Julius's death but somehow it was an enormous surprise. She felt sorrier than she had anticipated she would.

How weird it all was. The hushed sympathy at the hospital, the plastic bag of personal effects. The registering of the death, the form filling-in. Going to Julius's musty empty flat, creeping in and out as quickly as she could. The solicitors being a lot more friendly, thinking about their probate fees no doubt. The young female funeral director in a green suit who said call me Annette.

A week later Laura stood alone outside the crematorium. It appeared she was to be the only mourner and not a deeply grief-stricken one at that. She'd thought at least the chauffeur might attend but there was no sign of him.

What a gruesome, shiver-inducing place it was, both inside and out: like a nineteen-sixties council office or health centre (hardly an appropriate comparison, on second thoughts) – plate glass windows, ugly red bricks, single storey, different roof levels plus the inevitable tall chimney behind. The garden was large and flat with sad empty lawns bordered by straight rows of 'roses for remembrance'. She wondered if people ever came to visit the shrubs they planted, no doubt expensively.

It was nearly time for the service to begin. Reluctantly Laura went into the chapel. There was a free-standing bier for the coffin to one side of the altar. So it appeared they would be spared the ghoulish conveyor-belt scene when the coffin trundled away into a gaping mouth.

It all reminded Laura of how much she had hated her mother's cremation.

The piped hymn began and Julius was carried solemnly in by the professional pall bearers, preceded by the priest and the portly chief undertaker who wore full black morning dress and carried a top hat. With his young face and curly blond beard, he made a surreal vision.

The spray of white flowers Laura had selected from the florist's catalogue had been hugely expensive but looked, she now saw, mean and inadequate, covering only half the coffin. No one else had sent wreaths, so presumably Julius had no friends. Ashamed of these worldly and uncharitable thoughts, Laura tried to concentrate on higher things. She couldn't bring herself to intercede for Julius's soul, so she prayed instead for Charlotte, that she was happier.

Suddenly there was a clatter of high heels. She turned round to see Melanie hurrying in. She wore a rather unsuitable cherry-red suit with a black hat and looked marvellous. Laura's heart rose at the sight of her friendly face and then sank again as she realised the significance. So Mel was back home.

Mel came around the side of the pew to stand next to her. 'Thought you might need reinforcements in death's dark vale,' she whispered loudly.

Laura suppressed a giggle.

After Julius had been discreetly curtained-off to the tune of further solemn piped organ music and they'd escaped into the fresh air, Melanie gave her a hug. 'Would you look at this spooky place – isn't it enough to freeze a monkey's balls off?' she said. 'Let's go to the pub. No, no, don't worry, my love, I'm dry as a bone, sober as a Presbyterian judge, in fact, but I passed a reasonable-looking place on the way that was offering afternoon tea. It's just down the road. They must do a rip-roaring trade with people needing a double brandy to get over the heebie-jeebies.'

'Is a pub such a good idea?'

'It is,' said Mel. 'I have something to tell you.'

Surprisingly, Mel did actually order tea. 'Now,' she said, settling back in her chair. 'I'm a wee bit tired as I drove down from darkest Wales yesterday, and it's a bloody long way in that terrible noisy car I borrowed.'

'You look very well, all glowing and slim,' said Laura, half-delighted to see her and half-dismayed that she'd returned. 'Very nice of you to come. I didn't even know you'd met Julius.'

'Don't know him from Adam but I thought it was your turn for a bit of support.' She scrutinised Laura's face. 'So you left that husband of yours.'

Laura grimaced. 'Yes.'

'Permanently?'

'Yes, I feel a complete fool but – '

'Good for you. Jack said he was a right bastard.'

'He's not that bad but it just didn't work out.'

'So now what will you do? Or can you afford to be a lady of leisure now you're an heiress?'

'Hardly. Julius left his own money and his flat to some distant relation in Australia. I get my mother's, of course, but it's not serious money, not enough to live on. Enough to keep the wolf from the door and help set up a business, though, and to buy you a slap-up lunch, Mel, any time. We should celebrate your return.'

'Ah, but I'm not staying long, my love.'

Laura's heart leapt. 'Oh?' she said in a neutral voice.

'I came to fetch the rest of my clothes and stuff from home. I've decided to stay permanently in Wales. You see, they need me. It's good to be needed, good to feel you're doing a proper job of work. And, if I'm to stay off the hard stuff, I need them.' Then she gave a grin. 'Better still, I have a boyfriend. Hope you're not too shocked.'

'Course not,' said Laura, hanging on her every word.

'He's called Alun. He's a carpenter, all young and strong and lovely. Looks like a Rugby prop forward. He's a recovering alcoholic too, you see. So we understand each other the way normal people don't. There's no barriers between us, none at all. With Jack I was always conscious that he was a sort of controlling figure in my life – inevitable because someone had to try and control me since I'd lost it completely. But Jack was more of a father to me than an equal partner. It's hard to explain, but that's the way my counsellor has made me see it. Ruth, she's called. She's a good woman, ruthless Ruth. She talks in a terrible sort of psycho-speak like they all do, but what she says makes sense. And it seems that, to grow, I need to come out from under Jack's shadow, benign though it was.' Mel's eyes were shining with a new confident light.

'So what does he say to all this?' asked Laura in a strangled voice.

'Oh, maybe there's a wee bit of hurt pride but, let's face it, I've been a great burden to him and something tells me he'll get over it damn quickly. To tell you the truth, I even heard him singing to himself this morning.'

Laura felt unable to comment.

Mel went on to describe the farm and the weirdos and the shrinks and the darling wee children and the beauties of the mountains versus the unbelievable dreariness of the local shops. And it had all been a struggle which wasn't over but now she was determined to stick to the straight and narrow because finally she'd got back her self-esteem and she wasn't going to let go of it again, no way. She confided that she and Alun spent a lot of time having sex – it took their mind off the drink. He was good in bed, was Alun, as good as Jack himself, though it was not good manners to compare, was it?

There was no answer to that.

Then Mel looked at her watch and said it was time to go because she thought what with one thing and another she had to have another wee talk with Jack.

Before she drove away, she squeezed Laura's arm and said, 'Look after him for me, won't you, my love.' She winked, almost as if she knew something.

Laura gulped. 'I will,' she said.

She wanted to ring him the moment she got home but that didn't seem tactful. What do you say? Sorry to hear your wife has left you but how about coming round here? No, she would wait a day or two. In case Mel changed her mind and stayed on for a few days.

Better not to ring up on second thoughts. Better to let him make the first move because he might want time to himself. Of course, there could be another woman altogether in his life, like that frightful Arabella. Another long silent fidgety day and night passed and it seemed to Laura that he must be too heart-broken to see anyone at all, least of all her.

Then that evening when she had just come in from working in the garden, she heard the telephone. Jack's voice asked, 'Laura, I wondered if you'd like to come out to dinner?'

She flushed. 'Now?'

'Perhaps a bit later. It's only six o'clock.'

Babbling like a schoolgirl, she wiped her hands on her jeans. 'So it is. Well, yes, I'd love to.'

'Where would you like to go?'

'Oh, I don't know. Somewhere quiet. Or we could have dinner here.'

'I thought you might prefer to go out.'

They sounded like people who'd met for the first time at a cocktail party, a couple who were attracted to each other but still fencing around.

'I need to talk to you, Laura,' he continued.

'Yes,' she stuttered, her heart thumping. 'See you soon then.'

She rushed upstairs and bathed carefully and then smothered herself from head to toe with Dior body lotion. Telling herself that she was jumping the gun, she found her special lacy stockings and even more special lacy Paris underwear – *artillerie de nuit*, as Kiki used to call it – and the only little sexy Paris suit that wouldn't appear over the top in Hampshire. Then, after fixing her face in what she hoped was a minimalist kind of way, putting on lipstick and then rubbing it off again, she went down again to wait.

She had an awful last-minute thought – what if he was coming round to tell her that everything had changed, he and Mel were together again? Anything was possible. She paced around, straightening the furniture, then pacing again, for what seemed like half an hour before she finally heard his car. She looked at the clock. He was ten minutes' early. She hesitated and then rushed outside, watching him drive rather too fast up to her door.

'You look fantastic,' he said.

Then her head reeled as he kissed her until she was weak at the knees and breathless. 'Do you want a drink?' she whispered shakily.

'Later.'

'You said you wanted to talk.'

But talking didn't seem to be important. After more kisses they were in her bedroom, though she didn't remember how they got there.

Jack was undoing the buttons of the little Paris suit and all the rest, undressing her in tender appreciative haste, exploring her and covering her body with small sensual kisses. Soon every part of her was melting with anticipation and she told him she couldn't bear to wait a moment longer. She was his.

And his lovemaking was wild and exultant, full of pent-up passion and deliciously erotic, but at the same time skilful and tender, just for her. And she found herself responding in a turbulent joyful haze of love and lust.

Everything it should be, she realised afterwards as she lay beside him in dazed euphoria. Even in the urgency and the newness of their sexual love, she'd had the strange but good sensation they were already familiar with each other's bodies, that they had always been together.

Next day she woke up to the sound of birds. She thought he'd have go to the office and she couldn't bear to be parted, but then she realised it was Saturday.

'Sex in the morning is nice too,' she said cheerfully over breakfast, biting into her toast and marmalade with appetite.

'It is, very nice.' He smiled. 'I love the way you eat.'

They gazed at each other without speaking. Then, leaning forward, he said suddenly, 'When shall we get married?'

She flushed with sudden overwhelming happiness. 'I'd love to marry you. But, well, three husbands, it's rather embarrassing.'

'So what? Third time lucky, I hope.'

She took a deep breath and said cautiously, 'There's Mel, you may be on the rebound. Perhaps we should wait and –'

'It's not on the rebound. It was over years ago, Mel and me. I told you, I've loved you for a very long time. But I had to stay to keep her going. Now it's all changed. May be ungentlemanly to say so, but it feels damn good to be free at last.'

'That's what I mean. Maybe you need a break. You were the one who gave *me* a lecture about not rushing into marriage again when I was engaged to Oliver.'

'This is quite different. You and I, we know each other.'

'Yes,' she said. 'Quite different, but what if Mel relapses?'

'She really has turned the corner. She'll be OK now, I'm sure. Anyway, I've done my bit for her. It's my turn now, our turn, don't you think?'

She smiled. 'Yes, it is. It absolutely is. But – '

'Look, I think Mel even knew about us. She's pretty generous. She said something before she left, that she hoped I'd find someone nice, someone like you.' He took her in his arms again, and soon Laura forgot her doubts.

Later she said, again cautiously, 'I'd decided last week when I knew I would finally inherit a tiny bit of money that I'd go ahead with my B&B plans. Then I'd be sort of independent.'

'You want to be independent?'

'Yes, kind of. Independent but together. A partnership. Like a modern couple. You know. The thing is,' she paused, 'the thing is I sort of want...' She paused.

He smiled. 'Want what?'

'Well, I don't want to go back to the traditional dependent wife role and Mel always gave me the impression that...'

'Mm?' His voice had gone quiet.

'That you like to run the show,' she blundered on. Oh my God, she thought. I'm screwing it all up. He's asked me to marry him and I'm quibbling and moaning. She hardly dared look at him.

He took her hand. 'I tried to run the show with Mel because she had lost the plot. I tried to support her, to get her to stop drinking through my own willpower. A mistake I know. But you and I are completely different people and,' he said pushing back his chair and walking around the table to stand behind her, 'My lovely Laura, we can do anything you want. I am putty in your hands. Your every wish is my command.' He slithered his hands underneath her shirt.

She grinned, relieved. 'Liar. Bet you won't always say that. You're just blinded with lust. You're not taking me seriously and I can't concentrate when you...'

He was kissing her neck. 'I am taking you seriously. But I know we'll be OK, you and me. You can be as independent as you want, just as long as we're together.'

Later she said, 'You know, despite my so-called high moral stance, if you'd seriously tried to seduce me before, I would have succumbed immediately.'

He smiled. 'Me too. You could have pulled me at any point. Just flicked your fingers.'

'Wish I had. We wasted a lot of time. Should have gathered more rosebuds.'

'Still plenty left,' he said happily.

## CHAPTER 31

'IT IS A LITTLE CARELESS OF YOU TO HAVE ALLOWED your wife to run away after such a short time,' said Agnès, settling back on the drawing room sofa and lighting a cigarette.

Oliver didn't smile. Agnès's jokes wore a little thin sometimes. 'So you said, several times, and, several times, I told you the reason.'

'But you could have gone after her. You could have told her your liaison with me had ended, that it meant nothing, you could have promised to give me up.'

'But I *did* give you up.'

'Apart from your stag night.'

'Yes, but after that, *if* you remember, we didn't see each other until Laura took it upon herself to rush off in that idiotic manner.'

'Then why didn't you tell her so?'

'I don't think she wanted to listen.'

'How do you know?'

'Agnès, enough. I don't want to discuss it.'

'That, my dear Oliver, is your whole problem. You never want to discuss anything. Poor Laura. Maybe she will change her mind.'

'I think not,' he said.

'Do you miss her?'

'Naturally,' he said flippantly. In fact he missed her a good deal more than he was prepared to admit. Every day he thought of her face, her warmth and beauty, and every day he wished she would suddenly walk through the door.

'Poor Oliver... But, talking of these things, I have something to tell you. As life's clock is ticking, I myself have finally decided that marriage is a good idea.' She paused to light a cigarette.

Oliver smiled expectantly. It flashed through his head that it was typical of Agnès to take it upon herself to propose to him rather than vice versa, but he was going to have to turn her down. He really couldn't marry again so soon. He hadn't got over Laura. Far from it. She meant a great deal to him. And anyway, as he'd said to himself before, even if Agnès was a pretty good fuck he was still far from sure she'd make a good wife, now or in the future.

Suddenly her words began to penetrate. 'My fiancé is called Pierre-Yves and he comes from an excellent family. My mother approves because he has two *particules* to his name and is distantly related to her late godmother's sister. He is young, handsome and vigorous, and he adores children – I have seen him play nicely with my little nieces and nephews. So pleasant, so good-natured. Best of all, he is an artist who makes very little money and so he would be happy to stay at home as a househusband. He has no complexes or hang-ups whatsoever about the idea. As you know, I wish to pursue my career, so such a man is a rare gem who must be snapped up at once. Therefore, regretfully, my dear Oliver, I must bring our friendship to a close because I cannot risk losing him. *Mon Dieu*, did I say that? Sorry to sound over-sentimental but it must be love. It has never happened to me before so I didn't recognise it creeping up on me.'

Through clenched teeth, Oliver managed to wish her every happiness.

'Thank you.'

'But if you get bored with this handsome hulk...'

'No, I don't anticipate boredom, not with Pierre-Yves, but should I ever take a lover in the future, I think I will choose a younger man for a change,' said Agnès calmly. 'I'm sorry, Oliver. Pity in a way that I did not find my love a year ago then you would not have lost your little Laura but *c'est la vie.*'

It was next day that he received a letter:

*Dear Dad, My exams are finished, not that anyone cares. We're allowed to go home early and the school thinks I'm in Paris, but I'm leaving Europe, going abroad for a year, or maybe permanently if I find somewhere I like. I'll ring some time when I'm settled. No need to fuss – don't call police or Foreign Office or CIA or anyone. Charlotte.*

*PS. Please collect my trunk and stuff from school some time before the end of term.*


'You look worried, darling. What's the problem?' asked Jack.

'Oliver phoned. He said Charlotte had gone abroad and he wanted to know if I knew anything. Only wish I did. She hasn't spoken to me for months.'

He hugged her. 'She'll be OK.'

'You don't know that. She's only seventeen.'

'She sounds like a very competent young woman to me.'

'You don't understand. Anything could happen to her. Already has in fact.'

'If she's had an abortion, she's going to avoid another, that's for sure.'

'Yes but a million other things could go wrong. It's stupid I know, but when you have children you worry all the time.'

'Tell you what we'll do. I'll find us a wonderful old house, with lawns and paddocks and stables galore, then I'll do it up, build on everything a young girl might want, a swimming pool, tennis court, garages for their funky cars, a huge converted barn for raves, then when Alice comes back she'll come home and stay for a while, and Charlotte too. She can come any time she wants.'

'If I ever see her again.'

'You will.'

'I wish I was so sure. There's her father.'

'Their relationship doesn't sound that close. Anyway, she can see other people, not just her father. She's an adult, after all.'

'Mm. You mean, bribe her and Alice to come and see us?'

He smiled. 'Worth trying.'

'You mean, sell Pond Cottage?'

'Or re-let it to Bossy Bridget. But I'll dispose of my own house anyway and give Mel half the proceeds. Too many unhappy memories.'

Laura thought about her cottage and it occurred to her that – after Alice – it was once the most important thing in the world to her, but it didn't really matter any more. Not now. It was just a place and, of course, people are more important than places.

A while later she asked, 'So will you be able to set some rooms aside in our new dream house for my B&B guests? I want to contribute to the building costs in this partnership of ours, by the way.'

As usual, Jack ignored her financial offerings. 'There could be B&B rooms, but wouldn't it be better if they were in separate accommodation, like flats above the stable block, or something? After all, we don't want strangers interrupting when we're making mad passionate love on the drawing room floor.'

'On the hearth rug in front of a glowing fire, our bodies illuminated by the flickering flames and all that?'

'Absolutely.'

Laura smiled in anticipation.

Later in bed she said, 'In the new house – and don't forget I'm contributing – can we have a room for Charlotte too? As well as Alice's. I mean a bedroom that's always Charlotte's to use whenever she comes to see us, her own room. Not a spare guest room or anything. Though she might not ever come, I suppose.'

'She will. She'll forgive you eventually.'

Laura sighed. 'I'm not so sure, but I hope you're right. I'm sure she feels I deserted her when she needed me – which I am afraid I did.'

'Darling, you can't always be everything to everybody.'

'No, but – '

'You're everything to me though.'

She kissed him.

Later he added, 'I'll build you anything you want, my darling,'

Before she went to sleep she murmured. 'You know something, it's lovely, this dream house of yours, but I've already got what I always wanted.'

'Me too,' said Jack.


Laura was talking to Alice on the phone. They discussed how they were and then Alice said, 'Oh by the way, Mum, Charlotte was here the other day.'

'What! In Argentina? That's marvellous.'

'Yes, she suddenly phoned. Then she came to stay. We had a long talk about the abortion and everything. I think she's like coming to terms with it a bit.'

'Thank God for that. Alice, did she call her father to let him know she's OK?'

'Oh yes. Told her to. I wittered on about how neurotic and anxiety-prone parents are. You really don't need to worry, she's very cool and together for her age.'

'Poor girl. I feel so terrible about it all.'

'Well, I guess she's still kind of hurting, about you, I mean, but she'll get over it one day. Not yet though. May take a while.'

Laura sighed guiltily. 'So where is she now?'

'Gone off on her travels. To the States this time.'

'Oh, whereabouts?'

'California, I think, but she's aiming to avoid shitty Simon like the plague. Apparently he's shacked up with some oversexed old slag.'

Poor Kiki, thought Laura. The young always seemed to think sex was their preserve. 'Did Charlotte leave a contact number with you?'

'No, but, like I said, don't worry, she'll be back. She's going to go to a crammer and re-take her exams next year. Apparently she bombed this time.'

'I know,' said Laura, with another pang of guilt.

'Maybe we'll both turn up together – I'm a bit tired of Argentina. Roberto, well, he's so jealous and tiresome. You know the way men are. Probably not staying much longer.'

Laura smiled in delight. 'Darling, it would be lovely if you came home. Luckily, Jack's building a house with plenty of space for us all.'

'Great, but I wouldn't want to disturb your love nest for long, Mum,' said Alice cheerfully.

'I hope you'll be here in time for the wedding.'

'Just try and stop me,' said Alice.